The Cult of New Canaan

An Amari Johnston Novel, Volume 2

By R.A. Williams

Emma – Always in our hearts

i

Although the original concept for this novel was inspired by the Heaven's Gate cult, the characters and events in this novel are completely fictitious. Whereas some scientists and other people active in Shroud investigation during the period are mentioned by name, any other similarity to real persons, living or dead, is coincidental and unintentional.

Cover designed by www.ebooklaunch.com

Special thanks to Candace Sorondo, who has been both a source of encouragement and proofreading help over the last fourteen years.

Thanks to Joe Marino for his encouragement and research help. It was he, along with his late wife, M. Sue Benford, who inspired the Amari Johnston series by a discovery they made in 2000. To learn more about their story, you can view the Discovery Channel documentary called, *Unwrapping the Shroud*. For more detailed information you can read *Wrapped Up in The Shroud*, written by Joe Marino.

Thanks to my editor, Rachel Skatvold, who is not only an outstanding editor but a talented author as well. Here's a link to her Amazon page:
https://www.amazon.com/Rachel-Skatvold/e/B00NMSJTUO/ref=sr_ntt_srch_lnk_1?qid=1535207355&sr=8-1

Thanks to Nina Pykare, retired author of 56 novels. She reached out to me in kindness, graciously offering her experienced guidance to help polish not only this novel but my three previous novels as well.

Thanks to my dad, Ted Williams, not only for his keen proofreading eyes but also for seeing the writer in me long before I saw it myself.

And a very special thanks to my wife, Nilda, and daughter, Libby, who remain a source of encouragement as I pursue what I feel called to do.

From the Author:

I admit this book may seem strange compared to most Christian fiction. Although I indulge in an occasional episode of History Channel's *Ancient Aliens*, in no way do I subscribe to the beliefs represented by the cult in this novel. However, you should know that the premise of this book was inspired by actual events. As some of you may remember, in 1997, thirty-nine members of the Heaven's Gate cult were found dead inside a San Diego mansion. They had committed suicide in the hopes that their souls would be retrieved by a UFO that was hidden behind the Hale-Bopp comet. According to my research, Heaven's Gate's theology was a mixture of Christianity and science fiction, very similar to the beliefs held by the cult in this novel.

Other lesser known UFO cults exist, such as the Aetherius Society, who follow the voice of aliens they call the Cosmic Masters. And then there is the Ashtar Galactic Command. They claim to channel an alien being named Ashtar Sheran. Another cult called The Cosmic Circle of Fellowship believe in interdimensional travel. And most people are familiar with Scientology, founded by science fiction novelist, L. Ron Hubbard. According to Scientology, a powerful alien named Xenu was the dictator of a galactic confederacy of 76 planets. Population problems prompted Xenu to bring some of his people to Earth and stack them around volcanos, only to blow them up with hydrogen bombs. Seriously, I didn't make that up. So, compared to Scientology and other UFO cult ideology, the premise for my novel seems entirely plausible.

If you are interested in learning more about real UFO cults from a sociological perspective, I recommend reading *Heaven's Gate: America's UFO Religion*, by Benjamin E. Zeller and Robert W. Balch.

You should know, however, that every fact mentioned about the Shroud of Turin and the Sudarium of Oviedo is scientifically verifiable truth. I encourage you to investigate both relics and weigh the evidence yourself. For anyone who wants detailed scientific and historical information about the Shroud, I highly recommend *Test the Shroud: At the Atomic and Molecular Levels*, written by small-town attorney at law, Mark Antonacci. He makes a powerful argument for the Shroud—one that would stand up in any court of law and convince even the most skeptical of juries. His book is written in a way that allows you to get a basic idea of the content but skip the complex scientific details if you so choose. See his website for more information:

http://testtheshroud.org

For additional information about the Shroud of Turin, as well as the Sudarium of Oviedo, please visit my website. There you will find slideshow presentations with up to date research findings concerning both holy relics.

https://www.shroudstories.com/
https://www.facebook.com/rawwriter7/

John 14:6

Jesus answered, "I am the way and the truth and the life. No one comes to the Father except through me."

Chapter 1

October 23, 1989

Amari Johnston stared back in disbelief as she calculated the implication of his words. "*The owner's manual?* Kevin, you said you knew how to fly!"

Wind against the airplane's thin metal shell and the drone of twin-propeller engines muted Kevin's words as he calmly took inventory of all the knobs, switches, levers, and gauges.

"I thought you said you could fly!" she repeated, louder this time.

He raised his voice to match hers. "How hard could it be? There's the throttle, this here's the steering wheel, and one of those knobs or levers ought to control the flaps. Now just calm down and look for the flight manual."

"You said owner's manual."

"Whatever, it's the same thing."

"Kevin, this isn't one of those atom speeders you play with at work." She chanced a look out the cockpit window.

Roads and dry riverbed made faint lines in the greenish-brown landscape. Trees were nothing more than tiny random dots. "We're, like, a mile off the ground. You're going to get us killed." She cupped her hands over her face and shook her head in disbelief. So many plans, so many stories she wanted to tell her mother in heaven someday. Who would have thought she'd join her mother after only her second mission? Correction, before she'd even completed her second mission.

"That's Atomic Mass Accelerator," he corrected with his thick, Tennessee accent. "And if I can run that thing, this ought to be a cinch."

"You can't just flip through the owner's manual and learn how to land a plane."

"We got time. It depends on how much fuel we have." He frowned at one of the gauges. "Which doesn't look like much. Does that look like a fuel gauge to you?"

"Kevin, this is crazy!"

"You got any better ideas?"

"I don't know, but we have to do something, or we're going to die—along with forty other people too."

"A crash landing is survivable," he said in a strangely relaxed tone. "Maybe. Depending on the terrain, of course."

She watched him in dismay. He was so calm, so certain of God's intervention. 'Sometimes, you just gotta live by faith', he'd once told her. Deep inside, masked underneath fear-fueled adrenaline, she knew he was right. She'd chosen her path prayerfully. God wanted her to do this. He had her back now, just like he'd had it while she'd been stalked by a serial killer the year before.

She narrowed her eyes with firm resolve and buckled her seat belt. "Then crash land back at the compound. We have to stop those people before it's too late."

****

July 27, 1989

Adrian Agricola had earned the right to keep his given name—a name he'd given himself after his third arrest. Aside from the captain, the rest of the congregation had been stripped of their earthly identity. In return, they'd received a numerical equivalent based on an enigmatic biblical passage. The cult's founding leader had insisted that by stripping members of their earthly identity, adjustment to a transformed body would be easier. Then they would fully appreciate their new heavenly name, a sound which cannot be uttered by the human tongue.

Adrian stood atop a raised platform, directly in front of a small dry-erase board used for instructing the followers. A wooden podium stood off toward the right of the stage. Affixed to the dry-erase board, yet still obscured by a black curtain, was an image, that of the group's new, eternal home, which existed out in deep space, more than 1200 light years away.

The estate was financed by a trust fund bequeathed to Calvin Nettles, the thirty-eight-year-old son of a venture capitalist—*Captain* Calvin Nettles to his devotees. To say Calvin was eccentric was an extreme understatement. Unfortunately, he paid the bills. Suffering Calvin's peculiar quirks was unavoidable, at least for the time being. Adrian was sick to death of playing along, pretending to share in their perverted faith in exchange for three hots and a cot. Admittedly, it was more pleasant than San Quentin. After surviving that place, anything was tolerable.

The compound had a private airstrip, which included the services of a personal pilot. Not a believer, ex-army Captain Ian Somers stayed in a mobile home parked inside the corrugated steel airplane hangar. He spent most of his free time reading science fiction and tinkering with his airplane and helicopter.

Adrian watched the congregation settle around the stage. The high noon sun beamed into the rooftop atrium, casting shadows from the lattice of white, steel beams that held the glass pyramid together. A simple, unfinished cedarwood cross was carved from a thousand-year-old tree imported directly from Lebanon. It was suspended by a chain and hung down over the raised platform atop a plank floor that was painted a shade of gray that reminded Adrian of a space alien's skin.

The main house was a square, dormitory style building with a small, irrigated oasis of green grass surrounding it. The grass contrasted with the harsh, dry desert, and served as a reminder of the paradise awaiting them on their eventual new home. The glass pyramid atop the main house was exceptionally expensive and cost a fortune in electricity to cool during the heat of summer. The atrium was inspired by the Chrystal Cathedral in southern California. Calvin had become fixated on the design after watching *Hour of Power*, presented by televangelist, Robert Schuller.

Calvin had his good days and his bad days. Sometimes he was lively and spirited, other times he seemed withdrawn, aloof, spending days at a time confined to his bedroom, only opening the door for spartan nourishment of plain, white, gelatinous tofu. Today was a good day, as he was, in his own subdued way, ecstatic about a discovery that one of his flock had made during a fact-finding expedition to the outside world—a discovery Adrian planned to exploit to the fullest.

The thirty-five male brethren had their hair buzz-cut so short to the scalp that they looked like soldiers at boot camp. Each had a symbolic tattoo on their forearm. Their numerical identity was printed underneath the tattoos. The males wore understated coveralls, each assigned a unique color according to his rank. There were only five women followers. They stood behind the men with white veils covering their long hair—*for every woman who prays for prophecies with her head uncovered dishonors her head. It is the same as having her head shaved.* Instead of coveralls, four of the women wore simple blue dresses. Only 462 wore a white dress to signify she was the eldest.

Calvin ascended into the light-bathed pyramid, climbing into the atrium by way of a staircase that opened from a rectangular gap in the floor. His hair, disheveled and cowlicked like he'd just fallen out of bed, was a dirty blond and tinged with early onset gray. Since this was a special occasion, he'd exchanged his burgundy red coveralls for a white cloak instead.

As he strode toward the stage, his congregation parted like the Red Sea, as if Moses himself had commanded them to do so. He stepped onto the stage and faced the group. His normally expressionless face now seemed alive with enthusiasm.

There was a hush of silence as his followers awaited his first words. He lifted his face to the sky, squinting from the sunlight, gathering his thoughts before making his anxiously anticipated announcement. Finally, he began. "As you all know, several years ago I was caught up to the third heaven, ferried by an angelic spacecraft of silver and gold. I saw inexpressible things about which only this I am permitted to tell. It is both a warning and a promise of hope. Very soon, a time of tribulation will befall this planet. Men will look to the sky. They will see the fleet of Abaddon descending in great numbers, metallic discs from the abyss of space, armed with phasers and photon torpedoes. The earth will be scorched by the wrath of God. A thousand lasers from a thousand craft will boil the oceans and all life therein. The earth will be tilled under and prepared for new growth. The great recycling will begin."

A gasp arose from the followers, panicked eyes passing from face to face. Adrian couldn't help but be impressed by Calvin's gift of manipulation. Adrian had never been able to strike fear into the congregation the way Calvin could—fear and hope of redemption at the same time. And the reason was simple. Unlike Adrian, Calvin believed his own lies. Adrian's method of acting was worthy of an Oscar, but no amount of skill could match honest delusion.

"But God has set us apart," Calvin quickly added to dispel their concerns. "Brethren, we know this to be true. God will provide an ark, and I will be its captain."

"Calvin's Ark," one of the members said.

"What of the animals?" another asked.

"In the Kingdom of New Canaan, there is no predator nor prey," he explained. "A new order of beasts will roam the planet. A new kind of fish will swim in the sea. And a new people will rule New Canaan, purified of rebellion and sin. It will be the new garden of Eden. We will inhabit this garden. Us . . . ," he said, stalling for dramatic effect, "and the new Adam and Eve. For the new Adam and Eve are not yet of our fold. But soon, brethren, soon they will be."

"Who are they?" one asked.

"The new Adam holds a genius such as the world has never seen. The new Eve is a strong-willed and crafty woman, a warrior at heart. Their genes will combine to form a super breed of human, incorruptible, impervious to the temptations of sin." Suddenly, his eyes lost focus. He stood in silence, a puzzled look on his face as if he had just awoken from a dream.

"He is receiving another vision," one of the congregation suggested.

"The fires of . . . the . . . the fire." He mashed his palms into the eye sockets and twisted.

Here we go again, Adrian thought. *And he was doing so well.* He went over and whispered in Calvin's ear. "You were talking about New Canaan, remember? The new Adam and Eve."

Realization registered on Calvin's face, and he awkwardly continued. "Yes . . . of course." He coughed to clear his throat. "Brethren, as you know, we are the new root of humanity, and from us will sprout new generations. But not from one of our wombs, nay, but from that of the chosen, the new Eve of the new order, who is to receive seed from the new Adam. For we know that there can be only one father, only one mother. Our role is that of support, to build the city, to grow the food so that the offspring can flourish anew, free from the sin that stains the peoples of Earth."

"Where is this place?" Lieutenant Senior Grade 332 asked. He was clad in beige coveralls that zipped up the front. He was six foot, ten inches tall, a full head above the next tallest cult member. He reminded Adrian of Lurch from the Addams Family. Oddly, his nearly bald head gave him the appearance of a lumbering Uncle Fester. He was sort of the mouthpiece for the rest of the group, always asking the questions, probing for answers with his deep-set, sunken eyes.

"Unfortunately," Calvin replied, "our new home, the planet we call New Canaan, is not near to us, nay, not even in the same solar system. Our new home is many light years away. Adrian, if you will, please."

Given his cue, Adrian yanked the black curtain away from the dry erase board, revealing a photograph—a map of stars. "Most of you are familiar with this image," Adrian said with professor-like candor. "It's the Orion belt, some 378 parsecs from Earth. The visible stars of the Orion constellation are too large and too hot to sustain life. Rather, our new star is not visible by the naked eye, but it is very nearby, astrologically speaking. New Canaan orbits this sun-sized star that Calvin has aptly named the Star of Joshua. Once he arrives on this planet, the angels will provide a craft—an ark if you will. This craft is capable of sustained warp nine."

Another gasp arose from the congregation.

"That's right," Calvin said, "*Warp nine*. For with God, all things are possible, technology made perfect."

"But even at warp nine," Adrian added, "the journey will last 297 days."

"But how then shall you retrieve the ark?" Lieutenant Senior Grade 332 asked. "If it is so far away, will it be delivered to Earth?"

Calvin outstretched his hand toward Adrian. "Adrian, if you will."

Adrian got the wire bound report from atop the podium and handed it to Calvin.

Calvin held the notebook over his head for all to see. "This, brethren, is the secret. As you know, in early summer, my inner three ventured into the world on a fact-finding mission. They made many discoveries, not least of which is this." He waved the binder in the air. "This report holds the key to reaching New Canaan."

And mine too, Adrian thought. *It's my ticket out of here too.*

Chapter 2

Riverdale College, New Mexico. September 2, 1989

Situated in northern New Mexico, just east of the Navajo Nation boundary, Riverdale was a small farming community nourished by the San Juan River. The river fed a green band of land surrounded by desert sand, much like the Nile River did in Egypt. Riverdale was also home to the northwestern campus of New Mexico State University. Many of the students at this campus were Navajo, benefactors of Native American scholarships.

Amari Johnston's late mother was a full-blooded Navajo. However, Amari had grown up with her mother in Tucson with mostly white friends, co-raised by her own extremely Anglo father, a police detective for the Tucson City Police. Given her background, Amari had high standards to live up to. Not only was her Anglo father an aggressive police officer, but her great, great grandfather had been a renowned Native American warrior chief of the

Dine' people. His real name was Bít'aa'níí, but he was known as 'Manuelito' to the Spanish. He'd led attacks against the US Army in the Navajo Wars of 1863-1866. With his courageous blood thick in her veins, this mission in Riverdale was all the more appropriate. A serial rapist had been terrorizing the small town. The Sherriff and two deputies had been useless so far. She was the perfect solution—a college-aged girl who was an expert in martial arts, who also had ex-Army Special Forces soldiers to watch her back. It's like it was meant to be, like God himself had ordained this mission.

Like God himself called me for this, she thought to herself.

She closed her eyes and recalled the last conversation she'd had with her mother. Her mother was lying down with the head of her hospital bed inclined because it was less painful that way. Mother's hair was black, streaked with gray. Much of it had returned from the last round of chemo, but it was still short and thin, and her chest was flat after the double mastectomy. When the breast cancer returned, it had invaded her liver, and there was no point continuing the treatment, no point in prolonging her suffering.

Mother was gaunt, and her eyes were glassy, glazed over by narcotics to numb the pain. But her words were alive with hope, and that's what Amari chose to relish.

Amari knelt by her bed, holding her cold, weakened fingers inside her own.

Mother startled awake. Her eyes probed the dim light until they found her daughter. "Amari? Is that you?"

"Yes, Shimi. I'm here." She gently caressed her mother's hand.

"Before I go to heaven, I want to know something."

"Yes, Mother. What is it?"

"Tell me your dreams, Shiyazhi," she said, which meant my child in the Navajo language. "I cannot be here to see them come true, but at least tell me what they are."

"I don't know, Shimi." Her voice cracked as she strained to hold back the tears. "I don't know anymore."

"When the time is right, you will know, Shiyazhi. Trust in God. He will show you his purpose. Be open to his will. That is all you have to do."

"But God doesn't listen anymore. If he did, you wouldn't be dying." She fell against her mother's hollow chest as she wept.

Her mother stroked her hair as she spoke, her voice strained, but alive with emotion. "Diyin Ayóí Át'éii," Shiyazhi. Trust in the Great Spirit. Don't you give up on him. He will show you his will. One day, you will join me again, and then you will tell me all about it. Jesus will bring us together again, Shiyazhi. Someday, you will tell me all about it."

Tears burned at her eyes when she recalled her mother's final words. She swiped her eyes with the back of her hand and shook off the thought. She couldn't afford to be distracted by sentiment. She had to stay focused. So she drew a breath for courage, then pressed on down the darkened walking trail of Riverdale Community Park.

A rustling noise came from a thicket of bushes next to the river. She froze, turning her ear toward the noise, straining to see in the dark. She heard the gurgling water as it washed over stones. Another rustling sound startled her, and she hastened her pace down the dark trail. After all, she'd promised Bonelli and Parker that she'd stay close to the van.

It had been during spring finals when the first rape happened. A Navajo student had been cramming in the library until midnight. On the way home, she had passed through this same park. Not only had the rapist sexually assaulted her, but he'd also broken her jaw and two ribs. This student never took her finals and had yet to return to Riverdale. And then it happened again, on the last night of the semester. Some girls had been celebrating at a local bar. One of them crossed the park on her way home. No bones were broken this time, but she'd lost two teeth. She wasn't a Navajo but of Mexican heritage instead.

Then over the summer semester, it happened two more times. One of those girls was Chooli, Amari's own first cousin. Chooli had spent a week in the hospital and withdrew from her classes. Now it was fall semester, and she was still too frightened to return. Unfortunately, that didn't sway her second cousin, a freshman at Riverdale, named Doli, which meant 'bluebird' in English. The Sherriff had promised to increase nighttime patrols, but with only two deputies, they were stretched thin already. And because the rapes had occurred off campus, the college security wasn't any help.

Again, this mission seemed like a no-brainer to her. If anyone could bait this guy and take him off the street, it was Amari Johnston, world-famous sleuth who had debunked the carbon date performed on the Shroud of Turin while simultaneously fending off a serial killer. She was in peak physical condition and the hours spent with the personal martial arts coach had paid off. She'd prayed this through and was sure God had her back. Besides, Bonelli and Parker were just a few yards away, so what could go wrong? One way or another, she was taking this guy down. She owed it to her cousins. She owed it to the other female students.

I just hope he doesn't recognize me and get spooked, she thought to herself.

Her only misgiving was that she hadn't consulted her dad. Their relationship had improved dramatically since the serial killer ordeal, and now she felt guilty for leaving him in the dark. The last thing she wanted was to drive another wedge between them. Then again, if she had talked to him first, she'd still be sitting in Tucson, and more girls would be at risk. There was no way he would ever agree to what she was doing. And then there was

Kevin. If he had any idea what she was up to, he'd have a major conniption fit. His Tennessee accent was much thicker when he was pissed. With any luck, she could catch this guy and stay anonymous. The last thing she needed was to make headline news again.

A rustling noise came from the riverbank again. Probably a coyote. Or maybe a bobcat, if that was any comfort. She broke into a jog and moved toward a better lit area of the park.

The perpetrator had established a pattern, a taste for his flavor of victim. He preferred darker-skinned girls, like the Navajo or Mexican. Maybe he himself was Navajo. Or maybe this was a perverse reaction to childhood trauma, one involving an oppressive woman of Indian or Hispanic heritage, perhaps a teacher or authority figure who'd once humiliated or even abused him as a child. Maybe this was his sick means of payback—a way to reassert his dominance. Whatever his motive was, he had to be stopped, and she was the perfect bait to attract this maniac. As a just-turned-twenty-three-year-old, she had recently graduated with a degree in Criminal Justice from the University of Arizona. So it wasn't hard for her to pose as a student. And given his ethnic preference, her Navajo genes had given her the long, black hair and semi-bronze skin to play the part of one of the Navajo students, one that was naïve enough to walk alone at night in the park. Of course, if it was daylight, you could see the Caucasian in her, passed down from her father's Scottish heritage. But the rapist wouldn't be that choosy. For most of them, they only looked for opportunity.

She tried to act naturally as she strode down the riverside path, pushing back any misgivings she'd had about taking this mission. God had her back, she reminded herself again. And so did Bonelli and Parker, Ernesto's private security.

Ernesto Galliano was an Italian-American philanthropist who had discovered Amari after the ruckus she'd caused at the university over the carbon date they'd performed on the Shroud of Turin. Using the knowledge passed down from her mother—who was an expert in Navajo weaving—Amari had theorized that the portion of the Shroud used for the carbon date had undergone a repair at some point, which had mixed new fibers in with old, invalidating the carbon date that caused the world to believe the Shroud was a medieval forgery, a fact that infuriated her. It was a lie, after all, and she hated lies. So when the university administration had refused to let her examine their Shroud sample, there had been a major throw down. Then there was the angry protest she'd organized in front of the campus library—the one that was featured not only on the local news but the national news as well.

As fate would have it, Ernesto, a devout Christian, and believer in the Shroud, had seen Amari on the news. He admired her spirit and dedication to God, so he hired her to join Bonelli and Parker to form an organization that sought out people in need and helped them in the name of Jesus. Ernesto had tried to recruit her father as well, offering him top dollar. But her dad wasn't ready to leave his distinguished career as a homicide detective to work for some rich 'fanatical do-gooder who'd never worked an honest day in his life.'

It was true. Ernesto inherited his fortune from his father. But that didn't mean his motives weren't pure. And just because she and her dad didn't see eye to eye about Ernesto, didn't mean she was going to deny her destiny. God had called her to work for Ernesto—to make the world a better place, one victim at a time. And this was her first mission, despite Ernesto's reluctance to allow it. Instead, he'd wanted her to help investigate a crooked contractor who had conned flooding victims in the Florida peninsula, victims of a hurricane. The contractor had left them homeless after taking their insurance money and skipping town. Ernesto paid for the home repairs and was determined to track the conman down before more people could be swindled.

She had no problem taking the case of the swindling contractor, but the case involving the serial rapist was a top priority. She knew how these girls felt. Several years before, a jock from the wrestling team had tried to rape her—tried to. As far as she knew, his voice had still not recovered from damage her fist did to his Adam's apple. His groin hadn't fared much better. With her expertise in martial arts, the rapist would deeply regret sneaking up behind this Navajo warrior.

She wasn't a black belt in any particular discipline, like Karate or Judo. To her, the belt ranking was just for show, for winning contests and showing off staged achievements. Her mindset wasn't about competition. It was about apprehending the guilty—and about survival. She used a combination of Taekwondo, Krav Maga, police department self-defense, and brute strength from her workouts at the gym. Soon after she'd met Ernesto back in January, Amari had started working with a personal trainer, hired by Ernesto to prepare her for the job she would take once she graduated. After all, Ernesto had high standards.

She stopped just short of a dimly lit park lamp. It flickered and snapped as if it was about to burn out. She reached into her bra and pulled out a tiny earpiece and placed it into her ear. She propped her foot on a park bench and pretended to tie her shoe. "Nothing yet," she said softly into the Walkman's microphone. Bonelli and Parker's van was parked just out of view. They monitored her by microphone and transmitter cleverly built into the fake Walkman. Any sign of trouble and they would come running, guns drawn, eager for a violent take-down, providing she hadn't done the job already.

"You ready to head back?" she heard Bonelli say into her earphones.

"Let's give it another thirty minutes," she said. "I'll hang out under the light, so he can see me. If he doesn't take the bait, I'll start heading back."

"Are you sure?" Bonelli asked. "Parker has to go to the bathroom."

She could hear Parker mutter something in the background.

"Tell him to go," she said. "I can take care of myself."

"No can do," she heard Parker say. "We're not out here for your safety. We're here for the poor sap that tries to lay hands on you. We want him to go to jail in one piece."

"Oh, come on," she said. "I'm not that rough."

"Tell that to the tooth you broke last January in Turin," Parker said. "It still bothers me sometimes."

"Worse than the bullet you took in the chest?" she replied.

"That still hurts too," he said. "You better get back in character, kid."

"If you hear my kiai, then that's your cue," she said with a laugh. The kiai was a martial arts battle cry, designed as a yell of power when executing a move. The purpose was to focus the power of the strike while intimidating your opponent at the same time.

"Once we hear your kiai," Bonelli teased, "it'll be too late for him."

Again, Amari searched the darkened grounds with her ears, probing with her eyes. There was nothing but the faint sound of insects and a breeze passing over the brush. "If he's out there looking, then he's seen me already. We're probably just wasting our time. I'll start heading back. I wouldn't want you to wet your pants," she said with a snicker and clipped the Walkman back onto her waistband. She kept the earphones on to imply her state mind, one that said she was naïve, oblivious to the dangers of walking alone at night.

She started with a lazy stroll at first, then picked up the pace and jogged into the darkened path.

A noise from behind startled her. She slowed her pace and removed the headphones, so she could hear better. She nonchalantly slid them into her pocket. If the rapist was lurking in the trees, she didn't want to spook him. She heard it again, this time closer. Footsteps closed in fast. The next instant, a strong grip took her from behind, a sharp knife pressing onto her neck.

"Scream and I slit your throat," he growled into her ear, his breath hot on her skin.

Amari's reaction was immediate—no conscious thought, just muscle memory from countless repetitions. She grabbed his forearm with both hands and yanked down, hard and to the left, the blade away from her face. At the same moment, she thrust her right shoulder upward, forcing his arm away. Holding his forearm tight, she dropped her head down and lunged her body behind him, twisting his arm backward. With the blade still in his grip, she shoved the tip into his side. He yelped from the pain and turned to face her as he staggered away, clutching his wound. She stepped back, then planted a hard kick square on his chest. "Hi-yah!"

He fell backward, stumbling to maintain his footing. He wore what appeared to be a red wrestler's mask.

Refusing him time to recover, she moved in for the kill. The front kick was first. She swept her foot upward. "Hi-yah!" she cried, just as her foot connected with his groin.

The blade fell from his hand. He clutched at his stomach and hunched over from pain. He dropped to his knees, his head falling forward. She pivoted backward on the balls of her feet. In one fluid motion, looking over her shoulder for aim, she connected a spinning hook kick—a painful strike of her heal to the tender tissue of his ear. "Hi-yah!"

He toppled to the ground, rolling away in a panic, cupping his hand over his stinging ear. He struggled to his feet, snatched a pistol from his ankle holster, and attempted to aim. She spun around, connecting a roundhouse kick to his wrist, knocking the gun from his hand. "Hi-yah!"

Enough play, it was time to end this before he recovered the gun. Amari cross-stepped forward, drew in her left arm and spun around, leading with her right elbow, striking hard with an audible *clack* against the cartilage of his Adam's apple.

He gasped for air in a series of short, wheezing breaths. His eyes bulged in the eyeholes of his mask. He staggered away, attempting an escape.

Time for the taekwondo takedown. Amari grabbed his shirt and yanked him backward and off balance. She cocked her leg and swept it down heel first. She connected hard against his ankle, knocking his footing out from under him, directing his fall so that he fell face to the ground. She wrenched his arm behind his back and shoved it up toward his shoulder blade. A muted, guttural scream came from his injured voice box.

Bonelli and Parker rush onto the scene. "Woe, woe, hold on, Amari," Bonelli said. "Stand down. We'll take this from here."

Parker produced a pair of handcuffs and clamped them over the man's wrists.

She came to her feet, catching her breath, righteous rage turned to euphoria. "I got him! I can't believe this. I caught him," she said, her voice cracking with emotion.

"You got him all right," Bonelli said. "Now just pray the news doesn't find out this was you. Because if the news finds out, so will your father."

Euphoria gave way to dread. Bonelli was right. If this made the news, there was no way her dad wasn't finding out about this. No way whatsoever.

****

The sheriff pulled his car alongside the ambulance, got out, and went to the open ambulance door. He wore a khaki uniform with a gleaming gold star-shaped badge, pinned to a shirt that was missing a button. He was near retirement age. His gray mustache drooped down the sides of his mouth to make him look like Wilford Brimley. He stepped in beside Amari and the ambulance driver, but kept a leery distance from Parker and Bonelli, the palm of his hand resting on top of his firearm. "Came soon as a heard," he said. "There was a three-car pileup on Old Kirtland Highway. What's this about catching the rapist?"

"He's in the ambulance," Bonelli said. His jaw was square, his eyes piercing blue, and his black hair parted to the side. He reminded most people of the comic book depiction of Superman. Some people even called him Clark Kent just to get a reaction. "I wouldn't go in there if you have a weak stomach."

The sheriff eyed Bonelli suspiciously. "Who are you people? Vigilantes? Private investigators?"

"Something like that," Parker said. He was shorter, thicker built than Bonelli, and his hair was kinky brown. He sported one of those stubby beards like Sonny Crockett on Miami Vice wore, only his facial features looked more like a rugged version of George Michael.

The sheriff noticed Amari's disheveled hair and dirty clothes. "And you? You the victim? You don't look too shook up."

"I was *supposed* to be the victim." She cocked her thumb to the ambulance. "I'd say he's feeling like the victim now."

19

The sheriff ambled toward the opened back doors. Amari went with him and opened the ambulance door wide. The assailant wheezed under an oxygen mask that covered his mouth and nose. His shirt was cut away, and a blood-soaked bandage covered the wound from where she had shoved his own knife into his ribs.

"Looks like he's got a concussion, a dislocated elbow, and a crushed windpipe," the gruff female paramedic said.

"He'll also need a good urologist," Amari replied with a satisfied grin.

The sheriff returned his own puzzled grin, then focused on Bonelli and Parker. "You fellas do this to him?"

"Not quite," Bonelli said, nodding in Amari's direction.

"You don't say?" the sheriff said and studied the man lying in the ambulance. "I'm interested to hear his side of the story." The sheriff's eyes moved up the assailant's torso. "Well, I can tell you this. His clothes match the description. I see the red wrestler's mask on the floor. We didn't make that detail public."

Bonelli handed the sheriff a sharp blade, using a handkerchief to avoid contaminating the prints. "We found this on the ground not far from him."

"And this too," Parker said and held up a pistol, only using a ballpoint pen inserted through the trigger guard.

"Let me see that," the sheriff said and carefully took the knife by the handkerchief. He inspected it closely. "The knife matches the description. The Mexican girl was familiar with knives. Said her father collects them. She said it was a full-tang fixed-blade with a clip point and a saw back. That's exactly what this is." The sheriff moved closer to the ambulance to get a better view of the assailant's face. His eyes flashed wide with recognition. "Kesler?"

"You know this guy?" Bonelli asked.

"I'd say I do. I hired him about a year ago. He's one of my deputies."

Chapter 3

Tucson, Arizona

Detective Pete Johnston traveled south on Interstate 19. He watched a dirt devil spin and whorl in the desert brush, offset by blue sky and white clouds that offered little chance for rain. Chatter from the police radio played in the background. Just south of Tucson, the Osarca Mine was an open-pit copper mine—a massive hole forged by explosives, steel-tooth excavators, and giant dump trucks with tires the diameter of a small swimming pool. Unfortunately, one of those tires happened to turn one of the miners into a man shaped like a gingerbread cookie. The driver said it was an accident—evidence said otherwise.

Pete's partner, George Sanchez, had an acne-pitted face and wavy black hair that fell below his shirt collar. His real named was Jorge. In Spanish, the G and the J are pronounced like H, but nobody in the department seemed to understand that so to keep things simple, he always responded to George. He was a native Newyorican, meaning he was Puerto Rican by heritage but born and raised in New York City. He'd moved to Tucson a few years back. George sat in the passenger seat, chowing down on a mustard-soaked chilidog as he listened to Pete vent about his daughter's new boss.

"I don't care how much money that clown has," Pete continued. "I don't trust him as far as I can throw him. Think about it, George, he could hire a seasoned detective for that kind of cash. Yet, for some reason, he chooses my twenty-two-year-old daughter. She's just out of college, has absolutely no experience. Hasn't even been to the Police Academy yet. I've got thirty years in this line of work, for crying out loud. And he pays her close to what I'm making. And then he gives her a rent-free house in the Catalina Foothills. With a swimming pool to boot."

George took a two-inch chomp from his chilidog. He chewed for a few seconds and then used a napkin to swipe mustard from his thick, Tom Selleck mustache. "I thought she turned twenty-three last month."

"Whatever, George, she's still a kid to me."

"You think he's got the hots for her? She's like fifteen years younger than him, isn't she?"

Pete cringed at the thought. "Is that supposed to help?"

"I wasn't trying to help, man, I'm offering a motive."

"I doubt it. If he had any designs on her, why hire the boyfriend? Besides, I think this guy might be a eunuch."

"What? You mean one of those guys who's been . . .," George made a painful expression. "Man, I can't even say the word."

"Castrated?"

"Yeah, that one."

"I wouldn't put it past him. Amari said he wanted to be a priest when he was younger, but his father wouldn't hear of it. He wanted Ernesto to run his billion-dollar company. So when his dad died, what does he do? He sells the company and starts giving all the money away."

"Sounds like a righteous dude."

"Sounds like he's got a screw loose," Pete said. He exited the interstate, turning right toward the mine.

"Man, why do you always think the worst of people? Didn't he offer you seventy-five grand a year to help give that money away?"

"I got him to come up to eighty-five."

"That's more than twice what I make. Who's got the screw loose again?"

"I'm a cop, not a mercenary."

"You'd be a mercenary? Like a soldier for hire?"

"No, not exactly. Look, you ever watch that show, The Equalizer? It's something like that, only I'd have the use of a private jet and two goons for backup."

"Yeah, I watch that show. Robert McCall's a righteous dude too. You think you can fake the English accent?"

"George, this isn't a joke."

"The joke is you not taking this job. It can't be full-time work. Maybe you can take up golf in between missions."

"Oh, no, he's got my day all planned out. Amari says he's got several homeless shelters. In fact, he just bought an old motel in Tucson. He's renovating it and building classrooms. He only takes in people who are serious about turning their life around. If they're on drugs or alcohol, he pays for rehab. When she's not on a case, he wants her to work at the Tucson shelter. Says she'll be good at spotting a lie and weeding out those who aren't serious about getting clean. He wants me to be some kind of regional manager. Oversee security and make sure we keep the bad guys out."

George shoved the last couple inches of his footlong into his mouth and pondered the subject as he chewed. Finally, he said, "I don't know, Pete, sounds like a dream gig to me. You'd be helping people for a change instead of locking them up."

"I lock people up so innocent people don't get killed. I'd say that's helping."

"You said he offered to pay for a hip replacement. The Department's health insurance won't pay for that. At this rate, you'll be on disability in five years. Seems like a no-brainer."

"You got a point there," Pete conceded.

"And you say you're worried about Amari getting hurt working for this guy. Take the job so you can keep your eye on her."

"I tell you, that's the only other reason I'm considering it. When she took her Shroud case to the Vatican itself, I'm telling you it went to her head."

"She talked to the Pope?"

"Not exactly, but close enough. All I'm saying is now she's got delusions of grandeur. In her mind, she's on a mission from God."

"You mean like the Blues Brothers? With Dan Aykroyd and John Belushi?"

"George, I'm serious. This is no movie. She could get into some real trouble. And I can't seem to talk any sense into her. After the news about what happened in Turin broke worldwide, she's become an international celebrity. Then came the Johnny Carson show and then Larry King. Even Phil Donahue was interested in having her on his show. All that attention has gone to her head. She thinks she's invincible."

"So she believes in herself. What's wrong with that?"

"It's wrong if it'll get you killed."

"You call it ego, I call it faith. She's really on fire for God. Is that a bad thing?"

"George, you ever read the Bible?"

"A little bit."

25

"The Bible is full of people getting killed over their faith. Most of those apostles were martyred. I tell you, I lost my wife two years ago. If something happened to Amari, I couldn't go on. She's all I've got left in this world."

"Then you better take the job. That way you can keep her safe."

"If I didn't know any better, I'd say you were trying to get rid of me."

"I just want what's best for you and your daughter."

"And you think you'll get promoted when I retire? They'd have to fill my position."

"I could use the raise."

"You're too young, George. You've got a lot to learn. You don't become an expert until you've been in the field as long as I have."

"I'm pushing forty. It's not like I'm fresh from the academy."

"All I'm saying is you'll have competition, so don't get your hopes up."

Pete drove into a man-made valley created by two terraced mountains built of sandy excavated dirt. He turned left and crossed railroad tracks, then passed the entrance sign. On the way to the overseer's office, he passed murky, grayish blue circular pools that served some purpose of refining copper, then a graveyard for enormous, worn out truck tires. He followed signs that led past a long, white rectangular building lined with utility trucks. Finally, he found a standalone building that bore the correct address he'd been given over the phone, the office of the foreman in charge of the entire mine.

Pete parked his car in a gravel lot next to the office and glanced over at his partner. "You might want to wipe that mustard off your whiskers before you interview for my job."

George wiped his lips with a clean section of a napkin. "Did I get it?"

"Most of it. And get a haircut too. The chief's never going promote you with that shaggy mop."

George flipped down the vanity mirror and checked his mustache.

"We'll talk about this later," Pete said. "Right now we've got a potential homicide to investigate."

After they found the entrance, they stood inside an office with cheap, vertical wood paneling on the walls. A dead swordfish was proudly mounted on the wall, and a creepy looking stuffed raccoon stared at them from a table covered in magazines. The smell of burnt coffee left on a burner too long stunk in the air.

A secretary with overdone lipstick and a pencil behind her ear looked up from her computer. "You must be detective Johnston."

"That's right," Pete said. "We spoke on the phone. Is your boss available?"

"He's on a long-distance call. Have a seat on the couch, and I'll let him know you're here."

"Thank you, ma'am," Pete said and took a seat on the worn leather couch.

George sat beside him and picked up a newspaper from a coffee table. They sat for several minutes. George flipped through pages of the paper as Pete prodded the secretary to see if there was any good gossip going around the mine, gossip that could point to a motive.

George elbowed Pete for his attention.

"Just a second. Can't you see we're talking?" he said, tilting his head toward the secretary.

"Uh, Pete, I think you might want to see this," George said and handed him the paper.

"Does it have to do with this case?"

"Not *this* case. It's about that serial rapist up in Riverdale. Looks like he's been caught."

27

"Up in New Mexico? What's that got to do with us?"

"Because look who caught him," George said and pointed to a picture. "She look familiar to you?"

He snatched the paper from George and read the headline: *Notorious University of Arizona Graduate Apprehends Serial Rapist.* "I'm going to kill him," Pete uttered through clenched teeth. "I'm going to strangle that man with my bare hands."

"I'm sorry?" the secretary said, alarm flashing on her face.

Pete stammered for words, tamping down his internal rage. "Metaphorically speaking."

"I see," she said and pointed to the office door. "He's ready to see you now. May I warn him he's in danger?"

"That won't be necessary, ma'am," Pete assured her with a tight, insincere smile. "My partner and I were talking about a different case."

Chapter 4

In the backyard of her mountainside home in the Catalina foothills, Amari climbed the aluminum ladder, water dripping from her body as she got out of the kidney-shaped swimming pool.

In a lawn chair next to the pool, Jenny Brenner sat studying for an exam. "That's an impressive vastus medialis you got there," she said.

Amari stood on the edge of the pool and cast Jenny a curious stair. "How about in English this time?"

"I saw your leg muscles flex when you came up that ladder. Ernesto's getting his money's worth from that trainer."

Amari blushed, embarrassed by the attention to her body. "Thanks . . . I guess." She went to the poolside table, fed her arms into an absorbent swim robe, and tightened the sash around her waist. She picked a towel up from the table and dried her hair while gazing down into the hazy Tucson skyline that was situated in the valley between the

Santa Catalina Mountain and Tucson Mountain to the west.

"I wasn't trying to embarrass you." Jenny held up her textbook. "But your legs are helping with anatomy."

Amari laughed. "I'm glad I can help. I'll tell Tony you're impressed with his work." She pointed at an autopsy picture in her textbook. "That looks gross, by the way."

"It's Gross Anatomy, silly. It's supposed to be gross. I've got a test Friday."

Jenny was Amari's age, only instead of the mild Navajo tan and dark hair Amari had inherited from her mother, Jenny had hairspray teased blond hair, and her skin was still pasty white despite the Arizona sun, thanks to the gobs of sunscreen she applied underneath her makeup every morning.

Amari's mother had divorced her husband over an affair with another woman, so when she died from breast cancer, Amari had inherited her mother's house, along with a small amount of life insurance. When the insurance money ran out, she'd advertised for a roommate and Jenny was the first to knock on her door. They'd been best friends ever since.

Jenny had gotten her undergrad degree at The University of Tennessee with a dual major in pre-med and psychiatry. Her cousin—and now Amari's boyfriend—Dr. Kevin Brenner, was a prodigy in physics and had come to work at The University of Arizona the prior year. She'd followed him to town after he'd pulled some strings and gotten her admitted to UA's medical school. Her goal was to become a psychiatrist, and for that, she had to get a regular medical degree first, although if you didn't know any better, you'd think she was already a psychiatrist— she was that smart. Just like her cousin. Smart genes ran in their family.

It was Jenny who'd set her up with Kevin on their first date—not the romantic kind of date, but a date to discuss the physics behind the carbon dating of the Shroud of Turin. Needless to say, one thing led to another. They'd been dating for nearly a year now.

Jenny set down her textbook and stood, arching her back to stretch her muscles. "I'm going to get some lemonade. You want some?"

"Sure," Amari said. "That would be awesome."

Jenny went inside, and Amari sat watching the calming trickle of water from the pool fountain while combing her wet hair with her fingers, separating it into groups so she could do a quick braid. She was a master at braiding hair. She was especially good at weaving Navajo rugs and blankets, a skill her mother had taught her when she was alive. The Bible says that you entertain angels unaware. Sometimes she wondered if her mother had sent Jenny from heaven to watch over her in her absence. Jenny was that good of a friend.

****

Pete stomped on the gas pedal, his personal 82 Buick Regal's engine howling as it struggled against the steep incline of the Catalina Foothills. The closer he got to Amari's mountainside home, the more furious he became.

Northeast of Tucson, the Santa Catalina Mountains rose to an elevation of nearly 10,000 feet. Pete used to hike these mountains with his daughter when she was a kid. They'd even tried their hand at snow skiing on Mt. Lemmon. At the base of the mountain was the Catalina Foothills, where many of the wealthy citizens enjoyed estate-style homes with orange tile roofs, swimming pools, and sweeping views of the Tucson valley. These pricey homes were too expensive for a police detective's salary but easily affordable to the likes of Ernesto

Galliano. Mr. Moneybags rented a house up in the foothills for Amari and Jenny to live in. He'd never met Ernesto in person—just talked to him on the phone a couple of times. Mostly he knew about Ernesto from the way Amari sang his praises.

Pete found her driveway, and his tires barked as he left the main road and pulled up to her house at a quarter past six. Jenny's VW Rabbit was in the circular drive in front of the house, right behind Amari's 1978 Camaro, an exact duplicate of the one she had lost to a fire a few months back. How Ernesto found an exact match was a mystery. Then again, when you had Ernesto's resources, nothing was impossible. And sure enough, there was Ernesto's black Mercedes parked in front of the unattached garage. Upstairs from the garage, was a separate guest apartment. According to Amari, Ernesto and his men used it when they came to town. And unless he had loaned his daughter his Mercedes, it looked like they were in town now. That was good. It was high time they met face to face.

Pete got out of his car and went over to inspect Ernesto's fancy ride. He was surprised at what he saw. Up close, it wasn't what it seemed at a distance. The leather inside was worn. The paint was weathered and had scratches. Several small dents were on the doors and fender. It was an older model, maybe early '70s. You'd think someone like Ernesto would have the latest and greatest but apparently not.

"It's still a Mercedes," Pete uttered as he moved toward the front door.

Honestly, the house wasn't much either—not for Catalina Foothills standards. It was a simple three-bedroom rancher built back in the 60s. But like many Catalina foothills homes, it had a swimming pool that overlooked the Tucson Valley. Pete had been there once before, but never when Ernesto was around.

He pressed the doorbell button and waited. Nobody answered. He pushed it again and pounded on the door with his fist. He knew they were home. Unless, of course, Ernesto had hired a limousine for a night on the town. They were probably out celebrating their reckless victory in New Mexico.

Suddenly, the door swished open, and there was Jenny. She stood there with her typical makeup plastered face and teased up blond hair. She had her glasses on, so she must have been studying.

"Hey there, stranger," she said. "What brings you by?"

"You know good and well why I'm here," Pete said and brushed by her. "She in the pool?"

"Just got out," she called after him. "Can I get you some lemonade?"

"No thanks," Pete yelled back and slammed the sliding glass door behind him.

There she was, her tan legs stretched out on a lawn chair, not a care in the world, oblivious to the fact that she'd nearly given her father a heart attack.

Pete came up behind her and let her have it. "Are you out of your mind?"

Amari swiveled her legs around, and her nimble young body came off the chair in one fluid movement. A sheepish look dented her face. "Hey, Daddy."

"Don't you Daddy me. Did you think I wouldn't find out about this?"

"Dad, calm down. It's not what you think."

"Was this your first job? Is this what Moneybags is paying you to do? To be bait for a serial rapist!"

Her fists went defiantly to her hips. "It was my idea. He never brought it up. I did. You know that guy raped four girls," she said, holding up four fingers for effect.

"And were you trying to be the fifth?"

Her cheeks flushed red, and she squinted her eyes into narrow, determined slits. "I was trying to make sure there wasn't a fifth!"

Pete stepped back as a precaution. No telling what that martial arts trainer had conditioned her to do. "What did I tell you about that temper? It's going to be the end of you someday."

"My temper! You're the one who barged into my house and started yelling at me."

"I'm your father. I have every right to yell at my daughter, especially when I think it's for her own good. Wait till you're a parent. Then you'll understand."

Her face seemed to soften, and she just stared for several awkward seconds, the redness in her cheeks subsiding. "Did you know one of those girls was my cousin?" she said, her tone more sad than angry.

"I know, you told me right after it happened. Chooli, isn't it? Pretty girl. Felt awful when I heard."

"Then you can understand why I did what I did."

"No. No, I can't. Why put yourself in the same situation?"

"Do you remember Doli? She's my second cousin. She's starting there this fall. I did this to protect her."

"Amari, I know you mean well. You've got a big heart. But your cousins aren't my priority. You are."

"Well, it's over now. What's done is done. I got the guy. That's all that matters. And beat the crap out of him in the process."

"I'm sure he deserved it. I have no doubt. But you've got to stop thinking with your heart and start using your head. You could have been killed. Do you have any idea how dangerous that stunt was? Trust me, I've seen what a rapist can do to a girl. Not all of them survive. You're not Wonder Woman. You've just been lucky so far. But your luck is going to run out someday."

"It's not like I did this alone. Bonelli and Parker were just a few yards away. I had a microphone and transmitter. They could hear everything. And I've been training really hard with Tony. That's the black belt Ernesto hired to coach me. He's a fifth degree in taekwondo."

"And does all your karate-chopping make you bullet-proof?"

"That's why I learned the disarming techniques."

"And if you get it wrong? If you're too far away. What then?"

"Sometimes you just gotta live by faith. That's what Kevin tells me."

"Living by faith doesn't mean you have to test fate. You'd think after being stalked by a serial killer last year you'd want to lay low for a while. Getting on the news is what got you in trouble the last time, and now you've done it again. What if some other rapist out there decides to stalk you? Maybe payback for taking out one of his kind. You know rape isn't about sex, it's about control, about dominance. Some psycho out there might see you as a challenge."

"Then I'll put him in the hospital too," she replied with arrogance. "Or worse."

"It's that Ernesto character, isn't it? He's fueling that ego of yours. You never used to be like this. Sure, you could take care of yourself, but you never looked for trouble. Not until you got on his payroll. Where is he, anyway? It's time we had a face to face."

"Dad, I told you this wasn't his idea. He tried to talk me out of it, he really did. I told him I'd go up there by myself if he didn't send Bonelli and Parker with me."

He stood in silence and rubbed at the wrinkle trenches of his forehead.

"Dad?"

"Nothing, Amari, I'm just thinking."

"About what?"

"I'm still trying to get over what happened last year. You don't know the panic a father feels when he can't protect his kid. And you won't know until you have a child of your own. I don't ever want to feel that way again."

"I know, Daddy," she said, her expression full of empathy. "I know you love me more than anything. But we can't live in fear. You knew that when you took three bullets at a 7-Eleven—the bullet that's still lodged in your hip. When you responded to that robbery call, you knew you were taking a risk, but you did it anyway. Because that's who you are. And I'm just like you, admit it."

"That's what I'm afraid of."

"We all take risks. Every time we get on the road, we take the risk of getting hit by a truck. We can't live in fear. We have to walk by faith."

Pete gave a sigh of concession. "Well, you did get the guy. You may have even saved a life or two as far as we know."

"So you're not mad anymore?"

"I'm disappointed you didn't tell me about this."

"Can you see why I didn't?"

"Look, you're twenty-three years old. You're a grown woman. I can't expect you to ask my permission anymore. But if you're going to keep working for this Ernesto character, I want to have some words with him. If you won't listen to reason, then maybe he will."

"Of course, he will. Why do you think he wants to hire you? Because he values your judgment. He wants someone with experience on his team."

Pete nodded in disagreement. "It's not that easy for me. Being a cop is in my blood. When you've been doing this as long as I have, it's hard to change. Who's to say Ernesto won't fire me after a month? The department will fill my position. Then I won't have a job even if I want it back. Can't you see how risky this is for me? All you're giving up is waiting tables at Pizza Hut. But I've invested more than thirty years in my job."

"Then have him draw up a contract. Make him give you severance pay until you find another job. He'll do it, I promise. The least you can do is talk to him."

"For eighty-five grand a year and a hip replacement? It sounds too good to be true. That's not the way the real world works."

A figure suddenly appeared in Pete's peripheral vision. He turned to see a bearded man in blue jeans approach, holding a glass of lemonade. Pete fixed him with a smoldering stare. "Let me guess. You must be Ernesto."

Ernesto extended his free hand for a shake. "Finally, detective, we meet in person." He wore a cheap button-down shirt that looked like it could have been on sale at JCPenney. His wavy dark hair was long, parted in the middle and fell to his shoulders. A thick black beard fell an inch past his chin, and ugly scars marred his forehead.

Pete didn't answer but only eyed him with icy contempt.

"You look thirsty," Ernesto said and gave an uncomfortable laugh. "Would you like some lemonade?"

"Dad, be nice," Amari pleaded.

"Sure, I'll take some," Pete said sarcastically. He snatched the glass from Ernesto's hand and tossed the contents onto his face.

Chapter 5

Amari cupped her hands over her mouth in disbelief. She grabbed the towel she used to dry her hair and rushed to Ernesto's side. "Dad, are you crazy?" She dried lemonade from Ernesto's forehead. "I told you it wasn't his idea!"

Ernesto took the towel and finished the job, dabbing the pale-yellow liquid from his beard. "And you said your temper came from your *mother's side* of the family."

"You're lucky that wasn't my fist hitting your face," Pete said. "Who do you think you are, putting my daughter in that kind of danger?"

Ernesto held his hands up defensively as he staggered backward. "Detective Johnston, please, calm down. I tried to talk her out of it. She was going up there with or without my men."

"You should have called. You should have told me what she was up to."

"But I did try, Detective. You wouldn't take my calls."

"Because I told you I wasn't interested. There was nothing to discuss."

"If you were on our team, you could have helped us investigate those rapes. You could have found a safer way. My men are not trained in detective work. They are ex-Special Forces. They served together in Vietnam. They know how to kill, they know how to protect, but they know nothing of catching a rapist."

"I knew I could do it," Amari said. "And I did."

"That, she did," Ernesto said. "You have to hand her that."

Pete paused to gather his composure, wondering if those special-forces bodyguards were lurking nearby. If they felt their boss was threatened, he was no match for them. Besides, he was trying to teach his daughter to control her anger. He was setting a terrible example. "Listen, I'm sorry about the lemonade. But you have to understand where I'm coming from. With your kind of money, you can hire anyone you want for this little A-Team of yours. Why would a man with all your resources set your sites on my daughter, an inexperienced kid fresh out of college?"

"Because, Detective Johnston," Ernesto said and made a flustered sigh. "The reason should be obvious."

"Nothing is obvious about this. None of this makes any sense."

"She and I are kindred spirits."

"What's that supposed to mean?"

"We have a common passion—The Shroud of Turin."

Pete made a weary expression. Of course, this was about the Shroud. With her and Kevin, everything was always about the Shroud, even more so Ernesto. The three of them shared the same fixation, had the same vision of the future, the day the world would have irrefutable scientific proof that Jesus had indeed existed, and his words had been true. Such concrete evidence would be life altering for those who cared to listen. As a Christian himself, Pete couldn't dispute the logic.

"The first time I saw your daughter was on the evening news," Ernesto continued. "At that moment, I knew she was special. She had a holy passion for truth. So I sent my men first to investigate her claims, and then as it became necessary, to protect her from harm. After all, she had made a brilliant discovery, but one that many would not want to be revealed. Yet, she pursued her findings with uncommon courage. Dr. Brenner has a different theory as to what caused the carbon date to be invalid, but his theory is equally impressive. They both risked their lives to bring this truth to the world, and they did so out of the purest of motives. So tell me, detective, who else should I hire? If they can achieve so much with the scant resources at their disposal, God only knows what they could achieve with my financial support. Would you expect me to choose anybody else?"

Pete furrowed his brows and considered Ernesto's words. His rationale made sense. It was as if God had brought them together with a common goal. But what made little sense was Ernesto Galliano himself. He was a paradox. Wealth tended to breed indifference to the poor. In fact, Jesus himself had warned of the dangers of wealth. But Ernesto went against the grain. There was no logic to him. He was raised one way, yet he went in a completely different direction. No, his motives couldn't be entirely pure. There was a reason he was doing this. Perhaps he sought fame. Giving to the poor made better headlines than company takeovers. Maybe he'd figured out some way to profit from his philanthropy, if not now, perhaps sometime in the future. Maybe this was all some sort of publicity stunt he'd use to grow his fortune rather than give it all away.

But as Pete watched Ernesto in his simple, inexpensive garb, there was an innocence to his expression, a sincerity he'd rarely encountered in his years as an investigator. He could smell a lie—could feel the vibrations of deceit. But he felt none of that from Ernesto. He seemed pure as snow. But how? Everybody had demons. There had to be some dark motive behind his actions. He just hadn't discovered it yet, that's all.

"You okay, Dad?" she asked.

"I'm sorry, baby, it's just a lot for me to swallow. None of this makes any sense from my perspective. If something sounds too good to be true, then it probably is."

"Detective Johnston," Ernesto said. "I assure you, I'm no saint. If you think me too good to be true, then you are correct. For I am not good. No man is truly good. My behavior is not guided by inner goodness, but rather by torment."

"What are you talking about?"

"Guilt, Detective Johnston. If you must delve into my deepest motives, you may rest assured that your suspicions are correct. I do have my demons."

"I knew it," Pete said sharply. "Everybody does."

"Detective, have you ever heard the sound of a mother's cry the instant she learns of her child's death? And I don't mean at funerals. I mean the very instant she learned the terrible, irreversible news."

Pete had no idea where this was leading, but he wanted to crack the enigma that was Ernesto, so he humored him. "There was a case of a missing child back in '84. I had the unpleasant task of informing the mother that we'd found her son's dead body."

"And how did that sound make you feel?"

"Look, where are you going with this? That's not a memory I care to revisit."

"What did it sound like, Detective?"

"I told you that's a memory I'd just as soon forget."

"Answer my question, and you will better understand my state of mind. How did it sound? How did it make you feel?"

"It's hard to describe. Hell itself couldn't utter such a terrible sound. It gave me chills. It was a cry of despair like I'd never heard before. I had nightmares about that."

"Now imagine that you were the cause of this woman's grief. Imagine that sound was because of your poor judgment, because of your vain negligence."

Amari sniffled, and Pete saw the water building in her eyes. She didn't like to admit it, but deep inside, she was a softy. "I can't listen to this story again," she said and headed into the house.

Ernesto lowered his head and moved to the shade of the veranda. He wore a dire expression and rubbed his hands together anxiously. Pete's anger and suspicion melted, and he almost felt pity for the guy. "Look, if I've touched a nerve, I'm sorry. Maybe I should go."

Ernesto looked up with pleading eyes. "No, Detective, please. Hear me out. I know how suspicious I must sound. I don't blame you for an instant. Please," he said and motioned to the chair next to him.

Pete sat down and looked out at the Tucson skyline as he waited for Ernesto to gather his courage. What he was about to reveal was clearly upsetting.

"Do you see my beard? Some people say it makes me look like Jesus. The scars on my forehead are often compared to the scars Jesus suffered from the crown of thorns. Some say that I wear the beard intentionally so that I will look like him. The comparison humbles me, but nothing could be further from the truth. I wear this beard to hide my shame." Ernesto paused to collect his thoughts.

"I'm listening," Pete said.

"The scars on my head are not my only ones." Ernesto used his fingers to separate the hairs on his lower cheek.

Deep, jagged scars etched the skin under his beard. "I have to wear my beard long. Otherwise, the scars would still be visible. There are equally grotesque scars on my other cheek."

Pete cringed at the sight. "So what happened to you?"

"Wealth happened to me."

"You say that like it's a curse."

"In many ways, it is a curse." He drew a deep breath and drove into a painful recollection. "My parents are from the region of Perugia, just north of Rome. They immigrated to the United States after World War II. They relocated to Fresno, and my father started a small metalworking shop that he used to manufacture machine parts. Eventually, he had built an entire automotive parts factory. I was born in 1952. My mother had a complicated pregnancy and could no longer have children. At any rate, my father's wealth continued to grow. By the time he died in 1974, he had amassed several factories in the United States and Mexico, providing parts for GM, Chrysler, and Ford."

"Amari tells me you were the sole heir to this fortune."

"That's true. My parents divorced in 1970, and my father left his entire billion-dollar company to me. He'd wanted me to run the company, but I sold it instead. After all, I'd wanted to be a Catholic priest when I was younger. My mother supported me, but my father wouldn't hear of it. He insisted that I learn the family business and continue his empire when he was gone. Clearly, I had other intentions. Rather than become a priest, I realized that I could affect far more good in the world by using his wealth to further the cause of Christ."

"So what about these scars?"

"Aside from his mansion in Fresno, my father purchased another estate in his homeland, back in Perugia. When school was out, I spent my summers at his Italian estate. My father was proud of his wealth, and he enjoyed flaunting it in front of old friends and family that remained in Italy. So on my sixteenth birthday, he bought me a brand-new sports car—an Italian made Ferrari. At that time, we had a trusted family servant by the name of Luisa. She lived in a nearby village and brought her four-year-old daughter, Gabriella, to work with her. My mother and I adored the child and gladly watched her as Luisa went about her chores."

"So what does that have to do with the scars?"

"My father's estate was atop a mountain with sweeping views of the village below. There is a winding road that leads from the village to his home. I had a sixteen-year-old friend at the time. His name was Fabio. We had taken the car out for a spin one late afternoon. A car with such horsepower has no place in the control of a teenager. I was speeding along this mountain pass, more than twice the speed limit." Ernesto rubbed his palm against his eyes to smear away the gathering tears. "It all happened so fast. When I rounded the corner, there was Luisa's sedan. The momentum of my car forced me to veer into her lane. I tried to brake, but it was too late. Honestly, the only thing I remember is seeing her car. I don't even remember applying the brakes, but the authorities said I left a hundred feet of skid marks. The next thing I remember was careening down the hillside. It was a convertible, and I wore no seatbelt. These scars you see on my face were caused by stones and tree branches as my body tumbled down the mountain. Just before the edge of a cliff, my body slammed into a tree. That tree broke several ribs, but it saved my life. The tree stood alone, teetering on the edge of a cliff. I'm not sure how it grew into the rocks, but somehow the roots found soil. Sometimes I wonder if the angels had foreseen this event and planted that tree on purpose. I believe there is a reason for everything."

Pete let the story absorb. He was guilt-stricken. He was trying to make up for what he did as a child. "That's too bad about what happened to you. But you were a kid. It was your dad's fault for getting you that car."

"Did you not help Amari buy a sports car when she was sixteen?"

"She had to have it for work."

"And did she ever get into an accident?"

"No, not by the grace of God."

"I was not so fortunate. My next memories were of lying in the emergency room. My face was bandaged, my eyes covered with gauze, but my ears heard everything. It was a small emergency room and Luisa, Gabriella, and Fabio were in the same ward, on different beds. I will never, ever forget the haunting sound of Luisa's voice when they pulled the sheet over young Gabriella's body."

A tear leaked from Ernesto's eyes and was caught by his beard, "My sweet Gabriella. Such a sweet child," he said, his voice cracking with emotion. "She didn't deserve what I did to her. Luisa didn't deserve that. And it was all my fault—and my father's. Because of his money!" Ernesto pounded the arm of his chair in anger. He sat silent for a moment, breathing deep, steady breaths to quell the emotion. "Now and then," he finally spoke, "I hear Luisa's cry in my dreams, and I wake in terror. Every morning when I look in the mirror, the scars on my forehead are a cruel reminder of the foolishness of my youth—and the cost of stinking opulence." He turned to face Pete. "Now, Detective Johnston, do you see what motivates me? I have vowed to go to my grave penniless. I am like a camel trying to squeeze through the eye of a needle. I can squeeze through, but first I must unload my pack. Help me do that, Detective Johnston. Come work for me and help me right the world's wrongs."

Pete stood and shoved his hands into his pockets, contemplating the shocking story he'd just heard. He'd never for a moment expected this, and his defensive resentment gave way to pity. "Thank you for sharing that with me. I know that's gotta be hard to talk about."

"If it will help you make your decision, I will gladly repeat it."

"That won't be necessary. I just need some time, that's all. This isn't easy for me. Amari gave up being a waitress, but I'm giving up an entire career."

Ernesto stood and met Pete's gaze. "Do you believe in destiny?"

"In some cases, maybe."

"I believe that God brought us together, you and I. Everything happens for a reason. Now if you will excuse me, I think I need to lay down," he said and walked toward the fence's gate with his head lowered in despair.

Pete sank back into his chair to gather his thoughts. Just then, Jenny came back out with another glass of lemonade. Pete took it from her and sipped as he continued to ponder Ernesto's words. "Jenny, sit down for a minute, would you?"

Jenny sat next to him. "You want my take on this?"

"Sure, you're the one with the psychology degree. What do you make of Ernesto? Can I trust him?"

"I think so. I mean, he's no saint. Sometimes he drinks a little too much wine, and sometimes I even hear him cuss. And, honestly, I think he could find a better use for his money if he's really into helping the poor. His plane is one example. He says it belonged to his father, but it costs a fortune to maintain. Still, it's a useful tool, I suppose. It gives him easy access to any part of the world. I understand he flies to Africa and South America a lot. He sets up clinics and mobile dentists RVs down there. And he uses his estate in Fresno as an orphanage for abused children. He has ten kids living there last I heard."

"If that's the worst you can say about him, then he sounds pretty clean."

"In his actions, yes. But psychologically, he's got issues."

"You don't say?" Pete scooted forward in his chair. "Care to elaborate? Is this guy bonkers? Is he crazy?"

"I hate when people use that word."

"You got a better word for it?"

"Calling somebody crazy is just a lazy way to judge someone who's got challenges to deal with. I mean, think about it. Some people have diabetes. That's a problem with pancreatic chemistry. Some people have mental problems. That's a problem with brain chemistry. The brain is just an organ, like any other part of your body."

"So what's wrong with Ernesto's organ?"

"Isn't it obvious?"

"To you, maybe, but not me."

"Didn't you see the way he suddenly left? He went to go lay down, didn't he?"

"I guess he was tired. Maybe he just wanted to wash the lemonade out of his hair."

"Ernesto suffers from clinical depression. He's very hard on himself. He never thinks he's good enough. He has very poor self-esteem."

"He's got some sort of guilt complex?"

"Remorse is a better term for it. It's anguish he lives with daily. Remorse comes from the Latin word that means 'to bite with more force'. It refers to the gnashing of teeth that goes on in the mind of a person with a guilty conscience. As a psychological defense mechanism to combat the guilt, he relies on contrition. The word contrition comes from the Latin word meaning 'crushed'. In Ernesto's case, he feels crushed by the weight of what he caused as a teenager. But a contrite person takes responsibility for their actions. They don't make any excuses. Instead, they make a sustained, long lasting effort to make themselves a better person. And in Ernesto's case, he uses his resources as a tool for contrition. It's like an antidepressant for him. Kind of like Prozac without the side effects. When he sees suffering relieved because of his actions, it improves his self-esteem and relieves his remorse."

"Well that explains it, I guess. Like he said, there's a reason for everything."

"In most cases, that's very true."

"You know, he never did finish the story."

"What do you mean?"

"What about Luisa, the mother? And Fabio, his teenage friend?"

"He says Luisa had some internal injuries but recovered. His father paid her off, so she wouldn't press charges. Ernesto has yet to face her after what happened. He wants to, but it's too painful. It might provide closure for him, but he says he can't make himself do it."

"I understand. But what about Fabio? How bad was he hurt?"

Jenny's expression turned dire. "That's another reason he feels guilty. He had severe brain damage. He's conscious but just short of being a vegetable. On the bright side," Jenny said in an upbeat tone.

"There's a bright side to this?"

"On the bright side, Fabio lives in a very nice nursing home built by Ernesto. Conditions in state-run nursing homes are always disturbing, but Ernesto made sure this one has all the perks. There are 80 beds in this home, and only the poorest of the poor are allowed in. So at least they live their last years in luxury."

"At least there's that. So where's Amari?"

"She's in her room."

"Sulking?"

"Yep, she's mad at you."

"The lemonade stunt was a bit much?"

"Yeah. A little bit."

Chapter 6

Oviedo, Spain

The grappling hook was holding. Carl Mikolajczak crept up the side of the ancient stone bell tower, his climbing gloves gripped tight around the rope, his arm and back muscles straining as he made his gradual ascent. A skilled mountain climber, when he was young, he'd scaled the face of El Capitan in Yosemite National Park. That was before his enlightenment, before his escalation to the next level. Now Carl was known only as 876. Lieutenant Senior Grade 876 to be precise.

He heaved at the rope one final time and lunged his body through the arched window at the top of the tower. His breaths were quick and hard, a reminder that he was not young anymore and not nearly as physically fit. But that was just a temporary condition. When Calvin's craft reached the lush gardens of New Canaan, he would eat of the so-called technological tree of life, and he would be provided a glorified, new body.

He lifted the claws of the grappling hook from the concrete ledge, cringing at the noise it made. It was two in the morning, and he'd made his way quietly enough through the narrow side streets behind the Oviedo Cathedral, which were dark and barren of people. He had snuck from his hotel and through the Plaza Corrada del Obispo. Then he'd moved down the narrow alley of Travesia Santa Barbara undetected—as far as he knew. From there, it was simply a matter of climbing an iron gate, connecting the grappling hook, and climbing the tower.

The next phase would be tricky. The plan was to drop out the side window of the bell tower and jump onto the tile roof of the building below. This building connected to the tiny Camara Santa chapel that housed the Sudarium of Oviedo—the cloth that had wrapped Jesus' face as he was taken down from the cross. Once on top of the roof, he would fix the grappling hook onto the opposite edge of the roof that faced the courtyard. He would then drape the rope over the arch of the roof and lower himself down the other side of the building, setting down atop the Camara Santa. Then he would simply break an upper window that was near the roof line, drop himself into the chapel, cut the lock to the iron gate that separated the Sudarium from the chapel, pry open the case that held the Sudarium, stuff the relic into his backpack, and then escape by the same route. It was so simple, Calvin had explained. His success was assured, a prophecy fulfilled.

"By God's providence," he uttered to himself as he apprehensively stepped over to the side window of the tower. He leaned out and surmised the distance to the rooftop below. It was too dark to tell, so he pulled his flashlight from his backpack and risked being spotted, just for a necessary moment. He shined the beam down onto the tile roof and made calculations in his head. It had to be at least ten feet. If he didn't break an ankle, it would surely be painful. He would have used the grappling hook to lower himself, but how would he unhook it from below? Why didn't he bring two hooks? Calvin had assured him every detail was mapped out. Nothing could go wrong.

He dropped his backpack, rope, and grappling hook onto the tile roof below. He checked his pistol in his shoulder harness to ensure the safety was on. The last thing he needed was to shoot his leg during the hard landing. He stepped onto the window ledge and turned himself around. Gripping the ledge with his fingers, he lowered himself out the window until his feet dangled over the roof. Doing this would remove a few feet from his drop.

"One, two, three," he whispered and released his grip. His legs hit first but gave way as they struck the angled roof. He came down hard on his butt, wincing from the pain. He paused to evaluate his condition. Other than his throbbing tailbone, everything seemed intact. The Lord had delivered him.

His faith renewed, he stood and gathered his gear. Carefully planting his feet on the angled tiles, he hunched down low to reduce his center of gravity. He crept toward the edge of the roof that rose above the building's courtyard.

Suddenly, a deafening thunderclap overhead startled him. The rain fell lightly at first, then a torrent poured from the heavens, soaking his clothes in frigid water.

"Lord, what are you doing?" 876 said in a panic. Suddenly, his feet slipped out from under him. He hit the hard tiles and searing pain stabbed from his already injured tailbone. He tried to stand but quickly fell into an excruciating, bumpy slide down the roof. He flipped to his stomach and clawed at the tiles but to no effect. The roof's edge raced toward him. He careened over the edge but barely caught the gutter one-handed. He dangled from the ledge, kicking his feet wildly, hoping they would connect with a window, something as a hedge against gravity's pull. But there was nothing but air. 876 reached up with his free hand and snatched at the gutter's edge but fell short. He kicked his legs to provide momentum, rocking back and forth on the pendulum of his right wrist. On the third try, his left fingers connected to the gutter, and relief came when he held tight with both hands.

He caught his breath as the rain beat down on his face. He could feel the water rising on his fingers that curved into the mouth of the gutter. He had to act fast. If he could just muster his strength to heave himself back onto the roof. He braced his feet against the wall to displace some of his weight. Then he noticed it, just below him and to the right. It was a small balcony rail. If he couldn't find the strength to get back on the roof, maybe he could swing his body over and grab the balcony rail on the way down.

He shut his eyes to gather focus, breathing heavily to give his muscles oxygen for the task. God would rescue him. He was just being tested, that was all. He could do this. He drew a deep breath and held the air in his lungs. He heaved himself upward. The roof edge came to his waist. He started to pull his leg up and onto the ledge— when the gutter whined, and part of it popped loose from the roof.

"This can't be happening!" he cried as another gutter bolt failed. "The prophecy!"

His panicked eyes noticed a concrete support pillar extending from the wall. It was a long shot, but it was all he had. He braced his foot against the pillar, kicked off against it, and released his grip on the gutter. As cruel gravity pulled his body down, he reached out in desperation for the balcony rail. He caught it one-handed, his other hand and feet flailing wildly. His climbing gloves aided his grip—but the rail was too wet. One by one, his fingers slipped away from the rail.

"God help me!" he screamed looking down into the depth below, a concrete sidewalk awaiting his fall.

Something clapped around his wrist. He felt a tug on his sleeve.

"Dame tu otra mano!" a forceful woman's voice boomed from above.

"Please, help me!"

"Then give me your other hand!"

He brought his arm up, and she clasped her grip around his wrist. Then he wrapped his fingers firmly around her wrist as well. She braced her house shoe against the rail and heaved her weight backward. When his waist reached the top of the rail, he flung his leg over the top and fell onto the balcony floor.

"What are you doing out here?" the woman angrily asked. "Are you crazy?"

"Thank you," he said as he gathered his wits. "You saved me."

"I saved you from falling. But I'm calling the police."

The woman stepped back inside and started to close the door. But 876 was too swift. He came to his feet and blocked the door with his boot. The woman stomped on his toe, and he reflexively pulled his foot away, reeling from the pain. The door slammed shut, and he heard the lock engage.

"Please!" he cried, his face pressed into the window pane. "You don't understand. I am an instrument of God! And so are you! You saved me by divine providence!"

876 saw the curtain snap shut. He wasn't getting through. He balled his fist and punched at the square window pane next to the handle. The thin glass shattered. He reached in, unlocked the door, and used his hip to force his way into the apartment. The beefy, middle-aged

woman gawked at him through ugly black-frame glasses, stammering for words.

"Please, listen to me," 876 said. "You have a higher purpose. You and I both. It is no accident you saved me. It is so you can help."

She backed away until the kitchen table stopped her. "Help you do what?"

"I am one of the chosen. And now you have been chosen as well."

"Of course, I'm chosen. I'm a nun, and this is a church. Now, why are you here?"

"For the Sudarium, of course. I have come to retrieve the Sudarium. I have come to fulfill the prophecy."

"You're here to steal the Sudarium of Oviedo? I've studied the Bible. What kind of prophecy is that?"

"It is from the prophet of our age."

"And this prophet told you to steal the Sudarium?"

"No, not steal, borrow. Until its purpose has been fulfilled. Then it will be returned."

"I'm calling the police," she said and made her way for the phone.

He stepped in front of her and blocked her advance. "Please don't do that. You don't understand yet, but you will. Please, hear me out."

"All I've heard so far is crazy talk."

"I had thought I was supposed to break into the chapel, from a window. But now I know God's true plan. You'll help me gain access."

"And help you steal the Sudarium? You think they give me keys to the Camara Santa? You're out of your mind. Now, out of my way. I'm calling the police."

876 had tried to reason, but Satan was clouding her judgment. It was time to implement the backup plan. He unzipped his coveralls, pulled the pistol from his shoulder holster, and pointed it at the nun. "Don't make me use this."

54

"Now hold on just a second," she said, backing into the small kitchenette.

876 pursued her until she backed into the stove. "This is divine providence, Sister. Soon, you will see that."

She fumbled for something behind her. "No, this is divine providence!"

He saw the blur of an iron skillet just before it collided with his head.

Chapter 7

Pete sat at his work desk, peering through reading glasses at the report the Perugia Police department had kindly faxed over free of charge.

George stepped into the office. "You get it?"

"Got it right here," Pete said. "They were nice enough to translate the basics to English."

"So what's it say?"

"Looks like he was telling the truth. The police report agrees with his story. Said the charges were dropped."

"I bet his dad bribed somebody."

"I'd say you're right."

"So you taking the job?"

"I don't know, George. At least now I know the guy means well. I'm tempted to, but this is all I know." Pete gazed at a bulletin board covered with notes and pictures concerning ongoing cases. "If I resign, who's taking these cases? What about the guy who got flattened by the dump truck? Who's going to clear that case?"

"If you don't want the job, you think Ernesto would give it to me? Tell him I'll work for seventy grand."

Just then, the phone rang. "Hold on a second," Pete said and picked up the receiver.

"Chief Turner wants you in his office, pronto," Sergeant Novak said over the phone.

"The chief? What's he want with a peon like me?"

"Don't know. But I saw a couple of suits headed toward his office. Must be about one of your cases."

A sense of dread overcame him. He knew exactly which case this involved. "George, we'll talk about this later. But I have a hunch you may be getting your wish."

"You mean Ernesto's going to hire me?"

"No, I mean you getting a shot at my job. If this is what I think it's about, my position may be up for grabs."

****

"Have a seat, Detective Johnston," Police Chief Turner said as Pete entered the office. The chief wore the standard navy uniform coat with a gold badge and matching gold ranking stripes on his sleeves. His hair was one of those shades of gray that looked pure white. He was only sixty but could easily pass for eighty.

Pete took the middle chair in front of Turner's desk, flanked on both sides by men of a higher pay grade. Lieutenant Braden was to his left. He sat nervously popping his knuckles, stiff as a board, no part of his back touching the chair. Next to him was a lawyer named Tom something-or-another with his combed-over hair. He did work for Internal Affairs—another bad sign. To his right was Commander Bennett with his blotchy, pink skin, and next to him was a Terry Holtzclaw, with his black Armani suit and Gucci shoes. He was a well-known civil suit lawyer Pete occasionally saw around the courthouse.

"Detective Johnston," Chief Turner said, "do you know why we brought you here today?"

"I have a hunch," Pete replied and cleared his throat. "I'd say it's about the Spalding case." A few months back, a wealthy businessman was found dead, floating in his swimming pool up in the Catalina foothills, near Amari's new house. At first, it looked like the guy had a heart attack and drowned in the pool. But when the toxicology report came back, a heavy helping of valium was found in his blood.

Holtzclaw cleared his own throat and spoke first. "My client, Tina Spalding, is filing a two-million-dollar lawsuit against the Tucson Police Department."

"Two million dollars?" Pete blurted. "Is she out of her mind? For what?"

"Defamation of character," Holtzclaw said. "Suggest she's out of her mind to the papers and we'll make it three million."

Pete swiveled left in his chair. "Tom, can they do that?"

"I'm afraid they can," Tom said.

Holtzclaw held up a newspaper and said, "According to the Tucson Times, you said she was guilty as sin."

"And she is," Pete said emphatically. "The paper prints the truth, doesn't it? I told the truth."

"You also made a wisecrack about her being the *black widow* of Pima County," Tom said.

Pete swiveled back to Tom. "Whose side are you on, his or mine?"

"The truth of the matter is," Tom said, "she was cleared of all charges. There was insufficient evidence for trial. But unfortunately, in the court of public opinion, you convicted her with your careless words."

"Mrs. Spalding is a lady of high society," Holtzclaw said. "Now her reputation is ruined. She's been blackballed from several societal functions. She says you ruined her life."

"She ruined her own life when she killed her husband," Pete replied sharply.

"Detective Johnston," Chief Turner said, "you're not helping matters."

"I'm sorry, Chief, but the evidence speaks for itself," Pete said. "He had enough valium in his blood to kill a horse. Somebody must have spiked his drink. This is a classic case of a wife murdering her husband for money. He'd recently filed for divorce. Marital infidelity. She was about to be cut off. It's cut and dried—ready for an episode of Murder She Wrote."

"Mrs. Spalding states that she had been shopping for several hours," Holtzclaw said. "If he ingested the valium, then he did so from his own volition. He had a prescription. It was clearly suicide. He was distraught over the coming divorce."

"Who takes valium and goes for a swim?" Pete asked.

"You would if you wanted to make certain you died," Lieutenant Braden said.

"Now you're on their side too?" Pete said. "You thought she was guilty. Everyone in this department agreed with me."

"Unfortunately, the courts did not agree," Holtzclaw said. "They didn't even find it worthy of a trial."

"She says she was shopping," Pete said. "Yet she failed to produce one receipt. Not one. What rich lady spends hours shopping yet doesn't buy anything? And we checked with the clerks at the mall. They knew her well. She shopped there all the time. According to them, they never saw her that night."

"That's because she never rang anything up," Holtzclaw said. "The clerks were busy waiting on paying customers."

"She was lying," Pete replied flatly. "I can smell a lie, and she reeked of it."

"And who made you the one-man jury? Holtzclaw asked. "I see no gavel in your hand. Yet she was convicted by your careless words."

"Look, I'm sorry," Pete said. "I was under a lot of stress at the time. I was losing sleep. I wasn't in my right mind. A serial killer was stalking my only daughter, for crying out loud."

"Detective Johnston," Chief Turner said, "we are all very aware of your situation last year. For that matter, the entire world is aware. But that doesn't excuse your behavior. Now, I want to make this as easy as I can on you—and for the department. I've taken the liberty of drafting a letter of resignation. Ms. Spalding says she doesn't need the money, nor does she want to take funds from the very department that protects her. So instead of suing the department and dragging you into a drawn-out trial, she has agreed to drop the lawsuit if we terminate your employment."

"Well, of course, she wants me gone," Pete said. "She knows I'm still working this case. She's afraid I'll uncover more evidence and bring this to trial."

"Pete, you've had a good run," Lieutenant Braden said. "You should be proud of your service. You put a lot of bad guys in jail."

"And for that, you're firing me?"

"If this goes to trial and she wins, we'll take that two million dollars out of your pension—after we fire you," Chief Turner said. "Go easy on yourself. If you sign this resignation, then you can keep your pension. You've been with the department long enough to retire. Don't take this as quitting, just say you decided to retire."

Pete stared at the resignation letter the chief had slid in front of him. He laughed at the irony of it all.

"You see," Chief Turner said. "You're laughing because you know I'm right."

"That's not why I'm laughing," Pete said. "You see, I made this new friend the other day. And he tells me that everything happens for a reason. I think God put this in front of me for a reason. Hand me a pen, and I'll sign your paper. It's time I moved on."

Chief Turner handed him a pen. "You're doing the right thing."

"I am doing the right thing," Pete said and signed his name at the bottom of the page. He handed back the pen. "Thank you for showing me that."

Chapter 8

Lieutenant Senior Grade 876 sat in the passenger seat of Adrian Agricola's black Toyota Tacoma, seemingly engrossed in his delusions. Adrian had just picked him up from the Phoenix International Airport. They made the last leg of the three-hour journey home, turning off the main highway, traveling down the long dirt road that led to another dirt road, which eventually led to the compound. The closer to home they got, the more apprehensive 876 appeared to become. After all, he had failed to complete Calvin's mission. He would have some explaining to do and some humiliation to endure. Adrian hadn't heard from 762, the one who went to Turin. Most likely he was in an Italian prison, or even more likely, a mental asylum—or better yet, dead.

Adrian approached the turnoff to the compound but kept driving, never slowing down.

876 craned his neck, watching the long trail of dust billowing from the back of the pickup. "Where are we going? We just missed our turn."

"Actually," Adrian said, "I wanted to show you something. Last night I saw a light, steaking down to earth. At first, I thought it was a meteorite. Now I'm not so sure."

876 perked up, his curiosity aroused. "You think it was a UFO?"

"I can't say for sure. Whatever it is, it hit the ground hard. It's mostly buried, but I could swear I saw something shine like metal. I need you to help me dig it out."

"Have you consulted Calvin?"

"Not yet. We need to investigate first. Then we'll share our findings."

Adrian pulled his truck off the dirt road and drove several minutes into the open desert, his torso bobbing with the bump and jolt of the terrain. Finally, he came to a stop in front of a small embankment.

"It's over here," Adrian said and got out of the truck. "Just on the other side of that little hill."

876 got out of the truck and curiously followed Adrian up the mound. Once they reached the crest, they descended the other side and stopped just in front of a coffin-sized hole in the ground.

"It's inside there," Adrian said, forcing an edge of excitement into his tone.

876 peered into the hole. "I don't see anything metal. Just looks like a hole to me. Almost like a grave."

"Calvin can't know that you failed," Adrian said matter-of-factly. "I need him to believe you're still trying to retrieve the Sudarium. Trust me, none of this was my idea. I'm sorry it had to end this way."

"Of course it wasn't your idea. You are no longer the anointed. The glory belongs to Calvin. He had the vision from God."

"Do you see why you can't report to the congregation?"

"What are you saying? You're not making sense, Brother Adrian. Why have you brought me here?"

"Calvin must believe the vision."

"What are you suggesting?"

"I'm suggesting that you *can* eventually tell Calvin about your failure. Only, I prefer you do so later—when you see him again in New Canaan." Adrian reached into his pocket and produced a revolver. He leveled it at 876's head and pulled the trigger.

****

Adrian leaned against the chopper as he watched former army pilot, Ian Somers, taxi down the runway. The black Hughes MD 500 he leaned against was a light utility helicopter bought at auction for a bargain price considering its near mint condition. The used twin-engine Beechcraft Super King coming down the runway cost over a half million. Both aircraft were purchased during one of Calvin's manic spending sprees a couple of years before. Ian had helped Calvin make the selection.

As Ian approached, Adrian moved out of the hangar and stood off to the side with his fingers plugging his ears against the thunderous roar of the plane engines, curling his nose in protest to the engine exhaust. Inside the hangar, a mobile home was parked against the corrugated steel wall. Ian's emphatic condition of employment was that he had his own housing, separate from the main house, separate from the religious fanatics who called it home.

The eighty-acre property was enclosed by a twelve-foot fence with razor wire along the top. The fence served a dual purpose—that of keeping post-apocalyptic invaders out, and more disconcerting, it served as a prison wall for any of Calvin's forty followers who secretly wished to escape.

The main house was a square, dormitory-style building that was aligned perfectly to due North. A narrow swath of irrigated green grass surrounded the house on four sides, except for the pavestone driveway that led into the first story garage. Atop the building was its most striking feature, the glass pyramid that served as a chapel for worship. The pyramid shape was essential to focus the earth's energy, Calvin had insisted. At night, devoid of city light pollution, the stars were impressive to behold. It was the perfect vantage point for the faithful to dream about their imaginary new home, light years away.

Adrian had tried to convince Calvin to build his compound elsewhere, somewhere more convenient. But Calvin believed the coordinates, the exact longitude and latitude, must be strictly adhered to. At any other location, the energy would be insufficient. After all, it wasn't energy from the electrical grid he was after, but the energy of the Earth itself. Only the nexus would suffice.

Until recently, Adrian hadn't the faintest idea as to Calvin's rationale. He assumed it was something he'd dug up in one of those crazy books he frequently read, obscure books written by California New-Age types. So Adrian reluctantly played along, his smile faked, his faith insincere. What choice did he have? Calvin paid the bills. The food was crap, but Calvin was the one who put it on the table.

Naturally, the problem with such isolation was logistics. During the planning stages, Adrian had warned of the challenges of getting utilities hooked up. Providing provisions for forty people would be troublesome. The only road access was a three-mile dirt road that led to another eight-mile-long dirt road, which led to a two-

lane highway that tourists used to drive to the Grand
Canyon. It was a forty-mile drive to the closest town of
Williams. Provisions could have been trucked in from
Williams, but Calvin was paranoid that the frequent trips
would call attention to the compound. So he'd insisted
upon building an airstrip and having supplies flown in
from Flagstaff—an airstrip he would hypothetically use
later to land his space-ark. And if you needed a plane, then
you needed a pilot. So Adrian had suggested the services
of a pilot buddy he knew from the army. Ian was out of
work because of a technicality involving his vision so he'd
been willing to take what he could get.

Looking back, Adrian knew life after his dishonorable
discharge from the US Army would be uncertain, but he'd
never envisioned such a freakish outcome. The cult had
been something he'd stumbled upon, just one of several
ways he'd tried feed himself. He'd even resorted to
changing his name with the help of a guy named Gustavo
he'd met in prison. Adrian Agricola was just a name he'd
made up to evade arrest. After all, he was wanted for fraud
in three states. Unfortunately, getting an honest job
wasn't easy without a legitimate social security number.
Telephone scams were profitable but risky. Also, long
distance bills made for a ton of overhead that cut into
profits. So after another short stint in prison back in '81,
he'd come across this cult when one of its members was
handing out recruiting handbills outside a New Age
conference in Santa Barbara.

David White had been the leader back then. He'd
managed to brainwash his flock into believing that God's
angels were not majestic, musclebound creatures with
powerful wings of snow-white feathers, but rather little
gray creatures with a big bald heads, large black eyes, and
spindly arms and legs—just like those seen in the movie,
Close Encounters of the Third Kind. According to David, he'd

been abducted by one of these aliens and subsequently enlightened as to the true nature of the universe.

Adrian had felt silly playing along with their ridiculous belief system, but at the time he was hungry and desperate for housing. He was in no position to be choosy. Then, once inside, he realized the simplistic beauty of the con. The best way to make money wasn't to cheat people out of their cash, but to convince them that it was God's will that they hand over their life's savings. As L. Ron Hubbard had said after founding Scientology, you don't get rich writing science fiction. If you want to get rich, start a religion.

Frustrated by his spartan existence and lack of control, Adrian had considered starting his own church from scratch, but that was no easy task. Seizing control of his current cult would be more efficient. Acting had come easy for him. He'd gotten several leading roles in drama class in high school. Playing a gullible idiot was easy. The tricky part was getting rid of David and assuming his role as leader. How else was he going to get rich? It certainly wasn't from mowing yards and handing his cash over to David, which is what he'd been reduced to. He hated getting his hands dirty, the dust in his hair, grass clippings clinging to his pants. David needed to disappear. Or better yet, one of those little gray aliens needed to whisk him away to heaven in a flying saucer. But before that happened, David needed to make a recording that instructed the followers to accept Adrian as their new leader.

It's amazing what someone does with a gun pointed at their head, Adrian mused. Getting rid of the body wasn't so easy.

Life had been simpler back then, before Calvin joined the group. With David out of the picture, Adrian had taken control. They'd rented a mansion in Santa Barbara. All thirty of his flock worked dutifully at their day jobs and deposited all their earnings into the common fund with Adrian's name attached to it. All he had to do was play the part David had taught him. The drawback, of course, was sharing a house with thirty gullible dimwits. But he'd envisioned a brighter future. He'd been investing the common fund in stocks. Unfortunately, he got a tad greedy and made some risky buys. When his stocks tanked, the congregation was nearly bankrupt.

Adrian had considered selling his stocks for a loss and leaving in the dead of night. But just as he'd been packing his bags, Brother Kasper, aka, 792, had called from the facility—a court-ordered internment due to his mental instability. Kasper was excited because he'd just attended a sort of Bible study in the rec room, which was led by a man named Calvin Nettles, a man with a remarkably similar belief system—a man who was stinking rich thanks to his father's trust fund. Their meeting was by divine providence, Kasper had insisted. Not only was Calvin wealthy, but he already had ten of his own followers. It was a chance to join forces—to increase the size of the fold, and to ensure the common purse had sufficient funds.

At first, it seemed like a beautiful plan. Once Calvin had become one of the fold, Adrian could start siphoning off his wealth, the same way he'd absorbed the wealth of the rest of the group. Unfortunately, according to the rules of Calvin's trust fund, payments were to be made monthly, gradually correcting for inflation. The payments were enough to cover monthly expenses for what was now, including those ten who followed Calvin into the cult, forty members. Feeding that many mouths left next to nothing for him to embezzle without getting caught. Fortunately, Gustavo, his friend from prison who'd help change his identity, also specialized in forgery and bank fraud. Gustavo had managed to finagle Calvin access to his entire trust fund, which was paid out in cash in several installments during a one-month period. The problem was that Calvin's closest followers, his so-called *inner three*, were always present during the bank withdrawals, always ensuring the cash was delivered securely to Calvin's thick walled safe that one of his inner three had purchased. Still, with Adrian officially in charge of the cult, he assumed it wouldn't take long to lay hands on a good portion of Calvin's cash. He didn't need it all to retire comfortably. A couple million would do nicely.

Like all well-conceived plans, there was potential for unforeseen consequences. Who could have known Calvin could be such a charismatic and compelling preacher? Before long, he'd muscled his way to the top, reducing Adrian's role to second in command. Adrian had tried to resist, but cult members are like dogs. They seemed to smell intentional deceit. The difference between Calvin and Adrian was that Calvin believed the words that came out of his own mouth, whereas Adrian just pretended to believe. That difference was all it took. One moment Adrian was on top, and the next thing he knew, he'd been demoted to Commander, second in charge, as Calvin assumed the role of Captain. Adrian knew that a house divided couldn't stand. And so as far as the rest of the cult knew, he'd happily stepped aside and allowed Calvin to resume control. He made no waves when Calvin purchased the remote desert land, built his eccentric pyramid-topped estate, and then hired Ian and provided both a plane and helicopter. Meanwhile, Adrian waited, scheming for the perfect opportunity to secure a comfortable retirement—for the perfect chance to access the impenetrable safe full of cash in Calvin's bedroom.

The opportunity finally came last winter when a young couple down in Tucson had managed to refute the carbon date performed on the Shroud of Turin. Calvin had been obsessed with the Shroud of Turin for some time. And leave it to a nutjob like Calvin to translate their discoveries about the Shroud into his ticket into heaven.

Unfortunately, there was a hitch to Calvin's heavenward ambition. Plan A involved stealing two of the world's most valuable religious relics. Fortunately, Adrian had his own Plan B—a plan that if played out correctly, could easily fund his early retirement.

Once inside the hanger, Ian killed the engine and Adrian strode over to the plane. A door behind the wing fell open, and Ian appeared, standing next to stacks of boxes secured with a cargo net. Two seats had been removed to provide more space for supplies.

Ian walked down the short ladder holding a folded newspaper. Unlike Adrian's self-imagined aristocratic features with his falcon eyes and wavy black hair, Ian was thin as a pencil, his sandy-brown hair just as thin. Uncharacteristically nervous for a pilot, beads of sweat would form on his nose and caused his disturbingly thick glasses to slide down his face.

"Good, you got the papers," Adrian said.

"I found *USA Today*." Ian handed Adrian the paper and descended the flight of steps. He reached behind his back and pulled two more papers from under his belt. "Got the local papers from Phoenix and Flagstaff," he said and handed Adrian those as well. "You're not going to like what I read. Good thing they don't have a television in there. This might have made the evening news." He removed his glasses and swiped the beads of sweat from his nose with the cuff of his shirt. "*USA Today* ran a story about some crazy in Turin who'd threatened to blow up the Shroud if they didn't hand it over to him."

"That had to be 762," Adrian said. "So what happened?"

Ian pointed at the newspaper in Adrian's hand. "The guards at the church shot him. He survived, but he's in pretty bad shape. Says he's in a coma or something."

"Idiot," Adrian said. "I warned Calvin this wouldn't work, but he wouldn't listen. He never listens."

"You think he'll rat on us?"

"Not 762," Adrian said. "He'll die first. I know the guy."

"So what about the other one? What's his name again? You didn't have much confidence in him either."

"You mean Carl? 876?"

"Yeah, that one. Whatever happened to him? I couldn't find anything about Oviedo."

"I couldn't tell you," Adrian lied. "I haven't heard a word from him."

"That's strange," Ian said.

Adrian hiked a thumb toward the compound. "Does anything really strike you as strange anymore? You should be immune to it by now."

"That's true," Ian said with a smirk. "Oh, yeah, before I forget. I got another nitrogen tank. I'll pick up some more when the plane isn't loaded down so much. So what's Calvin want will all of those?"

"Beats me," Adrian said. "I heard one of them talking about needing nitrogen for cryopreservation. You know, so they can go into stasis for the year-long journey to New Canaan."

"That's funny," Ian said. "When I took the last tanks over there, one of them said they were for Plan B. What's that supposed to mean?"

"Curiosity killed the cat, Ian. If I were you, I'd mind your own business. It's safer that way."

Chapter 9

Amari parked her car in the staff lot beside The University of Arizona's Weiss Mass Spectrometry Laboratory, WMS for short. She locked up her white '78 Camaro and made her way down the sidewalk that ran alongside the four-story red brick building. White window shades were installed perpendicular to the brick walls, running down the entire length of the building, strategically placed over the windows as protection against the brutal Arizona sun. Students in light, colorful summer clothes mounted and dismounted bicycles secured with padlocks to a bike rack, which was shaded by the wide branches of date palms, making a natural canopy to keep the seats and handlebars cool.

Ernesto was back in town and wanted to see Kevin's latest research regarding new testing to authenticate the Shroud of Turin as the true burial cloth of Jesus Christ. She was meeting Ernesto at the lab, and then everyone was going out for lunch to celebrate Bonelli's birthday.

She found the entrance and pushed through the double door of the lab building. As usual, Ms. Embry, the elderly, semi-retired receptionist, sat at her desk reading a trashy romance novel through horn tipped reading glasses.

"Hey, Ms. Embry," she said. "Is Kevin here?"

Ms. Embry peered over the top of her glasses. "Look who's back. I see you've been in the papers again."

"Looks that way."

"Hey, next time you see that Italian fat cat, tell him I said thanks. I got a raise after his donation."

"He's actually from Fresno, California. He only spent his summers in Italy."

"I don't care where he's from. All I know is my grandson's getting that Sega Exodus he wanted for Christmas."

"I think you mean Genesis."

"It's the one with Sonic the Wart Hog, that's all I know. Tell your boss thanks."

Amari wasn't sure if she was kidding or not. "That's *hedgehog*. And you can tell him yourself. He'll be here in a few minutes."

She went to the elevator, got in, pressed the button to the fourth floor, and popped her knuckles as she ascended. She was dying to see Kevin. She'd talked to him over the phone, but he had been out of town, so this was the first she'd seen him in person after her return from New Mexico.

Kevin had come to the University of Arizona to do his post-doc work and, among other projects, he'd worked on the carbon date performed on the Shroud of Turin in 1988. As a child, he'd been a prodigy with a gift of genius that was handed down over the generations. His grandfather had worked in Oak Ridge, Tennessee, during the Manhattan Project to develop the atomic bomb. Then his father stayed in town to work as a physicist for the Oak Ridge National Laboratory. Kevin had graduated from Oak Ridge High School when he was only sixteen. Then, by the age of twenty, he'd graduated from The University of Tennessee with a double major in physics and mechanical engineering. He'd finished his master's degree at twenty-one and went on to get his Ph.D. in theoretical physics from MIT in Boston. He was twenty-three when he graduated. He'd won a bunch of awards and gotten a ton of accolades along the way. But you would never know it if you met him. He was a disorganized slob with long hair, shabby clothes, and a deep southern, grammatically incorrect, Tennessee accent. And she wouldn't have him any other way.

The elevator door opened on the fourth floor, and she strolled down the painted cinderblock-lined hall toward Kevin's office, hoping she wouldn't pass Dr. Rahal on the way. Even though she was now granted permission to visit the facility, encounters with that man were still awkward. One year wasn't nearly enough time to smooth the feathers she'd ruffled on that closeminded jerk.

After several showdowns of his own with Dr. Rahal last year, Kevin had abruptly quit his job, choosing to side with Amari over his work at the university. Doing this put Dr. Rahal in a bind because of the looming Dead Sea Scrolls carbon dating project the next month. Dr. Rahal had begged him to stay on until the Dead Sea Scroll project was complete. However, Ernesto was so impressed with Kevin's work to unlock the secrets of the Shroud that he'd offered him full-time employment and agreed to fund him for further Shroud research.

As it turned out, it was expensive and time-consuming to start a research lab from scratch, so Kevin worked out a deal with the university. He would stay and help with the Dead Sea scrolls and then stay on staff on an as-needed basis, serving as a consultant. In the meantime, thanks to a generous gift from Ernesto, the university agreed to allow Kevin to use their laboratory for his research. They even provided an upstairs office. Well, they rented it to him—for the sum of $120,000 a year from Ernesto's bank account. But compared to the cost of starting up a new lab, it was a bargain.

She reached Kevin's door and knocked.

"It's open," he hollered from inside.

She stepped in and hugged him from behind. He had papers strewn all over his desk, illuminated by the light of two computer screens and sunlight leaking between the flaps of aluminum window blinds.

"Hey," he said but never looked up from his papers.

"You're still mad at me, aren't you?"

"How can you tell?" He briefly glanced her way, then refocused on his work. "Detective skills?"

She twisted her fingers playfully in his shoulder-length brown hair. It was feather-cut and parted in the middle, making him look like a cross between Luke Skywalker and MacGyver. "You don't have to be a detective to see you're still pissed," she said. "You never look at me when you're mad."

"You should have told me what you were up to."

"Oh, come on, Kevin," she said and wrapped her arms around him. She pressed her cheek tenderly against his and looked down at his work. "I think it's sweet that you're still mad. It means you love me."

"I do love you, babe, more than you'll ever know."

"I love you too." She sat and swiveled his chair around so he'd be forced to face her. She took his hand and said, "Look at me. Do you remember last year when everything was going on? You kept telling me everything was going to be okay. 'Just believe', you told me. Well, I did believe, and I did what I felt needed to be done. God had my back on this."

"Would God want you to lie to me? I thought you hated lies."

"I didn't lie to you. I told you Bonelli, Parker, and I were headed up there to investigate a serial rapist."

"You didn't tell me you were bait."

"I may have left off one little detail. Would you have let me go if I hadn't?"

"I'd of gone with you and hid in the bushes."

She giggled and said, "I'm sure you would. Look, my dad's on board now. There's no way he's going to let me do something like that again. And I promise. In the future, I'll let you know every detail, okay?"

"Deal," he said and leaned in for a hug. "If I lost you, I don't know what I'd do."

She released her embrace and cupped his razor-stubbled chin in her hand, looking into those cute, half-moon shaped brown eyes of his. "I promise. You're stuck with me. Now, what's this you're working on? Ernesto's coming up in a few minutes. He wants to see it too."

He looked at his watch. It was 11:30. "He buying lunch? I'm starved."

"Of course. It's Bonelli's birthday. For dinner, we're grilling out by the pool, so make sure you come over. So whatcha working on?"

He sorted the papers into a stack. "Working on a new report. I'm gonna present this thing at the Dallas Shroud Symposium."

She made a leery expression. "Uh, Kevin, is this another report about wormholes?"

"Hey, it's a valid hypothesis. Scientific as it gets."

"Mmm, hmmm."

"I'm serious, babe. Just for pretend, let's say Jesus did fly to heaven through a Lorentzian wormhole. The radiation burst would explain the Shroud image. Which would also screw up the carbon date. Just ask Stephen Hawking. He'll back me up."

"Would he?"

"Maybe. In theory, anyway."

"You know, there's some people out there that read your papers. People see you as a genius. When you say something, they believe it. Somebody out there's going to read that wormhole paper and think it's real."

"Who said it isn't? With God, all things are possible."

"Sure, if he wanted to make a wormhole, he could. That doesn't mean he did. People are going to read that and believe it really happened."

"Everybody knows it's just a theory—not proven, just speculation. Besides, I didn't come up with the idea, some other guy did. I just elaborated on it. Personally, I favor the alternate dimensionality angle. According to supersymmetry and string theory, there could be from ten to twenty-six different dimensions. Let's say heaven takes up four of those dimensions. Theoretically, when Jesus crossed over, there'd be a small radiation burst. This theory also explains how he appeared and disappeared to the apostles after the resurrection. He simply slipped into an alternate dimension."

"Well, obviously," she said with a sarcastic grin. "So what else you got?"

"All right, this part's pretty down to earth. You know that trip to the particle accelerator I took over the summer. The Grenoble Nuclear Studies Center over in France?"

"Of course, you were gone for three weeks. My long-distance bill was over four hundred bucks. Good thing Ernesto doesn't charge me rent."

"Well, anyway, I wrote a report on what I found. We took regular linen like they used for the Shroud and hit it with a proton beam. At less than 1.4 megaelectron volts, the linen discolored the same way it did on the Shroud."

"So that proves it then. Radiation formed the image."

"It comes pretty darn close. I'll be going over that in Dallas. And here's the really interesting part. The carbon date actually confirms the Shroud is not medieval."

"What are you talking about? The carbon date is the only reason they think it is medieval."

"Well, think about it, babe. We've proven that the image was formed by radiation, right?"

"Right."

"And we know that when something is hit by neutron radiation, it screws up carbon dating. The extra neutrons make it appear younger."

"You've explained it a thousand times."

"So if someone really did forge this in medieval times, they had to forge it using radiation."

"Which was impossible back then."

"But if they pulled it off anyway, then the Shroud would carbon date into the future, maybe at around 2600."

"And you said the only ones who could have done that back then were aliens."

"That's right. As a practical joke."

She laughed and ran her fingers through his long hair. "You're so silly. Tell me about this other test your working on, the one you said would really prove your theory."

"Yeah, that's the tricky part—the part that's going to take time and cost some serious cash." He picked up a piece of scratch paper and started scrawling figures as he spoke. "See, the natural form of chlorine is chlorine-35. That's seventeen protons and eighteen neutrons. Chlorine-36 happens because it's hit with neutron radiation, and this adds a neutron. So it has nineteen neutrons instead. In nature, Chlorine-36 is extremely rare. So anytime you see something that's high in Chlorine-36, you know it was hit by neutron radiation. It's a no-brainer. The problem is, I need to take a scrap of that Shroud and figure the ratio of chlorine-36 to chlorine-35.

If I can do that, I can not only prove radiation screwed the carbon date up, but—"

"Don't tell me. That's because carbon-12 is the natural form of carbon. It has six protons and six neutrons. Neutron radiation adds neutrons to make carbon-14."

"Exactly. The sun's radiation is what causes carbon-14 in the first place."

"See, I'm catching on."

"Anyway, if I can calculate the chlorine-36 to chlorine-35 ratios, then I can crunch the numbers and figure out exactly when and where that radiation happened."

"The radiation that formed the Shroud image?"

"Exactly. And I bet I can prove it happened in the first century. Not only that, I can prove it happened in Jerusalem."

"Where it happened? How are you going to pull that off?"

"Ever heard of the Church of the Holy Sepulcher?"

"That's the one in Jerusalem they claim was built on top of Jesus' tomb."

"That's right. If I can get ahold of some of that rock from the tomb itself, I could run it on the mass spec downstairs. If there's an unusually high amount of chlorine-36 in the rock, I can prove it came from a neutron radiation burst. And if I can compare those numbers to the numbers on the Shroud, then I can prove the same burst of radiation caused both radioactive anomalies."

"Rahal's still got his piece of Shroud you did the carbon date on. Run your test on that sample."

"It's not that simple. It's easy to do that test on large samples like you would get with rock—especially since limestone has a bunch of chlorine. But linen doesn't have much chlorine, and there's never been a procedure developed to test linen for chlorine-36. And doing it with a small sample would be tricky."

"Then get cracking. I'm sure you can figure it out."

Kevin pulled a manila folder from his shelf. "Working on it right here. I'm collaborating with some guys from the chemistry department. A lot of this stuff's over my head."

"I don't believe that. Not world-renown experimental physicist, Dr. Kevin Brenner."

"Believe it or not," he said with a wry smile. "But I've got friends in high places. They can help me."

"Then go for it."

"I plan to, but then what?"

"Run your tests."

"That's the biggest problem. I got strategic locations I need to sample from, not just snip a piece off a worn-out corner. I'd need something from the image itself. Some of the blood too. That's the only way to be a hundred percent conclusive. You think the Vatican would ever go for that?"

She cringed. "I don't know, Kevin. Maybe if the samples are small enough. If you could prove without a doubt, this came from Christ, who knows?"

"Maybe. Either way, that option could take years. In the meantime, I've got some more ideas." He reached up to his shelf and produced another manila folder full of notes. "Now this is promising. I'm working on a test that'll show how tensile strength of linen fibers changes over time. I could compare the leftover samples from the Shroud carbon date to other ancient linen fibers known to come from the time of Christ."

"There you go. See, you're making a ton of progress. No wonder you're getting so famous."

He made a doubtful smirk. "I wouldn't say *famous.* Not like you."

"In the scientific community, you are. That's what Dr. Rahal says."

"You still getting along with him?"

"He tolerates me. As long as I don't make any waves."

Suddenly, Kevin's phone rang. He picked it up. "Hello? Already? Yeah, yeah, okay. I'll send her down." He hung up the phone and started sorting and stacking papers as if in a panic.

"What is it?"

"Ernesto's downstairs. He wants to see what I've been blowing all his money on. Help me tidy up."

"Relax, Kevin, he knows you're a slob. Besides, I don't know where any of your stuff goes." She handed him the stapler. "Tell you what. I'll go down there and stall him. I'll start up a chit-chat with Ms. Embry, then take him the long way around to your office."

"That would be awesome," he said as he stapled some papers. "Just give me ten minutes."

She went downstairs and found Ernesto pacing the foyer floor nervously as he spoke into his portable phone. "Quali altri protocolli di sicurezza sono stati avviati? . . . Uh, huh. . . E perchè no? . . . Allora se i Carabinieri non faranno qualcosa, e la Guardia Svizzera? . . . Certo che lo direbbero. Questo è ridicolo." He glanced up to see Amari and stopped pacing. "Ah, Federico, Grazie per la chiamata. Ma lascia che ti richiami più tardi." He flipped the phone's mouthpiece closed.

"Ernesto?" she said. "Is everything okay?"

"I'm afraid not. Something happened in Turin. Call your dad. Have him meet us at your house. We may have his first case. And bring Kevin. He's no detective, but sometimes he sees things we don't."

"Ernesto, what's going on?"

He glanced over at Ms. Embry, then back to Amari. "I prefer to discuss this in private

Chapter 10

Amari, Kevin, Bonelli, and Ernesto sat on a corner-hugging sectional couch in Amari's living room. It was a few minutes past one in the afternoon, and they were eating carryout pizza while waiting for her dad to show. Out in Fresno, Ernesto's neighborhood watch had reported a suspicious vehicle that seemed to be casing the street, so Parker stayed behind as a security precaution. Ernesto didn't seem to mind the wait. He was too enthralled by Kevin's work to care.

Kevin fingered the adjustment strap of his obnoxious orange University of Tennessee baseball cap as he waited for Ernesto to look through his research notes. The hat was dirty and worn, but Kevin wouldn't part with it, claiming it was his good luck thinking cap, the same hat he'd worn during his exams, the same cap he'd worn when the UT football team beat Alabama in '82 after a twelve-year-long losing streak. Kevin had a heavy southern accent, but Amari could swear his accent got even worse when he wore that hat, seemingly unable to utter a sentence without using the word ain't or some other country slang. His language and mannerisms were a strange juxtaposition to his legendary intellect. Amari wasn't sure whether he was aware of this, but his co-workers called him Bubba Einstein behind his back.

Ernesto sorted through Kevin's research. "This is incredible. I'm astounded by what you've accomplished in so little time. I can't understand of word of it, but I'm impressed nonetheless. In the Shroud community, you have become the talk of the town."

"It ain't like that at all," Kevin said with a sheepish shrug. "I've been dreaming this stuff up for years. But until I was on your payroll, I haven't had time to crunch the numbers, let alone test those theories."

"Then it was the best investment I've ever made," Ernesto said. "Can you imagine how the world would change if we proved beyond a shadow of a doubt that the Shroud came from Christ? And that the Shroud captures the powerful, miraculous moment of his resurrection?"

Bonelli made a skeptical frown. "People would still find a reason not to believe."

Ernesto nodded in agreement. "Yes, but for those who want to believe, this provides credible truth."

The front door slammed shut, and Amari watched her dad limp into the living room. He was apparently having a bad hip day. The sooner he got that fixed, the better.

"Sorry if I'm late," her dad said, scratching his thick, crew cut hair. He reminded people of that drill sergeant on the Gomer Pyle Show, only Dad's hair was speckled with gray, and he was taller with a lankier build. Heavy wrinkle trenches were etched into his fifty-five-year-old forehead, the product of years of stress and worry. "I was cleaning out my office. Didn't get the message until I checked my answering machine."

"Sit here, Dad," she said. "This chair's got more support for your hip."

Her dad sat and rubbed his hands together with greedy expectation. "So, you say you've got a case? Already? And here I thought this job would be boring."

"I'm afraid so," Ernesto said. "I'd hoped you would have a break between jobs, but this is an urgent matter."

"That's what you're paying us for," Dad said. "So let's hear it."

"A dear friend of mine serves as a deacon for the Turin Cathedral," Ernesto said. "His name is Federico."

"That's where they keep the Shroud," Amari clarified.

"So what happened?" Dad asked.

"My friend tells me there was an attempt to steal the Shroud. You may have read about it in the newspaper."

"Can't say that I have," Dad said. "Then again, I haven't been reading every page."

"It probably wasn't in the Tucson news," Ernesto said. "The local authorities in Italy seem more amused by the situation than concerned."

"Amused?" Dad said. "What's so funny about stealing a priceless relic?"

"It was the way he tried to steal it," Bonelli said. "That's what's funny about it."

"Yes," Ernesto continued. "A man had gotten to within feet of where the Shroud was being kept. It had been removed from its secure location and placed in the sacristy for repairs. Only wooden doors separated this man from the Shroud. Security caught him trying to break the lock. When they confronted him, he claimed to have had a bomb in his backpack. If they did not hand over the Shroud, then he would blow it to shreds."

Dad furrowed his brows. "And the Italian police think that's funny?"

"It was a fake bomb," Bonelli said. "That's what they thought was funny."

"And from his possessions," Ernesto said, "they reason he's a religious fanatic. They don't see any additional threat."

"I see," Dad said. "I can understand their angle. They see it as a fluke."

"No," Ernesto said emphatically. "It was not a fluke. Any other time and the Shroud would be safely secured in an underground, fireproof encasement. But the Shroud had been temporarily moved to the sacristy for repairs. These repairs were secret, not public knowledge. That means there was inside information. Otherwise, how would this man know to go to the sacristy?"

"You've got a point," Dad said. "I don't believe in coincidences. So what's this guy saying?"

"Not a thing," Bonelli said. "They shot him in the chest. He survived, but he's still unconscious."

"When this guy wakes up," Dad said, "we need to talk to him."

"If he wakes up," Amari said.

"There's something else," Ernesto said. "It could be totally unrelated, but it still causes concern nonetheless. There may be a bigger plot unfolding. If I'm right, we haven't seen the last attempt to steal the Shroud."

"You're paying me to listen," Dad said. "Let's hear it."

"Something else happened in Oviedo, Spain. My friend says there was an incident at the cathedral."

"Oviedo?" Dad said. "Amari, isn't that where your brother is now?"

"He's in a town just north of Oviedo," she said. "I know he's talked about going down there."

"So maybe he knows something," Dad said.

"He hasn't said anything. He usually calls me collect once a week. He's supposed to call me tonight when he wakes up. I could ask him about it then."

"Do that, would you? And tell him to call me too."

"Call collect?" she asked.

"I can afford it now," he said and winked at Ernesto. "So what's Oviedo have to do with the Shroud?"

"Must have something to do with the Sudarium," she said.

"You say that like I should know what you're talking about," Dad said.

"It's the cloth that wrapped Jesus' face while they took him down from the cross," Ernesto said. "It was mentioned in the Gospel of John. They keep the Sudarium in a small chapel on the Cathedral grounds."

"That's right," Dad said. "It rings a bell now. Seems like I heard Amari mention it before. So you think this cloth is genuine?"

"All the evidence says it is," Bonelli replied. "They recently did a comprehensive study of the cloth. The blood type and blood smears all match what's found on the Shroud. It even contains pollen from a species of thorn bush that grows in Jerusalem and pollinates during Easter. It's the same pollen that was found on the Shroud."

"Gundelia tournefortii," Amari blurted. "That's the name of the bush."

"That's right," Ernesto said. "All evidence suggests it covered the face of Christ."

"So what happened?" Dad asked. "Somebody try to hijack it too?"

"We don't know," Ernesto said. "I don't have any connections with the cathedral in Oviedo. If it has been in the news, I am not aware of it. Federico only mentioned rumors of an incident. That's all I know."

"Kevin," Dad said. "Use that computer brain of yours and tell me what time it is in Oviedo."

"Let's see," Kevin said. "Spain is nine hours ahead of us. I'd say it's about 10:30 at night."

"So Jason's probably in his pajamas," Dad said. "Amari, you got his number?"

"Of course."

"Then let's ring him up before he goes to sleep," Dad said. "Maybe he can enlighten us."

She went into the kitchen and came back with Jason's phone number. She picked up the phone, dialed in the long, international number, then hit the speakerphone button so everybody could hear.

The phone rang three times, then Jason's voice came on the line. "Digame."

"Hola, Padre Johnston. Como estas?" she said, meaning hello and how are you in Spanish.

"What's up, bro?" Kevin said. "We didn't wake you, did we?"

"En realidad pensé en llamarte pero no sabía si estarías en casa para aceptar los cargos," Jason replied.

"You gotta talk American, Son," Dad said. "Nobody here speaks Spanish."

"Actually, I do," Ernesto said. "And so does Bonelli."

"Hey, I talk some Espanola myself," Kevin said. "He was saying something about calling us too but wasn't sure anyone was home."

Dad looked impressed. "Spanish too?"

"And I-tal-yon," Kevin said. "Spanish ain't much different."

"Hi, Kevin," Jason said. "And is that Mr. Galliano I hear? I didn't realize you were in town."

"Ernesto, please. Just call me Ernesto. And yes, I'm here for a couple of days. We called to see if you could spread a little gossip."

"Pardon?"

"The rumor mill in Turin says there was an incident in Oviedo, perhaps concerning the Sudarium," Ernesto said.

Jason laughed. "You heard about that? All the way in Tucson?"

"You know how Italians are," Ernesto said. "We like our gossip. So tell us, what happened over there?"

"They did have a little excitement the other night," Jason said. "It's all anyone's been talking about. It was headline news in the local paper this morning. Not sure it was big enough to make the national news. I was going to tell Amari about it when I called. You know, since she's interested in the Shroud."

"We're all interested now," Dad said. "So what happened?"

"Apparently, some guy scaled an old bell tower and was on the roof when a thunderstorm hit. It washed him off the roof, but he got lucky and caught a balcony rail on the way down. It was like two in the morning or something."

"Two in the morning? What on Earth was he up to?" Dad asked.

"The nun said he was trying to steal the Sudarium," Jason said. "There's no way he could have pulled it off, but that's what the nun claims. They found his gear on the roof. He had cutting tools and climbing equipment."

"So what about this nun?" Dad asked. "How would she know what he was up to?"

"That balcony rail he grabbed onto? It belonged to a guest apartment," Jason replied. "A nun from the States was staying there. Mother Agatha's her name, I think. She heard him yelling and helped him inside."

"So what's he saying?" Dad asked. "What do the police think?"

"He didn't hang around," Jason said. "From what I understand, he used a gun to convince her to help him steal the Sudarium. That's when mother Agatha hit him in the head with an iron skillet."

"Ouch, that's gotta hurt," Kevin said. "Knock him out?"

"Unfortunately, no," Jason said. "He escaped down the stairs and found his way outside. He was gone by the time the police got there."

"You're right, Ernesto," Amari said. "I don't think this is a coincidence either. Jason, you said the nun was American. Did she mention if he sounded American too?"

"That's what I understand," Jason said. "That's what Mother Agatha seems to think. In fact, she said he sounded like a Yankee. Her words, not mine."

"Let's just for the sake of argument assume he is an American," Dad said. "So you got two Americans trying to steal the Shroud and its companion cloth, all in the same week. That can't be a coincidence."

"Of course, it's not," Amari said. "And I know why they're trying to steal it! They know it's probably real and they want to destroy it before we can prove it."

"Who would do such a thing?" Dad asked.

"Anybody who isn't a Christian," she said. "It could be an atheist, Muslim, Jew, or even Hindu for that matter. There's a ton of people who wouldn't want us to prove Jesus is real. Think about it, if you were a Muslim or a Jew, why would you want evidence that proves Christianity? Think about all the millions of church members who'd change sides."

"Then you'd lose billions of dollars in revenue," Bonelli said.

"Not so fast," Dad said. "That's just speculation. I know people. Most would choose to ignore the evidence."

"Maybe, maybe not," Ernesto said. "Either way, there are some powerful people would like the world to believe the Shroud is a hoax."

"If it's just speculation, we still need to investigate to see if it's true," Amari said. "These guys were probably part of some sort of organization. If they failed once, who's to say they won't try again?"

"Detective Johnston," Ernesto said. "Have you ever been to Europe?"

"During the Korean war, in the Army," Dad replied. "I'd love to go back someday."

"Then pack your bags," Ernesto said. "You have your first case."

Chapter 11

Oviedo, Spain

Three days later, Pete watched as his daughter gaped up at the soaring gothic bell tower of the Oviedo Cathedral. She was twenty-three years old, yet she still viewed the world with a child-like wonder. A father never got tired of seeing the majesty of God's creation through his child's eyes. Jason stood next to her, rattling off random historical facts about the cathedral and the city in which it was founded. Bonelli kept his distance, allowing for a private family moment.

A couple of hours earlier, Pete, Amari, and Bonelli had landed at the Asturias Airport, a landing strip in northern Spain that was a short distance from the Atlantic Ocean. Former Airforce pilot, Skip Townsend, no pun intended, was Ernesto's personal high-altitude chauffeur. He had flown Ernesto's Learjet from Tucson, making a refueling stop in Portsmouth, New Hampshire. It was a long flight for sure, but owning a Learjet afforded you the luxury of lying down or stretching your legs whenever the feeling struck, taking naps on and off to minimize effects of jet lag.

Bonelli had come along to serve as a guide, translator, and extra muscle should the need arise. Kevin had agreed to sit this one out, knowing criminal investigation wasn't his forte. Besides, he was busy preparing his lectures for the upcoming Shroud symposium in Dallas. He was going to be the keynote speaker and wanted to be prepared.

"In Spanish, it's known as the Catedral de San Salvador, or Church of the Holy Savior in English," Jason said. "Sancta Ovetensis in Latin. This front part of the church was constructed between the fourteenth and sixteenth centuries in the classic gothic style of the day. The older part of the church was founded in 781 by King Fruela of Asturias. That part has a more Roman feel to it."

"Son, spare us the history lesson," Pete said. "We're losing daylight. You can give us the grand tour later."

Jason glanced down at his watch. "This won't take as long as you think. I came down here yesterday to scout the place out. I talked to people about what happened and got permission to show you around. I even met Mother Agatha. She's agreed to meet us at her apartment."

"I was hoping you'd say that," Pete said. "The sooner I get to the hotel, the better. I'm beat. I tried to nap on the plane, but it's just not the same."

"Then follow me," Jason said. "I'll make this easy on you."

Jason was four years older than his sister. He was short like his late-mother, Haseya, which was unlike Amari who was taller than the average girl. Like his mother, Jason's hair was so black that when the light hit it just right, it reflected a white sheen. His skin was bronze like Haseya's, unlike Amari, who had fairer skin. Most people who met

Amari didn't realize she was half-Navajo, but Jason looked more the part.

It had been funny watching those two grow up together. Typically, it's the big brother who watched out for the little sister, but with those two it was the other way around. Jason had his mother's gentle temperament, which made him easy prey for neighborhood bullies. But the first time Amari saw the Jenkins kid pick on Jason was the last time he was bullied—at least by any kid who was familiar with his younger sister. That Jenkins kid was left with a broken nose and a deviated septum to remind him to watch his manners in the future. Fortunately, the Jenkins' weren't the suing kind.

Given Jason's gentle nature, it wasn't all that surprising he'd become a priest. He wasn't raised Catholic, but non-denominational instead. Missionaries from the Church of Christ had converted Haseya as a teenager and Pete had grown up Episcopalian. When the kids were born, Pete and Haseya had agreed to split the difference and raise their kids in a non-denominational church. Jason, however, seemed dissatisfied with the lack of structure and tradition of non-denominationalism, so when he got a scholarship to the Catholic University of Notre Dame, he converted to Catholicism. Then with the prodding of the Bishop of Tucson, he went on to become a priest.

They followed Jason down a path along the side of the church and stopped when they reached an ancient stone wall constructed of randomly sized field stones rather than the symmetrical cut stone like that of the Cathedral itself. To the left of the ancient wall was a small gated courtyard just in front of an old bell tower, constructed with the same irregular stones.

"This is called the Torre Vieja, or old bell tower," Jason said. "It's an example of Roman architecture. The police found a grappling hook and rope. They think he used it to scale the tower from here. Apparently, he jumped down from the top of the tower onto the building next to it. It's called the Claustro Bajo. That means lower cloister in English. This is the building he fell off of."

"And then caught onto the balcony rail," she said. "The nun's balcony?"

"That's right," Jason said. "The balcony overlooks a courtyard."

"That's a good forty, maybe fifty feet climb," Pete said.

"Back in my Special Forces days, we used to practice climbing and repelling walls like this," Bonelli said. "It takes a lot of skill and body strength."

"So you think he's military trained?" Pete asked.

"Or maybe he's into mountain climbing," Amari offered.

"Whatever he is, he's good with a grappling hook," Pete said. "That's pretty impressive how he managed to get that hook onto that tower window. He's got good aim."

"Then he must have practiced it," Bonelli said. "I'm sure he trained for this."

"Grappling hooks are pretty bulky," she said. "You think that's something he would carry on a plane? I mean, if he's really an American?"

"I see where you're going with this," Pete said. "He probably bought it locally."

"We should check the local sporting goods stores," she said. "Maybe he used a credit card. If he did, then we've got him."

"Good idea," Bonelli said.

"It's in her blood," Jason said. "She's got a nose for this kind of thing."

"We need to get his description," she said. "Jason, you said the nun was expecting us?"

"She said she'd be glad to help," Jason said.

"Maybe we can get a sketch artist and show the picture around the local stores," she said.

"I bet the police already have a sketch," Pete said. "Let's go have a word with her and then we'll chat with the detective handling this case."

Jason led them under a soaring, arched, open-air portico. They found a stairway, went up several flights and entered a hallway on the top floor, stopping when Jason found her room.

Jason knocked on the door. "Mother Agatha? It's Father Jason."

The door flung open, and a mammoth of a woman stood before them in a classic nun's habit. She looked to be late forties with streaks of gray in her black hair. Black framed, unstylish glasses sat over chubby, rosy cheeks, anchored on the bridge of her stubby nose.

"Hola, Mother Agatha," Jason said.

"Hola, Padre Jason. ¿Y quién es? ¿Tu padre y tu hermana?" she said with a thick, American accent.

"Yes, this is my father and sister. And this is Bonelli. He's come to help with the investigation."

"Ven adentro," she said. "Come inside."

They stepped into the tiny apartment. It was sparsely decorated with only a crucifix over the front door and portrait of Jesus on the wall, the kind with the Sacred Heart over his chest. The kitchenette had a small round table for two. A thick iron skillet sat on the stovetop.

"Mr. Johnston, Father Jason tells me you're a police detective," Mother Agatha said. "Or should I say, Detective Johnston."

"Retired detective. Just call me Pete. So what part of the States are you from?"

"Originally, I'm from Michigan, but I've been in Birmingham, Alabama for a few months now. I'm a nurse. I work for a free clinic run by Catholic Charities. We see a lot of folks from Mexico and South America. It's hard to treat someone if you can't talk to them. So they sent me over here to *aprender español*."

"And do they teach you to hit people in the head with an iron skillet in nursing school?" Amari asked, pursing her lips to keep a straight face.

"No, that I learned from living in Detroit," she said and returned a wry smile. "It didn't knock him out, but it sure convinced him to leave."

"That's what I understand," Pete said. "Listen, we don't want to keep you. We were just hoping you could tell us more about this guy and how he ended up inside your apartment."

"Well, I was sound asleep until the thunder woke me. The rain really started coming down, so I got up to look out the window. That's when I heard this racket from the roof. Apparently, our hard-headed friend was hanging from the gutter. I heard a sound like metal bending, and the next thing I see is him hanging one handed from the balcony rail and yelling for help. So I helped. I pulled him back onto the balcony, and he came inside. Well, forced himself inside is more like it." She pointed at the broken glass pane. "I tried to lock him out and call the police, but he forced his way in."

"So what did he say?" Amari asked. "I bet he was freaking out."

"You know, dear, he was surprisingly calm. He had this look on his face. Like he'd just had an epiphany. Like he'd suddenly realized the will of God."

"That's odd," Pete said. "And what was this epiphany?"

"He started babbling something about taking the Sudarium. About fulfilling a prophecy. He claimed God wanted me to help him. He said it was divine providence that I'd saved his life. That God had placed me here for a reason. And that reason was to help him steal the Sudarium."

"So he was trying to steal it," Amari said.

"Borrow was the word he used. He claimed they would return it when they were finished."

"If I may," Bonelli said. "Why does he think you would have access to the Sudarium? It's a tightly guarded relic."

"You tell me," the nun said. "It sounds just as crazy from where I'm standing. So I told him I was calling the police. Then he shows me his gun, and then I showed him the iron skillet. I must have knocked some sense into him because he scrambled out of the apartment after that. Then I called the police."

"Can you describe him?" Pete asked. "What did he look like? Any distinguishing features?"

"He was wearing beige, brown coveralls that zipped up the front. He unzipped the top to show me his gun. And his hair was buzz cut so close you saw more skin than hair. He was maybe forty years old, possibly older. He looked to be in pretty good shape."

"Not that good of shape," Amari said. "He got beat up by a nun."

"Well, I am a big woman. Six feet three in case you're wondering. There's not many men I couldn't take."

"Me either," Amari said.

"She's not kidding," Bonelli said.

"No, she's not," Pete said. "So is that all you got, ma'am? Anything else that could help us identify him?"

She tapped a finger on her forearm. "I noticed an odd tattoo on his arm."

"Oh, really?" Pete said.

"It was shaped like a flying saucer, only this one had Calvary crosses on it. A big one in the middle, with two smaller ones next to it, just like on Calvary Hill. Now here's the weird part."

"That's not the weird part?" Amari said.

Mother Agatha chuckled. "Well, equally as weird. On the bottom of the UFO was a three-digit number. Here, I'll draw it for you." She pulled a paper from the kitchen drawer and drew out what she'd just described. "Under the tattoo was the number 876," she said and wrote in the number.

"That is bizarre," Pete said.

"It's some kind of code," Amari said. "I bet Kevin could figure it out."

"When we get back, we'll show this to him," Pete said and held out his hand. "May I?"

The nun handed him the drawing. "Certainly. Anything I can do to help."

"There is something else," Pete said. "Do you think you can describe this guy to a sketch artist?"

"I already have," she said. "The Oviedo Police had me describe him to their artist. I'm sure they would let you see it."

"We'll talk to them next," Pete said. "Thank you, Sister. We won't take any more of your time."

"Gracias, Sor Agatha," Jason said as he left.

"De nada," she said and closed the door.

Chapter 12

Turin, Italy

The next day, Pete sat next to his daughter on a stone bench directly across the street from St. John the Baptist Catholic Church, otherwise known as the Turin Cathedral. It was surreal sitting in the open, pavestone square in front of the church that housed the very cloth that once covered the tortured, then risen Jesus. Electric streetcar wires stretched overhead, and people milled about, minding their affairs, seemingly indifferent to the holy relic just inside those stone walls.

Inside the church, it was fancier than all get out—the most ornate décor Pete had ever laid eyes on in person. However, the church had a surprisingly simple façade, just a white stone front with minimal etchings, overshadowed by an imposing bell tower off to the left. The tower's design, brown brick crowned with white Roman-style pillars at the top, apparently had nothing to do with the church, as it was built in 1470, nearly thirty years before the completion of the Cathedral in 1498.

Cardinal Ragazzi had been delighted to see Amari again. She and Pete had enjoyed a tasty lunch with the cardinal inside one of the buildings adjacent to the church. His eminence seemed like a nice man but didn't speak a lick of English, so some other priest named Father Como did most of the talking for the Cardinal.

Right now Bonelli was inside with the Cardinal trying to arrange access to the idiot who'd made this foolhardy attempt to steal the Shroud, or at the very least to allow Pete and his daughter to view any evidence relevant to the case.

Pete checked his watch, then glanced back up at the Cathedral, letting out a sigh of disappointment. "It's too bad they wouldn't let us see the Shroud. You'd think after you risked your life trying to prove it was real, they'd show a little more appreciation."

"Dad, they don't just pull it out for anyone to see," she said. "They rarely show it, and when they do, it's a really big deal."

"They had it out already. It was in the sacristy. I'm just saying it's too bad they had to put it up before we got here."

"And look what almost happened while it was out there. It's better to keep it secure."

"I suppose you're right. They showed us some great pictures of it. And I admit, it's kind of a thrill just being this close to it, even if we can't lay eyes on it."

"I know. I feel the same way. And at least they let us look around the church and even go into the sacristy."

"There was nothing to see, other than the jimmied door lock. All the evidence is over at police headquarters."

"Maybe Bonelli can pull some strings and let us see it. Here he comes now."

As Bonelli made his way down the Cathedral's steps, Pete and Amari crossed the square to meet him halfway. Bonelli gave the thumbs up as he approached.

"I take it you've got good news?" Pete said.

"Cardinal Ragazzi called the colonel in charge of the local Carabinieri," Bonelli said.

"The carabi-what?" Pete asked.

"The Carabinieri," Bonelli replied. "It's a kind of paramilitary force. They're the branch of police that handles major crimes."

"I see," Pete said. "So what's this colonel say?"

"He said to come by the department, and you can see the evidence. He'll give you a copy of the police report."

"You'll have to translate it for us."

"Of course."

"And what about the perp himself?" Pete said. "Any chance we can talk to him?"

"Cardinal Ragazzi arranged that too. He's still in the hospital, but he's finally awake. He's able to see visitors now."

"Awesome," she said. "I knew Cardinal Ragazzi could help."

"The colonel is Catholic," Bonelli said. "Did he have a choice?"

She laughed. "I guess not."

"They plan on transferring him to the prison hospital later today," Bonelli said. "So we need to hurry."

****

The Carabinieri officers had reluctantly cooperated with the colonel's instructions and left Pete and his daughter inside an interrogation room with all the evidence found both on the perp and at the scene. Bonelli stayed out in the hall, practicing his Italian with a lady from housekeeping.

101

According to the Carabinieri, there was no identification of any kind found on the guy, nor were there any hotel keys. The guy had stashed them somewhere just in case he was caught. He'd refused to give his name or nationality, although, from his accent, he was American. And who could blame him? If he were working for someone, his boss wouldn't want to be implicated. Maybe he feared for his life or even the life of his family. Then again, the guy hadn't talked to anybody but Italians. Maybe he'd warm up to Pete and Amari since they were both Americans, just like him. Maybe she could use her good looks to sway some words out of him. That is, if she didn't punch him in the throat. She wasn't too happy with this guy.

"Since he's got no ID and he's not talking, the next best thing is what he had on him," Pete said. "That can say a lot about him."

Amari put on a pair of latex gloves, pulled the evidence out of a box, and laid it on the interrogation table. It was everything the perp had on him when he was arrested. He'd been carrying a black backpack with several zipper pockets. Besides the backpack were tools a burglar would use—a crowbar, lockpick, screwdriver, pair of pliers, and a flashlight. Next, Pete saw a stack of metal pipes that were tied together with electrical tape. It was supposed to look like a fake bomb from the bulge it made on the fabric of the backpack. Next to the fake bomb was a pack of Big Red chewing gum, a wad of tissue, a bottle of mineral water, and a small pocket New Testament Bible. There was also a cardboard cylinder tube like architects carry to a construction site. Presumably, the guy planned to roll up the Shroud and transport it that way—and pray airport security didn't think to look inside.

His clothes included a pair of Reebok sneakers, white crew socks, and plain gray coveralls that zipped up the front.

"Those coveralls," she said. "That's the same kind the guy in Oviedo wore."

"I see that," Pete said. "Seems like these two guys were part of the same team. It's like this is some kind of uniform."

"Only the guy in Oviedo had beige coveralls instead of gray. I wonder if there's any significance to that?"

Just then, Bonelli stepped into the room and joined them. "Is that a Star Trek T-shirt?"

"Looks that way," Pete said. "This is what he wore under his coveralls. I guess he's a fan."

"It's safe to say he's not an atheist," she said. "Not with a copy of the New Testament in his pocket."

Bonelli leaned in closer and inspected the book's cover. "He's no Catholic. That version is NIV. Last I remember, the New American version is preferred by the Catholic Church."

"He's not a mainstream Protestant, I can tell you that," Pete said.

"Must be some kind of cult then," Amari said. "That may explain the tattoo. Maybe all the members have them. And they seem to be fixated with space. Think about it. The guy in Oviedo had a flying saucer on his forearm, and this guy has a Star Trek T-shirt. I've heard Kevin talk about UFOs before. He said there's books out there that claim UFOs are the work of God."

"If it exists, then it came from God," Pete said.

"Yeah, but there's people out there that think these UFOs are doing God's work on Earth," she said.

"Like they're angels or something?" Pete said.

"Something like that," she replied.

"Well, only one way to find out," Pete said. "We better get moving."

Chapter 13

A fiberglass half-wall partition separated the nursing station from the hallway. Standing in front of a gap in the partition wall, Bonelli spoke Italian to the nurse sitting behind a desk. A green screen computer was visible to her left, and hospital charts with aluminum, hinged covers were scattered about the counter. She wore a scowl on her face that reminded Pete of his eighth-grade teacher right before she broke out the wooden paddle. An unlit cigarette somehow clung tight to her bottom lip and bobbed as she exchanged angry Italian words with Bonelli. Judging from the nurse's defensive body language and tone of voice, there seemed to be a security issue. She had apparently been instructed not to reveal the location of the criminal in case someone wanted to bust him out. Finally, after making a phone call, she hung up the phone and spitefully barked instruction to Bonelli.

Pete and his daughter followed as Bonelli led the way down a hall that smelled like a blend of disinfectant and human excrement.

"Now, remember, Amari. You catch more flies with honey than vinegar," Pete said. "Control that temper of yours and be sweet to him. Get on his good side."

"Fine," she said, pursing her lips defiantly. "But if honey doesn't work, then he gets the vinegar."

"Amari, I'm begging you. The last thing I need is to bail you out of an Italian jail. Just keep your cool, understand?"

Her lips spread into a mischievous grin. "Okay, Dad. I'm just kidding."

"I hope so. And while you're in there, as hard as it may seem, try and flirt with him a little."

"You can't be serious."

"God gave you good looks. Use that to your advantage."

She shot him an incredulous glare.

"Well, at least don't punch him in the throat. That's a good place to start."

She tossed her head back and laughed. "Dad, give me some credit. I promise, I'll be good."

"I've heard that before," Pete uttered as they followed Bonelli down the hall. After rounding a corner, they stopped when they found two carabinieri officers sitting in chairs, one on each side of the door to the hospital room that held the prisoner. They wore navy blue berets on their heads with uniforms of the same color, complete with vest pockets for ammo.

Bonelli approached them with his outstretched passport and spoke first. "Il mio nome è Bonelli. Abbiamo il permesso di parlare con il prigioniero."

The officer with the most stripes on his uniform took Bonelli's passport, eyed it momentarily, then said in heavily accented English. "We expect you. Go," he said with a tilt of his head and handed back Bonelli's passport.

"Thank you," Bonelli replied respectfully in English. "We won't be long."

They found the prisoner asleep with an oxygen mask over his mouth and nose. An IV bag hung from a metal stand and fed into the vein of his hand. On the nightstand, a white, plastic straw was stuck into a Styrofoam cup. A TV was mounted on the wall across from the adjustable bed and softly played in the background.

The patient was young, mid-twenties. He was thin and nearly bald, his head shaved almost down to the skin. He looked as if he'd just left the barber's chair on his first day of army boot camp. Under his loosely tied gown, you could see the bulky pressure bandages that patched his bullet wound.

"Is he conscious?" Amari asked. "I thought he could talk to us."

Pete coughed and kicked the foot of his bed. The guy startled awake and eyed his visitors with suspicion.

"Hi, there," Pete said and took the well-worn visitor's chair next to him. "My name's Pete."

The patient anxiously rubbed the back of his neck and glanced around at the unfamiliar faces. He seemed particularly interested in Bonelli. The blips on his heart monitor started going faster, his pulse racing to a hundred and five beats per minute.

Pete motioned for Bonelli to come closer and whispered into his ear. "Why don't you step outside for a minute? You can be a tad intimidating."

"I understand," Bonelli whispered back. "I'll be waiting out in the hall."

Amari went to the other side of the bed and sat on a chair with the back against her chest. She rested her hands atop the chairback and leaned forward. "I bet it's scary being in a place like this, you know, with a bullet in your chest and everything. And nobody speaks English, right?

At least not very good English. I know I'd be scared if I were you."

The patient eyed her warily.

"Relax," she said and flashed a pleasant, disarming smile. "We're Americans, just like you. We're not with the police. We just want to ask you a few questions, that's all."

The kid can act too, Pete thought. It was another thing that made a good detective. The job required hiding true feelings—anything to get the bad guy talking. Sometimes detectives even had to lie.

She reached over and gently squeezed his wrist, forcing a concerned expression on her face. "You know you're in a lot of trouble. Big time. The Italian government's pretty pissed right now. That's the way they get when a foreigner tries to steal a cherished relic. They want to throw you in jail and never let you out."

"And these prisons over here," Pete added, "they're not like they are in the states. It can be really rough over here. And nobody's going to care that you don't speak Italian. Why don't you cooperate with us and maybe we can help?"

"My boss is a zillionaire," she said reassuringly. "If you help with us, I know he'd pay for a good lawyer. He's got some powerful friends over here. I'm sure he can help, but you've got to at least tell us who you are and who sent you."

Pete noticed he had a childlike, naive innocence to his expression, the kind who'd believe anything you told him so long as you had a straight face, the kind who could easily be brainwashed into doing something stupid—like trying to steal the Shroud of Turin.

She gave him another comforting squeeze on his wrist. "Can I get you some water or something? Fluff your pillow?"

Pete glanced up at the heart monitor. His pulse had dipped to ninety-five. It was working. They were gaining his trust.

"No, thank you," he finally spoke.

She eyed his bandages. "That must have really hurt. What you did took a lot of guts."

He pulled the oxygen mask from his face and formed a pious expression. "My faith gave me courage. It strengthened me for the task."

"Faith can move mountains," Pete said. "So are you a Christian? I know I am. How 'bout you? You had a New Testament with you, so I assume you are."

He looked to be considering the question, wondering how to answer. "Not only Christian but one of the Chosen."

"Chosen huh?" Pete said. "Someone chose you to steal the Shroud of Turin?"

"That's not a real Christian thing to do," Amari countered.

The patient got defensive, and his heart rate went up again. "No, I wasn't going to steal it. You don't understand. I just needed to borrow it, for a divine purpose. I acted by the will of God."

That confirmed Pete's suspicions. The kid had been brainwashed. Time to dirty the brain up again with a dose of reality. "The will of God?" Pete asked, shaking his head in disagreement. "Are you sure about that? Who told you this was God's will?"

"The Divine Conduit told us so."

Pete and his daughter exchanged amused glances.

"Divine what?" she asked.

"The Conduit. He is the channel, the messenger of God's will."

"You mean like a prophet?" Pete asked.

"Much more than just a prophet. He hears the message of God, but he is also the physical conduit. From the power of the earth, he will ascend to heaven, only to return for us, piloting a craft. It is he who will take us to paradise. He is the Divine Conduit."

Pete pointed at the bandages on his chest. "So does this conduit know you took a bullet for him? Does that feel like the will of God to you?" He thumbed out to the hallway. "There's a couple of mean looking Italian cops outside who want to take you to prison. They got a medical ward at that jail, and I guarantee it ain't as nice as this. You won't have a private room there. You won't ever have a private moment again, for that matter. Just cruel, hardened Italian criminals who'd probably find a young kid like you very attractive, if you know what I mean. Talk about losing your privacy."

He formed a stoic expression on his face. "Sometimes we are called to be martyrs. It assures my acceptance into heaven. Where I have failed, others will succeed. The prophecy cannot be broken. Otherwise, in the apocalypse to come, the seed of man would be lost."

"Prophecy, you say?" Pete said. "You know, some guy over in Spain tried to steal something too. He mentioned something about a prophecy. You mind showing me the underside of your arm?"

"I have nothing to hide. The truth will be revealed in due time." He rolled his arm over and displayed the tattoo, his face beaming with pride. Amari got up and came to her father's side, so she could see better. Sure enough, it was the same tattoo. A saucer-shaped spaceship with the three crosses of Calvary in the middle. Only this guy had 762 under the UFO instead of the 876 the guy in Oviedo had.

"Looks the same to me," she said. "Only with 762 instead."

"That's an odd tattoo, don't you think?" Pete said. "That guy in Oviedo must be a friend of yours. Those numbers over your tattoos. Is that some kind of code?"

"As one of the Chosen, we must relinquish all of our earthly possessions—as well as our earthly identities. 762 is my name now. We must lower ourselves now, so we can be elevated later. In the land of New Canaan, I will have a new name, and a new, glorified body."

"Canaan?" she said. "You mean like in the Bible? The Promised Land?"

"The new Promised Land. It is not of this world, even as Christ was not of this world."

"I see," Pete said. "So if I interpret your tattoo correctly, you intend to travel to this new Promised Land by flying saucer?"

"Whether it is shaped like a saucer, I do not know. But a spacecraft, yes. The Conduit must first travel through the gate. He will then return for us in his craft."

"The gate?" she said. "You mean like a wormhole or something?"

"Is that so hard to believe?" he asked. "The angels come and go at will. Do you think they fly from heaven by wings made of feathers? Angels are merely superior beings that travel by spacecraft. They pass through wormholes all the time. In heaven, there is ultimate technology. Anything that is possible technologically is routine on the planets of heaven."

"The *planets* of heaven?" she said. "You mean there's more than one?"

"Of course, there are many inhabited planets in the heavenly realm."

"You know, that makes perfect sense to me," Pete said, attempting to find common ground so he could gain his trust. "The universe is a big place. Why would God stop with this one?"

"Precisely," 762 said.

"So let me get this straight," Pete said. "This Divine Conduit of yours is going to pass through a wormhole and land on one of the planets of heaven."

"The Planet of New Canaan," 762 clarified.

"That's right," Pete replied. "Then he's coming back for you in a big flying saucer."

"Something like that," 762 said. "The Divine Conduit goes first, then returns for us."

"So this divine conduit is the leader of your cult?"

762 pursed his lips. The word *cult* must have offended him. "Of course you would say that. Most people have no understanding of who we are. Need I remind you that the first followers of Christ were considered a cult in their day. If only you knew, you would bend your knee to me in reverence. For I am crucial to the survival of humanity. During the great recycling, the entire planet will be tilled under as a farmer tills his old crops into the soil. So shall it be for the people of Earth, except for the Chosen."

"Then I'm afraid you're going to get tilled under with the rest of us," Pete said. "You're not getting onto that saucer while you're rotting in an Italian prison. Now, I'll make a deal with you. Give us the name of your *conduit* so we can have a talk with him. Who knows, if he follows proper legal channels, maybe he can borrow the Shroud." That was the lying part that went along with the job.

"I can't do that."

"Then I hope you enjoy the *recycling*," Pete said. "From what you're telling me, there's going to be a lot of weeping and gnashing of teeth."

"When I accepted this mission, I was assured that even if captured, I would escape the recycling. If I fail, I will enter the traditional way. I will choose Plan B."

"The *traditional* way," Amari said. "Most of us call that dying. There's no other way to get there. You're not going to kill yourself, are you? Is that your Plan B?"

"There is no death for those in Christ. Only transition. A change of location."

"That's right. In Christ, we inherit eternal life," Pete said. "We agree on that part. But you still haven't explained why you tried to steal the Shroud. How does the Shroud or the Sudarium of Oviedo involve your prophecy? Why do you need it so bad?"

"I cannot say. The new Adam holds the secret."

Amari scrunched her brows, looking utterly confused. "Come again?"

"The Adam of this age knows how to make them work."

"You mean like Adam and Eve, Adam?" she clarified.

"Yes, a new Adam is born. His seed will repopulate humanity. His seed and the womb of the new Eve."

"Oaaakay, then," she said. "That new Adam and Eve— I don't remember reading about them in the Bible."

"So who is this guy?" Pete asked. "Somebody we've heard of?"

"I cannot reveal that to you," 762 said. "For even the new Adam does not yet know his true identity."

"I see," Pete said. "We wouldn't want to ruin the surprise for him. So you're telling me you have no idea what the Shroud of Turin and the Sudarium of Oviedo have to do with all of this?"

"I only know the parts are essential. I was instructed to retrieve the Shroud, nothing more. The new Adam will know what to do."

"So what about the new Eve?" Amari asked. "Can you tell us who she is? Or does she not know either?"

"She is also unaware of her true identity."

"I'm guessing you know who she is," Pete said.

"Yes, but I am forbidden to tell."

This conversation was going a bit long. They needed to make progress before the nurse kicked them out. "Amari, what time is it?" Pete asked.

She glanced at her watch. "Ten minutes till 3:00."

"They should be here with the ambulance any time then. You know, the one taking you to prison," Pete said, trying to instill a little urgency so 762 would cooperate.

Suddenly, 762 became restless. The suggestion worked. He widened his eyes, fixed on Amari. Pete glanced up at his heart monitor and noticed that his pulse had shot back up to over a hundred. "You seem a little upset. Not looking forward to that prison, are you?"

762 stuttered for words and finally let it out. "What did you say her name was?"

"My name's Amari Johnston. You've probably heard of me. Especially since you're into the Shroud. I've been on the news lately. Maybe you saw me on the *Tonight Show*."

"You are kind of famous," Pete said. "Especially in the Shroud world."

Suddenly, the monitor alarm blared. 762 turned pale, and his breaths quickened.

"Hey, calm down," she said, placing his oxygen mask back over his nose. "I'm only a person, just like you."

"Must be a little star-struck," Pete said. "Hey, buddy, look at it this way. You'll be sort of famous too after this."

"Infamous, maybe," she countered. "How many people can say they tried to steal the Shroud of Turin?"

Suddenly, the nurse rushed into the room, followed by Bonelli and the two Italian police.

"Tu dovrai andartene," she barked. "Lo stai sconvolgendo!"

"She says you're upsetting him," Bonelli translated. "She says you need to leave."

The nurse ushered them out of the room. They strolled down the hall, out of earshot of the Italian police officers.

"Did you get anything useful out of him?" Bonelli asked.

"Just nonsense," Pete replied. "But I can tell you he's in cahoots with that guy from Oviedo. No doubt about it. They even have the same tattoo."

"I've got a bad feeling about him," Amari said. "He seems too relaxed about his fate. Dad mentioned him going to an Italian prison and there was no reaction. His heart monitor stayed the same. Well, until he mentioned it a second time."

"That was because of you," Pete said. "Because he realized he was in the company of Shroud royalty. If he tried to steal the Shroud, you know he's heard of you."

"Dad, I'm serious," she said. "Something doesn't feel right. I think he intends to take the *traditional* way out."

"What are you saying?" Pete said. "He's going to off himself?"

"It's what my gut tells me," she said and turned to Bonelli. "I think you should probably talk to those police and nurses. That guy should be on suicide watch."

"I'll see what I can do," Bonelli said.

Bonelli went into the room and spoke briefly with the nurse, then came out and had words with the carabinieri sitting in the hall. He finished his conversation and then met Amari and Pete at the nursing station.

"What did they say?" she asked.

"They inferred that they were aware of his mental state."

"And?"

"They basically told me to mind my own business."

****

"When we get back I'll ask Kevin if he knows about any crazy UFO cults," Amari said as she accompanied Pete and Bonelli down the sidewalk outside the hospital. The hospital was on a busy city street, so Bonelli had parked the car a couple of blocks away in a parking garage.

"You told me Kevin was into UFOs," Pete said. "Doesn't he have some books about them?"

"Several books," she said. "And he knows people too. I bet he could give us a good lead. And I've got another idea."

"Oh, yeah?" Pete said. "Let's hear it."

"I figure most cults don't advertise in the Yellow Pages, but New Age churches do. I'll call around. Maybe we can even visit some of those churches if they're not too far away. I bet they can help us."

"That's a good place to start," Pete said.

Smashing glass sounded from above. Glass shards rained down on the sidewalk behind them. They lunged away from the debris, hands overhead as protection. A loud thud came from behind, followed by screams and gasps from pedestrians.

Pete stepped in front of his daughter as a shield. There on the concrete sidewalk lay the broken body of 762, his limbs contorted from misshaped bones, blood spattered on the brick wall and pooling on the sidewalk around his head. Pete instinctively brought his hand over her eyes to protect her from the nightmares that would come after witnessing such a grizzly site. As a homicide investigator, he knew this to be true. Years after some of his most brutal cases had been solved, he still had the occasional nightmare.

She pressed into her father's chest, knowing she didn't want to see it either, but she knew what it was. "It's him, isn't it? 762?" she managed, her voice strained with alarm.

"It is, baby. I hate to say it, but it looks like our friend took the traditional way out."

"May God have mercy on his soul," Bonelli said.

"It's my fault," she said weakly. "I should have said more. I shouldn't have left until they took me seriously."

"No, baby, it's not your fault," Pete said. "We tried to tell them. They just didn't want to hear it."

"The fault lies with those who brainwashed him," Bonelli said.

"Then we need to get back and find them," Pete said. "Bonelli, call Skip. Tell him to fuel up and take us home."

Chapter 14

Fresno, California

Neal Barrett came highly recommended. His specialty was jewelry stores and expensive estates. Adrian knew him by reputation but had never, until that moment, worked with him. When Adrian had called Barrett to inquire about the possibility of stealing the Shroud and Sudarium, it was a no-go. Barrett had explained that he was good, but not that good, and neither was anybody else for that matter. But after hearing Adrian's explanation for needing the Shroud, Barrett had suggested an alternate, more practical solution, and Calvin would be none-the-wiser.

Barrett drove the four-wheel-drive Jeep Wrangler with the headlights off, using the lights that flooded multimillionaire Ernesto Galliano's ranch home as a guide. The Jeep was loaded with bolt cutters, glass cutting tools, and a wooden ladder, not the noisy aluminum kind.

Adrian sat in the passenger seat, contemplatively enduring the hard bumps and dips of the barren land behind the Galliano ranch. Ian jostled around in the back seat. This was a first for Ian, but every pilot was a thrill seeker at heart, and he was willing to participate, even if he did seem a little uneasy about the prospect of getting caught. Barrett had assured him that the likelihood of going to jail was extremely low. And Barrett ought to know. He was the best of the best, and he didn't come cheap. Adrian had to liquidate the stocks he'd invested in using the cult members' contribution to the common fund. But after the botched European heist, he wasn't taking any chances. He had to leave this to the pros.

Barret parked the Jeep just outside a horse fence. He opened his glove compartment and removed a pistol. He reached back in and retrieved a black, cylindrical sound suppressor and carefully screwed it onto the pistol's barrel. "This is a 22 Ruger Mark 2," Barret said. "It's not ideal for bringing down a man quickly, but it's perfect for silencing a medium to large sized dog."

"If they're not home, wouldn't they have kenneled their dogs?" Ian said.

"Do you want to take that chance?" Barret said. "Besides, they may have a housekeeper that stayed behind. We may have to use it on her too."

"Or I'll use this," Adrian said, pulling out his own gun, a short-barrel Astra 68 revolver chambered for .45 caliber rounds. "It packs a bit more punch."

Adrian noticed the sweat beading on Ian's nose. "Relax, Ian. Nobody's going to get hurt . . . probably."

"But you said nobody's home, right?" Ian asked again and nudged his slipping glasses back up the bridge of his slick nose.

"From my reconnaissance, the house looks like it's empty," Barrett said. "I watched a whole bus of them pull out this afternoon. But just in case, be on guard. They probably have a state-of-the-art alarm system, and there's no way we can defeat it. That's why we gotta work fast."

"Can't you just cut the phone line?" Ian asked.

"I plan on doing that," Barrett said. "I know where the junction should be. Still, they may have a radio backup. Houses like this usually do."

"Ian, I told you to relax," Adrian said. "This is going to be fun. Just pretend you're a kid again and you're rolling your neighbor's yard with toilet paper."

Ian laughed nervously. "I've done that a few times."

"All right," Barrett said. "Let's go over this again. We get what we came for and off-road it out of here, lights off, so there's no way the police can track us. Not until we're long gone. Remember, Ian, once we break in, you go to the front and watch for the police. If our prize is in a safe, then I'll crack it, but I'll need a few minutes. If the cops come, we're bugging out pronto. Sorry, Adrian, but I can't spend your money from prison."

"This is an isolated estate," Adrian said. "It'll take a good fifteen minutes for a patrol car to respond—unless of course, they happen to be in the neighborhood. And I always have this." He waved his revolver for effect. "You know, the irony of all ironies?"

"What's that?" Ian asked.

"Calvin claims he knows this Galliano guy. In fact, this guy is who introduced the Shroud of Turin to him years ago."

"Obviously, they lost touch over the years," Ian said.

"Obviously," Adrian said.

"If we're going to do this thing, we need to do it now," Barrett said.

"Then what are we waiting for?" Adrian said and opened the door.

****

Cain and Abel were ecstatic to see Bonelli. The black Doberman Pinschers wagged their stubby tails, whining and clicking their fist-sized paws against the mosaic tile floor. It was after two in the morning, and Bonelli had just driven in from the Fresno airport. It had been a long flight from Turin to Tucson. Skip, Ernesto's pilot, needed a break before making the last leg of the trip to Fresno, so Bonelli had gone into town and visited with Kevin and Jenny while Skip took a nap in the back of the plane. They flew out of Tucson around midnight.

Bonelli was exhausted. All he wanted was a hot shower and the cool sheets of his bed. Other than the dogs and the housekeeper who lived in a separate bungalow, the estate was empty. Ernesto had taken the ten children and two nannies to Monterey for the weekend to see the aquarium and Mitch had gone along for security.

He showered and threw on a T-shirt and pair of shorts. He was brushing his teeth when Cain and Abel went ballistic, frantically barking at growling. The dogs were trained to remain silent unless there was a human threat. Whatever they were mad at, it was no skunk.

He spat toothpaste into the sink, hurried into the bedroom, and snatched the shotgun from a wall mount. He ran down the hall towards the ruckus, pumping the gun to chamber a shell as he went. The dogs ravenously barked and snarled at the French doors that opened to the poolside veranda. Floodlights beamed onto the patio, triggered by motion detectors. Three dark figures hurried past the swimming pool and entered the veranda, dressed in black, wearing ski masks. They were burglars, apparently made aware of the empty house—or so they thought it was empty. Bonelli moved behind a support pillar and aimed the twelve-gage at the glass. One of the thieves produced a silencer tipped pistol and pointed it at the dogs.

"Cain, Abel, here!" Bonelli shouted.

Once the dogs were clear, he pulled the trigger. A deafening blast shattered the window. The gun toppled from the burglar's hand, and he stumbled backward.

"Cain, Abel! Behind me!" Bonelli ordered and braced his shotgun against the pillar, awaiting return fire.

No fire came, only muffled panicked words as the three figures retreated into the darkness.

THE CULT OF NEW CANAAN

Chapter 15

When Ernesto had heard about the attempted burglary, he chartered a boat trip to Catalina Island, so he could keep the kids busy until the investigation was finished, the blood cleaned up, and the French door repaired. Those kids had seen enough trauma in their lives. The last thing they needed was to hear about an attempted burglary and shooting in their backyard. With any luck and tight lips, the kids would be none-the-wiser.

Pete and Amari had arrived at the estate as quickly as Skip could get them there. By noon the local police had cleared the scene, and it was time for a more thorough investigation from the private sector.

Bonelli stood with Pete and his daughter on the patio, broken glass shards scattered on the orange tile patio floor. "Thanks for coming out on such short notice," Bonelli said. "Ernesto doesn't have much faith in the local PD."

"Another set of eyes is always helpful," Pete said. "I assume the locals will run a trace on that gun you blew out of his hand."

"I'm sure it'll come up stolen," Amari said.

"Of course," Pete replied. "These guys weren't fools. It's no coincidence they chose last night to break in. They were casing the place and knew the house was empty."

"Only they never figured on Bonelli showing up at two in the morning," Amari said.

They followed the blood droplets across the poolside tile. "It wasn't their lucky day," Pete said. "For one of these guys, this was a career ender."

Bonelli followed them into the grass lawn. "This is about where I lost sight of them. The floodlights go dim here."

"You can see two sets of footstep impressions in the grass, maybe three feet apart," Pete said. "In the middle, the grass lays down flat in a straight line."

"So the other two were dragging the guy who got shot," she said.

"From a 12-gauge shotgun blast?" Pete said. "You know they were dragging him."

"I was only trying to hit his hand before he could fire the gun," Bonelli said. "But he was moving forward. He walked into the blast."

"Nobody's blaming you," Pete said. "You were just doing your job. An armed burglar pulls out a gun, and you got every right to shoot first."

"I'm just glad you weren't hurt," she said. "Or the dogs."

They followed the blood and footprint trail to an iron gate that was flanked by an eight-foot concrete wall finished with tan stucco. The gate was open.

"The police found long-handled bolt cutters a few feet from here," Bonelli said, pointing at the small yellow evidence flag stuck into the dirt.

"Guess they were in too much of a hurry to grab them on their way out," she said.

"Getting hit with a shotgun will do that," Pete replied.

Outside the fence, beyond the range of the irrigation system, the lush grass had withered to dirt and weeds. They followed blood and footprints into an open field behind the estate.

"You can really see the blood now," she said. "He was bleeding out bad."

"The blood shows up a lot better when it's not hidden by the grass," Pete said. "Pull back the blades of grass, and you'll see more."

The blood trail stopped where off-road tire tracks began.

"Here's where the blood trail ends," Pete said.

"And the tire tracks begin," she said and pointed into the open field. "Looks like they turned around and drove out the same way they came in."

"There's a main road a half mile from here," Bonelli said.

"The tracks are from off-road tires," Pete said. "So they snuck up on the place from behind at night, no doubt with the headlights off. They probably had the taillights disconnected too. After the burglary, they could easily escape in the dark, especially since there was a full moon last night. If they saw police lights on the road, they'd either wait it out or go another direction. These guys were clever. Not like those idiots in Europe."

"We should check all the local hospitals to see if they got any gunshot wounds," she said.

"I'd say the police have already done that," Pete said. "But I doubt they'll find anything. This guy didn't survive his wound. I've never seen anyone survive a 12-gauge blast to the torso. From the amount of blood on the ground, I'd say he was dead before he ever made it onto the vehicle. They either dumped the body, or more likely, they buried it somewhere."

"You're probably right," she said.

"You think the three crimes are related?" she asked. "The two in Europe and this one?"

"Most likely it's a coincidence," Pete said. "Probably a random burglary."

Her face suddenly flashed with realization. "Oh my gosh! I know what it is! It sounds crazy, but I know what they wanted."

Chapter 16

Amari had spent some time at Ernesto's estate over the summer, so she gave Pete the grand tour. It was a 14,000-square foot Mediterranean style mansion with pale yellow stucco exterior and an orange Spanish tile roof. A swimming pool with a waterfall was out back. Adjacent to the home were horse stables and a small separate house for the head housekeeper. The estate had a total of fourteen bedrooms, eight of them in a separate wing of the home that was added onto the estate to house abused orphans and foster children. Two of those rooms were for the full-time nannies in charge of the children. A child psychologist worked with the children during the day.

"When Ernesto's father owned the estate, this used to be a game room," Bonelli said, ushering them under an arched mahogany doorframe. The mission style ceiling had thick wooden beams for support.

"It's more of a shrine now," Amari said. "He got rid of the pool table and poker table right after his father died."

A life-size, black and white, negative image of the Shroud of Turin hung on the far wall. Directly above the life-size photo was an intricately carved crucifix that bore a graphic depiction of the crucified Jesus, so finely detailed you could see the agony etched in the wooden face. The wall to the right had three stained glass windows with religious themes like you would see in a church. Scores of books about anything biblical lined shelves on the opposite wall. And dead center of the room was a long table, maybe sixteen feet in length and four feet wide. Draped over the top of the table was a blood-red silk sheet with gold fringes, sort of like a fancy tablecloth.

"Hold on a second," she said and closed some shutters over the stain glass windows. Then she went over and flipped off the lights, dimming the room so much it took Pete's eyes a moment to adjust. She removed the long red tablecloth, folded it into squares, and set it in a chair. She then set her hand above a switch built into the sidewall of the long table. "Ready?"

"As I'll ever be," Pete said. "What's all this about?"

She flipped a switch, and light glowed from within the table. Pete staggered backward and stammered for words. He couldn't believe what he was seeing. It was impossible, yet there it was in front of his own eyes. "Uh . . . if that's real . . . then Ernesto's got some explaining to do."

"It sure looks real," she said, beaming with pride.

"You bet it does," Pete said and moved in for a better look. There in front of him, underneath the protection of a sheet of glass, was the spitting image of the Shroud of Turin. He'd studied up on the Shroud since his daughter had introduced him to the relic. And this was identical down to the most minute detail. The image, every blood stain, every burn mark, even the corner they had sampled for the carbon date, was spot on.

"Ernesto wouldn't tell me how much this cost," she said.

"But it cost a fortune," Bonelli added. "I assure you of that. He hired some of the most skilled artisans on the planet."

"Just so he could gawk at this in the privacy of his own home?" Pete asked. "That doesn't seem like him."

"No, not at all," Bonelli said. "Ernesto is entirely too frugal for that. This is part of a traveling exposition. This Shroud replica, as well as the life-sized photo you see on the wall, has been on display all over the world."

"So he uses this to get the word out," Pete said. "To educate people."

"Exactly," she said. "Right now, his exhibit manager is busy setting up the next world tour. It's sort of in between gigs."

"I see," Pete said and moved to another smaller table, also with another red tablecloth covering it.

"Oh, yeah," she said and removed the cover. She flipped on the light. "You should know what this is."

"That's what the guy was trying to steal in Oviedo," Pete said. "The Sudarium. The cloth they used to cover his face when they took him down from the cross."

"That's right," she said. "Everybody knows about The Shroud of Turin, but not a lot of people know about the Sudarium. Ernesto's trying to change that."

Pete inspected the Sudarium replica more closely. It was a rectangular cloth about three feet long with a width of about twenty inches, give or take. The fabric seemed identical to that of the Shroud, and it was soaked in brownish red blood stains. Two of the stains looked like they could be from eye sockets.

"Okay," she said in her *listen up, I'm about to give a lecture* tone of voice. "We know that the Shroud has to be the authentic burial Shroud of Christ, despite the misleading result of the carbon date. I mean, a medieval forger wouldn't know about mineral fingerprints. Yet the mineral samples found on the heal of the Shroud image perfectly matched mineral fingerprints in Jerusalem. The scourge marks on the back match exactly to those found on a Roman flagellum. The gospels say he was pierced in the hands, and a forger would have made it that way to look authentic, yet on the Shroud, the blood comes from the wrist. Only now we know the hands couldn't hold the weight of a body, so it had to be that way. Not only that, but we see the bones in the hand. We can also see teeth and some bones on the skull. That's because of the energy that came from within the body. And this energy that radiated from the body formed a negative image—which is exactly what you would expect if it was radiation. Not only that, but the image encodes a 3-D image that can only be seen with a special camera they used to map the moon. That's exactly what you'd see if the cloth wrapped a body that sent out a burst of radiation. How's a forger going to do that?"

"I know, Amari, you went over all this before—several times. I even remember you telling me about the pollen on the head, the one that comes from a thorn bush that grows in Jerusalem."

"And blooms in Easter," she reminded him.

"That's right. And I know all the reasons the carbon date is wrong too. You're preaching to the choir. But what about the Sudarium? How do you know it's authentic?"

"First of all, the Gospel of John talks about this cloth. It says that when Peter went into the tomb, he saw strips of linen—as well as the cloth that wrapped Jesus' head. The strips of linen were the Shroud itself and the strip of cloth used to tie the Shroud close to the body. It's the strip you see sewn onto the right side of the Shroud. Now, the ancient Jews believed that everything needed to be buried with the body, including all the blood. That's why they didn't wash the body before burial. So the Sudarium was used to wrap the face of Jesus while he was still on the cross so they could catch any blood that came from his nose or mouth. They needed to make sure none of the blood was lost when he was taken down. Once they wrapped him in the Shroud, then they wrapped the Sudarium around the head, on top of the Shroud."

"Okay, I'll buy that," Pete said. "But it still doesn't prove this is the actual cloth they used."

"There's more."

"I'm sure there is," Pete said. His daughter always did her research.

"For one thing, The Sudarium of Oviedo can be traced historically back to Peter himself. Christian texts say Peter took the Sudarium. They also say that after Peter died, it was kept in Israel until the Muslims and Persians invaded. So according to the historical record, it was then moved to Alexandria in Egypt. Then it went to Cartagena, and then to Toledo in Spain. It was kept there until 711 AD but had to be moved again because of another Muslim invasion. That's when it went to the Cathedral of Oviedo, and it's been there ever since."

"So the historical records for this thing are better than the Shroud's."

"The records are clear about the Shroud too, only it was called other things like the *Image of Edessa* or the *Mandylion*. They didn't call it the Shroud of Turin until it went to Turin in 1578."

"All right," Pete said. "History says it must be authentic. But historical documents can be faked, you know."

"Both the Shroud of Turin and the Sudarium are linen, and they are both woven with a Z-twist. That was the common pattern of the day, and that suggests that both clothes were woven during the Roman Empire. It wasn't used during the period they claim the Shroud was forged, and they never used it in France, only in the Middle East."

"That certainly narrows it down," Pete said.

"The smoking gun is the pollen. There were a hundred and forty-one grains of pollen identified on the Sudarium and ninety-nine percent of them are native to the Jerusalem area, and three of the species grow only in that area. And then there's the pollen that comes from a thorn bush that only grows in Jerusalem and blooms in spring."

"Goundelia tournefortii," Bonelli said.

"Yes, that one," she said. "That pollen is also on the Sudarium, the same pollen that's on the Shroud. And not only that, but traces of myrrh and aloe were also detected on the Sudarium. The Gospel of John mentions that Nicodemus brought a mixture of myrrh and aloe so they could use it in the burial. And then there's the blood on the Sudarium. If you line the Sudarium up with the Shroud, the blood stains match perfectly. Also, the part of the Sudarium that was around the forehead is only blood, but the part that was around the mouth had both blood and a clear fluid from the pulmonary edema. This happened because he was hanging from the cross. When you're stretched out in that position, fluid starts to build in your lungs. When they took him down from the cross, that fluid would come out, and that's what we see on the Sudarium."

"And that's why they put it around his head to begin with," Bonelli offered. "To catch all the fluid they knew would be released. They were no strangers to crucifixion back then, so they knew how to do this."

"And do you know what the blood type on the Sudarium is?" she asked.

"I suspect you're going to tell me it was AB," Pete said. "That's the blood type on the Shroud, if I remember correctly. It's a rare blood type."

"Yes, it is type AB, and only about five percent of people have it. So we know that medieval forgers were unaware of blood types back then. And if the Shroud and Sudarium aren't real, then they must be forged. And since the Sudarium can be historically traced to the time of Christ, then a forger would have to have known the blood type on the Sudarium so he could put the same type blood on the Shroud."

"But why would he do that?" Pete said. "You said yourself they didn't have any idea what a blood type was back then."

"Precisely," she said. "And that meant it had to be a random chance. And if you crunch the numbers, the odds of that happening by random chance are about a hundred and fifty to one."

"Then I'd say you've proved your case beyond a reasonable doubt. If this was a courtroom, no jury in their right mind would say those cloths didn't cover the same man."

"Nobody in their *right mind*. Which brings me to why I brought you here. I think those guys were trying to steal this replica. There's nothing else of value in this house. All the jewelry went to Ernesto's mother, and he auctioned the artwork and donated the proceeds to charity. This Shroud replica is the only thing of value, so that has to be what they were after. And the fact that this happened right after the other theft attempt in Europe can't be a coincidence."

"So they figured if the real thing was unattainable," Pete said, "then this replica would have to suffice."

"I know it sounds crazy, but it has to be true," she said. "It's the only thing that makes sense."

"Not to me," Pete said. "Heck, stealing the real Shroud doesn't make any sense. It would be almost impossible to sell without getting caught. Maybe a wealthy collector."

"That's a normal person's motive," she said. "Remember, it looks like some UFO cult is after it, and there's nothing normal about that."

"You have a point," Pete said.

131

"Perhaps the motive was its power to heal," Bonelli said.

"Pardon?" Pete said.

"The healing power of Christ," Bonelli clarified. "His power to heal is so great that even touching one of his garments could heal. Do you remember the story in the Gospels of the woman touching the hem of his garment? She was healed of a bleeding disorder."

"Yeah, but he was actually wearing the garment," Pete said.

"Yes, but part of him remains on the Shroud," Bonelli replied. "His blood. Legends suggest that the Shroud of Turin has miraculous healing properties."

"That's true," Amari said. "I can tell you about one of those miracles. It's a documented fact. In 1954, an eleven-year-old girl from England was dying from a terrible bone disease. They'd already given her last rights. But when the girl saw a photograph of the Shroud, just looking at it made her start to get better. When the Catholic Church heard about this, they took her out to Turin to see the Shroud in person. They rolled up the Shroud and set it across the arms of her wheelchair. Then they let her touch it. Do you know what happened next?"

"She was healed?" Pete guessed.

"Completely healed," she replied. "There's been other reports just like this. If the woman from the New Testament can be healed by merely touching the robe of Jesus, then the cloth that bears his blood and image might also have power."

"Okay, I'll buy that," Pete said. "I can see why someone would want the Shroud itself—that is if they believed in that kind of thing. Maybe someone is dying from cancer or something, and they're desperate."

"A cult leader maybe?" she said. "You think maybe he's dying?"

"Maybe, maybe not," Pete said. "The healing part is just speculation. But if healing power is the motive, then why bother with a replica? It makes no sense."

"I don't know, Dad. Maybe they were just after jewelry. They saw nobody was home, so they tried to break in."

"Bonelli, how often has someone tried to break into this house?" Pete asked.

"Since I've been working for Ernesto, never. Not once."

"Then this is no coincidence," Pete said. "They were after this replica, and odds are, it was the same crazies who tried the steal the real Shroud."

"But why?" Bonelli asked. "Like you said, it doesn't make any sense."

"Nothing about this case makes any sense," Pete said. "We just have to keep digging, that's all."

Chapter 17

Deep in the California desert, a few miles east of the Sierra Nevada Mountains, Adrian and Ian discussed their uncertain future.

"So what now?" Ian asked. "We don't get paid unless we assemble the parts."

Adrian squinted against the intense sunlight. "Barret said that replica was between exhibits. Maybe we should wait until it goes back on tour. We can try again later. Or who knows, maybe there's another replica out there. I need some time to sort this out. This was my Plan B. I'll have to work on Plan C. What scares me is Calvin has his own Plan B."

Ian winced and shook his head in disbelief. "Please tell me it's not anything like his Plan A. Did he really think they could steal the Shroud of Turin?"

Adrian gave Ian a grave look. "Yes, Ian, he believed it."

"So what's his Plan B?"

"I have no idea. I only know this. If he doesn't get his precious parts in the mail by the end of the week, he says he's going to need to borrow your phone."

"My phone?"

"Is there any other phone on the compound?"

"Guess I better tidy up the place then. Hate for the boss to see my underwear on the floor."

"Please do," Adrian said and stepped closer to the Jeep. The VIN had been pried off, the license tags removed, and the gasoline poured. He lit the match, tossed it on the wet fuel-fuse, and watched as the flame snaked its way across the desert floor, erupting in a crackly roar when the Jeep ignited.

"Too bad we couldn't give him a decent burial," Ian said. "You think we dug the hole deep enough? I hope the coyotes don't dig him up."

"There was nothing *decent* about that guy," Adrian said. "He got what he deserved."

"If that's the way life works," Ian said, his voice tinged with remorse, "where does that leave the two of us?"

"I suppose if there is a hell," Adrian replied, "then I'll be in a particularly hot spot."

"Right next to Hitler and Ted Bundy."

Adrian snickered. "Fortunately for the two of us, there is no such place. All that matters in this world is survival. Survival of the fittest. We're doing what we have to do to survive, nothing more. Don't ever forget that." He climbed into the rental car and started the engine.

Ian stood, thinking wistfully as the watched the flames devour the evidence.

"You worry too much, Ian. Get in. We need to get out of here before someone sees the smoke."

Chapter 18

The Austin Ballroom of the Sheraton Hotel in downtown Dallas was filled to capacity. A projection screen hung on the wall behind the stage. A slide projector beamed the words Dallas International Scientific Symposium on the Shroud of Turin in bold, blood red letters. Next to the projection screen were the enlarged front and back negative photographic images of the Shroud. A podium stood center stage.

The ballroom was set up in the classroom arrangement with long tables in front of the chairs to allow attendees space for laptop computers, books, notes, or caffeinated drinks to help endure hours of tedious scientific discussions cluttered with technical jargon and speculative tangents. Over three hundred experts from around the world were in attendance, including several of the original members of the Shroud of Turin Research Project, also known as STURP. Most of the attendees were men, middle-aged and older. Amari was in the minority as only about twenty-five percent of the attendees were women. She was also the youngest person in the room.

Some of the biggest names sat on the front row, people like Professor Luigi Gonella of Turin, Italy. Any scientist who wanted access to the Shroud went through him first. There was a forensic expert on crucifixion named Dr. Fred Zugibe. Dorothy Crispino, publisher of *Shroud Spectrum International*, was in the front row too, sitting in between author Ian Wilson and Dr. John Jackson, a founding member of STURP. Several other priests and experts from Europe sat on the front row, but she had no idea who they were. But one person seated right dab in the middle was a man she knew well—none other than Dr. Michael Tite of the British Museum. He was one of the people who announced the Shroud's flawed carbon date to the world, the only test ever performed on the Shroud that suggested it was anything but authentic.

In between lectures, a moderator followed raised hands around the room, handing over a microphone to anyone who cared to ask questions or offer their own alternative opinion.

Dr. Whanger had just finished his presentation about faint images of Israeli flowers found on the Shroud, which were theoretically placed within the Shroud during burial. Next up was Kevin. It was his second lecture of the symposium. His first lecture the day before had been about his crazy wormhole theory. Nobody laughed out loud, but she saw a lot of doubtful expressions in the audience. This time he was giving a lecture about his more plausible theory, the one he'd proven possible over the summer at the particle accelerator in France. It was the theory about how the Shroud image was formed with proton radiation. For the next and final day of the conference, he was scheduled to give a two-part lecture concerning possible reasons the carbon date was invalid.

The first part of his lecture would be about the discovery that had thrust Amari into the national spotlight. It was her patch hypothesis that suggested the portion of the Shroud used for the carbon date had been done on a repaired section, mixing old fibers in with new, and, therefore, making the carbon date invalid. The second part of his lecture was about how neutron radiation released during the resurrection could have altered the carbon-14 results.

Kevin, who was sandwiched in between her and Ernesto on the far-left side of the front row, looked uncharacteristically nervous, unlike his typical laid-back manner. She could tell because he wasn't slouching in his chair but sat upright with a healthy posture instead.

"Almost time," Ernesto said with a wink. "You're going to do great. Just like yesterday."

She squeezed his knee. "You nervous?"

"Little bit," he said. "Not as bad as the first one though. The subject was a little farfetched. Some people were even laughing at first."

"They weren't laughing when you finished," she said reassuringly. "They were thoroughly confused, but they weren't laughing."

A lawyer from Missouri took the podium next and started to introduce Kevin.

Suddenly, out of the corner of her eye, she noticed a side exit door open. Two men stepped through and stood there as if they were looking for empty seats. One of them arched an eyebrow like Spock on Star Trek, and the other one just had a dumb look on his face. Yet, something about those guys seemed familiar. For one, they were relatively young, maybe early thirties. Most of the conference attendees were mid to late fifties, well established in their scientific circles. And she had a feeling these guys weren't invited. Otherwise, they wouldn't have snuck in the side door. And they both had the same hair, shaved close like they'd just come from boot camp—*like the cult member in Turin.* The only difference is they both wore casual dress clothes instead of coveralls.

She elbowed Kevin for his attention. "Kevin, look at those guys."

He glanced toward the door and shrugged. "So?"

"Did you invite them? They came in just now, right when you're supposed to talk."

"I got nothing to do with the guest list."

The lawyer spoke Kevin's name, and applause broke out in the hall.

"Gotta go, babe. Wish me luck," he said and made his way to the podium.

"Good luck," she said, but her eyes never left the two men by the door.

One of them raised his arm to point toward two empty seats near the rear of the hall. When he did, he exposed the underside of his forearm. And then she saw it—a flying saucer-shaped tattoo with three crosses in the middle. Numbers were written underneath. No doubt about it, they were from the same cult that had tried to steal the Shroud and the Sudarium. But why were they at a scientific conference?

Just as Kevin started to speak, a security officer wearing khaki pants and cowboy boots meandered over to the intruders with his thumbs tucked under his belt. He pointed to the door with the antenna of his walkie-talkie and appeared to be telling them to leave the same way they came in. The two cult members left without hesitation.

"Be right back," she told Ernesto and hurried over to the security officer. "Are you just going to let them leave? Detain them."

He regarded her with suspicion, a wad of tobacco bulging in the lower corner of his cheek. "It ain't no crime to walk in the back door. They got the wrong banquet hall, that's all. There's another convention in the Pearl room. I gave them directions."

"No, they tried to sneak in. They only left because you caught them. We need to keep them here until the police show up."

He spit into a garbage can, then hooked his radio back onto this belt. "You want them arrested, call the police yourself," he said and meandered away.

Distracted by the commotion, half the audience looked at Kevin, but the other half looked her way. Kevin noticed it too and stopped mid-sentence. He locked eyes with her and seemed to be questioning why she was out of her seat. "I'll be right back," she mouthed to him and backed out the door.

"Nature calls," he told the audience. "Too much coffee, I guess."

The door closed behind her, hushing the cackle of laughter filling the ballroom. Leave it to Kevin. She loved the guy, but he had no tact whatsoever.

Her embarrassment could wait. Right now, she had to find those guys. She scanned the hallway, looking both ways. She spotted them just as they rounded the corner, making their way to the hotel lobby. She hurried down the hall, her short pump dress shoes clapping against the tile floor, her legs kicking at her dress. She arrived in time to see them heading toward the exit. "Hold on! I want to talk to you!"

Everyone in the lobby turned to look at her, including the two guys from the cult.

"Stay right there," she shouted, plodding in their direction. "I just have some questions."

Suddenly, recognition seemed to dawn on their faces—recognition and fear. They spun around and walked briskly toward the front door.

"Wait!" She kicked off her shoes and sprinted barefoot after them. "Stop, I just want to talk!"

They quickened their pace and exited through a side revolving door, rather than the automatic double doors used by the bellhops.

Seconds later, she reached the revolving door. She started to shove her way through but collided with glass instead. "What the—" She regained her footing and leaned into the door with all her strength. The door slowly moved outward, giving a ton of resistance, like a wedge or something had been shoved underneath it. Finally, a crack opened, and she sidestepped out, immediately spotting the problem. There, stuck underneath the door like two rubber door jams, were two brown, leather shoes.

She huffed in exasperation and resumed her pursuit, her eyes passing from guest to guest entering and exiting cars, to bellhops unloading luggage. Where did they go?

She went to the valet desk. "Did you see two bald guys run out of the hotel? Through that revolving door. One of them doesn't have shoes."

"Like you?" the valet said, grinning at her bare feet.

"Yes, like me! Just tell me where they went!"

He recoiled defensively and pointed over his shoulder toward the sidewalk. "They went that way."

"Thanks," she said and sprinted in the direction he'd been pointing.

She reached the sidewalk and glanced back and forth as she caught her breath. To her right, she saw them climbing into a car parked at a meter. Cautiously, she crouched low and continued her pursuit. She had to be careful, though. They had no obvious weapons in the hotel, but now things had changed. No telling what they had in that car. She took cover behind a Chrysler minivan and peeked around the corner. The car was still sitting there, the engine off. If they were trying to escape, then what were they waiting for? Suddenly, all four doors opened, and four men stepped out. One of them was huge, towering over the other three. They went to the sidewalk, and she heard muffled conversation. *And one of them had a gun.*

Her dad was right. She wasn't Wonder Woman. God had her back, but she wasn't going to test him. No way was she taking on four guys, especially when one of them was armed. For all she knew, they were baiting her to their car so they could kidnap her.

Leaving the sidewalk, she went to the street, crouched low, and crept back toward the valet drop off, using the parked cars for cover. When she arrived at the last car in the line, she took cover behind the trunk and chanced a peek down the sidewalk. She watched them get back into the car. The engine revved, wheels barked, and a silver Ford Taurus lunged onto the street and sped away. It was too dark, and they were too far away to read the license plate.

She watched them as she gathered her thoughts. There wasn't anything left to do but call the police—and, of course, her dad.

She went back into the hotel lobby and found Ernesto standing there, dumbfounded, holding her shoes.

"You're sweating," Ernesto said, alarm registering on his bearded face. "And you're barefoot. What happened?"

She took her shoes from him, dusted the dirt off her feet, and slid back into them. "You need to call Skip. Tell him to fly back to Tucson and bring my dad here."

"But why? What's going on?"

"I'll tell you when Kevin finishes. Let's get back in there before he gets worried."

Chapter 19

Pete had arrived in Dallas just in time to see Kevin's lecture on his and Amari's theories as to why the carbon date performed on the Shroud of Turin was invalid. Given his special relationship with the speaker, Pete was allowed to view the lecture despite not having an invitation. After Kevin's lecture, the Shroud symposium broke for a two-hour lunch and Pete met up with Kevin, Amari, and Ernesto in the hotel lobby.

"Kevin, great job, by the way," Pete said. "But if you want to see the rest of this symposium, then we got no time for small talk. Now, on the way over I checked with the local traffic division. I was hoping maybe they wrote a ticket for a silver Ford Taurus in the area. If they had, then we'd have the license plate number. Even if the car was a rental, we'd still be able to get a copy of the driver's license from the rental agency."

"Excellent idea," Ernesto said. "Any luck?"

"I'm afraid not," Pete replied. "And I checked the sidewalk for anything like a restaurant receipt they might have dropped but found nothing."

"I didn't either," Amari said. "And the police were no help whatsoever. They just said it wasn't a crime to leave a hotel in a hurry."

"And the shoes they jammed under the revolving door?" Ernesto said. "That didn't strike them as odd?"

"Odd, yes," she said. "Crime, no."

"I can't say as I blame them," Pete said. "These big city cops have enough on their plate." He pointed to a surveillance camera mounted on the wall of the hotel lobby. "That's our best bet. Let me talk to the hotel manager and see what we can do about getting a look at those tapes. With any luck, we got footage of our suspects. If we can get a still of their faces, we'll put it over the wire and see if anyone bites. You never know. If these guys have criminal records, one of the police departments may recognize them."

****

The security office was the size of a walk-in closet, so Ernesto waited in his hotel room upstairs as Amari, Kevin, and Pete viewed the VHS tapes from the prior two days with Harold, head of hotel security. Harold was retirement age with a gray mustache over constantly upturned lips. He was one of those people who'd keep smiling after you told them you'd accidentally run over and killed their dog.

"Ma'am, I'm sorry my help wasn't any help," Harold said with his gap-toothed grin. "Bobby fills in for special events like this conference. On most days, it's just me and the weekend guy."

"He might have helped more if I had time to explain," she said. "He didn't know what happened over in Europe."

"So you were telling me," Harold said. "I can see why those fellas upset you. And you know, after you described them to me, I remembered seeing them in the lobby. They stood out. Most people their age have long hair, like Dr. Brenner over here," he said, casting a pleasant nod at Kevin. "Not shaved off like those two. They both had a funny expression on their faces too."

"That's great," Pete said. "Tell us anything you can remember."

"I remember it was Tuesday. They came in through the front door at about 1:30. I'm sorry to say we don't have a camera in the Austin Ballroom. All we have is the one in the lobby. Now, I saw them leave the Austin Ballroom maybe an hour and a half later. But I never watched them go inside. Just saw them in the lobby. I assumed they had tickets, so I thought nothing of it."

"Then they must have snuck in," Kevin said. "Mostly only scientists with credentials were allowed to attend. And these scientists paid for the entire conference, not just for an hour."

"Kevin's lecture was at two," she said.

"Sounds like they may be fans of his," Pete said. "They watched his lecture and then left. Show us on the tape, Harold. Let's get a look at them."

Harold pulled the plastic VHS tape from a shelf and confirmed the date written in blue ink on the white label. Several other dates preceding the current date had been crossed out with a black marker. "We keep these tapes for a week and then erase them with new footage if nothing exciting happens. Now, we record this using the Super Long Play mode, so we can squeeze eight hours out of a tape. That way we only change it three times a day. Of course, there's a drawback to that."

"Grainy video," Kevin said.

"It's better than nothing," Amari replied.

"Unfortunately, it makes it hard to get a decent still shot we can use for identification purposes," Pete said.

"Sorry guys." Harold inserted the tape into the VCR recorder. "There's only one of us on duty. We can't spend all our time changing these tapes out every two hours."

"I understand," Pete said. "So let's see what you've got."

Harold hit the Rewind button. He stopped when he found the right time. The date stamp on the bottom of the screen read: Sept. 26, 1989, 1:25 p.m.

They watched the tape as various guests and bellhops entered and exited the front sliding door, some carrying luggage, others with kids in tow. Suddenly, the two cult members appeared. "There! That's them," Amari said, her voice shrill with excitement.

Harold stopped the tape. A blurry image of two men with buzz cut hair was frozen on the flickering screen, their faces too grainy to get all the features down. One had black hair, the other blond. Actually, he could be a redhead for all they knew. The hair was too short to tell.

"You sure that's them?" Pete said.

"Yes, I'm sure," she said. "I never forget a face. Even if it's fuzzy. Hair's the same. One blond, the other's hair was black. They wore the same clothes too."

"I remember those guys now," Kevin said. "They were standing off to the side. I remember them because they had a tape recorder."

"So they recorded your lecture?" Pete asked.

"Looked like they were," Kevin said. "It was the one about Einstein–Rosen bridges."

Pete furrowed his brows. "What's that?"

"Traversable Lorentzian wormholes," Kevin clarified. "It could explain the radiation burst that formed the image."

"I noticed from your lecture today one of those scientists shared your radiation angle," Pete said. "The guy with the French accent."

"Dr. Rinaudo," Kevin said. "He's the head of Nuclear medicine at Montpellier Cancer Institute over in France. I talked to him this summer while I was over there. He's got the same take as I do. Alpha particles not only enriched the carbon-14 and made the Shroud date younger, but they also caused the 3-D image."

"And the negative photographic image," Amari said.

"That's right," Kevin said. "Only radiation could cause that image."

"Dr. Rinaudo share your opinion about the wormholes?" Pete asked.

"Not exactly," Kevin replied. "That idea came from a *theoretical* physicist friend of mine. That's why it's just a theory."

"Somebody thinks your theory's valid," Pete said. "Enough to record it with a tape recorder."

"Guess so," Kevin said. "I published a paper about that over the summer. Maybe they read it and wanted to hear it in person."

"I told you," Amari said. "There's crazies out there that take you seriously."

"I was serious. It's valid science," Kevin said defensively. "I didn't make this stuff up. I'm not that creative."

"All right guys," Pete said. "Whether it's true or not isn't the point. What matters is someone out there does believe it. Enough to sneak into a conference they weren't invited to. Enough to try to steal the Shroud itself—and for some reason turn around and try to steal a replica."

"What?" Harold asked, only now his smile had faded.

"Never mind," Pete said. "That's just a theory too."

"Fast-Forward," she said. "Let's see if we can spot them leaving."

Harold forwarded the tape until they saw the two guys exit the Austin Ball Room and reenter the lobby at 2:49 p.m. Next, they left the hotel altogether.

"My lecture lasted forty-five minutes," Kevin said. "It started at two."

"So these guys left right after," Pete said. "They got what they came for and left. They were only interested in you."

"And they tried to come the next evening," she said. "Right as Kevin started his second lecture."

"I can tell you this," Harold said. "They didn't show up today. After you talked to the police, I had my eyes peeled for them. If they came, they were wearing wigs."

"I didn't see them either," she said.

"Me neither," Kevin said.

"I wouldn't show either if I were them," Pete said. "Not after the scene they made high-tailing it out the front door."

"And leaving their shoes as a door jam," Kevin said.

"The jig was up," Pete said. "They knew we were looking for them. At any rate, we've got a rough idea what they look like, so that's something. Harold, you think you can make us a copy of that tape?"

"No problem. I make them for the police from time to time."

"That would be great," Pete said. "Hey, one more thing. What are the odds I can take those shoes you found lodged under the revolving door?"

"I believe they're in Lost and Found."

"Then I think I'll claim them," Pete said. "Thanks again for your help."

Chapter 20

"I don't understand," Calvin said. As was often the case, his expression was devoid of emotion. Sometimes the medication caused this, that is when he decided to take it—not that the medication helped anyway. Calvin was beyond the help of a few pills. And he was particularly ripe today, the sharp edge of body odor a sting to Adrian's nostrils. His hair was oily with dandruff flakes, and his clothes hadn't been changed in days.

"We haven't gotten them yet, but we will," Adrian assured him.

"And 876 and 762? Are they still in Europe?"

"Yes, I spoke to them personally," Adrian lied. "They called me on Ian's telephone. Security was tighter than expected. But they seemed optimistic. Only, it's going to take some time."

"Perhaps I should reach out to my old friend. If anyone can help, it is he."

"No, Calvin. I still don't think that's a good idea." It was a terrible idea. Doing so would immediately alert the police as to who was behind the attempted burglaries, not only in Europe but also at the Galliano estate in Fresno. Granted, the police had no idea as to Calvin's whereabouts. Still, it was too risky.

Calvin released a weary sigh. "Our current efforts are ineffective. It is time for a new strategy."

"You told me your friend had no influence in Oviedo."

"We haven't spoken in years. Perhaps he has gained it now."

"Are you sure you have to have the Sudarium too? Wouldn't the Shroud be sufficient?"

Calvin tightened his eyes, his normally flat expression morphing into anger. In a flash, he lashed out and slapped Adrian hard on the cheek. "I told you already! It was in the tomb! It is part of the machine. I must have it. Without all the parts, the apparatus will not function!"

Adrian bit back his anger, quelling his intense urge to strike back. "Of course, Calvin." He winced from the burning pain on his cheek. "Please forgive me. I wasn't thinking."

Moments later, Calvin's angry expression melted into one of pity. He reached out and caressed Adrian's reddened cheek. "Shhhh, no need for that. We do not all hear his voice. We are not all called to understand."

Adrian bowed his head in reverence. "Only you are the Divine Conduit." It was the same appeasing line he always used when Calvin frequently flew into a sudden, unexpected fit of rage.

"Jesus did not enter heaven spiritually, but in the flesh, as I must do also. It was no accident the Shroud of Turin and Sudarium have survived all these years. No, it is by providence. They were left for me. Otherwise, the seed of humanity would be lost to the Recycling."

"We'll get the Shroud. Like you said, it's divine providence," Adrian said, anything to defuse the situation. The last thing he needed was for Calvin to kick him to the curb now—not after he'd invested so much.

"We have been too timid," Calvin said resolutely. "That is why we have failed."

Adrian stared back in disbelieve, unable to reply. How could they have been any bolder?

"My spies have returned from Dallas. They recorded Dr. Brenner's lecture. After hearing it, there is no doubt in my mind. It is time we removed the veil," Calvin said, nodding his head with confidence. "We must awake the new Adam. It is time we made first contact."

****

Kevin sat across from Amari under an umbrella shade next to her swimming pool. Books about religious cults were haphazardly scattered atop the patio table. Four books had been checked out from the city library, and three had been special-ordered from Waldenbooks. There were dozens of case studies within those books, but what they were specifically looking for was information about UFO cults. They were trying to find similarities that might help them find the culprits, or at least eliminate some possibilities.

"Wow," she said as she read from one of the books. "Did you know that Scientologists believe that we're possessed by alien spirits who came to Earth 75 million years ago? L. Ron Hubbard taught that an alien named Xenu was the dictator of a galactic confederacy of 76 planets. There was a population problem, so Xenu brought a bunch of them to Earth and stacked them up around volcanos and blew them up with hydrogen bombs. So now a goal of Scientology is to rid yourself of the spirits they call thetans by helping each other recall the painful memories of being blown up."

"Man," Kevin said. "What was L. Ron Hubbard smoking?"

"Whatever it was, he wasn't the only one smoking it. There's other cults too." She flipped the pages in her notebook and recounted some of her research. "There's this Aetherius Society founded about thirty-five years ago. They claim to have contact with aliens they call the Cosmic Masters. More recently, a cult called the Ashtar Galactic Command claims they channel an alien named Ashtar Sheran. Then there's this Cosmic Circle of Fellowship. They believe in interdimensional travel by getting really relaxed."

"So they open up wormholes by chillin' out," he said with a thoughtful expression. "Sounds like they're smoking something too. You got any idea how much negative energy it takes to open a wormhole? Only God could pull something like that off."

"Yes, but these guys are delusional. Just like this cult founded nine years ago called Fiat Lux. Their leader claims to channel Jesus and his mother, Mary. They think an alien ship is going to save them from the apocalypse. Then the earth is going to be transformed into a paradise they call the Amora."

"That's pretty out there too."

"It's not either." She clapped her book closed and tossed it onto the table. "It sounds a lot like that guy we interviewed in Turin. Only this guy was babbling something about technology. He implied there was no magic, no miracles, only technology—ultimate technology."

"I know the type. They think angels get around on spaceships."

"I know, I remember you telling me about that when I first met you."

152

"Yeah, but I was just messing with you. I was repeating stuff I read. But these guys really believe it. Must be their way of making religion more 21st century. Their parents take them to church on Sunday morning, then they go home and watch reruns of Star Trek and Lost in Space. If you got a weak mind, that's a recipe for some weird beliefs."

"You're calling them weak-minded? You're a genius, and I've heard you talk about that kind of stuff."

"The difference between them and me is I ain't worshiping, just speculating. It's not that far-fetched if you think about it. I mean, why wouldn't God use technology to his advantage? He made everything, didn't he? The Book of Revelation says that when Jesus returns, everybody will see him coming in the clouds. Now they can. Just about everybody's got a television. It'll be shown all over the world. It'll be breaking news, and everyone will watch it live. That was never possible until now."

"Good point. I've thought about that too. But what if you're not around a TV? Then you're going to miss it."

"I think someday most people will have a TV in their pocket. And it won't be just a TV. It'll be a phone too. And not just a phone, but a TV phone. You could be in Italy, and I could be in Tucson, and we can talk to each other face to face. I think it'll be a computer too. I bet you could even play games on it. You could certainly use it to watch breaking news about Jesus coming in the clouds."

"Oh, come on, Kevin. All that can't fit inside your pocket."

"A supercomputer that fits in the palm of your hand. And if that sounds like a miracle to you, can you imagine what the people from the Bible would think about life today? They'd think TV and that car of yours are miracles from God. Not to mention airplanes and air-conditioning. I'm telling you, I don't think technology is a fluke. I think it's part of God's plan. For thousands of years, we stood still. Then all of a sudden, one day we're using a horse and carriage, and seventy-five years later we put a man on the moon. It's a blink of an eye compared to history. That's no coincidence. It's providence. We're setting the stage for the second coming. We're setting the stage for Jesus' millennial reign. These guys think the same way, only they take it to the extreme and involve other planets with even more advanced technology."

"Ultimate technology, according to that guy in Turin. But that's not all they need. Something about the power of the earth."

"Yeah, that's a new age thing. They think the earth is wrapped in some sort of energy grid. I've read a book about it. A friend of mine from the geology department gave it to me. He said it was pseudoscience. He implied that's why I'd enjoy it."

"And did you?"

"It was interesting, but he's right, it's all crap."

"Whether it's crap or not isn't the point. If a UFO cult believed it, then maybe it'll help us figure out who they are. Tell me about this grid."

"Some people noticed UFO sightings occur more frequently along what they refer to as ley lines."

"Ley lines?"

"Energy is supposed to be more focused along these lines. The lines make up a grid pattern around the planet. They came up with this idea when they noticed ancient monuments like the pyramids and Stonehenge seemed to line up when you look at them on a map. Supposedly, UFO sightings happen a lot along these lines. I'll bring you the book if you want to read it."

"I don't want to read it, but I need to. That guy mentioned Earth's energy. He had to be talking about the same thing. What if their home sits on top of one of those lines? It would definitely narrow the search area."

"It might. If these nut jobs were going to set up shop, I'd say a ley line was prime real estate. I'll bring you the book. It's even got a map of those lines in the appendix. Let me run home and get it."

****

Amari answer the door on the second ring. "There you are," she said to Kevin. "What took you so long? I was about to call."

"Here's the book," he said and handed it to her.

"What's with the videotape?"

Kevin held up the VCR tape. "This is what took me so long." The expression on his face was a blend of fascination and fear. "You gotta see this. And call your dad. He needs to see this too."

Chapter 21

It was a cloudless night sky, the stars shining brightly into the pyramid-shaped atrium. Calvin lay prone on a mattress laid out on the floor, gazing into the heavens in a meditative trance, mumbling incoherent babble. Astral projection was an attempt to disembody the soul and leave the confines of the earth to communicate with aliens, or in Calvin's mind, to the angels of God.

Adrian cleared his throat to break Calvin's trance. "You asked to speak with me?"

Calvin sat up and studied Adrian. At first, he seemed baffled by the intrusion, almost as if he didn't recognize the face. A moment later, his eyes flickered with recollection. "Yes, Adrian, I did indeed summon you."

"I came as soon as I was told. Is there something you need to tell me?"

"Yes, Adrian, there is. I have done something without your knowledge. As second in charge, I feel like you should know."

"Yes, I'm listening." Adrian braced himself. There was no telling what he had done now.

"Lieutenant 332 and I made a video tape."

"A tape? What kind of tape?"

"We have made first contact."

"What do you mean, first contact?"

"With the new Adam, of course."

Adrian fought to control his frustration. Calvin was a fool. One false move and the FBI would be on their compound like vultures to a carcass. "Calvin, what have you done? Please tell me you didn't tell him to come here. Did you give him our location?"

"I sent my scouts to him. He was speaking at a symposium in Texas."

Panic surged. Adrian fought to maintain composure. "Yes, you told me that, but they didn't speak to him, did they? I thought we agreed you would consult me first."

"I don't require your permission, Adrian. My permission comes from on high."

Adrian could bite his tongue no longer. "You do realize that trying to steal the Shroud of Turin is a crime. We could all go to jail. Please, Calvin, I'm begging you. You're wise to the way of the heavens, but I'm wise to the way of this world. Please consult me before you do anything else."

Calvin narrowed his eyelids into angry slits. He came off the mattress and shoved Adrian. "Get behind me, Satan!" He lashed out with a clenched fist, but Adrian was too fast, lurching backward just in time.

"Calvin, please, calm down."

"The devil seeks to control you! Resist him, and he will flee!"

"Please. Hear me out."

Calvin shouted, his face red with rage. "Where is the Shroud, Adrian? Where?"

Suddenly, Calvin fell silent and stalked off toward the exit. He paused, contemplating his words. Finally, he spoke. "Adrian," he said with eerie calm. It was creepy how he could turn off emotion like a faucet. "Go and pray. Pray to the Evolved Entity. Pray to his son, Christ Jesus. Then Satan will flee you. Tomorrow is another day," he said and headed down the stairs.

Like Dr. Jekyll and Mr. Hyde, Adrian thought. And tomorrow he'd act like nothing had ever happened. "There has got to be an easier way," Adrian mumbled to himself. "There's got to be another way to get into that safe.

Chapter 22

Amari opened the door and let Pete into the foyer of her home. He limped in, feeling the bite after climbing the steps to her front porch. Stairs were always the hardest. Ernesto had made an appointment to see a surgeon to discuss his hip replacement. The sooner the better.

"You want some ibuprofen or something?" Amari asked.

"I'll pass, but thanks anyway. All those do is give me a stomach ache on top of the hip pain. So where's this tape you told me about?"

"In here," she said. "Have a seat on the couch, and I'll get it."

Pete went into the den and admired the Navajo chief's blanket his daughter had just completed. It hung on the wall next to a picture of her mother, Haseya, Pete's ex-wife of nearly thirty years. Haseya's old loom stood in the corner of the room with another creation just begun, spools of yarn sitting on the floor underneath. His daughter was gifted at weaving most anything. She knew her stuff, but not like her mother. That woman was a master at the craft.

Amari came into the den using a tissue as a shield from her own fingerprints. "Kevin got his prints on it already. You should still be able to lift the prints that aren't his. By the way, about those shoes from the hotel," she said. "Find anything useful?"

"I had George take them by the lab and check for prints. Unfortunately, the hotel staff made a mess of them. Everything was smudged and who knows what came from who."

"That's too bad." She showed Pete the label affixed to the VHS tape. "It says for Dr. Brenner's eyes only."

Kevin came out of the bathroom and joined them in the den. "I chose to ignore those instructions. This is too good not to share."

"Did he send a letter with this or just the tape?" Pete asked.

"Just the tape," Kevin said. "But I got a feeling I'll be hearing more from him. Watch the tape, and you'll see what I mean. And get Jenny in here. This is right up her alley."

"I'm already here," Jenny said as she walked up behind Kevin. "I wouldn't miss this for the world."

"Should I make popcorn?" Amari asked.

"Amari, just play the tape, would you?" Pete said. "Ernesto's not paying me to eat popcorn."

"You're no fun," his daughter replied and loaded the tape into the VCR using the tissue.

The four sat on the L-shaped sectional couch and waited for the show to begin. Amari scooted to the edge of her seat, feeling the thrill of eager anticipation. Apparently, Kevin had refused to show it to her until Pete was there, just in case the VHS player ate the tape or something.

The screen flickered to life. A man who appeared to be in his late thirties stared into the camera. His unshaven face had about two days' worth of stubble. He had dirty-blond hair, disheveled and cowlicked like he'd just fallen out of bed. White specks of dandruff spotted the shoulders of his black T-shirt. He wasn't looking into the camera but seemed to focus on the edge of the lens. His left eyebrow was hiked higher than the other.

"Greetings, Dr. Brenner." He forced a tight smile. Other than the slight curve of his lips, his expression seemed flat, devoid of emotion, reminding Pete of a department store mannequin. "We have been watching world events, searching for a heavenly sign, in hopeful anticipation that we might discover the one who was called." Despite his disheveled appearance, the tone of his voice was smug and arrogant. "Several months ago, one of my fold discovered you while listening to your interview on NPR. We have since researched you, read your papers, and watched your lecture. We have no doubt that you are the one. There is no question as to your true identity."

His left brow fell in line with the right one, but his eyes drifted down to his extended thumb. He picked at his thumb's cuticle, seemingly unaware of the camera. He brought his thumb to his teeth and chewed, his eyes darting around the room like he'd suddenly forgotten where he was. The screen flickered, and the camera stopped filming, then immediately flashed back on. Now the man's eyes were fixed onto the camera lens.

"When you were a child, you spake as a child, and you understood as a child, and you thought as a child. Now that you are a man, you must put away childish things. You must embrace your divine destiny. Look closely at me, Dr. Brenner. Nobody else can see it but you, and you alone, because you have been chosen. Only you can see the glow of my aura."

"What?" Amari hit the Pause button. "His aura? He's talking nonsense. Kevin, is this some kind of joke? Where did you get this tape? You put one of your buddies up to this, didn't you?"

"Amari, I promise, hand to the Bible," Kevin said. "If this is a joke, then the jokes on me too."

"Not so fast," Pete said. "I think this may be for real. He just explained why they were at the Dallas conference. Maybe they wanted to talk to him, but you scared them off.

"I've never seen one this bad before," Jenny interrupted, her eyes sparkling with fascinated wonder. "I've read about them, but to actually see one in person. This is really cool."

"Care to enlighten us?" Pete said. "What's your diagnosis?"

"He's clearly delusional. It's a kind of psychosis. He can't tell the difference between imagination and reality. And he's obviously schizophrenic. That goes hand in hand with delusional disorder. I mean, most people with schizophrenia have delusions, but this guy is off the scale."

"So you really think he's a schitzo?" Pete said.

"Well, sure. Didn't you notice he has practically no emotional expression on his face? His poor hygiene? The way he lost track of his thoughts. They had to stop rolling the camera and let him start over."

"I still say this is a joke," Amari said. "Kevin, who gave you this tape?"

"I told you, it was mailed to me," he said and pulled brown wrapping paper from his pocket. A mischievous grin spread across his lips. "Here's the return address."

"Let me see that," Pete said, taking the paper from Kevin's hand. "One, two, three, four, Orion Belt Road. New Canaan, Milky Way, 10101."

"Kevin," Amari said with a scolding tone. "You're grinning."

Kevin raised his hands defensively. "I'm grinning because of the return address. I swear, I had nothing to do with this."

"All right, you two," Pete said. "Can we just watch the rest of this?"

"Fine," Amari said. She pointed the remote and hit Play.

"Search your heart, Dr. Brenner, and you will know this to be true. Only you can comprehend ultimate technology. Only you can serve as engineer." He reached out his hand, and someone handed him a stack of papers held together with a binder. He held the report up to the camera— Kevin's report about the wormholes. "Only you can construct heaven's gate. You will build it, and I shall pass through."

Amari snatched up the remote control and hit the pause button. "I knew it! Kevin, I told you somebody out there would believe you."

"Well, I didn't mean for *him* to read it," Kevin defensively replied. "I wrote that for other scientists. How'd he get ahold of that anyway?"

"I don't know," she said. "But he got it, and now he believes it."

"So that's what all this is about," Pete said.

"Must be why they're after the Shroud," Kevin said. "Maybe they figure it's got something to do with the wormhole. This ultimate technology he mentioned. I wonder if he thinks the *Shroud* opened the wormhole."

"I can't believe this is happening," Amari said. "I knew that paper of yours was controversial, but this?"

"Huh," Kevin said with a thoughtful scowl on his face. "This is all my fault."

Amari seemed to notice the hurt in his eyes. She reached over and drew him in for a hug. "No, Kevin, it's not. You only wrote the truth. Besides, you said the wormhole theory wasn't yours anyway."

"That's true," he said. "I only elaborated on it. But I had no idea this would happen."

"Nobody could have known that," Pete said. "God called you to find the truth. What people do with that information is beyond your control."

"He's right," Jenny said. "These people are grasping at straws, anything they can find to affirm their beliefs. They could just as easily latched onto something else and caused even more trouble."

"The important thing now is to catch them before they cause any more trouble," Pete said.

"This may be a blessing in disguise," Jenny said. "Now maybe we can stop them before it's too late."

"What are you talking about?" Amari asked. "Before what's too late?"

"If this doesn't go the way they plan," Jenny said, "it could escalate into something much worse."

"How could this get any worse?" Kevin asked.

"Have you ever heard of Jim Jones?" Jenny replied.

"Are you talking about the mass suicide in Guyana?" Pete asked.

"Yes," Jenny said. "That's a worst-case scenario, but with people like this, you never know. It already happened once in Turin—when the guy jumped out of the window. According to their theology, suicide seems to be an option."

"Perfect," Amari said, shaking her head in dismay, still trying to get the image of the dead cult member in Turin out of her head..

"Then we need to crack this case before that happens," Pete said.

"And get them the help they need," Amari said.

"Push that Play button," Pete said. "Let's see if we can find any more clues."

The screen flickered back into motion. "In God's divine scheme for the universe, it seems that our paths have converged, and it is here, at the nexus. I will pass into New Canaan, and from there I shall return for you and your bride, the new Eve. From your loins, a great generation will be spawned, numerous as the stars in the sky and the sand on the seashore. If only you will listen to God's voice, then you will know this to be true. Heed that voice, Dr. Brenner. I will contact you later with further instructions. I will do so in a way that only you can comprehend." The screen flickered, and the screen turned to static.

Amari's eyes grew wide with alarm. "His bride?" She gave Kevin a stern look. "I hope he's talking about me."

"Well, that explains it," Pete said.

"Explains what?" Amari replied.

"It explains why the cult member's heart rate shot up when I mentioned your name. He just realized he was in the presence of holiness—the Eve of creation."

"What? That's crazy," Amari said.

"Like I said," Jenny replied. "He's delusional. That's not uncommon with schizophrenia, especially delusions of religious divinity. Did you notice how he mentioned his *aura*? He sees himself as the next best thing to Jesus. Only his theology is a mix of Christianity and science fiction."

"Like you'd expect with a UFO cult," Amari said.

"What kind of nut job would join such a crazy group?" Pete asked. "Who in their right mind would follow this guy?"

"That's what puzzles me," Jenny said. "Most schizophrenics have trouble with organization. He might be the mouthpiece, but he's obviously getting some help."

"Upper management?" Pete suggested. "Someone helping him keep things together."

"That's my guess," Jenny replied.

"So what about the people who follow him?" Pete asked. "Who'd be crazy enough to call this guy their spiritual leader?"

"People with issues, obviously," Jenny said. "But not necessarily insane. Gullible and weak-minded, but not insane in the classical sense. I think these people just want to be loved. They need to belong something bigger than they are, like having a special purpose in God's eyes. And if that's what their heart desires, and if they're gullible at the same time, then they could easily be brainwashed if their leader has enough charisma. And then once they've joined the cult, they have to cut ties with family and friends. That way, the cult is the only family they have left. Under circumstances like this, it's not easy to get out, even if the teaching does get a little weird."

"And remember, they've got no money," Pete said. "Most cults make people sell everything they own and give the money to the leader."

"Exactly," Jenny said. "But it's not just about living expenses. If they left the cult, not only would they be losing the only family they had, but they'd feel like they've abandoned God's purpose in their lives. They would fear eternal damnation. That's a powerful motive to stay."

"And motive enough to die for the cause," Pete said.

"For them, it would be a blessing," Jenny said. "Sort of like how terrorists have no problem dying for their cause. They trade their meager earthly life for eternal rewards."

"That's not good," Pete said. "Let's say we found their house and wanted to ask a few questions. You think it'd be dangerous?"

"Absolutely," Jenny replied. "I wouldn't go to their house without a SWAT team."

"Then we need to proceed cautiously," Pete said. "If we find out where they live, we'll alert the local authorities, or at the very least bring Bonelli and Parker."

"You better bring more than that," Jenny said. "Maybe the FBI or something. For all we know, there could be a hundred of them."

"We'll cross that bridge later," Pete said. "Right now, we just gotta locate them. That's the hard part. So, Amari, you and Kevin find any clues in all those books you been reading?"

"I got one idea," she said. "Kevin, hand him that book, would you?"

Pete took the book from Kevin and eyed it skeptically. *The Universal Pulse: Earth's Energy Grid*, by Brent Cagle." He fanned the pages. "Why don't you give me the quick summary."

"Just to clarify," Kevin said. "I didn't buy that book. A geologist friend of mine gave it to me."

"He's a geology professor at the university," Amari said. "What was his name again?"

"Berry Stone," Kevin said and snorted a laugh. "No pun intended."

Pete didn't react.

"Stone?" Kevin said. "He studies stones for a living?"

"Yeah, yeah, I get it," Pete said. "So what about him?"

"Rocky gave me this book," Kevin said.

"I thought you said his name was Berry?" Pete replied.

"His nickname's Rocky," Kevin said. "Get it? Rocky Stone? Anyway, he gave me that book. He said I might enjoy it because I like a good laugh. It's all crap, really. Just pseudoscience."

"So why is this supposed to be helpful?" Pete asked.

"Because it's crazy, that's why," Kevin replied. "And so are these loons that tried to steal the Shroud. See, that book talks about the earth's energy and how it's concentrated along grid lines. Ley lines is the technical term for them. And according to that book, most of the UFO sightings happen along one of those lines. They think maybe the earth's energy give them power for space travel or even to open up a wormhole, so they can get back home."

Amari took the book from him and flipped to the index. She pointed to a map of the world that was overlaid with grid lines. "I bet this cult has a house on top of one of these lines."

Pete made a doubtful scowl. "That's the craziest thing I've ever heard."

"And you also said the cult member in Turin was the craziest person you'd ever met," she replied defensively. "If someone like that was looking for real estate, they'd buy a house on top of a ley line."

"Okay, maybe they would," Pete said. "Assuming they'd read this book. But first off, this map is so small, there's no way to pinpoint anything. We'd need exact coordinates. On top of that, do you have any idea how many miles of real estate you're talking about?"

"Rocky's got a more detailed map," Kevin offered. "He did some serious research on the theory before he gave up and decided it was bogus."

"Even if his maps are more accurate," Pete said, "we're still talking about thousands of miles to cover, and we have no idea what we're looking for."

Amari sighed and sank back into the couch. "I know, it's a long shot. Unfortunately, it's the only clue I've got."

"Not the only one," Pete said. "You mentioned checking out some of those New Age Churches. That's a great idea. We'll check with some of those next. Maybe someone there would recognize the flying saucer tattoo. I can think of one New Age church here in Tucson. I'll call and see if I can set up a meeting with the pastor. If he doesn't know anything, maybe he'll know of some churches that might."

Chapter 23

After a fruitless meeting with the pastor of the Unity Center of Peace, Pete and his daughter stood in the parking lot next to her car. The New Age church was no more than a rented space in a strip mall, right next to the empty shell of an old out-of-business Kmart. The pastor had agreed to meet them there before the Wednesday evening service.

"Well, that was a waste of time," Pete said. "I thought they were the weird ones. They acted like we were the ones out of our minds."

"You feel like driving up to Phoenix?" she said, looking at the list of churches the pastor had recommended.

Pete didn't relish the long drive with such slim odds of a payoff. "Two hours there, two hours back? I doubt it would pan out. These guys we're looking for aren't mainstream. They don't advertise in the Yellow Pages."

"Maybe not," she said. "But it's worth a few long-distance calls. I've got a copy of the Phoenix phone book at home. I'll look up the numbers and make some calls. What I can't find in the book, I can get from the operator."

Suddenly, a faint ringing sound chimed from nowhere. It rang again, and Pete searched for the source.

"Oh, that's my new phone!" She reached into her purse. "My first call ever!"

"Your phone?"

She pulled a small black device from her purse. "Yeah, Ernesto bought this for me. It just came out. It's called a Motorola Micro TAC. Cost three thousand bucks, but look, the battery is so small you don't need to carry that heavy bag around."

"I'll be danged," Pete said. "What'll they come up with next?"

The phone rang again.

"Well, answer the thing."

She extended the black antenna and flipped open a lid that seemed to be the mouthpiece. "Hello?" she practically yelled into the phone. "Can you hear me?"

Pete could hear a voice coming from the mouthpiece but couldn't make out the words.

"Hey, Ernesto. Yeah, it really works. It's awesome. So what's up?" She listened for a moment, then made a horrified face. "When? Is he calling back?" She listened for a few seconds and said, "Can you send Skip down to pick us up? We need to be there when he calls again." She nodded her head as she listened. "Okay, great. I'll tell him. See you soon." She flipped the lid shut.

"Tell me what?" Pete asked.

"Ernesto got this crazy call."

"About what?"

"Some guy who wants to borrow the Shroud."

"It must be the same guy on Kevin's tape."

"I don't know. Probably. We'll bring the tape with us and see if the voices match."

170

****

Ernesto's servant, Miranda, set a platter of finger sandwiches on the large, round, mosaic tile kitchen table. Pete and his daughter had shown up just in time for lunch. Along with Ernesto, Bonelli, and Parker, they sat around the table, every eye focused on the answering machine.

"Let's hear it," Pete said and reached for a tuna sandwich.

"Okay," Ernesto said. "Brace yourself. It's a little bizarre."

"If it's who I think it is, I'm sure it is," Pete said. "Wait till you get a load of the videotape. After lunch, we'll play it and compare the two voices."

"I doubt you'll need a side by side comparison," Ernesto said. "His voice is unmistakable. You'll see what I mean." He pressed Play to start the recording.

"Be of good cheer, Ernesto, for the Lord has seen your good works and found you worthy of his plan. Hear me and heed my words. The survival of humanity depends upon your cooperation."

Amari pressed the Pause button on the answering machine. "That's him. I'd know that voice anywhere."

"I agree," Pete said. "It's the same guy. Let's hear what else he has to say." He pressed the Play button, and the recording continued.

"It is no secret that you are a man of great wealth, a man of compelling influence with the Vatican. I understand you are friends with the cardinal who presides over the cathedral in Turin, the one which houses the Shroud in which Jesus was buried. Through this cloth, his body passed through during the resurrection. Now, bear with me because this may sound strange on the surface, but I would like to ask a favor, not just for me, but for the future of mankind. In short, I would like to borrow the Shroud of Turin. As well as the Sudarium of Oviedo. I must have both. I need you to ask permission to borrow them. Once they have completed their purpose, you have my word, they will be returned with only minimal damage. I will give you three days to consider my request. Pray to the Lord for his guidance. But you must first open your heart to receive his message. I will call again in three days." The line went dead.

"Minimal damage?" Amari said. "He can't be serious."

"I know," Ernesto said. "His request is preposterous."

"What a weirdo," Parker said.

"Wait till you get a load of the videotape," she said. "He's much creepier in person."

"I know that voice," Ernesto said. "It sounds so familiar, but I just can't place it."

"Sounds like he knows you too," Bonelli said.

"Maybe someone you met in college," Parker offered.

"You know any schizo's in college?" Amari asked.

"Pardon?"

"Schizophrenics," Pete said.

Ernesto's posture stiffened, and his mouth fell open in dismay.

"Ernesto?" she said. "What is it?"

"Lord have mercy," Ernesto managed to say. "That can only be Calvin."

Chapter 24

As Ernesto viewed Kevin's videotape, he sat with his hand cupped over his mouth, his expression a mixture of shock and pity. When the tape had finished, Pete hit the stop button, and everybody in the room waited for his response.

"The poor man," Ernesto finally said. "He looks awful."

"So it is him," Amari said.

"I'm afraid so," he said, nodding his head in dismay. "He looks so dirty and unkempt. This is not the Calvin I remember. He even talks differently. He was humble when I knew him, but now . . ."

"Now he's delusional," she said. "And it's gone to his head. It's like he thinks he's the new Messiah or something."

Ernesto sank back into the couch and silently contemplated the strange reality he'd just witnessed. "His full name is Calvin Nettles," he finally said. "He wasn't a college friend, but rather the son of one of my father's friends. We were merely acquaintances. I would only see him on social occasions. I haven't heard from him since he went . . ."

"Went where?" she prodded him. "Where did he go?"

"To a mental asylum."

"That's where he belongs," Pete said. "Only somehow he got out."

"Yes, he was deeply disturbed," Ernesto said. "Now you see why we were only acquaintances. His sister's wedding was the last time I saw him. My father had died by then, but because I remained in the same social circles, I was invited to the wedding. It was several years ago."

"I see," Pete said. "So if you haven't seen him in so long, then why is he calling you now? Why would he assume you could lay hands on the Shroud?"

"Because . . .." Ernesto sighed as if reliving a disturbing memory. "I'm partly to blame for his delusion."

"Come again?" Pete said.

"The last time we talked, I had been reading reports published by members of the Shroud of Turin Research Project. I was so excited by what I'd found. I remembered telling him all about it at the wedding. I think it was 1980. He seemed very intrigued, so I told him where he could find more information. At least that's the way I remember things. It was nine years ago, after all. That was the last time I spoke with him."

"Would he know you have a replica of the Shroud in your house?" Pete asked.

"My involvement with the Shroud is no secret, especially in a town the size of Fresno. I've been in the newspapers and even appeared on the local television news. My influence with the Cardinal of Turin was mentioned as well. And of course, since we ran in the same social circles, he had to be aware of my connections."

"Do you still stay in this social circle?" Amari asked. "Can you get us in touch with Calvin's dad? Maybe he knows where his son lives."

"I've been so involved with the children and my charities. I haven't attended any parties lately, but I do still have his address and phone number, assuming he hasn't changed it."

"Then I'd like to talk to Calvin's father," Pete said. "With any luck, he can help us find his son. But something tells me they aren't very close."

"You're right about that," Ernesto said. "They had a bit of a falling out."

"Even so, if you could give me that address, we'll go talk with him," Pete said.

"Of course," Ernest said. "I'll get it for you."

"That's great," Pete said. "In the meantime, I'm going to call in a favor from a guy I know in the FBI. When this Calvin guy calls you back, I'm going to see if we can trace his call."

****

John Nettles raked his fingers through hair-plugged, Grecian Formula-dyed hair. "My God, what's happened to him?" he said after viewing the videotape, the alarm barely registering on his tight, plastic surgery-tightened face. "He's aged so much since I saw him last. He looks twenty years older."

"You see why I didn't want to meet at the country club?" Pete said. "I wanted you to see this for yourself. That way you'd know how serious this was. Your son needs help. And if he doesn't get it soon, there's no telling what will happen to him."

"He looks gaunt—malnourished," Nettles said. "He used to be chubby as a young man."

"It's certainly not the way I remember him," Ernesto said.

"He looks like crap," Amari replied, just before catching Pete's look of admonishment. "Well, I'm sorry, but he does."

"She's right, he does look awful," Nettles admitted. "He needs to be back on his medication. He did better as long as he followed the doctor's orders."

"So help us find him," Pete said. "We'll get him the help he needs."·

Mr. Nettles stood, paced over to the wall, and thoughtfully inspected one of the paintings next to the fireplace. "Ernesto, your father always loved Van Gogh. I remember when he bought the original at a Sotheby auction. Paid a fortune for it. This is obviously a print."

"I confess it is a print," Ernesto said. "I sold the original for an even larger fortune."

"I'm glad your father wasn't alive to see that," Nettles said. "He loved that painting."

"He gave half that money to The Salvation Army," Amari said. "The other half went to Catholic Charities."

"It doesn't surprise me," Nettles said. "You know, they say Van Gogh was mad. Slam out of his mind. Sometimes I wonder whose son is crazier. My son or your father's," he said, casting a sideways glance toward Ernesto.

"Hey!" she said. "What's that supposed to mean?"

"Amari, your temper, remember?" Pete said.

"Young lady, I'm a capitalist. It took Ernesto's father a lifetime to amass his fortune. At this rate, Ernesto will have blown it all before he's fifty. From my standpoint, that's insane."

"The size of a bank account isn't the only way to measure wealth," Ernesto said. "How can one put a price on peace of mind? I do what gives me inner peace. Without inner peace, you live in poverty, no matter how much money you have."

Nettles locked eyes with Pete and pointed an accusing finger at Ernesto. "You see what I mean? That kind of hippy talk is just as crazy as what my son said on that tape."

Amari came off the couch and took one of those stances she made when she was about to go Karate crazy on someone and flip them over her shoulder. "We didn't ask you here for insults, you Godless jerk! If you're going to be like that, then you can leave."

"Amari, sit down and cool your jets," Pete scolded her.

She plopped down on the couch and folded her arms across her chest, casting an angry glare at Nettles.

Just then, Bonelli rushed into the room. "Is there a problem?"

Nettles tossed his hands up in exasperation. "I need a drink. Ernesto, please tell me you kept some of your father's wine."

"It's all gone. Sold in auction. This house is for children now."

"Of course," Nettles said. "I suspected that." He went back to the couch and rubbed at his temples as he composed himself. "I'm sorry guys," he finally said. "Watching that tape . . . seeing my son in that condition . . . saying such crazy things. You have no idea how hard this is."

"I can understand how you feel," Pete said.

"Can you really?" Nettles asked. "Has something like this ever happened to you?"

"I know what it's like to see your child in danger," Pete said. "Try having a pyromaniac serial killer stalk your daughter."

Nettles' eyebrows hiked upward, stretching his plastic surgery tightened face. "Was that you?" he asked Amari. "Over in Tucson? And then over in Italy?"

"Small world isn't it?" she replied.

R.A. WILLIAMS

"Apparently it is." He looked back over at Pete. "Then perhaps you do have some idea how I feel. Only in my case, my son is his own worst enemy."

Amari softened her expression. "Then tell us where he is. If we can find him, we can save him from himself."

"By sending him to prison?" Nettles said.

"No judge would declare him competent to stand trial," Pete said. "He'll go to a facility and get the help he needs."

"He was in one of those facilities before," Nettles said. "It obviously didn't help."

Pete pointed at the television. "It can't be any worse than this."

"Look," Nettles said. "I wish I could help you, but I can't. I have no idea where he is. We haven't talked in years."

"Okay," Pete said. "Let's start there. When was the last time you did talk to him?"

"The last time I saw him, he was at Atascadero."

"Atasca—what?" she asked.

"A mental asylum," Ernesto said. "It's about a hundred and twenty miles southwest of here."

"Calvin was a great kid," Nettles said. "He made straight A's all the way through high school. A real nerd, fixated on science fiction, Star Trek, all that stuff. Like most nerds, I guess. And he was a natural leader. Very charismatic. He was president of the debate team. Won almost every argument. And he was fine up until his sophomore year of college. That's when everything unraveled, and he started failing his classes. At the time, I blamed the Campus Crusade for Christ. He'd gotten all religious on me, and I thought they were brainwashing him. Although from what I heard later, it was him that started doing the recruiting. He'd started his own Bible study. It was almost like his own little church."

"So he wanted to be a pastor?" Pete asked.

"Apparently so," Nettles said. "Personally, I thought that was kind of crazy, considering his nonreligious upbringing. Only when he came home, I found out just how crazy."

"I'm sorry to hear that," Pete said.

"You and me both," Nettles said. "All he wanted to do was read science fiction novels. Well, that and the Bible."

"And that's why you think he was crazy?" Pete asked.

Nettles laughed off the suggestion. "I wish that was all. The real red flag was when his sentences didn't make sense. If you corrected him, he'd get frustrated. And he kept coming downstairs, asking if we were calling him. Apparently, he was hearing voices, only they weren't coming from us. So we sought professional help. That's when they told us he had schizophrenia. The doctor said it typically developed in early adulthood. Nothing could have prevented it."

"So he got the treatment he needed?" Pete asked.

"The doctor put him on drugs. He was seen on an outpatient basis. He seemed to be doing great. Little sleepy, maybe, but that was just the drugs. He got his own apartment and went to community college. When he graduated, just like we promised him, we gave him access to his trust fund."

"A trust fund?" Pete said. "How much are we talking about here?"

"Seven million dollars."

"Wow, that's a lot of cash for such a young fella," Pete said.

"With mental problems," Amari added.

"Like I said, he was doing much better," Nettles replied defensively. "The fund was set to pay out in monthly installments. That way he couldn't squander it all at once. And he was doing fine. Just ask Ernesto. Those two were almost friends."

"He seemed okay to me," Ernesto said. "I knew of his problems, but he seemed normal enough. Just a little slow from the drugs, like Mr. Nettles said. But he seemed to be functional. Until—"

"Until what?" Pete said.

"Until he wasn't," Nettles said. "For some reason, the antipsychotics stopped working. They tried different drugs, but they only helped a little. It eventually got so bad that he went missing for days at a time. One time a park ranger found him up in Yosemite National Park. He was famished and dehydrated. He claimed he was fasting in the wilderness for forty days."

"Like Jesus did?" she asked.

"I think sometimes he thought he was Jesus," Nettles said. "He would walk the streets of downtown Fresno holding a sign that said repent or go to hell, or something of that nature. It had gotten to the point where I didn't recognize him anymore. And he was prone to angry outburst. Real sudden, no warning. One time he punched me square on the jaw. Even his facial expression changed. It's like he was possessed by a demon—if you believe in that kind of thing. Anyway, long story short, one day he had a disagreement with a guy downtown, and Calvin whacked the guy over the head with the butt of his sign. The poor man went to the ER with a concussion. I settled the lawsuit out of court, but the judge still committed Calvin to Atascadero."

"That's the mental asylum," Pete clarified.

"That's right," Nettles said. "And you know what's even crazier?"

"What's that?" Pete asked.

"He'd started preaching in the recreational room. Very successfully, from what I understand. Had his own little congregation. Even with all the drugs they pumped into him, my boy still had charisma. Who knows? If he hadn't lost his mind, he might even be president someday."

"I suppose that explains his little cult," Pete said.

"So when did they let him out?" she asked.

"Let him out? Hardly. Somehow, he escaped. After that, I should have cut his trust fund off, but I couldn't bear the thought of him being homeless, begging for cash on a street corner. But somehow, over the span a month, he'd manage to drain the entire seven million. And vanish off the face of the earth. I haven't heard from him since."

"That's hard to believe," she said. "How does someone like Calvin commit bank fraud? That's not exactly his specialty."

"I'd say he had help," Pete said.

"He did have help," Nettles replied. "Someone very good at forging my signature."

"Jenny said he wouldn't be organized enough to form a cult," Amari said. "Not by himself, anyway. Someone else is behind this."

"I'd like to talk to these people at the mental hospital," Pete said. "Any way you can help with that?"

"I'll give you his doctor's phone number. His name is Dr. Fiszbein. You can call him if you want."

Chapter 25

Atascadero State Hospital was a massive facility. It was laid out more like a penitentiary than a hospital. A tall fence had razor wire along the top and encircled the entire compound. The hospital was so secure, in fact, that Pete and his daughter couldn't enter the facility to interview Dr. Fiszbein, but instead met him under the drive-thru portico in front of the main entrance.

Dr. Fiszbein stood before Pete, squinting from the sun. His gray hair was awkwardly long for a man his age, and his buck teeth called attention to a severe overbite, reminding Pete of Jerry Lewis' Nutty Professor.

"Thank you for meeting with us," Pete said.

"If he's a danger to himself or others," Dr. Fiszbein said, "I have an obligation to help. I just finished reviewing the Nettles file to refresh my memory. After all, it's been several years."

"I appreciate that, doc," Pete said and handed him a duplicate of Kevin's video recording. "Here's a copy of that tape I told you about. Maybe you can make sense of it."

"Perhaps," the doctor said. "I'll watch it and call you later with my conclusion."

"That would be great," Pete said. "In the meantime, you mind telling us about his condition?"

"He has severe schizophrenia. But you knew that already. He scored a thirty-eight on the PANSS scale."

"The what?" Amari asked.

"It stands for Positive and Negative Symptom Scale. Positive symptoms include delusions, hallucinations, and feelings of grandiosity. In Calvin's case, his feeling of grandiosity is religious in nature."

"You don't know the half of it," Pete said. "Look at that tape, and you'll see what I mean. So what's this you were saying about a scale?"

"Yes, the average positive scale scores for his disease are around eighteen. Calvin scored a forty-two, with a maximum possible score of forty-nine."

"That's really up there," Pete said.

"If not medicated," the doctor said. "He's one of the worst I've ever encountered."

"And medicated?" Amari asked.

"He's emotionally blunted, but his condition is manageable. With proper supervision, of course."

Pete pointed to the razor wire atop the fence. "So is he that dangerous? Does he belong in a place like this? Seems more like a prison than a hospital."

"He was placed here because of an assault. However, if I understand, he was confronted by a man on the street. People have fist fights for lesser things. It doesn't mean they belong here."

"Yeah, but what if one of those voices in his head told him to kill somebody," Amari said. "You think he'd listen to that voice?"

"Anything is possible. But you must understand, we can't keep somebody locked up here to prevent every unlikely scenario."

"So you let him out," she said. "I thought he escaped."

"Once we managed to get his symptoms under control, we transferred him to a halfway house, and I continued to oversee his treatment from there."

"So he escaped from the halfway house?" she said. "That I believe. No way was he getting out of this place."

"The residents of that home aren't prisoners," the doctor replied. "They stay because they know it's for their benefit. The doors to the halfway house are locked at night, but during the day they are free to wander the grounds. There is a fence, but it's kept unlocked during the day, so visitors can come and go."

"And Calvin decided he could benefit more somewhere else," Pete said.

"Not just him," Dr. Fiszbein said. "He and another patient left together. A staff member saw them get into the back of a van. The orderly tried to stop them, but the van drove away."

"You don't say?" Pete said. "So who was this other patient?"

"He was Calvin's roommate. He had a similar condition, only not as severe. Like Calvin, he had religious delusions. Before he came to us, he belonged to a religious cult."

"Let me guess," Amari said. "A UFO cult. They believe little green men are actually angels. Stuff like that."

"Precisely," Dr. Fiszbein said. "This cult's beliefs were a mixture of Christianity and science fiction. In our modern age of technology, it's a predictable scenario."

"So do you know where we can find this cult?" Pete asked.

"I can't tell you that. But his file did contain a paragraph concerning Calvin's roommate at the halfway house. His name is Kasper Wolff, with two F's. I remember this one well because he preferred to be called 792. In fact, unless you called him 792, he wouldn't respond."

"So that proves it then," Amari said. "Jenny was right."

"About what?" Pete asked.

"Calvin didn't form this cult. He joined it."

"Because of the number name," Pete said, now realizing what his daughter was inferring. "Those cult members in Europe had numbers for names. And this Kasper fella had a number for a name before he ever met Calvin."

"Exactly," she said.

"So if this was an existing cult, then they must have a history. Dr. Fiszbein, are you sure you've got nothing on the whereabouts of this cult?"

"As I recall, we sent the police to Kasper's last known address," Dr. Fiszbein said. "It was a rental house. They found it empty. The property manager said they left without notice and left no forwarding address."

"There's no telling where they could have gone," she said. "They could be out of the country, for all we know."

"That's why we gotta trace that call," Pete said. "Let's go. I need to call my friend from the FBI again and make sure it's a go before Calvin calls again." Pete handed Dr. Fiszbein a business card. "If that tape gives you any more clues, please page me using that number. Or if you'd rather, you can call on Amari's purse phone. That's her number handwritten on the card."

Chapter 26

Pete, Amari, Ernesto, Bonelli, and Parker sat around the kitchen table playing poker, waiting for the phone to ring. The kids were all in school, so hopefully, Calvin would call back soon before the place turned into a chaotic playground of laughter and distraction.

Suddenly, Amari's purse phone rang.

"That's probably Mike," Pete said and picked up the black Motorola phone. "How do you answer this gadget?"

"Just flip the mouthpiece down," Amari said.

"Like this?" he said and opened the bottom flap.

"Yes, like that," she said. "Get with it, Dad. This is 1989."

"Mike, you there?" Pete said into the phone.

"It's me," Mike said. "How much longer is this going to take?"

"Not sure. Should be any time now."

"I'm starved."

"Then have a pizza delivered. Send me the bill if you want. Just a couple more hours. You got a promotion out of what I did for you, so this is the least you can do."

"And you'll never let me forget that, will you?"

"Come on, Mike. Just a couple more hours."

"All right. But I'm sending you the pizza bill. The tip money too."

"Give the guy twenty percent. On me. Thanks, Mike," he said and handed the phone back to his daughter.

Finally, two rounds of poker later, the phone rang.

"Remember, Ernesto," Pete urged. "Keep him on the line as long as possible."

"I'll do what I can," Ernesto said. He answered the phone on speaker mode, so everybody could hear. "Hello?"

Static on the line crackled for a few seconds. Then words finally came from the speaker. "Ernesto?"

"Yes, this is Ernesto."

"Hello, old friend. Did you receive my message?"

"Yes, I did."

"And?"

"And . . . ," Ernesto said, clearly struggling with the morality of telling lies for the purpose of keeping Calvin on the phone longer.

"And what?"

"Cardinal Ragazzi hasn't decided. He needs time to discuss this with the Vatican."

"You should give them some incentive. If you do so, not only will you find a home on the promised-planet, but you will be repaid ten-fold. Offer your entire fortune if need be."

"Calvin, be reasonable. I can't *bribe* the church into handing over their most priceless relic."

"Of course, you can. How do you think we knew the Shroud would be in the sacristy for repairs? We bribed one of the staff."

Ernesto looked appalled at the idea. "You can't be serious. Who would take such a bribe? Surely not one of the clergy."

"I am not at liberty to say. We gave a solemn oath not to reveal their identity."

"Even so, bribing a staff member and convincing the Vatican to hand over the Shroud are two different things altogether."

"Ernesto, please, you don't have to wash paper cups— you throw them away."

"Pardon?"

Pete leaned over to whisper into Ernesto's ear. "Sometimes he talks nonsense. Just play along. Keep him on the line."

Ernesto stammered for words, then finally said, "Listen . . . Calvin, surely you know this isn't the Christian way. Judas took a bribe to betray Jesus. Is this what you're asking of me?"

"And Jesus told Judas to go ahead with his plan. He said, 'What you are about to do, do quickly'. It was a necessary evil. Now, Ernesto, your time has come. You should do what you need to do—and do so quickly. Call Cardinal Ragazzi back and make him a firm offer, up to your last dime."

Again, Ernesto stammered for words, looking to Pete for guidance. Pete twirled his index finger in small circles, telling him to keep it up a little longer.

"Look, this is going to take some time. I need to talk to my accountant. I think I have . . . gosh, I don't know what I can offer. I'm not sure how much money I have. You know, investments, dividends, depreciation, that sort of thing."

"Don't let your indecision rob you of your destiny. You are chosen just as I am chosen. We each have our roles to play. Search your heart, and you will know this to be true.

You have one week. I will call back at this same time one week from today."

The line went dead.

A moment later, the phone suddenly rang again, and every eye went to Ernesto.

"Do you think that's him again?" Ernesto said.

"Only one way to find out," Pete said. "Maybe he forgot to tell you something."

Ernesto hesitated.

"You did great," Pete said. "You're a natural at this."

Ernesto gave a hard sigh, then answered the phone in speaker mode. "Hello?"

"I'm looking for Pete Johnston."

"That's Mike," Pete said and scooted closer to the table. "Tell me you got him. Tell me he was on long enough to trace his call."

"Yes and no," Mike said.

"What does that mean?" Pete asked.

"He's calling from somewhere between Flagstaff and the Grand Canyon. I couldn't hone in on the address. I didn't have enough time. But he's definitely calling from northern Arizona."

"He said he's calling back in a week," Pete said. "Can you finish the trace, or do we have to start all over?"

"Wish I could help," Mike said. "But I'll be in Seattle next week. I've got a case up there."

"I understand," Pete said. "We'll figure something out. You've been a big help."

"So we're even?" Mike said.

"You only gave me half his address. Still owe me half a favor."

"Hey, my pager's going off," Mike said. "Call me later and tell me how things work out. Maybe I can return the other half of that favor."

"Will do, Mike. Thanks again," Pete said and pushed the button to end the call.

****

Ernesto's foster kids clamored around the kitchen table, enjoying a snack after returning home from school. It was joyful noise for sure, but Amari couldn't concentrate over the sound, so she retreated into Ernesto's game-room-turned-shrine. Her dad's hip was bothering him, so he'd gone to lay down in the guest quarters.

She closed the thick double mahogany doors to the shrine and the sound of laughter hushed, letting her finally be alone with her thoughts. Light from the stain glass window streaked into the room. She walked into the light and embraced its colorful warmth as she gathered her thoughts.

They knew for a fact that Calvin and his cult were located in the Flagstaff area. That was a huge help. She knew there were only about 50,000 people in Flagstaff. They could go up there and start asking questions. Then again, Mike had suggested it could be anywhere in northern Arizona. Amari went over to the bookshelf, pulled down a big atlas full of maps, and laid it out on top of the Shroud replica display case. She turned to Arizona's page and studied the map. Northern Arizona was huge. There were thousands of square miles to cover. Sure, the cult could live in Flagstaff, but they could also be in Sedona, Munds Park, Prescot, Bellemont, Williams, or any other Podunk spot in the middle of the desert. For all she knew, they could be hiding out on the Navajo reservation.

Still, this narrowed the area down. Now her energy grid idea made more sense. But then again, what were they looking for? Skip could fly his plane along the lines, but any one of those rooftops could be the cult's home base. She assumed it would be a big house, but she still couldn't just go knocking on the door of every big house in Northern Arizona. There had to be a better way.

She clapped the atlas shut and looked down into the Shroud display case. She flipped on the light, and the Shroud replica glowed below her, backlit by the lights underneath. "What do you think, Lord?" she uttered. "Any ideas?" She moved over to the wall and gazed up into the negative image of Jesus' face. "Tell me what to do."

She caught her breath. It was a long shot, but still, it might work—assuming Calvin was gullible enough.

She went to the phone and called home. When Jenny picked up, she told her everything that had happened, how Calvin wanted to borrow the Shroud, and how they'd traced the phone call to Flagstaff. Then she asked the question only Jenny could answer.

"Do you remember me telling you that Ernesto had a Shroud replica that went around the world on tour for exhibits and conferences? He uses it to educate people."

"Yeah, I remember."

"So what if we convinced Calvin that this replica was the real one. What if we told him he couldn't borrow the Shroud right now because it was on tour. In fact, it was going to be in Flagstaff soon. Of course, he has no idea we traced his call, so it being so close to home wouldn't sound fishy."

"So you're saying use the replica as bait. Have him believe it's real so he'll try to steal it. Then you can catch him in the act."

"Exactly. But would he go for it? Would the other cult members? You're the psychology major. Do you think he's gullible enough to fall for that?"

"Honestly, I think it might work. Not because he's gullible, but because he's delusional. In his mind, he'd see this as a sign from God. I mean, what are the odds of it showing up in his backyard by accident? He'll see this as

God's will. Like the Shroud had been delivered to his back door by divine providence."

"That's exactly what I was thinking. Thanks, Jenny. You're awesome. Let me run this by my dad and Ernesto. Be on standby to talk to my dad. When I throw this out there, he's going to think I'm crazier than Calvin is."

****

Amari had argued with her dad for over an hour. Of course, he thought the idea was nuts. Even after he'd talked to Jenny, he still wouldn't go for it. Finally, Dr. Fiszbein had assured him that the idea might work, that Calvin was indeed delusional enough to buy it, that he would be looking for a sign. Having the Shroud show up so close to home would leave him no choice but to act. Not doing so would be considered disobedience to divine will, and the consequences would be unthinkable.

****

It wasn't difficult for Ernesto to set the trap. His Shroud replica spent most of its time on tour anyway. He'd called his tour manager and asked him to book an event in Flagstaff. The exhibition was planned for Friday night at the Flagstaff Community Conference Center. An ad was even placed in the paper to make it look legitimate. And it *was* legitimate—well, except for the fact that the ad was worded to suggest it was the real Shroud, as well as the Sudarium of Oviedo, rather than mere replicas. Perhaps Calvin would bite and try to steal the Shroud replicas, or maybe he wouldn't. And even if the cult realized the Shroud was only a fake, there was still the fact that someone tried to break into Ernesto's house and the only thing of value in that house was the replica. Who knows why someone would risk their life for a replica, but that's

THE CULT OF NEW CANAAN

what they did so they must have a good reason. And if opportunity knocked again, there was a good chance they'd try again.

****

It was almost three in the afternoon, one week after their last conversation with Calvin, just before the time he had promised he would call back. Everyone, including Bonelli and Parker, sat around the kitchen table, watching the phone, anticipation building.

"Okay," Amari said. "So here's the way this is going to work. Since Ernesto prefers to avoid the sin of deceit—"

"Even if I did talk to him," Ernesto interrupted, "I am a terrible liar. He wouldn't buy my story."

"Well, I did a couple of plays in high school," Amari said. "I'll just pretend I'm on stage. I mean, I hate lies too. But sometimes you have to make a moral compromise and choose the least of evils. This is just a pretend scenario we make up so we can keep the Shroud safe. For something like this, I think God would understand."

"I pray that he does," Ernesto said.

"Listen," Amari's dad said. "Calvin is delusional. All we're doing is playing along with the lie he's telling himself. And once we catch him, he'll get the help he needs. It's for his own good."

"I suppose it is the least of evils," Ernesto said. "Just don't ask me to participate."

"You don't have to," she said. "Just sit back and listen. So the role I'm playing is your secretary."

"But I don't have a secretary," Ernesto replied.

"You do in this play," she said. "So when he calls, I'm going to tell him you're out of town and—"

Just then, the phone rang. Amari's pulse raced in anticipation. She'd rehearsed her lines, and now it was showtime. She drew a breath and pressed the answer button. "Ernesto Galliano's residence."

There was an awkward pause on the line, and she thought he might hang up.

"I need to speak with Ernesto," Calvin finally said. "He is expecting my call."

"Oh, I'm sorry. You just missed him. I'm his secretary. Can I take a message?"

"When will he return?"

"Not for a few days. He's gone out to Flagstaff, Arizona. Hey, have you ever heard of the Shroud of Turin?"

Another pause, then, "I have indeed. In fact, Ernesto and I were discussing the Shroud."

"Then you must know why he's in Flagstaff. Didn't he tell you?"

"He never mentioned Flagstaff."

"The Shroud of Turin is on tour in the United States. And the Sudarium of Oviedo too. They're both going to be at the Flagstaff Community Conference Center this Friday. Ernesto's gone out there to publicize the event and then help set up Thursday night. The truck's supposed to arrive around eight, and he wants to be there to help unload it. And if you know Ernesto, you know that's a big deal for him. Just imagine, this Thursday night, at eight o'clock, he will personally lift the burial cloth of Christ out of the van and help set it up. It's really an honor."

The line fell silent.

"Hello? You still there?" she asked.

"Yes, I was just . . . thinking."

"If you want tickets, you can call the conference center. I can get you the number if you want."

"Uh . . . no, no that won't be necessary. Thank you," he said, and the line went dead.

She looked around the table. "Well? Do I get an Oscar or what?"

"You're no Meryl Streep," her dad said. "But I think he got the message. Now let's work on our plan to nab him."

Chapter 27

BLIP ... BLIP ... BLIP ... BLIP

"This tracking beacon is only good for a couple of miles, three at the most," Bonelli said. "And that's assuming the radio signal doesn't get blocked by the mountains."

Pete and his daughter watched the light flash against a green radar-like screen mounted on the dashboard of Ernesto's Mercedes. Bonelli was in the driver's seat, Pete was in the passenger seat, and Amari sat in the back and watched from there. The homing beacon had been planted underneath the Shroud replica's display case.

The truck Parker was driving contained the two replicas, as well as poster-sized photos, information signs, and information brochures. On the side of the truck, a banner sign read, *The Shroud of Turin Exhibit.*

Bonelli put his CB handset to his mouth. "Parker, what's your location? Are you close?"

"I just got off Route 66, and I'm heading down North Eden Street. I'm coming up on East Bell Street. That's my turn, isn't it?"

"Roger that," Bonelli said. "Turn left on Bell, and the convention center is three blocks down on your right. Go to the loading dock and park the truck. When you get there, go inside like you're going to tell someone to open the door."

"Give me that for a second," Pete said. He took the handset from Bonelli and mashed the transmit button. "And leave the truck running with the driver's door still open. We want to lay down a welcome mat. And make sure you take your Walkie Talkie. There's a small park next to the conference center. We're parked at the north end of the park next to a cluster of trees to give us some cover. If they take the bait, radio us, then high-tail it through the park and get in our car. With any luck, this bozo will drive the truck all the way home. We'll call the local police to help with the arrests."

Amari scooted forward on the back seat and watched the flashing beacon on the green radar-looking screen. It moved closer and closer to their location and then came to a stop. And then she saw it the moment Pete did—the headlights of the truck, barely visible through tree branches. "That's Mitch," she said. "I can see his headlights."

"Parker, is that you at the loading dock?" Bonelli said over the CB.

"I'm here," he replied. "I'm going to back the truck in, so it'll be easier to steal."

"Look to your right," Bonelli said. "You see that patch of trees across the park?"

"It's dark, but I see them. I can barely make out the Mercedes behind it. The street light's reflecting off the windshield."

"That's us. Back the truck in and set the trap."

Once Parker backed the truck into the loading dock, there was radio silence.

"I hope these guys aren't listening to us with their own Walkie-talkies," Amari said.

"And they just happened to be on the right channel?" Pete said. "What are the odds of that?"

"Not good," Bonelli replied. "Besides, if they were on this channel, it would be so they can talk to each other, and I haven't heard anything."

"Are you sure we shouldn't have told the local police?" she said. "We might need some backup."

"The last thing we want these guys to see is a police car," Pete said. "Not while we're baiting them to make a heist."

"But they could use unmarked cars."

"The detectives who use those cars are home watching Doogie Howser," Pete replied sarcastically. "A patrol car is all we could get. It's too risky. Besides, I don't want any local interference. These guys are very territorial, and they won't appreciate some out of town private investigators setting up a sting in their jurisdiction. Trust me, I know."

"It's moving!" Amari spat out.

"What's moving?" Pete asked.

"The blip, the white blip! It's moving!"

Pete snatched up the CB handset. "Parker, is that you? Are you in the truck?"

No response.

"Parker?" Pete said louder this time. "Is that you moving the truck?"

No response.

Suddenly, banging came from the window. Amari unlocked the door, and Parker climbed into the backseat with her.

"Go, go, go!" Parker said, pointing frantically. "He's got the truck! He's heading east on Bell Street."

"Let's go, Bonelli," Pete said. "But don't be too obvious. Keep your distance. Remember, we want to track them all the way home. If they know we're tailing them, they might get spooked. They'll drop the truck, then cut and run."

"Gotcha," Bonelli said and started down the darkened street.

They turned left onto Bell Street. Pete and his daughter eyed the blip.

"There were two of them," Parker said breathlessly. "And one of those guys had a tattoo, just like the cult members have."

Amari could see the truck stopped at a red light up ahead. "I knew it!" she said, her heart thumping with excitement. "I can't believe this worked!" It was all she could do to keep from laughing. The thrill of the chase was intoxicating.

"Of course, it worked," Pete said. "You're my daughter, aren't you? This is in your blood."

"He's turning," she said. "Don't lose him. If he gets behind some buildings, we might lose the signal."

"I'm on him," Bonelli said and turned right.

"I bet he's heading back out to Route 66," Pete said.

They followed the truck back down Eden Street. Sure enough, he turned left onto Route 66 and picked up speed, with Bonelli trailing behind. As they approached a red light, the truck accelerated.

"He's trying to beat the light!" Amari cried. "Bonelli, punch it!"

"We won't make it," Pete replied. "Relax, we have the tracker, remember?"

They waited at the light for what felt like an eternity. "Bonelli, just run the light," she pleaded.

"There's too much traffic. I'll get into a wreck, and we'll never catch him."

"How far does that thing transmit?" she asked.

"At least two miles."

"Amari, I told you to relax," Pete said. "We don't want him to know we're following him. This works in our favor."

Finally, the light turned green. Bonelli sped ahead, weaving in and out of traffic to regain ground. They couldn't see the truck, but the radar blip remained strong.

"He turned already," she said, pointing at the flashing blip. "See, he's going to the left."

"But which left?" Bonelli said. "There's two left turns up ahead."

Amari watched the blip as they approached the intersection. As the blip moved to the left of the screen, she seemed to be calculating the distance. "It's the next one," she said. "It can't be this one. It's got to be the next one."

As they approached the first intersection, the light turned yellow. "Not this time," Bonelli said and stomped on the gas pedal. They passed under the red light, just in time to miss the flow of cars.

"We still got him," Pete said. "If it were that last turn, he'd be off the screen by now."

Suddenly, the cars stacked up in front of them, stopped by another red light.

"North Canyon Road," she said. "I can read the sign."

They watched the blip as they waited for the light to turn. Suddenly, the blip vanished.

"What?!" she cried. "Where's the blip?"

"He must have gone behind a hill," Parker said. "Without a direct line of sight, this thing is worthless."

Suddenly, Bonelli mashed the accelerator, jerked the wheel left, cut across traffic, and sped into a strip mall. He raced down the parking lot to bypass the red light. He cut left onto North Canyon. The rear wheels screamed as they spun, sending white smoke in the car's wake. They hit sixty miles an hour, barreling down the darkened rural backroad, chasing after the vanished blip. They reached the peak of a hill, and the bleep returned.

"There it is," she said. "And I can see him. I know it's him because of the red light at the top of the truck."

"I see him," Bonelli said. "He won't lose me again."

They broke out of the trees and city lights came back into view.

"Where's he going?" she said. "He's headed back into Flagstaff."

"Must be taking a shortcut," Pete said. "Or maybe he knows we're following him, and he's trying to lose us."

The truck veered right around a curve in the road. Suddenly, the passenger side door of the truck opened slightly, and someone leaned out. Two muzzle flashes. A bullet bit into the windshield.

"Amari, get down!" Pete cried.

Bonelli stomped the brakes. Mitch's strong arm jerked her head down to his knees. He fell on top of her for cover, protecting her body with his own.

"Everybody okay?" Bonelli yelled in a panic.

"Let me up!" Amari said and punched her way free. "Keep going! We're going to lose him!"

"It's not worth losing your life!" Pete yelled back at her. "Now do as I say and keep low!" He waited as the truck moved a safe distance away. "Okay, Bonelli, keep going. But keep your distance. He knows we're following, but he's got no idea we're tracking him. Let him get some distance, and maybe he'll keep leading us home. Just keep the car out of bullet range."

Bonelli cautiously drove forward, following the blip. Suddenly, the blip turned right, and he accelerated to keep up.

"A hospital?" she said as they approached the turn. A sign read Flagstaff Medical Center.

"Go easy," Pete said. "Follow him but keep your distance."

"Why would *he* go to a hospital?" Parker asked. "He was the one shooting at us."

"I don't know, but it's definitely a hospital," Pete said. "You see that helicopter coming in for a landing? It must be a medivac chopper. Probably a trauma unit."

"Look," she said, jutting her finger at the bullet-broken windshield. "He's pulling into the parking garage."

"I bet he's going to make the switch," Pete said. "They probably have a car waiting in the garage. They'll switch out, and we'll lose their trail for sure."

"Then let's go after them!" she said. "It'll take time to move the Shroud."

"Amari, they have guns," Pete said.

"And so do we," she snapped back. "*Four* guns between the four of us. We've got them outnumbered two to one."

"I've got a better idea," Pete said. "Bonelli, pull that car up to the entrance and turn it so it blocks both lanes, entrance and exit. Then get on the horn and call the local police for backup. We'll have them trapped like a rat in a cage."

"Uh, Dad? I thought you said that was a medivac chopper," Amari said as she looked out the side window.

"Well, of course, it is," Pete said. "What else could it be?"

"Then why is it landing on top of the parking garage?"

****

They reached the top of the garage just in time to see the chopper lift off and fly into the dark, starry horizon. Pete, Bonelli, and Parker got out of the car and cautiously moved toward the white truck, weapons drawn. Amari had reluctantly done what she'd been told and stayed down at the garage entrance and waited for the police. If there was going to be a shootout, Pete wasn't going to watch her take a bullet. Besides, Ernesto had hired him to protect her, not to put her in the line of fire.

They cautiously crept around to the back of the truck, guns cocked and ready. Bonelli shined a flashlight into the cargo area. Aside from exhibit décor, the truck was empty. Pete climbed up into the truck, putting his weight on his good hip. Bonelli handed him the flashlight. He shined the light down onto the smashed display case of Ernesto's expensive Shroud replica. The other case that held the Sudarium was also shattered. Both replicas were gone.

Suddenly, Amari clamored into the truck, breathless, apparently having just taken the stairs.

"I thought I told you to wait for the police," Pete barked.

"I told hospital security." she said, "They said the police were on their way."

She took the flashlight from her dad and shined it at the shattered case.

Pete reached under the case and removed the tracking transmitter, its red light still flashing. "Lot of good this thing did."

Amari cringed when she saw the shattered remains of the display cases, both expensive replicas gone. "Ernesto's gonna have a cow."

"I'd say you're right," Pete said. "You think he's going to fire you? And me too for agreeing to this?"

"Not a chance," she said. "Come on, let's go to the airport and see if they tracked the helicopter by radar. At least we can get some idea where they were heading."

Chapter 28

Underneath the apex of the glass atrium, Adrian inspected his work. He'd just stretched the Shroud replica out across a limestone slab that had been pieced together before the Shroud's arrival. The smaller Sudarium was folded up by itself on its own limestone slab, inches away from the Shroud, just as the Gospel of John had described. He'd folded the Shroud replica in two so that only the front part of the body showed. He and Ian had placed the replicas onto the limestone before Calvin and the rest of the congregation were invited to view it. The limestone slabs had been Calvin's idea because the tomb of Christ was carved from limestone.

Adrian glanced up to see Calvin ascending the stairs into the sunlit atrium. The rest of the congregation followed several paces behind. When his eyes met the Shroud, a subtle expression of wonder formed on his face. The rest of the congregation encircled the holy replicas and a clamor of exhilaration reverberating inside the atrium.

Calvin stepped forward and spread his arms wide, the white sleeves of his special occasion robe hanging down like the wings of an angel. The excited voices hushed as they awaited the profound words of their leader.

"Do you see, my children? Have my promises not been kept? Behold, The Shroud of Turin, the holiest and most technologically advanced of all relics—our gateway to the planets of heaven." He bowed his head in reverence and softened his voice. "I have but one regret, that Lieutenant Senior Grade 876 and Ensign 762 could not share in our joy. For as you know, they were martyred during their efforts."

"Then we will see them in New Canaan," Adrian said in a reassuring voice.

"Only in their gloried new bodies," Calvin said and listened to the happy chatter of his reassured flock.

"Will we recognize them?" the freakishly tall Lieutenant 332 asked.

"They will appear younger, without blemish or flaw. But assuredly, you will recognize them. For once on the planet of New Canaan, we will all be transformed. We will be as the angels in heaven, with incorruptible bodies. And just as with the angels, we will neither marry nor be given in marriage. It is for this reason that we must also bring with us the new Adam and new Eve. And now that we have the essential parts, we have sent the invitation, for surely now God speaks to their hearts as he does so to mine. In fact, as many of you know, I have already made first contact. I planted a seed in the new Adam's spirit. And so the seed grows as he awaits further instructions."

"But what of the girl?" Lieutenant 332 asked. "She was very aggressive in Dallas. Will she be so easily swayed?"

"When the Lord speaks to her, she will comply," Calvin assured him. "We have chosen to contact Dr. Brenner in advance so that he may soften her heart to the Lord's call. And when she heeds the call, her fierce determination will serve us well. It is all according to the divine plan."

"But when?" Lieutenant 332 asked.

"Soon, 332. If God wills it, they will see and understand our new message. If it is God's will, they will meet us at the Rock of Angels."

"And if he doesn't show?" Lieutenant 332 asked.

Adrian stepped forward and coughed for the group's attention. "Rest assured, we have a backup plan. If Dr. Brenner does not respond to this message, then we have other ideas. One way or another, by this time next year, you will be on your journey home."

"Next year?" Lieutenant 332 asked. "Will it take that long?"

"New Canaan is 378 parsecs from Earth," Adrian reminded them. "When Calvin boards the ark, his journey back home will last 297 days, and this is at warp nine. He cannot travel any faster."

"And as we await Calvin's return, who will assume leadership?" Lieutenant 332 asked. "Will it be you again?"

"Yes," Calvin said. "As he led you before I came, so shall he lead again."

A grumble of disdain rose from the flock.

"My children," Calvin continued. "I know that compared to me, Adrian is a poor substitute. Even still, he is my choice. And just so you know that his motives are pure, you should know that he will spend most of his time out in the world, ministering to the lost. For inside the ark, there will be many cryopreservation chambers, room for hundreds more. Any he manages to persuade will also be saved."

Again, the congregation grumbled their objection.

"Brethren, you know this must be so. Your glorified new bodies must never endure the pain of childbirth. And you know that when Cain was banished to the land of Nod, he took to himself a wife form the people of Nod. So it must be in New Canaan. The offspring of the new Adam and new Eve must intermarry with the refugees from this world. Yet you will be like gods over them, just as the Nephilim were in the days of old."

After another heated exchange of words, Lieutenant 332 voiced the group's concerns. "And when he's ministering to the world? Who will lead us then?"

"As Lieutenant Senior Grade, you have the third highest rank. Naturally, you will be in charge during Adrian's absence."

"I would consider it an honor," Lieutenant 332 said. "I will gladly take control."

Adrian suppressed a sinister smile and thought to himself. *You'll never get the chance, you ugly, nosey behemoth.* Not when Calvin resorts to Plan B.

Chapter 29

Kevin's apartment was situated just south of the Catalina Foothills, next to the river bed that was only wet during the summer monsoon season. Since Ernesto had doubled Kevin's post-doctoral salary, he could have easily afforded a nicer place, but he chose to stay put since he was just three miles from Amari's home.

Amari washed the last plate and set it in the yellow drying rack in Kevin's tiny kitchen. "Ernesto said he'd hire you a maid. Or you could hire one yourself for what he's paying you."

Kevin slouched on the couch with the remote control in his hand, channel surfing. "I'd of done those dishes, babe. Come here and sit with me. CNN's about to come on."

She dried her hands, went to the VCR, pushed the record button, plopped onto the couch, and snuggled under his arm. Part of being a good detective was keeping up with the news. The guys who stole Ernesto's replicas were guilty of at least three high-profile crimes, so she made it her routine to read every newspaper she could find, to watch and record every news show. With any luck, the cult would strike again and leave enough evidence to solve the case. But she had to be vigilant and not miss any news, even if it meant being up before dawn to watch CNN's Daybreak news show with Kevin, a routine she'd come to enjoy over the last week.

So far the news-watching had been a futile effort. Still, she enjoyed her morning time with him. She never seemed fully awake until she saw his face. One of these days, they would marry, maybe, if he ever got around to popping the question. Maybe one day she wouldn't have to drive to his apartment to see him every morning. Then again, they'd only been dating a year. Maybe it was still too early to rush into a lifetime commitment, but she couldn't see spending her life with anyone else.

"This is Daybreak on CNN," the announcer said as horn music played in the background. "With Dave Michaels from CNN center in Atlanta, and Norma Quarles in New York."

Most of the news was about the earthquake up in San Francisco. A double-decker freeway in Oakland had collapsed and trapped a bunch of people under the rubble.

After a commercial break, Dave Michaels returned to the screen. "A bizarre act of vandalism occurred in Utah over the weekend. Just north of the small town of Thompson, ancient Indians had left their mark by painting or carving petroglyphs onto the walls of Sego Canyon." CNN switched from Dave to a video feed of a rock wall with something that looked like cave drawing using red chalk. "Features of these petroglyphs include ghostly human-like forms," Dave continued, "some without arms or legs, and others with large bug eyes or no eyes at all. Some UFO conspiracy buffs even claim these paintings are depictions of space aliens, proof that we have been visited in the past. Unfortunately, despite severe penalties for vandalism, a recent addition was made to the eight-thousand-year-old canyon art." The camera panned down the rock wall to show the graffiti— two stick figure drawings with numbers underneath. Just below the numbers was some indecipherable scribble. "In vibrant color," Dave continued, "two more human-like figures have been painted onto the rock wall. One appears to be a male, the other a female, given the wide shape of her hips and long hair. Numbers are painted underneath each painting. Authorities are baffled as to the meaning of those numbers. If anyone has any information regarding this vandalism, a reward is available for information leading up to an arrest."

"That really ticks me off," Amari said. "I hope they catch those guys."

"Now that's interesting," Kevin said as he rubbed the morning razor stubble on his chin.

"Are you okay?"

"Huh," he said, watching the screen with a dumbfounded look on his face.

"What is it?"

"Rewind that and play it back for me."

"Hold on a sec." She got off the couch, changed the VCR to view mode, then rewound the tape to the right spot and hit Play.

"Right there. Pause it right there."

She hit Pause, and the stick-figure rock paintings froze on the screen, blurry and flickering, but clear enough to read the numbers.

Kevin came off the couch. "That's us."

"What are you talking about?"

He pointed at the television. "That's us. You and me."

"What do you mean, us? It's just two stick figures. Besides, my hips aren't nearly that big. Are they?"

"Well . . ."

"Answer carefully," she said with a balled fist.

"The numbers, Amari. The numbers underneath are what I'm talking about."

"What about them?"

"It's a code."

"A code?"

"Yes, a numeric code that stands for a word."

She gasped at a sudden realization. "You mean like the UFO tattoos? You think that's a code too?"

"Yes, that's what I'm driving at. Only the numbers under those stick figures are our numbers."

"What's that supposed to mean? Our numbers?"

"Have you ever heard of St. John's Code?"

She gave him a blank stare.

"Gematria. That's another word for it. In fact, I mentioned it in one of my papers."

"St. John's Code talks about the Shroud?"

"Not really. It was more of a mathematical tangent. I used it as an example of how math can be a language of its own. In ancient Babylon, they came up with a number system that assigned numerical values for every letter of the alphabet. Since the Jews spent so much time over in Babylon, they started using it too. In fact, it's right there in the Book of Revelation—the number of the beast. That's just a numerical code."

"You mean like in the Omen? The movie with the little devil kid?"

"Yes. Those three sixes identified him as the antichrist. Only he's not alone. Everybody's got a number. You just have to do the math. And those two numbers we saw on television under the stick figures belong to us. They spell out our names."

"How would you know that?"

"Cause, I crunched the numbers. I obviously knew my own number. Figured that out a long time ago. Then when

I met you, I ran the numbers in my head and came up with yours too."

"Why would you do that?"

He shrugged, and his cheeks flushed.

"To make sure I wasn't the antichrist?"

He shrugged again.

"Kevin, how could you think such a thing?"

"Hey, I didn't know you from apple butter. I do it to everybody I meet. You know me, I'm always crunching numbers in my head. It's what I do."

"And you're sure those numbers identify us?"

"In English, your number is 942. That was the number underneath the painting with the big hips and long hair."

The paused image was too blurry, so she rewound it and played it again.

"You see there, the girl has a 942, and the dude has 822 under him. That's my number in English. In Jewish gematria, mine's 1016 and yours is 1099."

"Hold on." She rewound the tape and hit Play. As she watched, she hit Pause again. "What does that say? It's underneath the numbers."

"I don't know. It's too small. It almost looks like Hebrew, but I can't be sure."

"Hebrew? Like in the Jews?"

"Why not? The numbers are a Jewish code."

"Then we need to get up there before someone cleans it off."

"That would be awesome. I know right where it is. Call your dad and see if he's up to a road trip."

"My dad's in California. Ernesto's taking him to see a hip surgeon. He's supposed to be the best in the business."

"When's he gonna be back?"

"It doesn't matter," she said defiantly. "We're not waiting for him. We don't need him for this. Besides." She laced her fingers into his. "We need some time to ourselves. It'll be like a mini-vacation. It'll be fun."

"Awesome, I'll call work and tell them not to expect me."

"I'll go home and pack an overnight bag." She pecked him on the cheek. "Pack yours too and meet me at the house."

Chapter 30

Amari adjusted her side-view mirror and eyed the car behind them with suspicion. "Kevin, I think that car is following us. When we stopped to eat in Monticello, I noticed they stopped at the restaurant across the street. And now they're behind us again."

He glanced at the car through his rear-view mirror. "So, they were hungry too. Probably tourists heading up to Newspaper Rock."

"In a Ford Taurus?"

"So? Those cars are everywhere."

"A silver Ford Taurus?"

"Ain't that the car you saw in Dallas? The one you said those cult members got into?"

"Yes, it's the same car. I think they followed us all the way from Tucson."

"Are you sure it was a silver Taurus? It was dark that night. It might have been white for all you know."

"Kevin, I know my cars. I'm sure it's the same."

"Then I'll try to lose them," he said and mashed on the gas.

"In a Honda Accord? Are you crazy? We should have brought my Camaro. Why didn't you let me drive?"

"Cause your car's a gas hog, that's why."

"Oh, I forgot. My car's making the planet hotter. The icebergs are melting because of me."

"That's what they're saying now."

"Whatever." She reached into her purse and removed her pistol. It was a compact 9mm Beretta registered to her dad. She dropped the ammo magazine to confirm it was fully loaded. She snapped the magazine back into the gun. "If it is them, I'll recognize their faces. Well, at least two of them. Have you got your gun?"

"Now, hold on, don't go shooting that thing."

"Just answer me. Have you got your gun?"

"It's in the glove compartment. You know I always carry it, especially on long trips."

"Good, cause we might need it."

"You're just being paranoid, babe. Relax. Enjoy the trip."

"Yes, I'm paranoid. Getting stalked by a serial killer kind of does that to you."

"I tell you what. You see that trailer park? I'm going to pull into it, and I bet you anything they keep on driving."

She chambered a round in her gun. "And if they don't, they'll wish they had."

He turned right into a small trailer park on the outskirts of Monticello. They waited and watched. Sure enough, the car kept driving.

"Told you so. Now put the safety back on that thing before you shoot me in the leg. Everything's going to be fine, I promise."

****

They'd stopped for gas in Moab. The small town was a green, river-fed oasis, situated in a valley surrounded by barren desert mountains on both sides. After filling up, they both went to the restroom before continuing their journey.

She stepped out of the smelly restroom at a quarter past five. It was one of those restrooms on the side of the gas station rather than inside. A block of wood was attached to the key she'd gotten from the clerk. She stretched her back muscles, then bent over to stretch her hamstrings as she waited for Kevin outside the men's room. When she came up from her stretch, she spotted it—the silver Ford Taurus. It was parked across the street at a Chevron, only nobody was pumping gas. They were just sitting there, watching.

When Kevin started to come out of the restroom, she pushed him back inside and closed the door.

"What are you doing?" he said. "This is the *men's* room."

"It's them!"

"Who?"

"The guys in the Ford Taurus."

"Again?"

"Yes, it's them. Look." She cracked the door open.

He cautiously stuck his head out. "I don't see anything."

She leaned out of the bathroom and pointed—at nothing. They were gone. "Seriously, I saw them. They were parked at that Chevron across the street."

"So they needed gas too."

She exhaled in exasperation. "I know it was there."

"I'm sure it was. They got their gas and went. You're being paranoid again."

"Maybe you're right. Jenny said I need counseling."

"Doesn't she counsel you every day?"

Amari laughed. "And every night too."

"Come on, let's hit the road. If we hurry, we'll be there before it's dark."

Chapter 31

A plume of brown dust billowed in the wake of Kevin's car as they worked their way up the barely paved road into Sego Canyon. They were in the middle of nowhere. Amari had seen a water tank a couple of miles back, but since then, nothing. The only thing in sight was spotty patches of green desert brush weeds and barren, crumbling mountains and rock pillars.

"Kevin, we better turn around," she said. "It's getting dark. We're going to get lost."

"It's gotta be around here somewhere," he said. "The dude at the RV park said it was just up this road."

"This isn't a road. It's more like a trail. Let's stay at a hotel for the night and come back in the morning."

"Did you see a hotel in the metropolis of Thompson Springs, population thirty-nine?"

"Then we'll go back to Moab. Wasn't that the plan anyway? We were going to stay there the night and drive back home."

"That's forty miles from here. There and back again is eighty miles. We're already here. We might as well check it out. It's just seven o'clock. There's still enough light to see. Besides, we've got flashlights."

"You know there's coyotes and wildcats in these hills."

"So, you know self-defense," he said with a grin. "I'll stand behind you."

"Kevin, I'm serious."

"Tell you what, if we don't find it in twenty minutes, we'll head back and try again tomorrow."

Moments later, they topped a hill and rounded the dusty corner. The headlights hit a small brown sign that said no camping allowed.

"That's gotta be it," he said. "The guy said it was about three miles up this road and I've been watching the odometer."

"Just hurry."

He pulled left and parked in a gravel lot next to the smooth face of a rock wall. He got out and shined a flashlight at a small wooden sign. "This is it," he yelled and waved for her to join him.

She got the Polaroid camera from the backseat and met him at the trail. They followed a dirt path that wound through the bushy desert brush. About thirty yards into the trail, the rock-face canvas came into view. The setting sun illuminated the stone like a spotlight onto a stage. About fifteen feet off the ground, twenty or so humanoid-like creatures were painted with red paint on the side of a smooth sandstone cliff. Some had insect features such as antennas. Others had heads shaped like space aliens with large hollow eyes. Some were faded with time, but others were surprisingly well-defined after so many years. No wonder UFO buffs considered these paintings proof of past visitation from the stars. They sure looked out of this world.

"What do you think those mean?" she asked. "They look like red, people-shaped insects."

"Beats the heck out of me," he said. "You're the Indian. Don't you know?"

"These weren't Navajo Indians, so I couldn't tell you."

"Maybe they're just self-portraits," he said with a smirk. "Maybe they're just awful at painting."

"Kevin, you're terrible."

"It's why you love me."

"It's one of the reasons. Hey, look," she said and pointed at the base of the cliff. "There's our paintings."

She shifted her attention to the newly added addition. They weren't up with the rest of the petroglyphs, but rather on a smaller rock ledge that could be reached from the trail. The paint used to draw the stick figures that were supposed to represent her and Kevin wasn't colored red like that used by the ancient Indians. Instead, they were painted vibrant yellow. And unlike the paintings left by the ancients, these drawings had arms and legs. Kevin's 'petroglyph' had hair that was parted in the middle, and falling to his shoulders, just like his real hair. The petroglyph with the big hips had hair flowing past the shoulder blades, just like her own hair. And of course, underneath each were the numbers 822, gematria for Kevin Brenner, and 942, the code for Amari Johnston.

"Not exactly Michelangelo," he said, musing at the artwork.

"At least they had the decency to mess up the wall down here instead of up with the rest of the paintings."

"They would need a ladder to do that," he said and hopped a rail fence.

She climbed the fence to join him. She touched the paint with her fingers. "It's definitely not spray paint or acrylic." She licked the tip of her finger and rubbed at the paint. "It's just watercolor. It would have come off with the next rain."

"That was thoughtful," he said.

"Well, they are a Christian cult—sort of."

"Do unto others," he replied. "Least they got some scruples."

She folded her arms across her chest and pondered the odd paintings. "So if they didn't mean to leave a permanent mark, then maybe this was some kind of message. It's in bright yellow to grab attention."

"We're here, aren't we?"

"Exactly. It's like they knew we would see this. Maybe they're even the ones who reported it to CNN."

"I mentioned the gematria code in one of my papers, remember?"

"So maybe they knew you'd recognize the numbers. Because they know you're a mathematical genius—a Christian mathematical genius. I bet they were trying to send a message only you could decipher."

"Could be, but it seems a little farfetched."

"You mean like a little crazy? Think about who we're dealing with."

"You have a point. Look here," he said, pointing to the line of foreign looking text underneath the numbers. The size of the lettering was smaller than that of the numbers. "This is what we saw on CNN, only we couldn't read it."

האדם החדש was painted in black paint underneath Kevin's petroglyph. ערב החדש was written underneath the figure representing Amari.

She moved in for a closer look, scratching her head as she pondered the gibberish. "What in the world?"

"It's definitely Hebrew."

"Hebrew? Can you read it? What's it say?"

"Heck if I know. It ain't a math equation. Tell you what, take a picture of it, and when we get back to Tucson, we can go by the synagogue and see if someone can read it."

"Good idea." She pointed her Polaroid camera at the numbers. A bright flash popped from the camera, then it whined as it ejected the picture. "Here, hold this," she said and handed him the picture. The sunlight was getting dim, so she flipped on her flashlight and searched the ground beneath the paintings.

"What are you doing?" he asked.

"What we came here to do," she said. "I'm looking for evidence. Maybe they left a paintbrush or a paint can, something with prints."

"Maybe they dropped a credit card carbon copy with their name on it."

"Funny."

She searched the entire area but found nothing except a weathered paper cup and some cigarette butts. Anybody could have left those there.

"See anything?" he asked.

"Nothing useful. Come on, let's get out of here before it's completely dark."

When they got back to the car, a soft twilight had settled over the gravel parking lot. She flipped on the dome light and inspected the Polaroid picture. "Can you read that?" she said and showed it to him. "Maybe I should have taken two pictures, one of each line, closer up."

He took the picture and eyed it. "Nah, it's fine. Someone who speaks Hebrew won't have any problem reading it. In fact, I know a Jewish guy. I bet he knows what it says."

Suddenly, a glint of light pulled her attention to the rear-view mirror. She looked out the back window and watched car headlights approach and come to a stop, blocking the parking lot's exit.

"Oh, crap!" She yanked the glove compartment door open and handed him his gun. "Get behind the car!"

"Amari, relax. They're probably just here for the petroglyphs."

"At night? I told you they were following us. When are you going to listen to me?"

She quickly climbed out, snatched her pistol from her purse, and took cover behind the car. He got out and met her on her side of the car, his gun holster in one hand, the flashlight in the other. They both watched as four figures stepped out from their car and slowly moved toward them, casting long shadows as their bodies blocked light from their headlight beams. One of them was huge, his shadow twice as long as the others.

"Stay where you are!" she yelled. She made sure her safety was on to prevent an accidental discharge.

"We mean you no harm," the tall one shouted.

Kevin shined his flashlight on them. "Hey, fellas, I wouldn't come any closer. She knows how to use that thing. My aim's not bad either."

They slowed their pace but kept walking toward them nonetheless.

"Are you deaf?" She clinched her pistol tighter and knelt into a shooter's stance, so they'd know she meant business. "I told you to stay there! Don't make me shoot."

Finally, they stopped their advance, just close enough for her to make out their appearance. They all had heads shaved close to the scalp. Three wore dark navy, one-piece coveralls, and the tall one wore beige coveralls. She recognized two of them—the ones at the Dallas Shroud symposium. The tall one had to be one of the guys who waited in the car.

"Let me see your hands," she shouted again. "Don't make me shoot you."

"Please, Ms. Johnston, we are unarmed," the tall one in beige shouted back. "Search us if you like."

She considered the offer. This was her chance to stop them. She'd be a fool to pass up the opportunity. "Okay, but you're going to do this my way. I want you each to come forward on your own, one at a time. You, the tall one. Come forward first, slowly, your hands on your head. When he checks you, go to the rear of the line, and the next can come forward. And don't try anything funny."

"Kevin." She waved her gun in their direction. "Pat them down. I've got you covered."

Kevin handed her the flashlight. "All right, fellas," he said, cautiously moving toward them. "She's got an itchy finger, so don't test her."

One by one, he searched them as Amari held the flashlight in one hand and her pistol in the other. When Kevin finished, he came back to her. "They're clean. Let's just talk to them and see what they want."

"Did you check them good?"

"You saw me. I even checked their calves for sock holsters."

She stalled for a moment, considering her options. "Hold this on them," she said and handed him the pistol. She reached into her purse and retrieved her compact, Motorola cellular phone. She flipped the lid open, dialed 911, and held the receiver to her ear.

"Uh, hate to tell you this, babe, but those things need transmission towers to work. You see any around here?"

"That must be why it's not ringing," she said, feeling a little embarrassed that she hadn't considered that before dialing the number.

She put away her phone, got her gun back from Kevin, and motioned for him to follow. She stood about five feet away from them and spoke in an authoritative tone, her flashlight trained on their faces. "I'm making a citizen's arrest."

"Ms. Johnston, please," the tall one said. "You must search your heart. Listen to God's call. The fate of humanity depends upon your cooperation."

"I thought it was Kevin you were after," she replied suspiciously. "Now I'm special too?"

"Yes, the divine plan depends upon your cooperation as well."

"The divine plan? Give me a break," she said and laughed. "I'm just a cop's kid from Tucson. Kevin's just a really smart nerd from Tennessee. You guys are delusional."

"And Jesus was born in a simple manger," the tall one said, his deep-set eyes probing her knowingly. "From humble beginnings, greatness is born."

"That's Calvin talking," she told him. "You've all been brainwashed. There's nothing special about me or Kevin. And you either, for that matter."

"One way or another," he said, "you will accompany us. By your own free will—or otherwise." He motioned for the others to follow, and they all headed back to their car without another word.

She took the shooter's stance again and aimed. "Hey, where are you guys going?"

They ignored her and kept walking. She pursued them toward their car. "You stop right there, or I'll shoot, do you hear me?"

Just then, the tall one faced her as the others got back into the car. "You're not going to shoot us, Ms. Johnston."

"How do you know?"

"Because the chosen of God would never break his sixth commandment. Your will is strong, a trait that makes you ideal for the challenges ahead. God has chosen you well, only now he must open your heart." He turned his gaze to Kevin. "And you, Dr. Brenner? Do you still resist your destiny?"

"Honestly, I think you guys are from the shallow end of the gene pool."

"Pardon?"

"You're a few sandwiches short of a picnic. Five cans short of a six-pack?"

An amused grin spread across his lips. "You are full of wit, Dr. Brenner. We will so enjoy your company. At first, even I resisted. I eventually heeded his call. And so shall both of you."

Without another word, he got into the driver's seat. He spoke a few words into the handset of a CB radio, then backed out of the parking lot and started to leave.

Chapter 32

Headlights streaked through dust as they descended the hill out of Sego Canyon. The red tail lights of the silver Tauris were getting farther away.

"Faster!" Amari cried. "This isn't a school zone."

"You want me to run off the road? There ain't much of it, you know."

Kevin accelerated a little, then slowed back down.

"Why are you slowing down?"

"You remember that water tank we saw on the way up here?"

"So?"

"There's a van coming down that road. His road merges into mine, and he don't look like he's stopping."

She glanced left and saw what he was talking about. A van was coming down the road, and he wasn't slowing down. If one of them didn't slow down, Kevin's Honda would be on the losing end of a collision.

He eased off the gas as the van approached. The van merged onto the road, then suddenly skidded to a stop.

"Look out!" she cried.

He stomped on the brakes. Tires dragged against dirt. The car came to a halt, just avoiding a rear-end collision.

The back door of the van flew open. A man wearing blue coveralls leapt out and rushed to Amari's side of the car, pointing a gun at her head. She recoiled away, her hands instinctively in the air.

"Get out of the car!" he yelled. He grabbed the handle and yanked the door open. "I said get out of the car. Keep your hands where I can see them. Both of you."

"Just do what he says," Kevin said, his voice strained with panic.

"Okay," she replied. "Don't shoot!"

She got out of the car, careful not to make any sudden moves, her hands overhead.

"Dr. Brenner," the man said, waving his gun to give directions. "Over here, next to your girlfriend."

Kevin walked around the rear of the car and stood by her side, hands reaching for the sky.

"Why couldn't you two just play along?" the man said. "It would have been fun. Like a little game."

"You think this is a game?" she said.

"Of course, it is," he replied. His face was acne pitted, and he had shark-like eyes, cold and indifferent. Unlike the other cult members, his hair was longer, black with hints of gray around his ears. "It's all a game—all pretend. You know that, and I know that, but those four guys you encountered just now think it's real. So why spoil the party?"

"I don't know what you're talking about," she said. "You're not with them?"

"Yes and no," he said. "It's complicated. I'll explain on the way. Now, in the van. We've got a long drive ahead of us."

"We're not going anywhere with you," she said.

Kevin stepped in front of her as a shield. "You heard her. We ain't going nowhere with you."

"You *ain't* going *nowhere*? This is the *brilliant*, Dr. Kevin Brenner?"

"So, I'm from Tennessee, what of it?" Kevin replied.

"Well, come on inside the van, and we'll chat a spell," the man said in a mocking tone, mimicking Kevin's accent.

"I told you we ain't going."

"Then you'll die right here," he said, narrowing his eyes like he meant business. "Game over."

Amari pulled Kevin out of the way. "Let me handle it. I've been trained for this."

"Trained for this?" the man said. "What, are you in the FBI or something?"

"We work for Ernesto Galliano," she said. "I'm a private investigator."

"Ernesto Galliano? You?"

"Small world isn't it?" Kevin said.

She pointed an accusing finger. "You know him, don't you? That was you who stole the Shroud replica. That was you who shot at us from the truck. It was you who flew off in the helicopter."

"Trevor, did you hear that?" he shouted toward the van. "This girl works for Ernesto Galliano." An amused grin of realization spread across his lips. "That was you on the phone. You were his supposed secretary, the girl that told Calvin about the exposition in Flagstaff. You're right, Dr. Brenner, this is a small world."

"Not really," she said. "We both have a passion for the Shroud. It's not that big of a coincidence. God brought us together."

"Did he now? Tell you what, get into the back of that van, and you can tell us all about it on the way."

"On the way where?" she said. "Where are you taking us?"

"Why, to fulfill your destiny, of course. You're one of the chosen," he said sarcastically. "Both of you are. Now, please step into that van before I choose a different destiny—a much shorter one." He cocked the hammer of his gun and aimed. "Now, please."

She glanced over at Kevin, and he shrugged back at her, clueless as to a solution. One thing was for sure, there was no way she or Kevin were getting into that van. She'd trained for this. She knew how to handle it. In his adrenalized state, the tiniest flinch on her part could cause him to reflexively pull the trigger, so timing was crucial. She had to find the right psychological break state, the moment his thoughts were distracted from the trigger, and do the unexpected. It would briefly take him off guard. And the best time to act was the moment after he ordered her to move. That way, he was expecting her movement and less likely to pull the trigger.

"Okay, fine," she said. "Just don't shoot. What do you want us to do?"

"I want you to get in the back of that van," he said, anger rising in his voice.

Now or never. "Okay," she said and turned toward the van. In a flash, she flung herself to the side, out of the line of fire. Her left hand gripped the barrel, and her right palm smashed against his wrist. The gun exploded a split second before she wrenched it free, sending it toppling to the ground.

She spun around and smashed her elbow into his jaw. He fell backward, giving her room to work. Her left leg anchored, she pivoted her hips and slammed his ribs with a roundhouse kick, the heel of her boot connecting hard against bone. She followed through, spinning around, connecting a 360-tornado kick to his head, her foot connecting square on his temple. He staggered backward, dazed, hobbling toward the van.

She snatched his gun from the ground and took aim just as he climbed through the back door.

"Don't move," she shouted. "Don't move or I'll shoot!" This time she meant it.

Suddenly, the van spun its wheels, sending dirt and rocks into the air. The rear doors slammed shut, and she watched them speed off toward Thompson.

"Oh, yeah!" Kevin yelled excitedly. "That's my girl!"

She caught her breath, smiling with satisfaction as she watched her attacker flee.

"Dang, girl, that trainer paid off big time," he said and folded her in his arms.

She hugged him back. That's when she felt it. Something warm and wet. She glanced down and noticed a crimson stain expanding on his white shirt.

Chapter 33

"We just got out of there," Amari told the Moab city deputy taking the police report. He was Native American, probably from the Ute tribe, located southeast of Salt Lake City. "I would have brought the gun, but I didn't want to disturb the crime scene. Besides, all I could think about was getting Kevin to the hospital."

"You did the right thing," Deputy Chee said. "The sheriff and I will head up there now. Probably contact the FBI since this was an attempted kidnapping. We'll be in touch with the Tucson authorities. They can follow up with any more questions." He tipped his hat and walked out the door.

Seconds later, the ER physician, Dr. Levine, walked into the exam room. He peered down through the thick half of his bifocal lenses at Kevin's chart. A black Jewish yarmulke fit perfectly inside the round bald spot on the top of his head. "When you get back to Tucson, I want you to follow up with your personal physician. I'm going to write you a prescription for antibiotics and something for the pain."

"Thanks, doc," Kevin said. "But it doesn't hurt much."

"Just the same, I'm going to keep you overnight for observation. If in the morning you don't show any signs of internal bleeding, I'll release you. I typically do my rounds at six in the morning, so if everything looks good, you can leave by seven."

"Thank you, doctor," Amari said. "I think that's a good idea."

"Come on, doc," Kevin pleaded. "There ain't no internal bleeding. It barely grazed my side. Hardly hurts at all."

"That's because of the meds we gave you already. We put it in your IV. Trust me, you'll feel it once that wears off. There's a pharmacy just down the street. You can get your scripts filled on the way home if you like."

When the doctor had left the room, Amari seemed to shut down, unable to maintain her outward illusion of strength. Careful not to mash his wound, she embraced him, grappling with emotion, struggling to hold back the tears. "Kevin, I'm so sorry. When I saw that blood, I was so scared."

He pulled free from her embrace and cupped her face in his hands. "Hey, it's okay. I didn't even feel it until you pointed it out. I was too hyped up on adrenaline."

"That's not the point. Just a couple more inches and that bullet would have hit your kidney. You could have died."

"And if we'd gotten in the van with that guy, we could have both died. You did what you had to do. And you were amazing at it."

"Still, I should have thought about you standing there. I should have been more careful."

"Hey, we're alive, aren't we? That means God wanted us to live. Everything happens for a reason."

"I don't know, Kevin. Sometimes I think the only reason is my own ego. Who am I to think God wants me to do this? I've been so arrogant to think he even noticed me, let alone had his hand protecting me. Maybe I shouldn't have taken this job. Like my dad said, it's too dangerous."

"And done what? Kept being an art major? The only people who paint worse than you are those cult members with their yellow stick figures."

"Hey," she said, playfully jabbing him in the arm with her index finger.

"Well, it's true. But this is in your blood. You were meant to be a detective. And you think being a real cop is any safer? Life is risky. We take risks just driving to work."

"I know, you're right. And I don't mind risking my own life. It's you I care about. I don't want to put you at risk."

"Your wants have got nothing to do with it. We're in this together. This is my choice, not yours. And if I get a scratch every now and again, so be it. We're going to be fine, Amari. Trust me. Someday in heaven, we'll both tell your mom all about this."

"I know," she said. "I'm just afraid at this rate we won't have many stories to tell."

"We will, Amari. Just believe. Sometimes, you just gotta live by faith."

Dr. Levine walked back into the room. "The nurse will be in shortly and take you to your room. I'll have your prescriptions ready before you're discharged."

"Won't need them," Kevin said. "Got a high tolerance for pain."

"At the very least, take the antibiotics. Otherwise, you'll get an infection."

"He'll take them," she said. "I promise, he'll take every last pill."

"Hey, thanks for everything," Kevin said. "But before you leave, can I ask you to look at something?"

"Something else hurting you?"

"No, nothing like that. I noticed that beany on your head. I take it your Jewish."

Amari's cheeks flushed, and she gave him a stern look. "Kevin, please, that is so inappropriate."

"That's just the pain medication talking," Dr. Levine said with a knowing grin.

"No it's not," she said. "He's always like that."

"Hey, sorry, doc, I didn't mean nothing by it, I just want to show you something." He pulled the Polaroid picture from the side pocket of Amari's purse and showed it to him. "Any chance you can read Hebrew?"

Dr. Levine took the photo and studied the image. "I know a little. Especially words that appear in the Torah."

"And those words? Underneath the two yellow stick figures?"

The doctor looked amused. "Is this some kind of joke?"

"Something like that," she said with a wry smile. "So can you read it?"

"Certainly," he said and handed the photo back. "It says the new Adam and the new Eve."

"The new Adam and new Eve?" she said. "Are you sure that's what it says?"

"I'm positive. I'll see you first thing in the morning. The nurse will be in shortly," he said and left the room.

She sat in stunned silence for a moment and then turned to Kevin. "So, it's true then. They really do believe I'm the new Eve. That's what Calvin implied on the videotape. And you're the new Adam."

Kevin just sat there, thinking, searching that brilliant mind for an explanation, seemingly in a daze.

She poked him on the arm. "Kevin, did you hear me?"

He shook out of his trance. "Oh, I'm sorry. I was just imagining what you'd look like wearing a fig leaf."

Amari snickered, caught off guard by his humor. Somehow, he always managed to make her laugh. "Kevin, I'm serious."

"So was I. Must be the pain meds."

"Must be," she replied. "But seriously, why would they think that about us?"

"Cause they're crazy, that's why."

"No, it's not that simple. There's a reason they believe it."

"Don't know, babe. Just do me a favor, would you?"

"Okay."

"You run across a snake, and he asks you to eat an apple, just pull a Nancy Reagan on him."

"Nancy Reagan?"

"Just say no, Amari. Just say no."

****

Amari had slept next to Kevin's hospital bed on one of those recliners that converted into an uncomfortable bed. She woke up with a backache, but no way was she leaving him, certainly not for a cheap motel. First thing in the morning, Dr. Levine had shown up as promised, and seeing that his wound was doing okay, he'd promptly discharged them. They were back on the road to Tucson by eight in the morning. He still had IV pain medication in his system, so Amari didn't trust him to drive. She took the wheel during the nine-hour trip home.

"I'm starved," he said as they approached the Tucson city limit. "You want to grab something to eat before we get home."

"Jenny said she'd have dinner waiting for us," she said. "I talked to her this morning in Moab before we left. I tried calling her again in Phoenix, but she didn't answer. She was worried about you and wanted me to keep her updated. We should have a signal now. Give me my phone, and I'll try again."

"Hands on the wheel," he said and pulled the phone from her purse. "I'll call her and tell her we're close." He dialed the number and waited with the receiver to his ear. "Hey, Jenny, it's Kevin. We're about thirty minutes out, so start setting the table," he said and hung up.

"That was rude. Why didn't you let me talk to her?"

"Cause it was the answering machine."

"That's weird. She said she was making meatloaf. She wouldn't leave the house with it in the oven."

"Probably in the bathroom. You worry too much. Why are you so paranoid?"

"Like I was paranoid about Sego Canyon? When you're a detective, you learn to listen to your gut."

"And what's your gut say about this?"

"Like yours. It's hungry. I'm sure you're right. She was probably getting the mail or something."

Chapter 34

At half past six in the evening, they were finally home. Amari parked the car in the circular driveway of her house, and they walked the steps to the front door. If Kevin was in any pain, it didn't show. If it weren't for the slight bulge the bandage made under his shirt, you'd never know he'd been shot. Good thing they'd packed an overnight bag. The other shirt was soaked in blood.

Just as they reached the top step, she stopped, turning her ear toward the door. "Kevin, you hear that?" Smoke alarms screamed from within. And then she noticed it—smoke seeping from the top seam of the doorframe. She rushed to the door and tried the handle. It was unlocked—not like Jenny. She shoved the door open, and they rushed into the foyer. The smoke was heavy and smelled of burnt meat. The oven timer chimed from the kitchen.

"Jenny!" Amari cried, waving smoke from her face as the alarm shrieked in her ears. She raced to the kitchen and saw the smoke billowing from the oven. She donned her oven mitts and flung the oven door open, smoke and heat assaulting her face. He grabbed the pan, dropped it into the sink, and doused it with water. A plume of hissing steam rose from the charred remains of meatloaf.

"I'll open the windows," Kevin said and hurried out of the kitchen.

"Jenny!" she yelled as she went about the house, searching every room.

She met Kevin in the master bedroom and helped him open the sticky window. "She's not here," she said and coughed, waving away smoke.

"Maybe she ran to the grocery store," he said.

"And left the meatloaf in the oven? That's not like her."

"Well, she ain't in the house. Let me run out to the garage and see if her car's there."

"Okay, I'll keep opening windows," she said and moved toward the guest bedrooms. "And see if you can shut that alarm off!" she yelled after him.

Finally, he silenced the alarms, and as she slid open the bathroom window, she noticed a man with glasses walking up the driveway. He was skinny, maybe late thirties. He moved toward the front door, but hesitated, as if reconsidering his actions.

She hurried to the front door. Maybe he knew what happened to Jenny. She opened the door and waited. "What are you doing here?" she said when he'd reached the top. "If you're selling something, this isn't a good time."

His face flashed with surprise, and his thick glasses slid to the end of his nose. He pushed his glasses back up to his eyes and opened his mouth to speak, but words seemed to escape him.

"I'm looking for my roommate," Amari said. "She's short with blonde hair. It's all teased up with hairspray. Have you seen her?"

He forced a toothy grin. "Uh, Amari Johnston, right?" he said, his Adam's apple bobbing on his thin neck.

"That's right." Her fists went to her hips. "Who are you?"

"Uh, do you mind if I come in for a second?"

"Do you know what happened to my roommate?"

"That's what I'm here to talk about," he said, an apologetic expression forming on his razor stubbled face.

"What do you mean—that's what you're here to talk about? If you know where she is, tell me now."

He held up his hands defensively. "This is complicated. Give me time to explain."

"Complicated? What's so complicated about going to jail?"

"Please, just let me talk."

She glared at him suspiciously, pondering the wisdom of letting this stranger into her home. Of course, he was no match for her. Not many men were, certainly not this skinny little twerp. So she finally stepped aside to let him in.

"Thank you, ma'am," he said and passed under the doorway. "Smells like something burned."

"All right, start talking. Who are you and what do you know about Jenny?"

"Let's just say my name's . . . Gary. Just call me Gary."

And then she noticed it—just north of his skinny behind, a pistol was tucked under his belt. Her reaction was automatic. She shoved her right palm into his shoulder, knocking him backward and off balance. With her left leg securely planted, she swept her right heel into his ankle, and down he went, clapping hard onto the floor. With ease, she flipped the skinny torso of the stunned man over, his chest to the ground. She wrenched his arm behind his back, and applied a firm hammerlock, pushing his wrist upward, sending a stab of sharp, restraining pain to his shoulder. With her free hand, she plucked his gun from his belt and sent it skidding down the tile floor.

"Wait, wait!" Gary cried in agony. "You're hurting me! Please, I'm here to help!"

Kevin rushed onto the scene. "Amari, you gotta stop this! Just tell him you don't need a vacuum and shut the door."

"Ouch!" Gary cried out again. "Please, you're going to break my arm!"

"It's your own fault," Kevin said. "Sign down the street says, 'no soliciting or handbills'."

"Kevin, that's not why he's here," she said, her knees firmly over his legs. "He's with that cult."

"Are you sure about that?" Kevin said. "His hair's too long, and I don't see any tattoos. His clothes are all wrong too."

"Please, I can explain," Gary said with a whimper.

"Go get my handcuffs!" she told him. "And get his gun. It's over there on the floor."

A moment later, Kevin returned. She cuffed Gary, helped him to his feet, and shoved him onto the couch. Kevin handed her Gary's gun, and she leveled at his chest. "Tell me what you did with Jenny!"

"I didn't do anything with her," Gary replied. "Not me. But I know who did. I'm here to help you get her back."

"I knew it!" she said. "Kevin, give me the phone. I need to call my dad."

"I thought he was in Fresno," he replied.

"He is, but I still need to call him."

"Before we call the police?"

"Yes, before that."

"I wouldn't do that," Gary said, an urgency in his voice. "If you call the police, or tell anybody, Jenny's life could be in jeopardy."

"Tell me where she is," she demanded, squeezing the gun handle hard. "Tell me now, or your life is in jeopardy." It was a bluff, of course, but he didn't have to know that.

"Okay, I admit it. I'm with the cult. Well, sort of, but not really. And they do have your roommate. But I can get her back. You just have to cooperate. Do us one small favor and you'll all be freed. Nobody will get hurt."

"Oh, really? Just like that? Is that why you tried to take us by gunpoint?"

"That gun doesn't have any bullets. Check it if you don't believe me."

The gun did feel too light now that he said it. She dropped the magazine and inspected it. He was right, no bullets. "Why would you carry a gun with no bullets?"

"Because Adrian told me I had to take a gun. So I did. But I never wanted to hurt you. So I took the bullets out. He said I had to take the gun. Never said anything about bullets."

She studied him as she digested his words. His facial expression and body language said he was telling the truth. Still, nothing about this guy made any sense. "That's crazy. Nobody brings a gun without bullets. That's a good way to get yourself killed."

"I'm sorry, but I'm not good at this. I'm just a pilot stuck between a rock and a hard place."

"Enough talking. Just tell me where you took Jenny."

"In my shirt pocket," he said, struggling against the cuffs behind his back. "There's a picture. Pull it out."

She set the empty gun on the coffee table and took the picture from his pocket. It showed Jenny with a gag over her mouth while someone pointed a gun at her head. She gasped at the sight. "If you hurt her, so much as leave a bruise on her arm, so help me God, you'll regret it!"

"Amari, cool that temper of yours," Kevin said. "Listen to what he's got to say."

"Okay," she said. "Spill it. You can start with your real name."

"My real name's Ian. Do I have to give you my last?"

"Of course, you do."

"Amari," Kevin said. "If he gives you his last name, then how's he going to get away with this? If they're going to let Jenny go, then obviously they don't want us to know their names."

"Fine, Ian, if that's your real name. Tell me what's going on."

"First of all, I don't belong to that cult. I'm a pilot—just a hired hand. Calvin's compound is in the middle of nowhere, out in the desert. He hired me to fly supplies in and out and take him places when he feels like it. Which isn't often. He's paranoid, always thinking people are following him. He's afraid if he goes out by car, someone will follow him back to his house. That's why I mostly fly stuff in and out."

"Now that, I can believe," Kevin said. "The paranoia goes with schizophrenia."

"You have no idea," Ian said, shaking his head in dismay.

"Believe me, we do," Kevin said. "We've seen his videotape."

"Then you know he's unstable," Ian said. "Then you know he's capable of anything if he doesn't get what he wants."

"Then what does he want?" she asked.

"Listen," Ian said. "These cuffs are cutting off my circulation. You know I'm no match for you. I promise, I mean you no harm."

Amari's pulse normalized, and she considered the request. This scrawny guy would be powerless against her and her martial arts training. There was no way he could take on both her and Kevin. Besides, she could spot a lie and so far, other than the name he gave her at first, this guy seemed to be telling the truth. Something about his demeanor told her he was sincere. And like he said, if he intended to hurt her, he would have put bullets in the gun. "Fine," she finally said. "Turn around. Kevin, hand me my purse."

After she got the key from her purse, Ian stood from the couch and turned his back to her while she uncuffed him.

"Thanks," he said, rubbing the red marks on his wrists.

Now that her adrenaline had subsided, she knew she'd been taking the wrong approach. Like her dad always told her—you attract more flies with honey than vinegar. "Let's go into the kitchen. Can I get you something to drink? A Coke or something?"

"Do you have diet? I'm a diabetic. Can't have the sugar."

They went into the kitchen, and she got a Diet Coke from the fridge and handed it to him. "Next time you guys kidnap somebody," she said, "could you at least turn off the stove?"

Ian took the Coke and sat at the table. "I promise, I had nothing to do with that. I was only sent here after the fact."

She and Kevin sat at the table with him. "So why are you here?" she asked.

"I'm here to convince you to help them. To help you get your roommate back."

"So what do you want from us?"

"First of all, like I said, I'm not a member of that cult. I'm just an employee. You see these glasses? I've got a condition called retinopathy. It comes from the diabetes. And unfortunately, I'm one of those rare people whose diabetes makes them nearsighted."

"So how are you a pilot if you can't see?" Kevin asked.

"I can see fine with glasses. I have no problem flying as long as I wear them. For now, anyway. The problem is, my condition will only get worse. So they yanked my pilot's license. Then a couple of years back, I get a call from an army acquaintance of mine. Adrian Agricola is what he calls himself now. I don't think he'd want me to tell you his real name."

"Was that the guy in Sego Canyon?" she asked. "The one who pulled a gun on us?"

"That was him," Ian said. "I had nothing to do with that either, by the way. Trevor, one of the cult members, he was driving the van. After they couldn't convince you to come with them, they came down here and took your roommate."

"You mean after she kicked the crap out of your friend, Adrian," Kevin said.

Ian snickered at the thought. "Yeah, after that, he realized he needed some leverage. He figured since you didn't mind risking your own life, maybe you would mind risking your roommate."

"How did you know where I lived, anyway?" she asked.

"It's no secret Dr. Brenner works at the University. They just followed him from work. Led them right to your house. They watched Jenny come and go, so they knew she lived here. They figured taking her would pressure you into helping."

"Well, it worked," she said. "You have my attention. Now, tell me more about this Adrian Agricola—or whatever his real name is."

"I knew Si . . . I mean, Adrian, from the army. I was a pilot in Vietnam. We were stationed on the same base. He was a paratrooper and jumped out of my plane. When Calvin built his desert compound, Adrian looked me up and asked if I was interested in being their pilot. I told him I lost my license, so he forged one for me. Well, not him, but he knows a guy. Cause that's what he does now. He's basically just a conman. All this started a few years ago after he got out of jail again. He was desperate to find a place to live. So he conned his way into a UFO cult. Eventually, he became their new leader."

"I'd rather be homeless," Kevin said.

"Sometimes Adrian would agree with you. Only back then, he saw an opportunity. Before long, he was the leader of the cult and keeping all the money for himself. Only now, Calvin's risen to the top. It was like some sort of mutiny, like they all seemed to identify more with Calvin's message than Adrian's. Now most of them follow Calvin and Adrian's getting paranoid. He thinks they're out to get him."

"So why doesn't he just get out?" she asked.

"That's what we both plan to do. Only we could use a little spending money. You know, to reestablish ourselves in society. Rent deposits, get a car, stuff like that. Fortunately, Calvin's loaded. He's got a trust fund from his father. He bought the airplane and helicopter."

"Hold on," she said. "You have a helicopter too?"

Ian held his hands up defensively. "Yes, that was me, but I had no idea what they were up to. They just told me to land on top of the parking garage, so that's what I did."

"So you and Agricola stole Ernesto's replica," she said, just to be sure she understood.

Ian shrugged and lowered his head in shame.

"But why?" she asked. "You didn't flinch when I just told you that was a replica. Obviously, you know it's fake. So first you try to steal the real thing, now a replica will do? That doesn't make any sense."

"Faith can move mountains," Ian said. "In Calvin's case, it can move his cash. All that matters is that Calvin believes it's real."

"That still doesn't explain why he wants it so bad," she said. "Is he sick? Does he think the blood on the Shroud can heal him?"

"No, nothing like that," Ian said. "That would be normal rationale. There's nothing normal about this guy."

"So why would he want it?" she asked.

"To get to heaven, of course."

"By committing grand theft?" Kevin said. "That ain't in the Bible."

"You have to understand their rationale," Ian said. "For them, everything is about technology. Christians might believe angels are watching over us. For these guys, angels are aliens hovering in UFOs, using cloaking technology to make them look like clouds. For them, the Shroud is nothing more than a complicated machine. It's how Jesus beamed himself into heaven—through a wormhole. Then he came back three days later once they'd fixed his body."

Amari snapped her head around to Kevin and gave him one of her *I told you so* looks. "A wormhole, huh? Wonder where they got that idea."

He shrugged. "Sorry, babe. I just report the facts. Ain't got no control over how people interpret them. We've talked about this before."

"I know, Kevin. I'm not mad, just a little weirded out." She refocused on Ian. "So let me get this straight. This cult believes the Shroud is some kind of portal. Like a gateway to heaven?"

"Something like that," Ian said. "Only for them, heaven is a system of planets they call New Canaan. You know, like the land of Canaan in the Bible?"

"So they basically believe Earth is Egypt and the new Promised Land is out there in the stars," she said to be sure she understood.

"You got it," Ian said. "In the Orion Constellation."

"*While he was still speaking, a bright cloud covered them, and a voice from the cloud said, 'This is my Son, whom I love; with him, I am well pleased.'*" A well-pleased smirk spread into Kevin's lips.

"Kevin, where did that come from?" she asked.

"It's verses like that that make them think about UFOs," Kevin clarified. "Only instead of God's voice, it was a loudspeaker on a flying saucer."

"Exactly," Ian said. "They take stuff from the Bible and mix it with science fiction. For them, there are no miracles, only technology—ultimate technology. The Shroud isn't a burial cloth. It's a technological portal." Ian pointed at Kevin. "And only Dr. Brenner here has the know-how to activate the portal."

Kevin's face flashed with surprise. "Calvin wants me to turn this thing on? You can't be serious."

"Only the great Dr. Kevin Brenner, the new Adam himself, has the knowledge to do so."

"This is insane," she said.

"Yep," Ian said. "And it's going to make Adrian and I a lot of cash. $200,000 to be exact."

"Now, hold on a second," Kevin said. "You're not getting a dime unless I can turn this thing on, right?"

"Exactly," Ian said.

"Then you ain't getting a dime," Kevin said. "What you want is impossible."

"Of course, it is," Ian said. "But Calvin doesn't know that. Look, don't worry about it. Adrian and I have this all planned out. We've got the parts. All you have to do is help us put it together and flip the switch. Then Jenny and the two of you can leave."

"Ian, you're not making any sense," Amari said. "Why is he giving you two hundred grand when Kevin's doing all the work? For a portal that won't work anyway?"

"That's the real crazy part," Ian said. "See, once Calvin beams over to New Canaan, he plans on flying a big spaceship back and land it on the airstrip behind his house. He's going to take his flock and anyone Adrian, and I can round up to come with him. He says there's room for hundreds on this spaceship."

"So you're going to be, like, missionaries?" she said. "You're going out to minister to the lost?"

"I know," Ian said, "Isn't it crazy?"

"So the money is for your expenses," Kevin said.

"That's right. Lodging. Advertising costs. It takes money to book lecture halls. How else are we going to recruit hundreds of people? We need cash to do that."

"Wow, it's always about the money," she said. "It makes total sense now. All of this is just a clever scheme to separate Calvin from his trust fund."

"He'd just blow it on something else if he didn't give it to us," Ian said as if that justified their actions.

"You know what, I don't care what the two of you do, or why you're doing it," she said. "I just want Jenny back. Tell us what we need to do."

"I need both of you to come with me to Calvin's compound," Ian explained. "But not as captives. As enthusiastic participants in God's divine plan. Trust me, you'll be treated like royalty."

"That's very flattering," she said. "And then what are we supposed to do?" A creaking sound came from the foyer, like a squeaking of a hinge. She turned her head toward the sound. She remembered she'd left the door open to air out the house. Maybe the wind was blowing it or something.

"Dr. Brenner builds the portal and flips it on," Ian said like it was the most natural thing in the world. "Then we give you the keys to a car. You take Jenny and leave while Adrian and I fly out in my plane. Call the police, have them raid the compound, and get Mr. Galliano's replica back. Send Calvin back to the mental hospital he escaped from."

"That sounds too simple," she said. "Like you said, Adrian's a conman. How can we trust him? How do I know he's not going to shoot us all once he gets his money?"

"Because you're the New Eve of Creation," Ian said. "Calvin and his followers would never allow you to be harmed. Adrian may have a gun, but so do they. And not one of those members wouldn't give their life to save yours. Trust me. You're safer inside that compound than you are out here."

"Oh, great," she said. "A crazy cult with weapons. And that's supposed to make me feel safer?"

"And like I said, every one of them would die so that you could survive," Ian reminded her.

"So what about Jenny?" she asked. "Will they allow her to be harmed?"

"Yeah," Kevin said. "She ain't royalty like us."

"They don't even know she's there. Adrian called me an hour ago. He has her locked in my trailer in the airplane hangar. Just do as I say, and I promise, Jenny will not be harmed. If you don't, who knows what Adrian is capable of. I wouldn't test him if I were you. I think your only option is to cooperate."

Amari sat pondering the offer. It seemed a small price to pay for Jenny's life. She opened her mouth to agree, but a rush a realization hit, and common sense prevailed. She couldn't believe she was actually falling for this. No way was she going with this guy. It could end up getting her and Kevin killed along with Jenny. There had to be another way. "No, it's not my only option. Kevin, hand me that phone. I'm calling my dad."

Just then, she felt a sharp pinch on her forearm. "Ouch, what the—" Then two baldies in jumpsuits came up from behind her—*cult members.* She clamored to her feet and took a defensive position beside the refrigerator, knees bent for balance.

Kevin sprang from the table and made for the door—probably to get his gun. One of them stuck out his foot and tripped Kevin, sending him hard to the floor.

"Kevin, you all right?" she asked, eyes darting back and forth between Ian and the cult members. She was trapped in the corner of the kitchen. The only way out was through them. "Get out of my house!" she yelled. "Or you'll be leaving by ambulance!"

The two cult members took the hint and backed off.

She chanced a glance down at her stinging arm and noticed something fuzzy and red stuck into her flesh. A wave of nausea hit, and the room seemed to undulate, clouded in a shadowy, white fog. She glanced at Kevin and saw him picking himself off the floor.

Ian stepped over and plucked the thing from her arm and showed her the needle tip. "I'm so sorry about this." His face appeared distorted. He seemed to be talking in slow motion. "This was plan B. We didn't want to do it this way, but you gave us no choice."

She dropped to her knees, unable to bear her own weight. She felt her muscles go limp. She felt like she was falling. And then the blackness closed in.

Chapter 35

Amari brought up her hand as a shield from blinding sunlight.

A surprised gasp of voices emanated from around her. "She's awake," one of them said. "Go get Calvin. She has awakened from the Lord's sleep."

She sat up slowly, dizzy, her mind in a stubborn fog. Her eyes adjusted to the light and she surveyed her surroundings. She lay on a mattress underneath some sort of glass structure, held into place by a lattice of white, steel braces. The wooden plank floor was painted gray. The sun-drenched structure was the shape of a pyramid, reminding her of the glass pyramid at the Louvre in Paris. Only in this version, a wooden crucifix hung from a chain from one of the corners, like a bizarre New Age style Christian church.

At least two dozen people stood whispering around her. The men's heads were shaved down to stubble, each dressed in coveralls. A handful of women were there too, only their hair was longer, and most wore light blue dresses that looked like they came from a uniform shop.

She locked her gaze on a woman with wrinkly, puffy bags under her makeup-free eyes. Her hair was long, streaked with gray, and covered with a light blue veil. Unlike the other women in blue, she wore an old-fashioned white dress, similar to those worn by Mennonite women. "Who are you?" Amari managed. "Where am I?"

The woman in the white dress knelt beside her. "I am known as 462."

"No, what's your real name?"

"My earthly name is irrelevant now. I look only to the future." The woman gripped Amari's wrist firmly. "Have you slept well? The Lord cast a sleep upon you so that Satan would flee. Now that you are here, your eyes are finally open. It is here that your destiny awaits."

Amari yanked her wrist free. "It wasn't the *Lord's* sleep. You drugged me. Where's Kevin?" She stood up slowly from the mattress, still a tad dizzy from sedation. Her eyes darted around the room at the clueless, brainwashed devotees. "Tell me where you took Kevin!"

"Right here, babe."

She turned around to see him standing, bathed in sunlight. She stepped off the mattress and fell into him for a hug. "I can't believe they did this."

"I know," he said as he returned her embrace. "I hardly slept a wink last night." He pulled away and looked at her with concerned eyes. "How could I when you wouldn't wake up? What if they overdosed you? For all I knew, that dart was meant to take down an elephant. What if you lapsed into a coma or something? What if you never woke up?"

"But didn't they . . ."

"Tranquilize me? No, they just overpowered me and tied my hands behind my back. You're the one they're afraid of. After you kicked Adrian's butt at Sego Canyon, he didn't want to take any chances. He's got a nasty, boot-heel-shaped bruise on the side of his head."

"I don't care about him. What about your wound?" she said, laying her hand gently on his side.

"Hardly notice it, not with everything going on. Stings a little when I twist too much."

"Careful not to pull the stitches out. And where's Jenny? Is she here?"

"She's fine. I've been with her all day."

"They didn't hurt her?"

"Not a scratch. She knew better than to put up a fight. She tried her psychobabble on them, but that's all."

"And did it work?"

"What do you think?"

"Kevin, we need to get out of here."

"And we will. Just as soon as I build their contraption. The parts were already here. Ian and Adrian dreamed this up ahead of time. They had everything waiting on me, including some rough blueprints of what they wanted. I'm about halfway finished already."

"Kevin, this is insane. What time is it anyway? How long have I been out?"

"It's 4:30. You've been out for nearly twenty-one hours."

"Twenty-one hours? Are you serious?" She looked down and took stock of her own body. Her black boots were still on, her stretchy, form-fitting jeans and long sleeve black shirt all remained intact. She hadn't been violated in any way, but the thought of being asleep with all those weirdos watching creeped her out.

"I was up at the crack of dawn," he said. "Come on. I'll show you. Stuff's in the hangar. I'm putting it together there since that's where all the tools are."

Suddenly, a sickeningly familiar voice called from behind. "He has left you. I can see it in your countenance."

Amari spun round to see none other than Calvin Nettles himself, strolling toward her with the slightest grin on his lips, a touch of joy glinting in his eyes. "Your trance has lifted. You are free at last. Rejoice and be glad," he said, his arms spread wide. He wore burgundy red coveralls, and his hair was clean, his face shaven. It wasn't at all like the man she'd seen on the video. He looked more like a man who'd been primping himself for a first date.

Amari stammered for words as she peered into his crazed blue eyes. "You must be Calvin," was all she could think to say. "Nice to meet you . . . I guess." She fell short of offering her hand.

"I am he. You are safe here, Miss Johnston. Satan has lost his grip. For this ground is holy, a sacred place of immense power. The devil dares not approach. Doing so would draw him like a magnet, back to the pit of hell."

She pondered her reply while glancing around at each naïve, eager face. There wasn't a trace of malice. Only benevolence showed in their childlike expressions as they regarded her and Kevin with awe. She felt oddly flattered—not angry and defensive like she had every right to be. Nobody in the room, Calvin included, seemed to realize that she had been drugged and kidnapped against her will.

"Now that the influence of Satan has abated, we welcome you to our family, as you must surely realize your destiny," Calvin said.

She replied with the only words that came to mind. "Calvin, you need help."

"I do indeed need your help. Both you and Dr. Brenner are crucial to the fate of humanity."

"That's not what I meant," she said, referring to the fact that he needed mental help. But because about three dozen of his devotees surrounded her, she decided to tread carefully, test the water a little before she said anything else.

"Then what did you mean?" he replied.

"Never mind. We'll talk about that later. Could you at least tell me where we are?"

"Somewhere safe," Calvin said and strolled over to the sloped glass wall of the pyramid. "No one uninvited may enter this place."

She followed him to the glass and studied the scenery. They were several stories off the ground, so she had a good view. Still in the desert, she assumed they were on the outskirts of Flagstaff, since that's where the call had been traced to. She noticed a runway and an airplane hangar in the distance. Surrounding the entire grounds was a tall fence with razor wire running along the top, reminding her of a maximum-security penitentiary.

"You see what I mean?" Calvin said as he pointed to the fence. "No one may enter, except through the narrow gate."

The razor wire fence reminded her of the one at Atascadero Mental Hospital. Getting over it would be impossible, so she had to find another way out. But the first thing she needed to do was locate Jenny and make sure she was safe.

She made assertive eye contact with Calvin. "I want to see Jenny. Now. Otherwise, I'm not going to help you."

A confused expression formed on Calvin's face. He didn't have a clue. "Who is Jenny?"

She glanced over at Kevin, and he was nodding his head vehemently as if to tell her to change the subject. She went to his side and whispered in his ear. "I forgot, Ian said he didn't know."

"That's right. Adrian hasn't told him," he whispered back. "He's afraid Calvin would go ballistic. They say he's got a nasty side."

Calvin spun around and stalked over to Amari and Kevin. "Are you discussing the portal? Is it almost finished? Last night, the voice said the time was upon us."

"Oh, yeah, right on schedule," Kevin said. "The Lord hath breathed his genius into my nostrils. The vapors of his knowledge settled onto my cerebellum. I went straight to work."

"Now who's talking crazy," she whispered.

"Just trying to fit in," he whispered back. "You ought to try it."

Calvin digested Kevin's words. Suddenly, his deadpan expression came alive with enthusiasm. "It is the power of the nexus. It repels evil and entreats the Holy Spirit." His face suddenly went blank as if he'd forgotten where he was, what he had been saying. Then he uttered some nonsense about a raccoon climbing the side of a skyscraper and stalked off toward a stairway that opened from the floor.

Chapter 36

Pete pounded on Amari's front door. "Open up, it's your dad!" This wasn't like her. Something was wrong. Kevin's car was in the circular driveway, and her car was under the carport, right next to Jenny's VW Rabbit. Unless they left by taxi, they should be home. He'd called her several times since returning from Fresno earlier that day, but nobody answered, not even Jenny. He'd even tried her portable purse phone but still no answer. She was concerned about his hip. She would have called to check on him, not the other way around. He tried the doorknob—it was unlocked, also not like her.

He stepped into the house cautiously and withdrew his sidearm, pointing toward the ceiling for safety. The air stank of burned dinner. "Amari," he called into the house. "Jenny, Kevin? Anybody home?" He listened intently for the slightest noise. There was nothing but the faint hum of the air conditioning. Thinking they could be out by the pool and unable to hear his voice, he stepped out onto the back patio. A trickling sound from the pool's irrigation and the dull drone of city traffic in the valley below was all he heard—no sign of his daughter. He went back inside and checked every room but found nothing suspicious, only windows that were left open to vent smoke. Then he remembered Ernesto's apartment, located above a separate garage, away from the main house. Maybe they were up there. He went into the kitchen with the intention of going out the side door. Something red on the floor caught his eye. He picked it up and inspected it. It was a hollow bore needle attached to a metal cylinder the size of a bullet shell casing. On the end was a red, feathery substance. He felt unsteady as realization dawned. It was a tranquilizer dart.

****

The Tucson police department had just wrapped up their investigation, leaving nothing but yellow crime scene tape in their wake. Pete's old partner, George, had stayed behind for moral support.

"They're calling the FBI on this," George said as he sat on the living room couch. "Field agents should be here tomorrow, maybe the next day."

"You and I both know the FBI will be useless," Pete said. "Other than that dart, there's not a shred of evidence to go by. The neighbors saw nothing. There's no sign of forced entry."

"Maybe we'll find some useful prints."

"Maybe so, but it'll take days for that to lead us anywhere. I'm about to crawl out of my skin, George." And then he remembered it. It was a long shot, but he'd take any shot he could get.

"What is it, Pete? You think of something?"

"It's not something I thought of. It was Amari's idea. Honesty, I thought it was a hairbrained notion, but right about now, I'll go for any idea at all. Help me find that book."

"What book?"

"It's some New Age nonsense book about the earth's energy." He went to the bookshelf and scanned the titles.

"Is this it?"

Pete turned to see George holding up a book.

"It was laying on the coffee table." George read the title. "*The Universal Pulse: Earth's Energy Grid*, by Brent Cagle."

"That's it," Pete said. "There's a map in it. Flip it open and see if you can find it."

George fanned the pages until he found a map in an appendix in the back of the book. "Right here."

Pete took the book from him and inspected the map. It was a round, black and white illustration of the earth. Lines crisscrossed the planet reminding him of a ball of yarn. He flipped to the next page and found an image of the United States, blown up to show more detail.

"X marks the spot," George said, pointing at the map.

"What's that?"

"You said you traced the call to somewhere around Flagstaff, right? Look at the map. One, two, three, four, *five* lines converge right under the Grand Canyon. That's just north of Flagstaff."

Pete pulled his reading glasses from his shirt pocket and used them to get a better look. His pulse quickened at the prospect. Suddenly, Amari's idea didn't seem so farfetched after all. "We need a better map."

"I agree. There's not enough detail in this one."

Pete inspected the map closely, then ran his finger the short distance to Flagstaff. "As a crow flies, I'd say that's less than fifty miles from Flagstaff. That's easy helicopter range."

"Then I say this is no coincidence. What are the odds?"

"Still not great, but it's all we've got."

George flipped to the front cover of the book. "I wonder if this Brent Cagle has a more detailed map. Maybe we can look him up."

"Or go see Rocky," Pete said.

"Balboa?"

"No, Rocky Stone. He's a geology professor at the university."

A grin spread on George's mustached lips. "You're kidding me. A geologist named Rocky Stone?"

"That's just Kevin's nickname for him. He's got another first name, but I can't think of it."

"How many Dr. Stones could there be in the geology department?"

"Not many. He's the guy who gave Kevin this book. He knows all about this supposed energy grid."

"Then I bet he's got a better map."

"Exactly. With any luck, he can give us exact coordinates."

Chapter 37

Amari followed Kevin down a stairwell as they made for the ground floor. "We can go out the garage since that's the side closest to the hangar," he said. "The roof's just a big glass atrium, so they do their living on the first four floors. There's a kitchen and dining hall, maybe two dozen dormitory rooms, and a big den with a bunch of couches and chairs. They've even got a rec room with air hockey, pool tables, and foosball. Calvin's got a big ole bedroom all to himself, and Adrian has his own room, only it's a lot smaller."

They reached the ground floor, and she noticed a couple of guys go downstairs into some kind of basement or cellar underneath the house. They carried a large gas tank between them.

"There's a supply room and laundry down this hall," he continued. "All the way to the end is a little barber shop so they can keep their hair short." He stopped at a door and opened it. "This is it—the garage."

She followed him into the garage and immediately noticed several more gas tanks lined up like big bowling pins in one of the corners. "What are all those tanks for? Is that propane or something?"

"If they were propane, it wouldn't be so weird," he said. "Those are nitrogen tanks."

"Nitrogen? What do they use that for?"

"Don't know for sure, but I've got a theory."

"Let's hear it, then. This ought to be good."

"Cryopreservation."

"You mean like freezing themselves?"

"The Orion Belt is over a thousand light years away. One of them told me that even at warp nine, it would take nearly a year to get there. That's a lot of food and water to carry. It's more efficient to freeze yourself and thaw out once you get there."

"This gets weirder and weirder by the minute."

"At any rate, it's just my theory. Nothing's better at making a human popsicle than liquid nitrogen. And they better be careful playing with that stuff. You can suffocate on pure nitrogen gas and not even know it. You'll go to sleep and never wake up. That's why they use it sometimes to euthanize animals, even human executions. It's considered a humane way to die."

"Has anyone warned them?"

"You think they'd listen?"

"I doubt it. But right now, I just want to see Jenny. I'll worry about them later."

They walked out of the garage and crossed the desert floor, heading toward the airplane hangar. On the way, they encountered a large white satellite dish jutting from the desert ground. Under the shade of the dish, wires converged inside a metal junction box. One wire came out of the bottom. She followed the black wire with her eyes as it stretched along the rocky soil toward the main house.

"So what's with the satellite dish?" she asked. "From the size of this thing, they ought to get good reception."

He smirked. "Yeah, that's not what you think it is. They got no TV. It's for listening to God."

She held up her hand to silence him. "I've heard enough. Just tell me where Jenny is. I want to see her. Now."

"Before we go, I need to warn you about something," he said and squinted his eyes against the sun, gazing warily at the metal airplane hangar that stood off next to the runway. "Adrian's in there with Ian. The three of us have been working all day, assembling the portal."

"You're working with the guy who shot you? You can't be serious."

"Have you looked around? We got no choice. It's our best way out. I'm telling you this because I don't want you to freak out when you see them in there. We just gotta do this thing, and then we can leave, understand?"

"I'll try. But it's not like me to stand by while Ian and Adrian play their stupid charade to cheat Calvin out of his money. I'm a cop's daughter, remember? They're breaking the law."

"You want them to add murder to their crimes? You go in there throwing Kung Fu kicks, and you're going to get us all killed. There's two more cult members over there, and they have guns."

"They're not going to touch us. Remember, they worship us."

"Not these guys. They're not believers anymore. When Calvin took over, they sided with Adrian. They might be a little crazy, but they aren't the Calvin kind of crazy, and they wanted out. But look around you. They're trapped, just like we are. So Adrian's going to give them a cut of the money, and they're bugging out too. Only they want their money first. So I'm telling you, unless you want another tranquilizer dart in your arm, you need to mind your manners."

"Fine, Kevin, I'll go along. But I'm known for a lot of things, and being polite isn't one of them," she said and trudged toward the hangar.

He rushed to her side and matched her hurried gait. When they reached the tall, wide opening to the corrugated steel structure, a heavyset cult member dressed in dark navy-blue coveralls blocked their entrance. He had a severe underbite that reminded her of a bulldog. He was also the guy who had tripped Kevin in the kitchen and one of the guys who had kidnapped her. She eyed him with contempt and took a defensive stance.

"It's okay, Trevor," Kevin said. "She's on our side now." He gave her a stern, coaxing look. "Isn't that right, Amari? We're on the same team, remember?"

"If it'll get Jenny back," she said. "So why did you call him Trevor?" She pointed to the tattoo on his arm. "What about 438?"

"Yeah, Trevor here had a little crisis of faith," Kevin said. "He's gone back to his real name. You mind letting us pass, Trev? Adrian's expecting us."

Trevor grunted his approval and stepped aside so they could pass. Inside, a white airplane with twin propellers was parked to the right side. A black, Toyota pickup truck was parked next to the plane. Farther back in the hangar was a helicopter, no doubt the one used to steal the Shroud replica. In the very back of the hangar was a small mobile home, apparently belonging to Ian so he could keep his distance from the rest of the cult. Then she noticed another member dressed in gray coveralls, standing next to the helicopter with his arms folded across his chest.

"That's Darryl," Kevin said. "AKA, Lieutenant Junior Grade 342."

"Another backslider?" she said sarcastically.

"Yeah, well, this backslider is the one who shot you with the tranquilizer dart. He's got the gun sitting in a chair over there next to him."

"I'll remember that," she said, rubbing the raised welt on her arm where she'd taken the dart. She was still groggy from the last one. Maybe Kevin was right. She should go along for now and see how this played out.

"Those ranks sound familiar to you?"

"You mean Lieutenant? Ensign? It's like in the military, only the crazier you are, the higher the rank?"

"No, like the United Federation of Planets. They got those ranks from watching Star Trek. Each rank gets their own color coveralls."

"It figures," she said.

"See that guy in seal-blue coveralls over by the workbench? The one with the blowtorch?"

"Adrian Agricola," she said, eyes narrowed in disgust. If she didn't recognize his face, then she'd recognize the boot-heel shaped bruise on the side of his head.

"Commander Agricola," Kevin corrected. "That's what the seal-blue represents. He's the equivalent to Commander Riker on Star Trek. He's second in charge, right behind Captain Calvin, who gets to wear burgundy red, like Captain Picard's shirt."

"You mean, like, Jean-Luc Picard?"

"You got it."

"It figures. So why don't Calvin and Agricola have numbers for names?"

"Jenny says the number system is meant to dehumanize. It strips their individuality, so they'll feel like cogs in a big wheel. They do what they're told, no questions asked. Once you rise to the top like Calvin and Agricola, you get to be human again. It means you're a cut above the rest."

"Well, well," Adrian said, apparently just noticing who had walked in. He snuffed the flame on his blow torch and set it on a workbench covered with tools. "Look who we have here. Did you sleep well?"

"Where's Jenny?" she snapped. "Tell me where she is. Now!"

"Relax, she's fine," Adrian said and walked closer. "In fact, she's enjoying herself."

Her eyes were drawn to the bruises on his face.

"I know, I look terrible. It hurts as bad as it looks."

"You deserved it," she said. "Now tell me where Jenny is, or this time I won't be so gentle."

"Sassy. I like that. But unless you're ready for another nap," he said glancing over at Darryl, "I wouldn't try anything. Not every member belongs to Calvin's camp. Trevor has a real gun. He won't hesitate to use it if he needs to."

"Are you going to tell me where Jenny is or not?"

"She's learning to fly," Adrian said, pointing to the airplane.

Just then, Jenny climbed down from the plane with Ian right behind her.

"She wanted to see inside," Ian said.

"I've never sat in a cockpit before," Jenny said. "It's so cool. All those buttons and knobs. How do they ever keep them straight?"

A wave of relief washed over Amari, and she rushed over and gave Jenny a hug. "Are you okay?" She released her embrace. "I figured you were tied up or something."

"Where am I going to go?" Jenny replied. "There's a twelve-foot fence with barbwire surrounding the entire compound. And they have guns, did I mention that?"

"You're not going along with this, are you? Do you know what they're planning to do? They're conning that man out of $200,000."

"It's actually $240,000," Adrian clarified. "I reminded Calvin that inflation would be high during the apocalypse. Talked him up forty-grand. Twenty apiece for Trevor and

Darryl. A little something to start their new lives once they escape this prison."

"I don't like it any more than you do," Jenny said. "But what am I supposed to do? Might as well get along. Isn't that right, guys?"

"Jenny, this is crazy."

"No," Adrian said. "Calvin is crazy. And he'll never miss that money. You might as well stop resisting and go along." He pointed to the silver Ford Taurus. "Once we get our money, then you can take that car and drive on out of here. The keys to the front gate are in the glove compartment."

"And why would you let us go, just like that? We can identify you. You couldn't take the risk."

"Calvin's not going to hand us the cash until the portal is ready. You and Dr. Brenner will be surrounded by his followers. They would never allow me to harm you. If I tried, it would cost me my life. I'm expendable, but you're essential to the plan."

Amari looked at Jenny. "What do you think? You believe him?"

"He has a point," Jenny said. "If they're going to kill us, they'll have to kill all forty of them. Those people in there worship you and Kevin. Literally. When they put on their show, you'll be right in the middle of them. Just go along with this so we can get out of here. Ian's couch is murder on my back. And I really need a shower."

"Fine," Amari said with contempt. "I'll do it, but I don't have to like it. You guys may get away with this for now, but someday you're going to get caught. You can't run forever."

"Finally," Adrian said. "I knew you were a smart girl. Almost as smart as Kevin."

"So let's see this thing," she said, glancing over at the workbench. A welding torch stood off to the side, next to an air compressor. A cooler labeled *dry ice* was sitting next to it. Sheet metal and wooden planks leaned against what looked like a tanning bed. She did a doubletake and inspected it more closely. "Is that a tanning bed? *That's* your wormhole maker?"

Adrian and Ian snickered. Jenny shook her head in dismay, and Kevin just looked a little embarrassed.

"You're going to get Calvin into heaven by giving him a tan?" Amari said.

"I can't take credit for the tanning bed idea," Adrian said once he'd regained his composure. "That was Ian's idea. And a good one too. The Shroud is fourteen feet long and three and a half feet wide. It's a perfect fit. We attach the bottom part of the Shroud to the foot of the tanning bed and lay it flat on the bed. Calvin will lie down on this just like the man in this Shroud."

"That's sacrilegious," she said. "Only Jesus has the right to lay on that cloth."

"It's only sacrilegious if you are religious. Do I strike you as a man of faith? Besides, this Shroud is only a fake, remember? It's a fake of a fake. Now how is that sacrilegious?"

"You're going to burn for this," she said.

"Ironically, that was the tricky part—keeping it from burning, that is. Let me show you." He reached into a box and pulled out Ernesto's Shroud replica. He carefully unrolled the tan linen and smoothed it out over the lower glass panel of the tanning bed. It was the underside of the Shroud that revealed the bloody scourge marks from the Roman flagrum. The top portion of the Shroud that contained the face and front of the body was still rolled up. He gripped the Shroud at the point where it folded over Jesus' head. "We had to redo the hinges, so it would fold down like scissors. You know, like a clamshell," he said, mimicking the action with his hands. "Ian special ordered these heavy-duty hydraulic pistons. They weren't cheap, but it was the only way. Now the trick was getting the spacing just right so that the back of the head and the face would line up perfectly when Calvin laid down on it. We have some double-sided tape to affix the front of the Shroud along the top glass panel. When it folds down, it'll make contact with Calvin, just the way this cloth supposedly made contact with Jesus' face. All we have to do is energize this thing, and Calvin will be on his way to New Canaan," Adrian said sarcastically.

Amari stared, stunned beyond words at what she was witnessing. She could see the anguish on Kevin's weary face too. He was only going along because he had no choice, not if he wanted to get his cousin and girlfriend out alive.

"Another tricky part is deciding what to do with the Sudarium," Ian said. "The Bible said it was folded off to the side. There's no indication it was on the body during the resurrection."

"Supposed resurrection," Adrian corrected.

Ian never replied, seemingly lost in thought.

"I suggested they just lay it on a table off to the side," Kevin said. "Just like in the Gospel of John. Any miscalculation and this thing ain't gonna work. Well, I mean if it was ever going to work."

"If you had any idea how offensive that is to Christians," she said.

"And if Christians are right, then I suppose I will burn," Adrian replied with nonchalant arrogance. "But as I said, that's the challenge. Not burning the replica before Calvin has a chance to lay down on it. Turn it on, Ian. Let her see what I'm talking about."

Ian went to the workbench and picked up what looked like a standard wall light switch. Wire ran from the switch to the control panel of the tanning bed.

"Fire it up," Adrian said.

"It's not groundbreaking science," Ian said. "But it's pretty cool to watch. Here goes." Ian flipped the switch.

A popping sound came from the tanning bed. Underneath the glass of the upper panel, a blue electric arc stretched the width of the glass. Starting at the bottom, the glowing arc bent and contorted as it moved along the length of the bed until it terminated at the top. Almost immediately, the arc reappeared and the bottom, and danced its way to the top again, popping and spitting as it went.

"This thing is going in the cellar," Adrian said. "It'll be dark so the light from the electric arc will show right through the Shroud replica. The bottom panel will do the same thing. Only we haven't hooked it up just yet."

"It's called a Jacob's Ladder," Kevin said. "One pole is positively charged, and the other has a negative charge. That causes the electric arc to jump the distance, just like when lightning is attracted to the ground. We had to put it underneath the glass. Otherwise, it would catch the Shroud on fire—and electrocute Calvin, of course. That wouldn't be good either."

"Isn't that ironic?" Adrian said. "The Jacob's Ladder is the Biblical stairway to heaven. It's exactly what Calvin wants."

"Only this isn't a stairway, but a wormhole maker," Ian offered.

"We have black lights built underneath the Jacob's Ladders to bathe the room in an eerie purple light. Smoke will billow from the portal and spread across the ground, thanks to a block of dry ice."

"You can't be serious," Amari said. "Is that what you came up with to fool Calvin?"

"Not just me. I hired an electrical engineer to draw up the designs." He pointed to schematic drawings laying on the workbench. "And he wasn't cheap, let me tell you. I told him this was going inside a haunted house next Halloween. Of course, I didn't have the know-how to put this together. That's why I needed Dr. Brenner's help. Conveniently, his first degree is in engineering."

"Mechanical, actually," Kevin said. "But I've read up on electrical too."

"Calvin's never going to fall for this," she said. "This is about the stupidest thing I've ever seen."

"He'll believe it if Dr. Brenner tells him to," Adrian insisted. "After all, he's the new Adam, remember? He's a modern-day prophet. What he says goes."

"And then what?" she asked. "What happens when he realizes the portal doesn't work? What are those forty people going to do then?"

"What do I care? He's handing over my cash before he gets in. Ian and I will be taxiing down that runway before he figures it out."

Amari looked to Jenny for her opinion. "Do you really think this is going to work? Is he that crazy?"

"I hate to say this," Jenny said, "but yes. Sometimes, people believe what they want to believe, and he wants badly to believe this. They all do. In their minds, their very survival depends on it."

"There, you have a professional opinion," Adrian said. He picked up the blowtorch, turned on the gas, and held a flint lighter to the tip. Blue flame jetted out of the torch with a muted roar. "Now, if you don't mind, we have work to do."

"Then let us go home, and I'll stop bugging you," Amari said.

Adrian pointed to the main house. "That's your new home until we finish our performance. If you hurry, you'll just make it in time for dinner."

"I'm not going anywhere without Jenny and Kevin."

"I can't leave, Amari," Kevin said. "Sooner I finish this thing the sooner we leave. Besides, Ian's got frozen pizza in his trailer. I ain't eating their crap ever again," he said and pointed to the main house. "But you're a health nut. You'll probably like it."

"Then I'm taking Jenny."

"Not a chance," Adrian said. "If Calvin finds out about her he'll go nuts, pardon the pun. Besides, she's my collateral. She's the only leverage I've got. Let's just do this thing, and all three of you can be on your way back to Tucson. Now run along, you don't want to miss dinner. Trevor, Darryl, go with her. Make sure she behaves."

Chapter 38

The spartan dormitory style bedroom Amari had been assigned had only a twin bed and a nightstand with a lamp. A small closet offered storage. A community bath down the hall served the needs for the entire floor, just like the typical college dormitory. Ironically, she noticed that her room was directly underneath Calvin's large bedroom. She had a feeling they did that on purpose, some sort of symbolic meaning.

It was after three in the morning, and she was still wide awake, her thoughts racing, pondering the best strategies for escape, wondering what to do if everything didn't pan out the way Adrian had said it would. She thought about Jenny and Kevin over in that hangar, wondering if either one of them were asleep, wondering if both of them were safe.

Of course, after being knocked out for over twenty hours, she wouldn't be sleepy under any circumstances. The gnawing hunger in her gut didn't help. She never did eat Jenny's meatloaf, and the tasteless block of tofu and multivitamin they'd served up for dinner did little to satiate her appetite. Not that she even noticed the taste when she was surrounded by so many strange admirers. It was a surreal experience. They'd treated her with utmost reverence and respect despite her insistence that she was just a girl like anyone else. Concerning their beliefs about her being the next Eve, she chose to stay off the subject, knowing that there are two things you should avoid during dinner discussion—politics and religion. The last thing she needed was a heated argument, especially since these people had guns. Like Jenny had insisted, when you are this outnumbered, the best thing is to just play along.

The strangest part of the evening had been her own feelings. She'd only known these people for a few hours, but already she'd found an emotional connection. They were like children, really. So kind to her and so innocent in their motives. And there were certainly no signs of the arsenal of weapons Adrian had mentioned, not that she could see, anyway. All they seemed to want was to belong to something greater than themselves, just like any Christian. They just wanted to obey the will of God, like the original disciples, and if need be, they would freely give their lives for the cause. And that's what bothered her the most. It was their seeming detachment from reality and equal willingness to detach from the flesh if called to do so. In fact, several expressed their fear of being frozen in cryopreservation. And if no cryopreservation was offered—nobody really knew what to expect—others were concerned about the monotony of a yearlong voyage in a cramped spaceship. Naturally, they wondered why they couldn't just go to New Canaan in the spirit, to be granted a new body after arrival instead of waiting to have their current bodies glorified.

She couldn't help flashing back to the conversation she'd had with Jenny about Jim Jones and his cult—the ones who killed themselves in Guyana back in 1978. These people had no problem going to heaven by committing suicide. Neither did that cult member in Turin. And what about those nitrogen tanks? Cryopreservation? Really? Was that their real purpose? Or was their true purpose something much more sinister? When the portal failed to transport Calvin to New Canaan, would they use that nitrogen as a humane way to end it all? After all, if there was no spaceship, then cryopreservation wouldn't be an option, would it? How long would it take them to realize that the only way to heaven was death?

Suddenly, a voice caught her attention. It was loud enough to penetrate the walls, but where was it coming from? She heard more muffled voices, like a conversation. It sounded like two men. She sat up and strained to hear. It was coming from up above, from Calvin's room. One of the voices seemed to be Calvin's, but the other was distorted like an echo had been added to the voice for dramatic effect. The sound seemed to cast vibrations into the wall and ceiling—like speakers would do. Maybe Calvin was just speaking into an intercom, perhaps instructing one of his minions to get him a glass of milk or something. There was no telling. She pressed her ear against the wall to see if she could hear better, but as soon as she did, the conversation was over, and a blanket of silence fell over the room.

****

Amari startled awake. A knock came from her door, and she heard Kevin's voice on the other end. She had managed to doze off after praying herself to sleep. Talking to God always soothed her anxieties. Even after the trauma of being drugged and kidnapped, his comfort still managed to offer her a couple hours of sleep.

Kevin stepped into the bedroom holding a carton of milk and something greasy wrapped in a paper towel. "Brought you some breakfast," he said. "The rest of the congregation have already eaten—more tofu with orange Tang. Ian said to bring you this. It's a microwave sausage biscuit and some milk."

"Ian gave you that?"

"Yeah, he didn't think you'd like what they were serving. I think he feels kind of bad about tricking you."

"He ought to feel bad." She took the biscuit and inspected it.

"It ain't poison. I had one too. Better eat up because this is the big day. I've been working most of the night. We got the portal in the cellar already. For this thing to work right, it's gotta channel the earth's energy. The ground of the cellar is nothing but dirt. That way the portal makes direct contact with its mother."

"Its mother?"

"Mother Earth. We're sitting right on top of the nexus—the convergence of ley lines. Can't get any more intimate than that. The portal's plugged into a 220-volt outlet, but you need a whole lot more juice to form a wormhole. That's where big mama comes in."

"I think you're actually enjoying this."

A wide smirk spread across his lips.

"Kevin, this is not funny."

"I know, but you gotta see the humor."

"I think you're delirious from not sleeping."

"Probably right. My brain's pretty much toast. At any rate, I need to hurry. We're putting up the metal frame so it ain't so obvious it's just a tanning bed. Calvin claims he heard the voice of God last night. Says this is the day and not to delay."

"The voice of God? That's what he said?"

"Well, sure, God talks to him through that satellite dish outside. A spaceship beams him the message from orbit," he said like it was the most normal thing in the world.

"Kevin, that wasn't the voice of God. I heard it too. It didn't sound like the Creator of the Universe to me."

"We'll talk about it later," he said. "Eat up because I think they expect you to join them for morning prayers. Darryl and Trevor said they'd come get you after you ate."

He kissed her on the cheek and started to leave. She grabbed his arm and stopped his advance. "Where are you going?"

"Gotta finish the portal. The sooner we finish, the sooner Calvin gives Adrian the cash. Then we get the keys to the car."

"What about Jenny?"

"Her hair's an awful mess. Other than that, she's fine. She just wants us to finish up and head on out of here."

He broke her grip and went to the door.

"Kevin, wait, I'm not done asking questions."

"We got plenty of time for that later. Let me finish up and I'll come get you when we're ready."

Chapter 39

George and Pete waited in the hallway of the geosciences department at the University of Arizona. They stood in front of Professor Stone's office. According to one of the grad students, Dr. Stone usually showed up at 7:15 in the morning to prepare for his first lecture. It was 7:30 already and Pete was getting anxious.

"Maybe he went straight to the lecture hall," George said. "Maybe he doesn't always stop at his office first."

"Give him ten more minutes," Pete said. "If he doesn't show, then we'll find out where he teaches class. I'll pull him out of his lecture if I have too."

Jangling keys sounded down the hall, and a thirty-something-year-old man approached carrying a tattered, leather briefcase. The buttons of his shirt were misaligned, giving it a lopsided appearance. His trousers were too long, and they raked the ground as he walked, causing the bottom hem to be worn and dirty. The man went to his office door and started to insert the key into the doorknob but paused to glance over at Pete and George. "Can I help you with something?"

"I sure hope you can," Pete said. "Are you professor Stone? I can't remember your first name, but Kevin calls you Rocky."

"You must mean Dr. Brenner," he said with a knowing smile. "People with brilliance in one discipline normally have a deficiency in other areas of thought."

"Oh, yeah?" George said. "What's Kevin's flaw?"

"His tragically corny sense of humor. I've heard the psychology department wants to study his brain. So how do you know Dr. Brenner?"

"He's dating my daughter," Pete said.

"So you're Amari Johnston's father? Detective Johnston?"

"Former detective," Pete said. "Retired. I'm in private investigation now."

"I'm not retired," George said and showed him his badge. "Mind if we come in and talk?"

"Be my guest. I'm curious to hear what Dr. Brenner said that has you up so early."

Pete wasted no time. He pulled the book from his pocket and dropped it on Dr. Stone's desk. "I was hoping you could answer some questions about this."

Dr. Stone sat at his desk and picked up the book. "The *Universal Pulse: Earth's Energy Grid*, by Brent Cagle. I thought Kevin would enjoy that. It's right down his alley."

"Dr. Brenner studies geology too?" George asked.

"No, I gave him that book because of his corny sense of humor. I thought he would appreciate it more than me."

"So you think this is crap too?" Pete said.

"I wouldn't say all crap. Just mostly. Certainly, the earth has powerful magnetic properties. It's what protects us from the sun's radiation. But the notion that there are highly energetic ley lines that offer some sort of supernatural power is nonsense. I published a paper debunking such a notion. That book was part of my research."

Pete picked up the book and fanned the pages until he found the dog-eared map of the United States. "Since you researched this, I was hoping you could provide a little more detail. In particular, this map. You see how all the lines converge in northern Arizona? I was hoping you had a more detailed map, something with actual coordinates."

Dr. Stone frowned in thought. "That's an odd request. You're not one of those UFO hunters, are you?"

"Listen, Dr. Stone," Pete said. "I don't have time to explain my rationale. But I'm telling you, this is life and death. It involves my daughter and Dr. Brenner. They've been kidnapped by a religious cult, and I have good reason to believe those coordinates could help us find them. Please, could you just give me the coordinates?"

Dr. Stone's face flashed in surprise. "I see."

"Don't tell me I need a warrant for this."

"No, no, not at all. Just a moment." He went to a filing cabinet and started sorting. "What did I file that under? I have a map somewhere." He slammed the drawer shut, jerked open the drawer just beneath it, and sorted files again. "Got it," he said and removed a map. He went to his desk and spread it out. It was a black and white rendition of the Southwestern United States. He pointed to the part where several curved lines converged. "That's the nexus. Where all the ley lines come together. Hypothetically, this spot should be the source of great power—if you believe that kind of thing. It looks like it's just south of the Grand Canyon."

Pete and George leaned in for a closer look. "And the coordinates? I need some exact coordinates, something a pilot could use."

"They're penciled in right next to it," Dr. Stone said, tapping on the map with his finger. Latitude 35.962, longitude minus 112.031. You say you're going to have a pilot fly over this?"

"We think that's where the cult calls home."

"Makes sense, if they believed in that sort of thing. Just keep in mind, according to the pseudoscience behind this nexus point, anywhere in a radius of twenty miles from these coordinates would hold great power. So even if you don't find anything at these exact coordinates, keep searching. I went up there a couple of years ago with some equipment to see if I could measure this energy. It's a desolate area. Almost no houses, just a few mobile homes. If it's a religious cult, then they should have a fairly big house. If you fly low enough, I'm sure you could spot it from the air."

"You mind if I borrow the map?" Pete asked. "I promise I'll bring it back."

"Keep it, if you need to. Anything else I can do, just let me know."

"Thanks, Dr. Stone," Pete said and folded up the map. "If I find Dr. Brenner, I'll tell him he owes you one."

****

Later that morning, Amari found herself with the cult members, upstairs in the atrium. Darryl and Trevor had escorted her there, then abruptly left so they could help finish up the portal downstairs. The rest of the congregation faced the crucifix hanging down from the white steel ceiling trusses. Instead of their rank designating color-coded coveralls, this morning they all wore white robes with leather sandals strapped to bare feet. The room reverberated with the sound of singing, like Gregorian chants from a Roman Catholic church. They seemed in a meditative trance as they took turns singing well-rehearsed verses. It was hauntingly beautiful, and she couldn't help but be spiritually moved, surprised by their sincere, yet misguided dedication to Christ. And then she wondered what would happen when the portal failed. Would that same misguided faith lead them into mortal sin, that of taking their own lives?

The sound of their voices brought her thoughts back to other voices—the two she heard upstairs last night—Calvin's voice and the voice Calvin believed to belong to God. What if she could prove the voice of God was no more than part of an elaborate, greedy hoax? Then, when the portal failed, maybe everyone would leave the cult altogether and rejoin their families and attend a traditional church. All she had to do was find the speakers hidden somewhere in Calvin's bedroom. Maybe they'd still need more convincing, but finding those speakers was a good place to start.

Chapter 40

Ryan Airfield was a small airport fifteen miles west of Tucson. Serving as the general aviation reliever airstrip for Tucson's International airport, it served mostly recreational pilots with smaller aircraft. Pete had called the night before, requesting the use of Ernesto's plane. Skip had the plane fueled and ready when Pete and George finally arrived at the airport. Bonelli and Parker had come along for support. Skip was prepared to circle Northern Arizona until he ran out of fuel if necessary, anything it took to get Amari, Kevin, and Jenny back.

At a quarter past nine in the morning, Pete followed George up the ladder of Ernesto's twin-engine Learjet. Skip sat in the pilot seat doing his preflight checks. Bonelli and Parker sat in the front two seats, eager to help, with binoculars in hand.

Pete went into the cockpit and handed Skip the already unfolded map. "All right, Skip, the coordinates are right here." He pointed to the numbers penciled onto the map next to a red X. "You think you can get us there."

Skip read the coordinates. "No problem," he replied. "This plane has a cruising speed of 500 miles per hour. I can be at those coordinates in thirty minutes. Twenty-five if I floor it."

"Then put the pedal to the metal," Pete said. "The sooner we find this place—if there's anything there to find—the sooner we can get cars on the ground to investigate."

"I'll call in the flight plan," Skip said. "We'll be in the air as soon as we get the all clear."

"What do you mean, the all clear?" Pete asked. "What if they deny your flight plan?"

"Then I'll tell them the radio had a lot of static and I misunderstood," Skip said with a wink. "We'll get a fat fine and Ernesto will pay it." He started flipping switches, and the engines whined to life. "Better buckle up, Pete. This could get bumpy."

****

Amari sidestepped slowly toward the staircase. Nobody seemed to notice. She hurried down two flights of steps, ran down the hall, and stopped in front of Calvin's bedroom door. She hugged the wall with her back and listened, glancing back and forth to be sure no one followed. Amari found the door unlocked and stepped inside, cringing at the sound of squeaky hinges. She gently closed the door behind her and surveyed the room. Sitting atop an ornate oriental rug, a king-size canopy bed with thick wooden posts stood against the wall. A purple curtain hid the mattress within. Next to the bed was a large, closet-sized combination safe. It rivaled a bank vault, and she wondered how they could have carried such a heavy safe upstairs. What could be inside that Calvin felt so compelled to protect? Money, jewelry, or something more? She could only imagine.

She shook off the thought and went to work, scanning the walls and ceiling for any sign of speakers. She went to the nightstand and inspected the lamp, then picked it up and looked underneath. She slid open the top drawer of the nightstand and flinched at what she saw—a silver Colt .45 pistol. A thought occurred to her. Maybe she should take the gun and hide it. She could tuck it into her jeans and pull her shirt over the top. And then what? Shoot her way out? And have Jenny and Kevin get caught in the crossfire? And what if Calvin discovered his gun missing? Wouldn't she be the first suspect? No, she wasn't that desperate yet. But if she ever needed a gun, at least she knew where to find it.

Suddenly, the faint sound of singing came to an end. She knew it was only a matter of time before they discovered she was gone. She had to hurry. She closed the drawer and kept searching. She pulled back the purple curtain and inspected the massive wooden headboard. Then she went to her knees and searched under the bed, looking for speaker wires. Nothing. She crawled across the floor to inspect the other end of the bed, the hardwood floor under the rug firm against her knees—until it wasn't. She eyed the floor suspiciously and knocked on the soft spot with her knuckle. A satisfied smile spread onto her lips.

"Gotcha," she said and pulled back the rug. Sure enough, there it was. Embedded into the hardwood floor was a speaker underneath a protective perforated metal plate, just thin enough to give a little under the weight of her knee. This was the other voice she'd heard last night. And it was so loud because it was only inches from her ceiling. Poor Calvin wasn't hallucinating at all. He didn't just hear voices in his schizophrenic head, but a real voice emanating from the floor. All this time, Adrian had been giving Calvin instructions, pretending to be the voice of God.

From the bathroom, she heard a toilet flush. "Crap!" she said and dropped the rug. She hadn't seen Calvin upstairs in the atrium, and now she knew why. He was on the toilet instead. She went to her feet and peaked around the canopy curtain. She heard water running. He was washing his hands. Now or never. She made for the door, but before she reached it, a voice called from behind—Calvin's voice.

"Miss Johnston? Is that you?"

She spun around to face him. His hair was disheveled, pillow marks making a crease on his cheek. His normally expressionless face now registered surprise.

"Oh, hey, Calvin. I was uh . . . just looking for the bathroom," she fibbed as she fumbled for words. "All that Tang I had this morning went right through me." She couldn't believe she just said that, but she couldn't help herself. She'd never felt more awkward in her life.

"And there for a moment, I thought you wanted in my safe," he said with the slightest of grins, his feeble attempt at humor.

"Yeah, I see that," she said. "It's a nice one. You'd need a pound of C-4 to crack that sucker."

"I can't be too careful. My last dime is inside that safe. Over two million dollars."

"Did you say two million? In that safe?"

"I don't believe in bank accounts anymore. Just a few forged papers and your money disappears."

"Well, can't be too careful . . . I guess." It was getting more awkward by the second.

"Would you like to use my restroom? It's far more private than our other facilities."

"You know what, I don't feel like I can go anymore. That ever happen to you?"

"Are you sick? Did our dinner not agree with you? I couldn't imagine a blander meal."

"No, no, the tofu was excellent. It's just . . ." She closed her eyes and sighed, pondering her next move. She hated lies. She'd always prided herself in telling the truth, and now here she was, telling a lie, to avoid the cold, uncomfortable truth. It was time to up the ante. "Look, I'll be honest. I wasn't looking for a bathroom. I'm here because I heard voices last night. Coming from this room."

Calvin caught his breath. "You heard it too?"

"How could I not hear it. My room is right underneath yours."

"Then you know the time is near. Even at the door. Perhaps even today."

"Honestly, I couldn't hear that well. I just heard muffled voices."

"Yes, one voice was mine, the other of God himself."

She straightened her posture and made firm eye contact. She had to confront his delusions head on. "No, Calvin. Not the voice of God. There's something you need to see. I think Adrian is conning you."

"Whatever do you mean?"

She bent down and pulled back the rug to reveal the speaker underneath. "That's the voice you heard last night. It wasn't coming from God. It was coming from that speaker."

"Well, of course, it was coming from that speaker."

She dropped the rug, his response taking her by surprise. "Excuse me?"

"There's another speaker on the other side of the bed. I had those installed myself, one on each side of the bed. That way I can hear the voice of God in stereo."

"I don't get it. You know that's only a speaker?"

"How else would I hear the voice? The satellite dish outside receives his signal, and the speakers convert the signal to sound. God uses technology for his divine purpose. In heaven, there is ultimate technology. There are no miracles, child, only misunderstood technology."

Of course, he would say that. She should have realized that before. "Calvin, please. This is crazy. You need help. Let me get the help you need."

"Indeed, I do need your help. That is why you are here. The future of humanity depends upon your womb."

"That's not what I mean. Calvin, what if the portal doesn't work? Then will you believe me?"

"Have faith, child."

"But what if it doesn't? What will you do then?"

A somber look crept into his face. "The thought had occurred to me. I suppose in that case we would all arrive in New Canaan simultaneously. No spacecraft would be needed. If the portal fails, we would simply take the traditional path. New bodies will be provided. Incorruptible bodies, robots made to look human."

The nonchalance in the way he spoke chilled her to the bone, as his words confirmed her fears. He wouldn't hesitate to take his own life, as well as the lives of his entire flock. To him, it seemed the only pragmatic choice.

Suddenly, Trevor appeared in the doorway. "Calvin, the portal has been installed. Dr. Brenner says it's ready to go."

"Excellent," Calvin said. "The sooner I reach New Canaan, the sooner I can return for you."

"Come with us, Ms. Johnston," Trevor said. "You are about to witness history."

Or be a part of history, she thought. *Just like Jim Jones.*

Calvin and Trevor jogged down the hall. "The time has arrived!" Calvin yelled. "Everyone to the cellar, the time has arrived!"

She knew what she had to do. She went to the nightstand and removed Calvin's Colt 0.45. She lifted her shirt, tucked it under her belt, and dropped the shirt back over it. One way or another, she was getting Kevin and Jenny out of there—before it was too late.

Chapter 41

The Learjet's engines thundered as Skip had the throttle wide open, racing to the exact coordinates indicated on Rocky's map, the convergence of energy ley lines, the nexus believed to focus the power of Mother Earth.

"Hey, I can see the Grand Canyon," George said as he looked out the window.

Pete sat in the seat directly behind him. "I see it too, but somehow I doubt their compound is on the canyon floor." Turbulence rocked the plane, and Pete knocked his head against the window. He shook off the pain and brought the binoculars back to his eyes. "Never mind the canyon. Keep a lookout for a big house, maybe several houses clustered together."

"How about a runway?" Bonelli said. "You see it? You can just make it out. Over there by the dry streambed."

Pete spotted what he was talking about. Sure enough, what looked like an airstrip was smack in the middle of the desert. He went to the cockpit and tapped Skip on the shoulder.

Skip pulled off his headset so he could hear. "You see something?"

"Over to your left," Pete said and pointed. "There's an airstrip. Do you see it?"

Skip searched the ground until he spotted it. "I see it now. Have a seat and hold on. I'll veer over there for a better look."

Pete took the copilot's seat. The plane banked left, and he could feel the drop in altitude in his gut. "When you get close, turn the plane so the windows face it."

Skip hiked a thumb in agreement and continued his descent.

Pete went back to the seat behind George and waited. After a couple of minutes, the plane banked to the right. Now, out the plane's left window, the runway was clearly visible. Only a small dirt road led away from the airstrip. There was fencing as well. Sunlight glared on the roof of the main house. It looked to be some kind of atrium, maybe a greenhouse or something, only it was the shape of a pyramid.

"Is that a satellite dish?" George said.

Pete grabbed his binoculars and saw what George was talking about. "It sure is. And it's a big one. Too big for satellite TV."

"You're right," Parker said. "That dish is NASA grade."

"It's like they're listening for signals," George said. "From little green men."

Pete went back to the cockpit. "Skip, is that runway long enough to land a jet?"

"I'll have to really lay on the brakes, but sure, it's long enough."

"Then take it down. If it turns out we got the wrong house, we'll tell them we got lost."

"Or engine trouble," Skip offered.

"Or whatever. Just get us on the ground."

****

Amari peeked around the corner, watching the cult members eagerly walk down the stairs into the cellar. She wondered if Kevin was in there. If he was, then she had to get him out. With everyone huddled around the portal, it offered a perfect chance to escape.

Then she noticed the door to the cellar. It was made of steel with thick heavy-duty hinges. Affixed to the door was a handle, but the lock was one of those that didn't have a knob, but rather a key was needed to open it from either side. Once the door was locked, only that key offered a chance of escape. She had no time to waste.

When the last cult member descended, she made her move. She went to the top of the doorway and peered down inside. Tiki torches were stuck into the dirt ground, emitting eerie, flickering orange light, black smoke rising and settling into the ceiling trusses. Other than the torchlight, the cellar was completely dark, giving it sort of a primitive feel, like it would have looked in the days of Jesus when they gathered at night, illuminated only by the light of oil lamps.

She spotted Kevin by the portal. He was fiddling with some wires on the back. She waved for his attention, but he never noticed. She didn't like it, but she was going to have to go in. At least she had Calvin's gun. That offered an advantage.

"Don't be shy," someone said from behind.

She turned to see Adrian Agricola, standing several feet way—safely outside the range of her roundhouse kick. He made no indication that he noticed the bulge of a gun under her shirt.

"The performance is downstairs," he said. "Don't you want a front row seat?" He waved her down the steps with the barrel of his gun. "I have no intention of staying for the encore. I hear this show is overrated."

Reluctantly, she descended into the darkness with Adrian several steps behind. The air was already stale from lack of ventilation, even though the smoke from tiki torches was still confined to the ceiling rafters.

Kevin noticed her and rushed over. Nobody from the cult seemed to notice him as they were enthralled by the newly unveiled portal. He pulled her aside and stood between her and Adrian. "Remember our deal," Kevin said. "Once he hands you the check, you leave, and then we leave right behind you."

Hands him the check? she thought. Calvin said he had no bank account. Something wasn't right. And then she saw them, in each one of the four dimly lit corners—the nitrogen tanks she'd seen in the garage.

The door slammed shut, and Trevor and Darryl descended the stairs, weapons drawn.

She turned to Kevin. "We need to get out of here!"

"As soon as I flip this thing on," he said. "At least wait for the fireworks."

"That's so true," Adrian said. "What's the hurry? Trevor and Darryl will keep you company." He turned his attention to Kevin. "Maestro, if you will," he said sweeping his hand dramatically toward the portal.

Kevin looked to her as if asking permission, clearly leery about leaving her back there with Trevor and Darryl.

She widened her eyes to give him a warning, tilting her head toward a cluster of nitrogen tanks.

He got the hint. "I'm not flipping that thing on until I talk to her," he told Agricola. "In private."

"But you're not the one holding the gun," Adrian replied. "I make the rules."

"Listen, buddy. I'm in no mood for this. I've hardly slept in two days, and my side still hurts from where you shot me the first time. And your food tastes like crap. I'm not touching that switch until I talk to her first."

Surprise registered on Adrian's arrogant face. "Temper, temper, Dr. Brenner".

"You ain't seen nothing," Kevin shot back. "We both know you're not going to shoot me down here. Not till I flip the switch. Now back off before I get ugly."

"Have it your way," Adrian replied. "But the only exit is that door," he said and pointed to the stairway. "And it's locked tight." He then walked over to speak to Trevor and Darryl.

"Kevin, we have to get out of here. Now!" she said just above a whisper.

"I know, I know," he said. "I saw the tanks too."

"When that portal doesn't work, they intend to kill themselves—and take us with them!"

"I know, babe. Looks like they've got their Plan B. But I think we should let this thing play out. When the portal doesn't work, there's gonna be chaos. We'll make our break then. Only problem is that lock. Did you notice? We need a key to get out."

She remembered Calvin's Colt 0.45 tucked under her belt. "Don't worry. I have a key. A big one. Just hurry and do what you need to do."

He looked confused.

"Trust me," she said. "Go do your thing so we can get out of here."

"Brethren!" Calvin's voice boomed. "Hear my voice!"

Adrian came up to them, his gun leading the way. "Chat's over." He pointed to the portal. "Dr. Brenner, if you don't mind. You gave me your word you would do this—in exchange for Jenny's safety." He nodded toward Amari. "And hers as well."

"Let's do it then," Kevin said. "And then we're out of here, understand?"

"Understood," Adrian said. He waved for Trevor and Darryl's attention. "Keep an eye on her. Keep her back here with you."

Kevin followed Adrian to the far end of the cellar where the portal was set up. Amari moved in for a better view, but Trevor and Darryl were still close behind. The portal sat on a raised stage, right next to a breaker box. It was plugged into the wall with one of those big plugs you see with a clothes dryer. The lower part of the portal was obscured by a black, rectangular box to provide the illusion that it was far more than just a tanning bed rigged with an electric arc generator. Another deceptive casing masked the top section of the tanning bed. Sturdy hydraulic hinges held the top panel up and away from the bottom, forming an angled opening.

The Shroud replica was stretched along the bottom of the portal, then wrapping around the hinge and onto the top section. The Sudarium of Oviedo was folded and set off to the side, atop a stone pillar to bring it to the same level as the portal. Ironically, the Sudarium seemed to have nothing to do with the rest of the portal. It was merely placed to the side, just as described in the Gospel of John. As Kevin had told her earlier, they didn't have the time or imagination to figure out how to incorporate it into the portal. If Calvin were to ask, Kevin had planned to tell him the Sudarium was a homing mechanism used to direct Jesus back to Earth during the resurrection. Since Calvin planned his return in a spaceship, no extra rigging was necessary.

Adrian stood front and center, his hands raised in celebration. "Finally, the time has arrived! The portal is complete, and Calvin will soon be in paradise! But rest assured, he will return and land his craft just outside these walls. Then you will see him again. Finally, you will be on your way, to your new home—to the glorious planets of New Canaan!"

Adrian stepped aside and gave Calvin the stage. Shouting and cheers came from the congregation, and one of them pressed the record button on a video recorder that sat atop a tripod.

Calvin hushed them with his hands, and the group gradually fell silent. "As you know, my brethren," Calvin said, a somber look on his face, "the time for my departure has come. You will look for me but will not find me. Where I am going, you cannot come. But this is only for a time. For as soon as I am permitted, I shall return for you, God willing, in no longer than one year. Until such time, just as he led you before my arrival, so shall Adrian lead you again. As previously discussed, he will leave intermittently to minister to the lost of this world. He must gather more sheep unto our flock. And so, to lead effectively, Adrian will also require all of my resources. As I promised him earlier, before my departure, I will allow him access to my safe, so that all your needs are met. I trust you all will be good stewards of my fortune. Store up food and water for our journey."

Calvin placed a trusting hand upon Adrian's back. "Adrian, it is time for you to resume control. Until now, I have kept the combination to my safe a well-guarded secret. But no more. Go to my bedside. In the nightstand, you will find a Holy Bible. Turn to Matthew 19:24 and you will find the combination to my safe written on that page. Use the balance of my wealth to sustain the flock. Then, upon my return, whatever remains shall be donated to the lost sheep of this world. For in order for us to enter New Canaan, we must first unload our pack."

Amari's jaw fell open as she understood Calvin's words. He was giving Adrian his entire fortune of $2,000,000. That was Adrian's plan all along—not to get just part of Calvin's money, but all of it.

Adrian faked a solemn expression. "Thank you, Calvin. Matthew 19:24. I swear to you, I will be a good steward of your fortune. May God bless your journey. I look forward to your return." Adrian bowed respectfully, stepped off the stage, and moved back into the congregation.

"Dr. Brenner," Calvin said. "You may now activate the portal."

Amari watched Adrian slip to the back of the cellar and quickly ascend the stairs. She had no doubt where he was headed.

Next, Kevin stepped up onto the stage and went behind a podium that was next to the portal. She waited for him to speak, expecting a flowery bon voyage speech Adrian had written for him.

"Here goes," was all he said, and he pushed the first button. Lights on the portal flickered on. Long fluorescent bulbs along the top and bottom edges of the box came to life. They were black lights, emitting a purplish glow, causing the white robes of the congregation to glow in contrast to their now darkened faces. Surprised gasps came from the group, and they clamored quietly among themselves.

Kevin flipped another switch. Heavy, odorless dry ice fog billowed from vents at the base of the portal and hugged the ground as it steadily spread across the dirt floor, obscuring the feet of the congregation. More gasps and louder chatter filled the room. Calvin was silent, but his eyes were wide with anticipation.

Then Kevin flipped a final switch. A crackling sound came from the portal. A blue electrical ark was visible underneath the Shroud replica. Simultaneously, on both top and bottom halves of the portal, radiant blue, jagged lines of an electrical ark stretched the width of the portal, wavering as they danced the distance of the tanning bed. Once the blue arc reached the end, it repeated the process, starting over at the other end, the spooky wavering blue light dancing underneath the replica's image of Jesus.

More gasps rose from the group, and the chatter got even louder.

Transfixed in awe, Calvin stood there for a long moment, mumbling to himself. Finally, he looked to Kevin for guidance.

"All you gotta do is lay down in it," Kevin said. He went behind the portal and retrieved a cylinder hand switch with a red button on top. "Climb in, she's all set to go. When you're ready, lower the top part using this handle, take you a deep breath, then push this red button." He turned his focus to the rest of the group. "Now, I recommend everybody stand at least five feet away. For safety reasons. Wormholes ain't nothing to play with." He stepped off the stage and ushered everybody back. Once they started to comply, he slipped through and joined Amari in the rear. "Now would be a good time to leave," he told her.

"What happens when he pushes the button?" she asked.

"Absolutely nothing. That's why we need to leave." He looked around the cellar as if he'd lost something. "Where's Adrian? Did he give you the keys to the car?"

"What do you think? But I know where he is." She reached behind her and retrieved the handgun. "Cleaning out Calvin's safe. We'll catch him in the act."

"Where'd you get that thing?"

"I'll explain later." She glanced over to see Calvin laying down in the portal, the top section lowered, the blue electric arc flashing over his crazed face. He was mumbling something, perhaps a parting prayer. "We gotta get out before he pushes that button. I don't want to be here when nothing happens."

They made for the stairs. Trevor and Darryl stepped forward and blocked their advance. She leveled the gun on them, and their faces registered surprise. They instinctively raised their hands.

Kevin reached over and took the tranquilizer gun from Darryl's waistband, then took the gun away from Trevor.

"Get out of the way," she said.

"We were told . . .." A tranquilizer dart struck Darryl before he could finish the sentence. He staggered backward, clutching at his neck.

"That's for Amari," Kevin said. He dropped the tranquilizer gun and leveled the real gun at Trevor's leg. He pulled the trigger, but nothing happened, not even a click. He pulled it again—nothing.

Of course, Adrian had rigged it so it wouldn't fire. If he were going to cheat Trevor out of twenty grand, no way would he give him a working gun.

Suddenly, Darryl collapsed to the ground. As Trevor watched him fall, she landed a hard kick square on his kneecap, causing him to topple in agony, clutching at his knee.

"Let's go," she said and hurried up the stairs.

Kevin ascended with her. When they reached the top, they found the door standing open. They rushed into the hall and stopped to get their bearings.

"This way," she said. "Calvin's room is upstairs."

He grabbed her arm to stop her advance. "Leave him. We don't need his key. I'll hotwire the car."

"He'll be busy digging the cash out of the safe. I'll have the high ground."

"Amari, just leave him," he pleaded.

"No, he's not getting away with this!" she said and headed up the stairs. He ran up behind her.

They reached Calvin's room, but she stalled at the door, gun readied, building her courage. She turned the knob and rushed in, gun out in front. The safe's door was open wide, only a few stray hundred-dollar bills left on the floor.

"We're too late," he said, breathless from climbing the stairs.

"Wow, that was fast," she said.

Kevin spotted something out the window and went to investigate. "Ian's got the plane parked outside. I bet they're flying out. Just forget the money. Let him have it. We gotta check on Jenny."

"You're right. Only . . . what about the cult?"

"What about them?"

"Kevin, they're going to kill themselves. We can't let that happen."

"You really think they'll do that?"

"Would you take that chance? All it takes is for one of them to lock the door and for another to open the gas canisters. Most of them won't know what hit them. They'll just fall asleep and never wake up."

"All right, tell you what," he said. "Take that gun and blow the lock off the door. That way, anyone who wants to leave is welcome to it. But if they're determined to kill themselves, I'm not sure there's anything we can say to stop them."

She pondered the thought and knew he was right. "All right, we'll do it your way. It's better than nothing."

They raced down the stairs and went to the cellar door. It was shut. She reached for the handle—locked.

"I knew it!" she said. "Stand back. I'm going to blow the lock!" She aimed and squeezed the trigger. A shot rang, but nothing happened. "What the . . ." She shot again, still nothing. "I can't believe this." She flipped the switch to drop the magazine, letting it fall into her hand. She inspected the bullets. "Blanks! They're nothing but blanks!"

"Of course, they're blanks," Kevin said. "Adrian wouldn't give Calvin a live weapon either."

"You have a pocket knife. Can you get the hinge pins off with that knife?"

"Not a chance. Those are thick hinge bolts. The blade would bend like a wet noodle."

"Then what are we going to do?"

"Crowbar. The van's in the garage. You know it's got a crowbar for changing tires. We'll pry the hinge pins off with that."

"Kevin, you're a genius."

"I know," he replied and made for the garage door.

Chapter 42

They rushed into the garage and stumbled mid-stride, stopping just short of running into Adrian and Ian. Startled by the intrusion, Adrian and Ian stood quickly and locked eyes with their unexpected guests. They had been stooped over the garage floor pulling stacks of hundred dollar bills out of overstuffed backpacks that were so full the zipper wouldn't close. Adrian stuffed bundles of cash into his coveralls, and Ian stuffed money into his flight suit.

Adrian leveled his gun at Amari and Kevin. "I was afraid you wouldn't stay for the party downstairs. Now back away, please. We've come this far, don't make me shoot you now."

She and Kevin complied and moved to the back of the garage.

"We should have brought bigger backpacks," Adrian said. "Can't get the zippers closed."

Amari glared at him in outrage. "Because that's more than $200,000!"

"It's ten times that," Ian offered with a grin.

"So that was your plan all along?" she said.

"Pulling this scheme off was a lot of trouble," Adrian said defensively. "If you're going to do something, then do it right. And where's Trevor and Darryl? I thought they were looking after you."

"They're a little incapacitated," Kevin said.

Adrian went back to work and stuffed two more stacks of hundreds into his coveralls and zipped it tight, lumps of cash bulging underneath. "That's a shame. But, more money for us, I suppose."

"Look, I don't care what you do," she said. "Just take your money and go. All I care about is Jenny and those forty people down there."

"They're going to be disappointed," Adrian said. "I was hoping to not be around when Calvin found out. Those guys can be dangerous, you know. Very unpredictable."

"They're not a danger to anyone but themselves," Kevin said. "We think they're gonna take their own lives, using that nitrogen gas."

"Is that what they wanted the nitrogen for?" Adrian asked, acting all innocent and unaware. "What about cryopreservation?"

She pointed her gun at him. "You knew exactly what they plan to do."

"Don't worry about them," Ian said.

"You know that gun has blanks in it," Adrian said.

She tossed it aside. "Tell me something I don't know."

"You're right," Adrian said. "You take care of your friends down there. It'll give you something to do, something to pass the time while we fly out of here."

"That's all I want," she said. "Take your money and leave."

A high pitch roar shrieked from outside, vibrating the closed aluminum garage door. Adrian quickly glanced at the door, then returned his watchful eye to Amari. The thunderous sound only grew louder. Adrian went to the garage door button on the wall and mashed it. As he watched the door rise, he recoiled at the site.

Amari gasped in surprise. Ernesto's Learjet came to a stop maybe fifty yards away. The hatch came open immediately, and four men clamored out. Bonelli, Parker, George, and her dad.

"Just in the nick of time," Kevin said.

"Dad!" she shouted. "Careful, he's got a gun!"

Adrian quickly stepped behind Kevin and shoved the gun into this back. "Out in front, Miss Johnston. Don't think I won't shoot him."

"Hey," Kevin said, clearly offended. "You're supposed to take the girl hostage. She's the damsel in distress."

"You think I'm stupid?" Adrian said and hefted up the backpack stuffed with cash.

"You want my honest opinion?" Kevin replied.

"Shut up!" Adrian shouted. "Miss Johnston, out in front or he gets it in the back."

"Okay, okay," she said and moved to the front.

"Ian," Adrian said. "You get behind me."

"Why me?" Ian said. "So I can stop the bullets?"

"Don't argue with me," Adrian shouted. "Just do it!"

"Amari?" Dad called out. "Is that you?"

"Stay back!" she cried. "He's got a gun!"

"Faster," Adrian said, prodding them toward Ian's plane.

Amari hurried toward the plane without protest. Once inside, it would be a confined space. She could get the jump on them then—unless he shot her first. She glanced over her shoulder and noticed that her dad, Bonelli, Parker, and George had fanned out, putting distance between themselves. Her dad shouted orders, but he was too far away to understand, especially over the Learjet's idling engines.

When they reached Ian's plane, the rear door was already open.

Adrian waved them both up into the plane. "I haven't got all day!"

Kevin climbed the short ladder up into the plane first, then Amari went in after him.

Adrian tossed his cash-loaded backpack inside but stalled at the door before climbing in. "Go to the rear of the plane! Into the cargo hold."

"Better do what he says," Kevin said and ushered her to the rear.

Adrian clamored into the plane and quickly retrained his gun back to her and Kevin. Ian tossed his bag of cash inside, came up the ladder, and turned to close the door.

"Leave it open," Adrian shouted. "Go start the engines and get us out of here!" Once Ian went to the cockpit, Adrian leaned out the door, aimed his handgun, and fired off four shots.

"Dad!" she cried and started to her feet.

Adrian slammed the door shut and leveled the gun back at her. "Relax, I was aiming at their plane's front tire."

"I can't outrun a Learjet!" Ian cried back from the cockpit.

"I shot out the front tire," Adrian called back to him. "Or at least I think I did," he uttered to himself.

"What was that?" Ian called from the cockpit.

"Never mind. Just get us off the ground!"

The twin engines sputtered to life and growled as the plane lurched forward and to the left. She grabbed onto the cargo net, holding on against the inertia.

Adrian fell into a seat, but as soon as the plane righted itself and began accelerating down the runway, he went to the cargo hold and latched the netting into place. "I know this netting won't hold you for long, but it'll hold you long enough for me to shoot you if you try anything funny. Now sit there and relax. When we start to land, I'll tell you when to hang on."

"Where are you taking us?" she demanded to know.

"Just stay on the floor and keep your mouths shut." Adrian strained against the acceleration, then finally relented and sat back down on a leather seat that seemed to hide a toilet underneath.

The G-force from takeoff forced her and Kevin against the carpeted rear of the cargo hold, which angled up with the shape of the tail section.

Adrian waited for the plane to stabilize before talking again. "I've got a buddy meeting me at an isolated airstrip. Once we land, Ian and I will drive off with him. There's a small town maybe five miles away. By the time you two make it there, we'll be long gone. The sheriff can take you back to Calvin's compound, and you can meet up with your father and Jenny. Like I promised you, everything's going to be fine as long as you don't cause any more trouble."

"That sounds like a plan," Kevin said. "We'll be good, won't we, babe?"

"Where are you taking us?" she asked. "What town are you talking about?"

"I understand you're half Navajo," Adrian replied.

"So?"

"So you'll appreciate where we're going. It's a little town called Borrego Rock. It's on the Southwest corner of the Navajo Nation. Maybe I'll buy lunch there and leave a big tip. Help your people out a little."

"There's an airstrip in that town?" Kevin asked.

"Like I said, it's five miles away. It's been abandoned for years, but Ian swears he can land on it."

"Sounds like you got it all worked out," she said. "But what about those people back at the compound? They're going to kill themselves. Doesn't that bother you?"

"That was never part of my plan. But it's always been part of theirs. I was powerless to stop it."

"You could have called the police."

Adrian smirked and nodded his head in disbelief. "So young. So idealistic." He stood up and checked the cargo net latch to make sure it was secure. "Do you think you can behave while I go up and talk to Ian? If I see you stand to reach this latch, I'll shoot you in the knee."

"Scout's honor," Kevin said. "We won't move a muscle."

Adrian cast a doubtful glare at them, then went up to the front of the plane and sat in the copilot's seat. As he spoke to Ian, he frequently glanced back toward the cargo area. Amari strained to hear but couldn't make out a word because of the engine noise.

A few minutes later, Adrian still sat sideways in the copilot's seat, keeping a wary eye toward her. Then Ian raised his voice anxiously, casting his own concerned glances toward the plane's tail section. He yelled into the headset microphone, flailing his hand in protest. Then his voice trailed off as if it was useless to argue. Next, he and Adrian had a heated exchange of words. When the two had stopped arguing, Adrian seemed to mull his options as he stared down at his wristwatch. He shook his head in disbelieve and let out a reluctant sigh. Then he got up and came to the rear of the plane, once again aiming his gun in Amari's direction. He unhooked the cargo net and stepped back into an open space where two chairs had been removed, probably to increase cargo capacity.

"Get up," he said sharply. "Change of plans."

"What's going on?" she asked.

"Just shut up and move to the front seats," he said, waving his gun toward the cockpit.

She widened her eyes in alarm, and Kevin returned the concerned expression. Something didn't feel right about this. But what choice did they have? The last time she'd tried to disarm Adrian, Kevin ended up getting shot. She wouldn't put him at risk again. Besides, if he were going to kill them, he would have done so by now. Amari took Kevin's hand and pulled him down the center aisle and stopped at two leather seats directly behind the cockpit.

"Yes, there," Adrian said. "In the front. And buckle your seatbelts."

Adrian waited for them to comply, then went to the cargo hold. He stooped down to the floor and opened the lid of a storage compartment. Seconds later, he emerged from the cargo area holding two more backpack looking things, only they didn't seem to have any zippers. They were army green, looking like something he'd bought from an army surplus store. The buckling system was extreme for a regular backpack. It looked more like a . . .

"Hey, is that a parachute?" Kevin asked.

"I can't fool you, can I, Dr. Brenner?"

She leaned into the aisle and craned her neck to the back of the plane. "Are you kidding me? You're going to jump!"

"Who do think you are, D.B. Cooper?" Kevin replied. "You're going to just bail with all the money?"

Just then, Ian walked down the aisle, and Adrian handed him one of the parachutes. "Correction," Adrian said. "We're *both* going to bail with the money."

"What?" She started to stand, but her seatbelt held her down.

Adrian pointed the gun her way. "I told you to stay put!"

"I thought you were meeting your friend," she replied.

"That's what we thought too," Ian said. "We were keeping tabs on each other by radio. He said the local sheriff caught him on the old airstrip and made him leave town."

"And not only that," Adrian said, "but Ian reminded me that your friends in the Learjet most certainly notified

309

authorities after we kidnapped the two of you. There's a good chance they're tracking us by radar. They'll see where we land. The state police will have all the roads blocked. We can't take that chance."

"Then who's going to fly the plane?" she cried.

"Kevin's a smart guy," Adrian said. "I bet he can figure it out."

Ian's glasses slid down his sweaty nose. He pushed them back to his eyes and wiped the sweat with the cuff of his flight suit. He looked conflicted, anxiously pondering his options.

"Oh, I almost forgot," Adrian said and went back into the cockpit. He lifted the radio headset, pulled the connection wire taught, took a knife from his pocket, and severed the cord. He did the same with the other headset and went back to the rear of the plane.

"You cut the radio wires?" Ian asked. "Now how are they going to call for help? I figured if Dr. Brenner had a little help, he could land the plane."

"And have them radio the location we made the jump?" Adrian tapped his head with his index finger. "Think, Ian. You've got to think these things through."

"Then they don't stand a chance," Ian said. "You promised me nobody would get hurt."

"Oh, come on, Ian. Dr. Brenner can figure it out. He's a genius, remember?"

Ian looked to Kevin as if expecting an answer.

"I've flown a little," Kevin said. "I don't have a license. But my uncle has a Cessna. It's not rocket science. I can do it."

"There's a difference between watching your uncle fly and actually taking the controls," Ian said. He shot Adrian a defiant glare. "You know what, I'll land the plane. I'll drop them off in Borrego Rock and meet up with you later."

Adrian scolded Ian with his eyes but said nothing.

"You know what else?" Ian said. "Here, take my money too." He hefted up his backpack full of cash and dropped it at Adrian's feet. "Just take it all. I don't care anymore. I'm done with this."

Adrian stiffened his posture and gave Ian an incredulous glare. Suddenly, a greedy grin crept into his lips like he was the Grinch that stole Christmas. "That's very generous of you, Ian. But there's only one problem." In a flash, he raised his gun and pistol-whipped Ian on the head.

Ian fell against the cabin wall and sunk to the ground, unconscious.

"The problem is you know my real name. You know too much about me. If you get caught, you'll sing like a canary."

Ian lay slumped against the cabin wall, unresponsive.

"Just go!" Amari cried. "Take your money and go!"

"But what happens when he wakes up?" Adrian leveled the gun at Ian's chest and pulled the trigger. The shot was deafening in the enclosed cabin.

She gasped at the sight. "You monster!"

Kevin reached across the aisle and took her arm. "Take it easy. I'll handle this."

She felt the blood rush to her face, her pulse pounding in her ears. He just shot his best friend in the chest. What chance did she and Kevin have? She had to do something and do it fast. Then a thought occurred. That was a six-round revolver in his hand. He shot Ian once, and four times at the Learjet. He had only one bullet left.

"If I were a monster," Adrian said. "Then I would shoot the two of you as well."

"You only have one round left," she said. "You can't shoot us both."

"And I'd prefer to keep that bullet—just in case I run into trouble on the ground. But don't think I won't use it on you if I have to." He leveled the gun at Kevin's head. "Now back into the cargo hold. Or he gets it."

She tossed up her hands in surrender. "Okay, okay, I'm going." She got out of her seat and moved to the back of the plane.

"Your turn, Dr. Brenner."

Kevin held up his hands and joined her in the rear of the plane.

"Now, attach the cargo net." He watched her clip it into place. "Thank you, Ms. Johnston. For that, you get to survive."

"Until when?" she replied. "Until the plane crashes?"

Adrian shrugged and set the gun on the chair next to him. "At least I'm giving you a chance."

"Which is more than you gave Ian," she said.

"Let it go," Kevin said. "Just let him suit up so he can jump. Trust me. I can fly this thing."

Adrian hefted the parachute up and fed his arms into the harness. "You know how I met Ian?" He buckled his parachute securely. "We met in the army." He hefted up one of the cash stuffed backpacks and secured it to his chest rather than against his back. "I was a paratrooper in Vietnam. He was the pilot." Next, he grabbed Ian's backpack and put the shoulder strap around his neck, with the pack bulging under his arm. Then he picked his gun up and squeezed it into his front pocket, which was also stuffed with stacks of hundred-dollar bills. He gave the airplane's door a wary look.

The door panel was a ladder that folded out when the door lowered to the round. Two hydraulic piston hinges stabilized the door and dropped it softly to the tarmac. Two black cables furled out to hold the ladder taught and could be pulled on from the inside to raise the door back up.

"Of course, I never jumped out of one of these doors before. This might be tricky. These doors aren't designed to be opened while the plane's off the ground." He glanced back to her and grinned. "I'm sure you won't mind giving me a shove if I lose my nerve."

"Would you just jump, already," she said.

"Like I said, that's the tricky part." He studied the door again, apparently calculating the consequences of opening it midair. "Well, here goes nothing."

He pulled the release lever and pushed. A violent burst of wind rushed into the cabin, knocking her off balance. She grabbed the cargo net to keep from falling. She squinted against the hard wind, her eardrums feeling like they would burst. Her long hair flailed around her face and head, and her shirt rippled like she was in a wind tunnel.

Adrian braced himself against the wind by gripping both hydraulic hinges at once. He pushed the door down with his foot, the ladder steps unfolding as it went, the steel cables providing support.

As Amari watched him build his nerve to jump, anger flared when she thought about him living a life of luxury, spending all that stolen cash. She worried about this driver that was supposed to pick him up once he landed. Why else was he saving that last bullet? She glanced over to see his dead friend, Ian, lying on the floor, head covered in blood. She recalled those forty cult members who may have been dead by now—all because of Adrian's greed. As she watched his cheeks flapping in the wind, anger boiled from within, and she couldn't control herself anymore.

Adrian put both hands on one of the hinges and rotated around to face her, one last taunt before he leapt into ill-gotten prosperity, one last look to see the expression on her face before he jumped. A devious grin spread onto his lips. "Say hello to Calvin for me," he yelled over the wind. "That is when you see him again in New Canaan."

Chapter 43

"You're not getting away with this!" Amari yelled back. "And you're not going to be rich!" She unlatched the cargo net and lunged for him. With both hands, she clutched the back-pack zippers and thrust them down. Wind-driven hundred-dollar bills fluttered about the cabin and rushed out into the open sky.

Fury flashed in Adrian's eyes, and he reached for his gun. But she was too fast. She reached for him and yanked the parachute ripcord, then fell back into one of the chairs and held on so she wouldn't be sucked out. Startled, he braced himself for the violent yank that would rip him from the plane. To his surprise, the parachute had deployed, but nothing happened. He stayed put, still holding onto the hinges. Through the open door, she noticed the chute wrapped around the tail wing, keeping it from inflating.

Again, Adrian let go of one of the hinges and tried for his weapon. Without hesitation, she did a 360 spin and landed her elbow hard against the bridge of his nose, feeling the sickening crack of breaking cartilage. Mustering all her strength, she grabbed hold of the door's hinges for leverage, cocked her knee, and landed a hard kick square in the cash deflated backpack strapped to his chest. The force propelled him backward, releasing him to the brutal wind.

Just then, Kevin came in behind her. He grabbed onto the support cables and thrust his weight backward, pulling the door up and into place. He reached for the locking lever, pulled the door tight against the door frame, and engaged the lock. The wind abated, and the deafening sound hushed. She heard only the relatively quiet sound of wind against the hull, the drone of twin-engine propellers—and the muffled cries of terror coming from outside.

She immediately went to the window and gawked at the site. Cash fluttered like confetti onto the impoverished Navajo town below. With Adrian's parachute caught on the wing, he dangled helplessly, buffeted by the wind. Suddenly, the chute split open and pulled free of the wing. He plummeted momentarily, only to be caught by the tattered parachute. He fell in a spiral motion, hurtling toward the earth in corkscrew circles, plums of cash still spilling from his coveralls.

As her anger abated, she searched her soul for pity, knew her Christian faith required it, but little came, only curiosity as to his fate. "You think he'll survive the fall?" she asked Kevin.

"Maybe, maybe not. If he does live, he'll spend a year in a body cast."

"Good," she said, catching her breath. "When he gets out of the hospital, he'll go to jail, where he belongs."

"You're lucky you weren't sucked out of the plane. What were you thinking?"

"I don't know. I was just mad. You know I have anger issues."

"Trust me, I know. Worked out this time, though. Adrian got what was coming to him."

She puckered her lips to contain her smile, knowing she shouldn't find joy in Adrian's outcome, but it wasn't easy. He deserved what he got. She glanced over at Ian, who was slumped against the wall, and Agricola's fate seemed all the more appropriate. When she noticed Ian's cash-stuffed flight suit, a sudden realization dawned. "Kevin! Who's flying the plane?"

"Oh, yeah," he replied with an uncanny calm, a thoughtful look on his face. "There is that. Autopilot maybe?"

"On a plane this small?"

"Maybe."

"Kevin, you said you could fly this thing, right?"

"Oh, yeah, piece of cake."

And then she noticed it—the rise and fall of Ian's chest. "Kevin, he's still alive! Maybe he can land the plane." She went and knelt next to Ian. She felt the artery on his neck. The pulse was strong. "Ian," she said and smacked him on the face. "Ian, wake up!" She slapped him again, harder this time. But it was no use. He might still be breathing, but for all she knew, he was about to breathe his last.

"Ease up on the man," Kevin said. "He's been hit over the head and shot."

She stood and paced up to the cockpit. "What are we going to do? I think we're losing altitude."

He came up and plopped down in the pilot's seat. "Just relax, babe. I told you I can fly this thing." He glanced around the instrument panel. "Just be looking for the owner's manual."

She sat in the copilot's seat and stared at him in disbelief, calculating the implication of his words. "The *owner's manual*? Kevin, you said you knew how to fly!"

Wind against the airplane's thin metal shell and the drone of twin-propeller engines muted Kevin's words as he calmly took inventory of all the knobs, switches, levers, and gauges.

"I thought you said you could fly!" she repeated, louder this time.

He raised his voice to match hers. "How hard could it be? There's the throttle, this here's the steering wheel, and one of those knobs or levers ought to control the flaps. Now just calm down and look for the flight manual."

"You said owner's manual."

"Whatever, it's the same thing."

"Kevin, this isn't one of those atom speeders you play with at work." She chanced a look out the cockpit window. Roads and dry riverbed made faint lines in the greenish-brown landscape. Trees were nothing more than tiny random dots. "We're, like, a mile off the ground. You're going to get us killed." She cupped her hands over her face and shook her head in disbelief. So many plans, so many stories she wanted to tell her mother in heaven someday. Who would have thought she'd join her mother after only her second mission? Correction, before she'd even completed her second mission.

"That's Atomic Mass Accelerator," he corrected. "And if I can run that thing, this ought to be a cinch."

"You can't just flip through the owner's manual and learn how to land a plane."

"We got some time. It depends on how much fuel we have." He frowned at one of the gauges. "Which doesn't look like much. Does that look like a fuel gauge to you?"

"Kevin, this is crazy!"

"You got any better ideas?"

317

"I don't know, but we have to do something, or we're going to die—and forty other people too."

"A crash landing is survivable," he said in a strangely relaxed tone. "Maybe. Depending on the terrain, of course."

She watched him in dismay. He was so calm, so certain of God's intervention. 'Sometimes, you just gotta live by faith', he'd once told her. And deep inside, masked underneath fear-fueled adrenaline, she knew he was right. She'd chosen her path prayerfully. God wanted her to do this. He had her back now, just like he'd had her back while she'd been stalked by a serial killer the year before.

She narrowed her eyes with firm resolve and buckled her seat belt. "Then crash land back at the compound. We have to stop those people before it's too late."

"Listen . . . I know this ain't the time, but there's something I need to say."

"What can be more important than flying this plane?"

He pulled her hand in close and enclosed it tenderly within his own two hands. "Amari, I had this all planned out. Really, I did. But now maybe I should just go ahead and spit it out. Wait, take the spit part out. I'm trying to be romantic. Definitely, strike out the spit."

"Kevin! The plane. Remember? Can't this wait?"

"Maybe it can, but maybe not." He reached for her chin and forced her to look into his eyes. "Amari, will you marry me?"

Her jaw fell open, and she started to say something, but instead, found herself speechless. She saw it in his eyes. He was serious. His timing was awful, but he was dead serious. "Marry you?" she said with a laugh, her eyes watering with strange, ill-timed emotion. "Kevin, you know we're about to die, right? And you're asking for my hand in marriage?"

He waved off the thought. "Relax, Amari, we're not going to die. Well, probably not. But just in case we do, I gotta at least know what you would have said, you know, had I asked you in a more romantic kind of way. Will you marry me?"

She cupped her hands around his face. Her conflicted emotions of terror and joy worked against her, and she struggled to get the words out. "Well . . . this isn't the way I imagined this, but . . . but, yes! Yes, of course, I'll marry you, silly. It's what I want more than anything in the world. I'll marry you the moment we land if you want. But for now, can you just get us on the ground?"

He clenched his fists in victory. "Thank you, Lord. Hey, maybe I ought to land this baby on the Las Vegas strip. They got twenty-four-hour chapels."

"Kevin, I'm kidding. I want a real wedding, with bride's maids and all that crap. We'll talk about that later. Just focus on what you're doing and land this thing."

"Then keep looking for the owner's manual."

"What does it look like?"

"Sometimes they have an aluminum cover. I think they call it a flight manual."

She glanced around the cockpit and caught movement out of the corner of her eyes. She snapped around to see Ian—and he was trying to stand.

"Ian! He's awake!"

Kevin looked to the rear of the plane. "Huh, well I'll be darned. Why don't you ask him to fly it? He did offer."

She made the short dash to the rear of the plane and steadied Ian.

"I don't feel so good," Ian said, holding his head and wincing as he fingered his chest. "What happened?"

She helped him to the chair. "Adrian hit you on the head, that's what happened. And then he shot you in the chest. I can't believe you're still alive."

"Is that why it hurts?" He cringed and unzipped his flight suit. Stacks of hundred-dollar bills tumbled to the floor.

She picked up one of the cash bundles and inspected it. "Oh, my gosh, Ian, the money stopped the bullet!"

"Then why am I bleeding?" he said, showing her his bloody undershirt.

"I guess it went through. Can you breathe okay?"

"It hurts when I inhale, but yeah, I can breathe."

"Bullet's dead center of your chest. I bet it's stuck in your breastbone. The money must have slowed it down."

"Not enough," he said and cringed from the pain.

Kevin came out of the cockpit and knelt next to them. "Ian, do you think you can fly this thing?"

"I don't know," Ian replied. "My head's killing me. I feel dizzy."

"He's got a bad concussion," she said. "If we help you to the cockpit, do you think you can land?"

"I can try," he said.

"Kevin, help him up."

When they stood Ian up, his eyes rolled back in his head, and his legs fell out from under him, his dead weight on her and Kevin's arms. They lowered him back to the chair.

"Ian?" she said and shook him. "Ian, wake up!"

"He needs to be in a hospital," Kevin said. "He's in no shape to fly. Don't worry. I told you I can do this." He went back to the pilot's seat and took the controls.

She sat next to him and cupped her hands over her face. "Oh, God, please, help us." Her next prayer was a silent one, not to God himself, but to one of his angels instead. *Mother, I don't know if you can hear me, but if you can pull any strings up there, now would be a good time.*

"Ask and you shall receive," Kevin said.

She removed her hands and looked his way.

"Don't look at me, out the window," he said and pointed.

She gasped in surprise. It was Ernesto's Learjet. Her dad, George, Bonelli, and Parker were all waving frantically for their attention.

"I bet they've been following us this whole time," she said. "They had to have seen Adrian bail out. That's why they pulled along beside us. They're trying to tell us something."

"They're trying to say talk to them on the radio," Kevin said.

"How are we going to do that?" she said. "Adrian cut the wire."

"Dang it, why didn't I think of this before?" He reached into his pocket and produced his Swiss Army knife. "All I gotta do is strip the wires and splice them back together."

"Then what are you waiting for? Just do it. Skip can tell you how to land."

"I told you I can land this thing. I don't need his help."

She balled her fist and socked him on the arm.

"Ouch," he said, rubbing at his muscle. "That kind of hurt."

"It got your attention, didn't it?"

"All right," he said and cut into the black wire with his blade. "We'll do it your way."

Chapter 44

Chain link fencing clanged against the nosecone as the plane came to an abrupt halt. Twin propellers churned dirt into the air. Kevin hit the kill switch, and the engines wound down. They'd overshot the runway, but by the grace of God, Kevin had managed to safely land without crashing. *Thank you, God,* she prayed. *And you too, Mother. And you too.*

"Man, that was crazy," Kevin said, his eyes full of zeal.

Amari sat stunned, her heart throttling down in her chest. "I think you actually enjoyed that."

"Didn't you?"

"We gotta go," she said and unbuckled her seat belt. "We have to get that door open—if it's not too late already."

He unbuckled his belt and followed her back to Ian. He was conscious again, but just barely.

"Ian, can you hear me?" she said as she shook him. "Stay here. We'll get help. But we gotta get that cellar door open first."

"Why . . . what's the hurry?" Ian said, a confused look on his blood-streaked face.

"The nitrogen," she said. "If we don't get them fresh air, they're all going to die."

Ian shook his head in disagreement. "No, no, don't worry about that. They may find another way to die, but it won't be because of any gas."

"What are you talking about?" Kevin asked. "That cellar was full of nitrogen tanks. They breathe that stuff long enough, and they'll take an eternal dirt nap."

"I know about the gas. I'm the one who delivered it."

"Then you know what they plan to do with it," she said.

"Yeah, I know," Ian said. "I suspected that. That's why I did what I did."

"Did what?" she said. "What did you do?"

"Remember seeing that air compressor by the workbench in the hangar?" Ian replied. "Next to the blowtorch?"

"Yes," she said. "I remember. What about it?"

"I sort of used that compressor to fill the tanks with regular air. I figured they'd never know the difference."

She contemplated his words, and it took a moment for them to sink. When they did, she felt relief wash over her. "Are you serious?" she said with a laugh, shaking her head in disbelief. "All this time, I thought they were going to die. And you put regular air in those tanks?"

"Of course, I did. I'm not a monster. Not like Adrian."

She was moved to emotion by his selfless act. She now knew that he'd only acted out of fear of Adrian. But he'd overcome that fear and risked his own life in a selfless act of redemption. "Ian, I know you've made some mistakes, but deep inside, you're a good man. If I wasn't engaged," she said and cast a playful grin towards Kevin, "I would kiss you on the cheek."

"That's right," Kevin said. "This here's my fiancé." He drew her close and planted a messy kiss on her forehead.

"Congratulations," Ian said. "If I wasn't going to jail, I'd sing at your wedding."

"I promise," Amari said, "after what you did, I'm sure Ernesto will get you the best lawyer money can buy. You may get your wish."

"I'd appreciate that. By the way, the key to the cellar is stuck to the top of the door frame with a piece of masking tape. While Adrian was cleaning out Calvin's safe, I was on the radio with the Williams Police Department. Told them everything. I figured we'd be long gone before they ever showed up."

In the distance, Amari could hear the police sirens as they approached the gate of the compound, and she knew Ian had told the truth.

****

The sun had just retreated over the western horizon and the first stars shined dimly in the dusky evening sky. Sheriff Hicks from the town of Williams was in a heated exchange with Captain Ogden from the Coconino County Police. The cult was like a hot potato that nobody wanted to hold. Captain Ogden wanted Sheriff Hicks to house at least ten of them in the small Williams jailhouse while they decided upon more permanent arrangements. The sheriff vehemently insisted that they all go to the larger Flagstaff facilities or possibly stay at the compound under house arrest until they decided who was guilty of what, who needed to be in prison, or who needed to be in a mental facility.

Amari, Kevin, and Jenny leaned against a squad car, watching the events unfold. The wall of the main house reflected flashing blue and red lights from a dozen police cars and two ambulances that were parked outside. Bonelli and Parker were inside the house to provide extra muscle in case the cult members tried to overpower the outnumbered police. Amari's dad was standing a few feet away, giving his side of the story to the Arizona State Police.

Ian had been taken to the Flagstaff hospital with minor injuries, but, according to one of the paramedics, Adrian had not been so lucky. They'd found him conscious and alive, several bones in his body broken, including his spine. He was expected to survive, but with a long recovery ahead. In all likelihood, he would serve his lengthy prison sentence in a wheelchair.

Amari glanced over toward the house to see two police officers escorting Calvin toward a squad car, his hands cuffed behind his back. Just before they put Calvin in the backseat, Amari walked over, feeling the urge to say something.

"Calvin, I'm sorry it had to end this way," she said.

"No, child, it is I who should apologize. The portal failed because of my unbelief."

"No, Calvin," she sternly replied. "The portal would never have worked. Calvin, I know you meant well, but Jesus said, '*I* am the way the truth and the life.' Nobody gets to heaven except through faith in him, not his burial cloth."

He stared back at her as if she spoke a foreign language.

Amari felt Jenny's gentle squeeze on her forearm. "Just let him go," Jenny said. "He's not ready."

The officer pushed down on Calvin's head and forced him into the car.

"I'll keep you in my prayers," Amari said just before they closed the door. She watched in silent contemplation as they drove him away.

Her dad came up behind her and put his arm around her in a loving gesture of approval. "Mission accomplished," he said. "I'm proud of you, baby."

She looked up at him, water building in the corner of her eyes. "You mean it?"

"You know I do. I know your mother would be too. I've heard you say that someday in heaven, you're going to tell her all about your adventures as a detective. Wait till she hears about this one. It's a real doozy."

Just then, a burst of light lit the sky as a meteorite streaked toward the horizon.

Amari placed her hand over her heart and gazed in awe at the beautiful site. In a strange, yet wonderful moment, she sensed her mother's presence—felt her loving, spiritual embrace. "I don't know, Dad. I have a feeling I won't have to tell her anything."

"Oh, yeah?" Dad said. "How's that?"

"Because something tells me she's been watching the whole time."

The End

If you enjoyed this story and recommend it to others, please leave a review on Amazon.

If you would like to know more about the Shroud of Turin and the Sudarium of Oviedo, please visit my website: www.shroudstories.com

If you have any questions, comments, or suggestions, feel free to contact me from the bottom of my webpage. I'd love to hear from you!

THE CULT OF NEW CANAAN

Made in the USA
Lexington, KY
09 October 2018